He was incre

Or maybe she was having that nervous breakdown she'd contemplated earlier. *Do people having nervous breakdowns suffer from hallucinations about incredibly handsome men showing up in their bedroom?*

"Oh, my God. What are you doing in my . . . who are . . . how did you get in here?" Cate demanded, slamming her glass down onto the dressing table and jerking the chair out in front of her. The little chair wouldn't do much to stop someone his size, but somehow it made her feel better.

He paused for a moment, just staring at her before he spoke. "I am Connor MacKiernan. I've crossed time seeking yer assistance, milady. Only you can help me."

He had the most wonderful Scottish brogue. Cate leaned toward him for a moment and then shook her head to clear it.

"Right." Stall for time and this hallucination would probably go away. "Through time." Oh my, he was gorgeous, and with that accent . . . !

But one of them must be crazy.

He was dressed like an ancient Scots warrior, boldly standing there with his legs apart and his hands on his hips, in a bubble of green light, in the middle of her bedroom.

Thirty Nights
with a
Highland
Husband

MELISSA MAYHUE

POCKET BOOKS
New York London Toronto Sydney

The sale of this book without its cover is unauthorized. If you purchased this book without a cover, you should be aware that it was reported to the publisher as "unsold and destroyed." Neither the author nor the publisher has received payment for the sale of this "stripped book."

An *Original* Publication of POCKET BOOKS

 POCKET BOOKS, a division of Simon & Schuster, Inc.
1230 Avenue of the Americas, New York, NY 10020

This book is a work of fiction. Names, characters, places and incidents are products of the author's imagination or are used fictitiously. Any resemblance to actual events or locales or persons, living or dead, is entirely coincidental.

Copyright © 2007 by Melissa Mayhue

All rights reserved, including the right to reproduce this book or portions thereof in any form whatsoever. For information address Pocket Books, 1230 Avenue of the Americas, New York, NY 10020

ISBN-13: 978-1-4165-3286-6
ISBN-10:   1-4165-3286-2

This Pocket Books paperback edition July 2007

10 9 8 7 6 5 4 3 2 1

POCKET and colophon are registered trademarks of Simon & Schuster, Inc.

Cover design by Min Choi
Art by Jaime DeJesus

Manufactured in the United States of America

For information regarding special discounts for bulk purchases, please contact Simon & Schuster Special Sales at 1-800-456-6798 or business@simonandschuster.com

To my mother, Beatrice Alexander,
for instilling in me an early and lasting love of
the written word, and especially for introducing me
to the world of Romance novels.

And to my husband, Frank,
for his encouragement and for never doubting
that I could do anything I set my mind to.

Acknowledgments

Many people have helped make this book possible, but I'd like to specifically thank the following:

My sons, Nick (for being the first to read my books!), Chris (for forcing me to learn how to update my website guest book!), and Marty (for answering that phone call!).

The best critique partners in the world, the Soapbox Divas: Irene Goodell and Kirsten Richard. They never let me slack.

The women who were instrumental in the process: Terri Valentine, Kally Jo Surbeck, Sue Grimshaw and Maggie Crawford. You are all special ladies.

And of course, my editor, Megan McKeever. She made the terrifying task of revisions easy.

Thank you all!

The Legend of the Faerie Glen

Long, long ago on a beautiful spring day in the Highlands of Scotland, a Prince of the Fae Folk peered through the curtain separating his world from that of the mortals. There, deep in a glen Pol thought of as his own, he saw a beautiful young woman gathering herbs. He watched her for a very long time, until her basket was nearly full, and he knew he had fallen in love with this innocent mortal. His love was so great for this woman that he was able to slip through a crack in the curtain between their worlds. Pol appeared to the maiden in his true magnificence, making no effort to disguise himself, for he knew she must love him for what he was.

Rose had wandered deep into the forest that day, gathering her herbs, and she had become entranced by the serenity of the glen. When Pol appeared before her, his beauty stole her breath away, and she knew at once that this was her own true love.

Pol and Rose dwelt happily in their idyllic glen next to the little stream where first he had seen her. But after a mortal year together, Pol was forced to return to his own world, for in those days, far in the misty recesses of time, the Fae abided by very strict rules.

One of those rules governed how long one of their own could remain outside the Realm of Faerie. Once returned to his own world, Pol would be unable to pass through the barrier again for a full century. And though one hundred years was nothing in the life span of a Fae, Pol knew his Rose would be no more at the end of that time.

Rose returned to her family, knowing her prince was lost to her forever. At first Rose's father, the old laird, was ecstatic that his little Rose had returned to him, even hearing her fantastic story of the Fae prince with whom she had spent the past year. Soon, however, it became apparent that Rose was with child, and her father and brothers were furious. Not only was their Rose a ruined woman, but to their way of thinking she had been defiled by a devious, unholy creature of magic. They began to treat her not as their beloved daughter and sister, but as their most reviled servant.

Rose toiled in the hot kitchens from sunrise to sundown each day and suffered all manner of indignity, but she didn't care, because her heart was gone from her. Her reason for living had disappeared with Pol.

Meanwhile, Pol could only watch with growing dismay, unable to pass through the curtain separating their worlds, as his beloved Rose slipped farther and farther away.

Finally the day came when Rose delivered her babes— three strong, healthy, beautiful girls. But Rose, whose spirit was damaged by the loss of her one true love, did not survive their birth. Rose's father refused to look upon the faces of the infants and decreed that they should be taken deep into the forest and left for the Faeries to whom they belonged—or the wolves. He cared not which claimed the infants first.

The old laird himself led the small party deep into the forest. As fate would have it, they were in the very same glen where Pol had watched Rose for the first time. The old laird ordered the infants to be laid on the grassy forest floor near a small shallow stream. Rose's brothers, who had each carried an infant, laid the babes on the ground and remounted their horses in preparation to leave the glen.

Pol, watching at the curtain between the worlds, was livid with rage and wracked with grief. Not only was his beloved Rose gone from the world, but now her children, *his* children, were being cruelly abandoned. His tormented cry of anguish reached his queen, who, in a rare moment of pity, broke the rules and opened the curtain just enough to allow Pol to slip through.

The wind suddenly began to howl through the tiny glen and thunder rumbled ominously. The ground around the old laird's party heaved and shook, and the old laird himself was thrown from his horse to the forest floor. He and his sons watched in horror as boulders pushed up from beneath the earth in the very center of the stream, piling higher and higher, one upon another. There they formed a magnificent waterfall and a deep crystal pool where only moments before a shallow stream had flowed.

Pol rose slowly from the depths of the pool, choosing to play upon the individual terrors of the men by appearing to each of the mortals as that which they most feared.

"I am Pol, a prince of the Fae. And you"——he swept his arm to include the brothers as well as the father—"have incurred my wrath. Now you will pay the penalty." His gaze turned to the helpless infants lying nearby, all three strangely quiet and untouched by the tumult around them. "These are my daughters. My blood runs strongly in them." Pol moved to the infants, gently picking up each one in turn. "I name each of you for your mother, my beloved Rose. For all time, your daughters shall carry a form of her name to ensure that her memory will live on in this world forever. I give each of you my mark and my blessing. Know this glen as the home of your mother and your father."

Pol turned back to the old laird. "I charge you with the care and the safety of my daughters."

"Never," the old laird hissed. "They are yer abominations. You take them. Neither I nor my sons will shelter yer spawn at our hearth."

"Oh, but you will, old man, and you'll be grateful to do so."

The shape of the Fae prince shimmered and grew until it filled the entire glen, surrounding the old laird and his sons, weighing them down with the power and the fury of the being they had angered, blocking everything else from their view and their minds.

Pol smiled with evil satisfaction. Well he knew the weaknesses of mortal men. His voice rang in their minds, all the more terrible for not being spoken out loud. "Should you or any male of the family fail to nurture and protect my daughters, hurt them or allow anyone else to hurt them, prevent them from making their own choices in life, or deprive them of finding their one true love, you shall suffer my curse. You will bear no male offspring. Any sons already living will suffer the same fate. You will be unable to enjoy the intimate company of any female ever again. Your line will die out and your name cease to exist in your world."

Pol waited for the full impact of his words to sink into their minds. Then he continued. "My blessing on my daughters, and thus my accompanying curse, will carry forward for all time, passed from mother to daughter. As even the smallest drop of my blood flows in their body, so they will have the power to call on me and all Fae to aid them. My mark upon them and upon all the daughters of their line guarantees all men know the penalty they will suffer for harming my beloved daughters."

As Pol's terrible voice reverberated in the minds of the old laird and his sons, his form shifted and shimmered around the infants, enveloping them for the first time, and the last, in the emerald glow of his love.

The old laird still lay on the ground where he had fallen, trembling with fear. And although he could not see the infants through the green mist surrounding them, he could hear what sounded impossibly like children's laughter.

Just before the mist faded, each of the men present felt an ominous warning echo through his mind.

"Never forget."

Later, much later, the old laird and his sons crept close to the infants to find them sleeping contentedly, each one bearing the mark of the Fae prince. The old laird gently gathered up his granddaughters—for so they must now be to him—and hurried from the glen.

Pol's daughters grew and prospered and eventually married, having families of their own. In time to come, though many generations of the Fae prince's offspring traveled and spread to varied parts of the world, all the men of all the lines continued to honor the Legend of the Faerie Glen.

CHAPTER 1

Sithean Fardach
The Highlands of Scotland
1272

The clatter of metal on stone rang through the air even as the goblet spun slowly to a stop on the floor where it had landed.

"Tantrums will no be helping you, laddie." The old warrior shook his head, warily eyeing his companion sitting at the far end of the great table. "You only waste good ale."

Connor MacKiernan glared at him. It was a look that had weakened the knees of many a strong man. "Nothing will help me now. I am as the weak, helpless fool, all my options closed save one." He dropped his head into the crook of his arm on the table. "I am a king's knight, yet my sword might as well be a woman's pretty feather for all that I can do." He spat the words as if they soured and burned his mouth. "I dinna want to involve Rosalyn. This is no my aunt's trouble, Duncan, but mine. I am to protect my family, no to place them in greater danger."

Duncan pushed back from the table laughing. "The Lady Rosalyn would, I wager, see things verra differently, Connor. Dinna she tell you her plan would make everything work out just as you need?"

"Aye." Connor lifted his head only enough to peer up over his arm. "And that's what worries me. There is no regular way out of this mess. You ken that as well as I do." He raised an eyebrow and leaned toward the older man. "She takes a terrible risk."

Duncan took a long drink from the tankard in his hand and shrugged. "So she'll use her gift." It was a statement of fact, not a question, and required no answer from Connor, who simply continued to glare at the older man. "It is what she does, laddie, as did her mother and her mother before her. She disna deny who she is." Duncan took another long drink and smiled. " 'Tis no good reason to waste such fine ale." Duncan strode to the far end of the table, placing his hand on Connor's shoulder as he sat down next to him. "It's no she disna ken the risk to her if she does this, Connor. It's that well she kens the risk to all of you if she does nothing. You must remain here with yer sister, laddie."

"Aye, it's my duty to see her protected and happy."

Duncan lowered his head, speaking quietly. "You ken there are men who would follow you. Men who would fight for you if you choose to oppose yer uncle. To take back what's rightfully yers. You do have a choice."

"And how many would die then, Duncan? How many innocents would be caught in the middle of that great battle? We've been over this many a time. I'm no willing to sacrifice the lives of so many of my people." Connor groaned, dropping his head back down to his arm. "It disna matter, Duncan. I've failed my family yet again. Rosalyn was right. In order to save Mairi without bringing death to my people, I hae no choice but to risk my aunt's use of the magic." He shook his head, sighing with resignation, and sat up straight. "Rosalyn bids us leave this night. She'll be down soon."

"She's down."

Both men jumped to their feet at the authoritative sound of the female voice coming from the entryway. A tall blonde woman, with a bearing equally as authoritative as her voice, strode toward them.

"Quit yer sulking, Connor. We've been all through this. You ken it's the only way out. I promise you, this will be the answer to all yer problems. Do you hae the trinket I requested?" Rosalyn MacKiernan smiled at her nephew, ignoring his glare much as Duncan had. Fully expecting his compliance with her earlier instructions she held out her hand.

"Aye." Connor reached into his sporran and handed over a small velvet pouch.

Rosalyn opened the little bag and dumped the contents into her hand. "Oh, verra good, Connor. It's exactly the piece I had hoped you would choose." She glowed with happiness as she lifted the emerald pendant, light from the candles reflecting in the facets of the jewel. "I remember when Dougal gave this to yer mother. It was at the dinner when they announced they were to be married." Her soft blue eyes glazed over with memory for a moment as she began to turn away, but she quickly turned back. "Oh. I almost forgot." She smiled at her nephew then, in a way that always worried him. "I need a small something of yers." Again she held out her hand expectantly. Seeing his momentary confusion, she explained, "Something of yers, Connor. Something personal. The magic willna work without it." She paused and looked around the great hall. "I know . . . yer plaid. A piece of yer plaid will do nicely." At his frown, she sighed. "Just a small bit, Connor. Honestly, nephew, must you make everything a battle?"

Connor shook his head, knowing it would do him no good to argue. He tore a strip of material from the end of his plaid and handed it over to Rosalyn. "I trust that's the last thing you'll be needing of me, Aunt."

"Indeed it is."

Rosalyn paused and Connor could feel the forces of fate gathering around him.

"Weel, except for yer presence at the glen." She looked remarkably innocent for someone so devious.

Duncan choked and spit out the ale he had just taken into his mouth. "The Faerie Glen?" he managed to croak. "Och, I should hae guessed that was where you'd be wanting to go." He looked at Connor. "You may hae had the right of this, laddie. I'll go see to the horses." He paused and raised an eyebrow. "And just where do I tell the others we'll be headed? Yer uncle will ask them when we've gone, you ken?"

Connor considered this for only a moment. "Tell them we head to the port in Cromarty. We'll be back within a fortnight."

Duncan MacAlister, although easily twenty-five years Connor's senior, was closer to him than any man alive. The grizzled warrior had served Connor's father from his youth. Only Duncan could be trusted with the truth of their destination.

Duncan nodded. "Lady Rosalyn"—he bowed slightly in her direction—"I'll be in the courtyard awaiting yer readiness."

"I suppose it's the Clootie Well you'll be wanting?" Connor's ice blue eyes reflected his irritation. He shook his head in disgust. "I will regret this, I am sure," he muttered.

Rosalyn beamed at her nephew. "My things are at the foot of the stairs. You can take them out and see that Duncan has our horses ready. I'll join you shortly."

Watching Connor stomp out of the great hall, Rosalyn smiled. How like his father he was. Both of them handsome and strong, just as her own father had been. Both of them clung rigidly to ideals of right, wrong, honor and responsibility to the family. Both held themselves to standards higher than those against which they measured anyone around them.

Those lofty ideals had brought her older brother an early death on a lonely battlefield. She would do anything in her power to prevent that same fate for Connor. Knowing the sacrifices her nephew had already made for his family, and the burdens he carried, she loved him all the more. This one time, however, she wanted Connor to get what he needed.

She carefully tucked the strip of cloth from his plaid into the velvet pouch with the emerald necklace and tied the strings, smiling broadly. She had very special plans for that little piece of cloth. And for her nephew.

When they reached the Faerie Glen she would tap into the source of the power and say the words that would allow the magic to travel within the pendant, guiding it wherever it needed to go to find the very special one it sought.

CHAPTER 2

❧

"Damn it. Why couldn't I do something, say something?" Caitlyn Coryell slammed her front door and threw her keys across the room, where they bounced off the wall.

This is just great. Now she was talking out loud to herself. Surely just one more thing for Richard to criticize. " 'Just who do you think you are?' That's what I should have said to Richard." Cate shook her head. "I should have said something, anything, to Richard." Instead she'd just let him usher her out, like she was a small child. Like nothing at all had happened.

Cate walked woodenly down the hall to her bedroom, kicking off her sandals and tossing all her packages onto the middle of her bed. She went back to the living room and flopped onto the sofa, pulling her legs up until she could rest her forehead on her knees.

"I'm so pathetic." *Maybe Richard is right.* Wasn't he always? Maybe it was all her fault. If she could just be more . . .

"More what," she mumbled, absently twisting the diamond ring on her left hand. "Not more. Less. Less like me." Cate heaved a deep sigh and sat up. "Less afraid." Afraid and powerless to make even the simplest decision.

I sound like a sulky little girl. She picked up the telephone and dialed.

The hollow echo of the telephone ringing sounded for the third time. *Pick up.* Jesse should be in his room by now. It had to be around midnight in Barcelona. She needed him to answer. Though she was close to all three of her older brothers, she was closest to Jesse. He wasn't just her brother; he was her best friend.

There was no reason for him to still be out. They had contacted the office this morning. The mission had gone well and the hostages were safe. The team should have been at the hotel long ago.

Fourth ring. *Come on, Jess. Pick up. Pick up. Pick up.* Cate paced anxiously across the living room, stopping to tuck a box of tissues firmly under her arm. She'd need them for the good cry she was planning later.

Fifth ring. "PICK UP THE PHONE!" Cate yelled desperately, just as she heard the answering click on the other end of the line.

"Whoa there, no need to . . . Cate, is that you? What's wrong?" Jesse's sleepy confusion was evident.

"Sorry, Jess. I was just being impatient. Nothing's wrong." *Unless you count finding my fiancé having sex on his desk with his receptionist the week before our wedding as something.*

"Well, baby sister, you dragged me out of bed at . . . what time is it anyway? What's going on?" That was more like her Jesse. He sounded annoyed.

Maybe calling Jesse wasn't the smartest thing for her to do but she had already started. "Richard said, that is, we sort of had a disagreement, and, well, I've been thinking about what Richard said, and . . . " Her voice trailed off as she vividly recalled the "disagreement."

She had thought to surprise Richard with a picnic lunch since he'd told her he was too busy to get away from the office and meet her. He was busy all right. And all three of them had certainly been surprised. The blonde on the desk had screamed and Cate had dropped the basket of food, lemonade darkening the pale, thick carpet after the glass container shattered.

Jesse's voice brought her back to the present.

"Answer me, Cate. What did he do? You say the word and I am so on the next plane home. I'll have my foot up his ass before he can even think of another thing to say."

At least Jesse was completely awake now.

"No, Jess, you know I don't want that." Not that her brother couldn't do it, with his black belts in God only knew how many martial arts.

She closed her eyes and watched it all happening again.

She had backed out of the office into the hallway, but couldn't seem to think to move from the spot outside Richard's door. This couldn't be happening to her. The door had opened and Richard had grabbed her arm, pulling her into the office as the blonde receptionist sidled past on her way out. She didn't even have the courtesy to look embarrassed.

"Why?" she had asked him, hating the hurt in her voice. "Why would you do this to me?"

"I wasn't doing anything to you, Caitlyn. It meant nothing. You know I'm under pressure with the new cases I've taken on.

How many times have I asked you to have sex with me? If you had, I wouldn't have been forced to find my relief elsewhere."

"You're blaming . . . that"—she pointed to the desk, unable to find the words to describe what she'd seen   *"that . . . behavior on your work?"*

Richard had led her to the large leather sofa in his office, waiting for her to be seated before he perched himself on the arm. Always the perfect gentleman.

"No. If there's any fault to be placed here, it's yours. I'm a man with needs. I've made that clear to you."

Cate shook her head to banish the memory. On second thought, it might not be a good idea to share the whole scenario with her brother. "Besides, Richard says it's my fault anyway."

"That's bullshit. Richard's full of it, and you deserve better than him." Jesse always ended up here when they talked about Richard.

"All I need from you is, I need to ask you a question, and I need your promise that you'll be completely honest with me. Will you do that?" She might as well get on with this.

"That's what big brothers are for, Caty Rose. I excel at being honest, given the chance. Fire away."

"Richard says I'm not adventurous, that I'm stuck in a rut, doing the same things day after day, until I'm not even living life anymore."

"My fault?" she'd asked Richard. "How can your doing . . . that . . . possibly be my fault?"

Richard had given her that haughty look she'd seen him use on others in the past, the waiter who took too long to bring the wine or the sales clerk who didn't jump fast enough. "You live life like some kind of spinster. The only thing you show any enthusi-

asm for is Coryell Enterprises. I constantly have to take a back-seat to your daddy's company and your work there."

"What my father and brothers do is important. They risk their lives to save people."

"I'm not saying it isn't important, Caitlyn. I'm saying that you treat me as if it's more important to you than I am. You have no adventure of your own. You spend ten to twelve hours a day running that office, coordinating everything that goes on there. You deal with some of the most powerful people in the world, but look at you. You're in a rut. You don't fix yourself up unless I re-mind you to. What am I supposed to think? How can I pursue a career in politics without a wife at my side who understands my needs? One who's willing to sacrifice for my career?"

"I'm adventurous." She'd desperately grasped at the only part of his censure she could, her stomach clenching in horror as he criticized her passion for her work, the one thing she truly felt she excelled at.

His cold laughter stung. "Really? Then prove it. If you have any adventure in you at all, you'll have sex with me right here, in this office, right now." He'd stood then, straightening his tie. "But you aren't up to that, are you? That's simply too out of the ordinary for Caitlyn Coryell."

Her fault. He'd said it was all her fault.

"Do you think he could be right?" She hated the wimpy, pleading note she heard in her voice.

There was a long pause on Jesse's end. "Okay, fine. You know I don't like Richard. I never have. How many times have I told you he's not right for you? You want honesty, well here it is. No, honey, you aren't adventur-ous anymore. Your last big adventure ended up with you ass over end flying off a horse."

She shuddered at the painful reminder. It had been so exciting to sneak out for a ride on her father's horse, at least for the first few minutes. What is it they say? It's all fun and games until somebody almost gets killed. She'd spent weeks recovering from that accident.

"But more important, Caty, is the change in you since you met Richard. The longer you've dated this guy, the more withdrawn you've become. You're so busy trying to be exactly what he wants you to be, you're like some 'Richard robot.' You should listen to yourself talk. You can't go more than five minutes without a 'Richard says' in your conversation."

Jesse was on a roll. "You fix your hair the way Richard wants, you attend the society functions Richard wants, you're forever starving yourself trying to lose weight because Richard wants, you wear the clothes Richard wants. Hell, you aren't even going to wear Grandma's wedding dress, and you and I both know you've wanted to do that your whole life."

"Richard said he only wanted the best for me, that he loved me." She barely noted that she'd referred to him in the past tense.

"I am so sorry to be the one to say this to you, but it's way past time someone did. Richard doesn't love you. Anyone can see it. If he did, he wouldn't be trying to change everything about you. You're great just the way you are. Richard only loves Richard. And the Coryell money. That and all the potential political allies he can meet through Coryell Enterprises. He's slime, Caty, and you need to drop him like a bad habit." Jesse stopped to draw in a ragged breath.

"He's simply an ambitious lawyer." She defended him now out of habit, though that wasn't really much of a defense for the man she was supposed to love more than anything.

"Lawyer or not, Richard is just plain slime of the earth. And, Caty?" Jesse waited until he knew he had her attention. "I don't really believe you love him either. I haven't seen you seriously happy since you agreed to marry this creep. I think you just want to be in love because you think it's supposed to happen now. But love doesn't happen on schedule. It sneaks up when you least expect it. You can't plug it into that little day planner of yours. You can't make it happen. You need to ask yourself some pretty serious questions about how you honest to God feel before that wedding next week."

"Okay, enough. Thanks for your honesty. I know you don't understand my relationship with Richard. I just . . ." She paused and took a deep breath. How could he understand? She wasn't sure she understood why she'd agreed to marry Richard. Or why she was still considering it. "So will you guys be finished up in time to get home by the end of the week?" He would know she was changing the subject, but she couldn't bear anymore right now.

"Sure." His deep sigh was clearly audible on her end. "You know we will, Cate. We won't let you down. So, I guess that means you're still going through with this?"

Still going through with it? That was the question she'd been asking herself for the last couple of hours.

After listening to Richard tell her how it was all her fault, how he forgave her, how he loved her, and how they needed to put this incident behind them, she had risen from his sofa without comment and crossed the office, dazedly stepping over the broken glass and the spilled basket that had been her carefully packed lunch. Lemonade had squished into her sandals as she'd opened the door.

"Don't forget the dinner tonight," he'd said as he strode toward her. "Remember there will be some very important people there, Caitlyn. Try to be ready when I come to pick you up. I don't want to keep them waiting. Oh, and why don't you put your hair up tonight? You look more polished that way." He'd kissed her on the forehead and ushered her out the door, closing it behind her as if nothing out of the ordinary had happened.

Was she still going through with it? She'd been too numb to think, too shocked to fully accept what had happened. Even now she avoided the decision, rattling off the first thing that came to mind in response to her brother's question.

"I finished my last prewedding detail today. I wandered into this little antiques shop in LoDo and found the perfect 'something old' to wear. I can't wait to show it to you. It's this beautiful old necklace. It looks like an emerald, although I know it can't be because I only paid ten dollars for it." Cate forced some lightness into her voice. "Oh my gosh, it's almost five thirty. I've got to get off the phone and start getting ready for tonight."

The senior partner of Richard's firm was giving a dinner in honor of their upcoming wedding. If she were late, there would be such a scene.

"All right. But at least promise me you'll think about what I said, okay? It's not too late to change your mind. You don't have to go through with this. I'm not hanging up until you promise."

As if I'll be able to think of anything else.

"Don't worry about me, Jesse. And yes, before you get all upset, I promise to think about it. I love you. Give my love to Dad and the guys."

"Love you, too, baby sister. You remember to think about what you really want. Just because Mom and Granny were both married at your age doesn't mean you have to get married right now." Allowing no time for her to protest, he quickly continued. "We should be on our way home in a couple of days. We're just tying up loose ends here. But when I get home, we're going to continue this conversation, whether you want to or not." He hung up before she could argue the point.

She put down her tissues, deciding she didn't have time to spend on tears, and shuffled off to the shower, deep in thought.

Why couldn't she decide what to do?

On a daily basis Cate negotiated contracts, met with clients of her father's company, and compiled sensitive background information for negotiations or hostage rescue. She even handled the business side of Coryell Enterprises whenever government agencies contracted them for civilian covert operations. How could she possibly be so weak willed and indecisive now?

"Because that's business and this is personal."

Cate stood wrapped in a towel in front of her bedroom mirror, examining her reflection. She'd spent thirty minutes in the shower, trying to decide what was wrong with her. If she hadn't used all the hot water, she'd probably still be there.

"I'm not that bad. Maybe not model or movie star material, but not totally ugly. I'm smart. I'm good at my work. I'm not mean and I don't smell bad." Cate smiled ruefully at her image. "But I might be crazy, because I'm talking to myself again. Maybe this is what a nervous breakdown feels like."

It was then the thought hit, stopping her in her tracks. *Do I really, honestly love Richard enough to have a nervous breakdown over him?* No.

Such a simple word. *No.* And yet for the first time, it allowed her to see her situation quite clearly. No. She didn't love Richard that much. In fact, right now, she didn't even like him. Maybe that was why it had always been so easy to tell him she wouldn't sleep with him before they got married. Jesse was right. Richard was slime. But she couldn't lay all the blame at his doorstep. She had chosen to ignore all the things that bothered her about him because she should be in love by now. And Richard should have been the perfect one. He was tall, strong, blond, intelligent, and very handsome. He opened doors for her, held her hand, took her to the places she wanted to go. He had been attentive and affectionate. More important, he instantly took command of every situation and people flocked around him. He had power over any circumstances, always smooth and in control. Not only was he everything she should want in a man, he was everything she wanted to be herself. And he had loved her.

No. He had used her. He had never loved her. He loved being with her and meeting all the important people she took for granted because, thanks to her father's company, they had always been part of her life. All the powerful, famous people who could make things happen for an ambitious lawyer with political aspirations. And everyone around her had seen it all along; watched as she let him make a fool out of her—no, as she'd made a fool out of herself.

Cate sat down on the end of the bed, her legs literally giving out under her. Richard might have used her, but she had used him, too. She had wanted to be in love, and when Richard came along she convinced herself that she was. She hadn't loved him any more than he had loved her. What had she been thinking for the past year?

"You know, for an almost genius, Cate Coryell, you're pretty stupid." Just because you could make it through school a few years ahead of everyone else certainly didn't mean you had learned anything about life.

She wouldn't need to straighten her hair or put on makeup or get dressed. She wasn't going out to dinner with Richard tonight.

And she wasn't going to marry him.

She stood up and headed for the kitchen. There was a bottle of some kind of alcohol she had never opened in the cupboard over the refrigerator. Her brother Cody had given it to her on her twenty-first birthday, warning her to be careful with it, but, since she didn't drink, it had languished with the cobwebs for the past three years. Now she deserved a celebration. She was declaring her freedom.

" '*An dram buidheach*,' "she quoted out loud, reading the back of the bottle. " 'The drink that satisfies.' Exactly what I need. A little satisfaction. 'Product of Scotland.' "

She had wanted to visit Scotland since her college Medieval History classes. Such a tragic, turbulent past, and yet so romantic. She had loved those classes, soaking up the history of the times, immersing herself in the lore.

Cate shook her head in disgust, remembering that she had even recommended Scotland for their honeymoon, but Richard was set on Belize, where the senior partner in his law firm liked to vacation.

Well, that isn't a problem anymore.

After struggling to open the dusty bottle, she poured some of the amber liquid into one of her pretty wine-glasses and headed back to the bedroom, taking the bottle with her.

"It's time to straighten out a few things in here."

She took a quick sip of the Drambuie and gasped for air, coughing. Cody had been right. She'd need to be careful with this stuff.

First she went to her closet and, climbing on an over-turned wooden storage box, brought down an old dress box, tied with an emerald green ribbon. Gently she laid the cardboard box on the bed and untied the ribbon, lifting out an antique ivory lace dress. Her grandmother had worn this when she married her grandfather. Her mother had worn it when she married. To think, she'd almost given up the opportunity to wear it herself.

Never again. Never again would she sacrifice her dreams. Never again would she accept anything less than the real thing. And if she ended up being one of those women for whom there was no true love? Well, so be it. Being without a man would be better than being with the wrong one for the wrong reasons.

She strode firmly to the closet and took out a huge garment bag, unzipping it and tossing its frothy white contents to the floor next to her trash can.

"Without a doubt, the most hideous excuse for a wedding dress ever, regardless of what Richard thinks." It had been vastly expensive, and she had waited three months for the designer to meet with her for a fitting. So what if it had cost a small fortune? It had been her money. She could do what she wanted with the white netted horror.

No doubt some charitable organization would be calling in a few weeks. They always wanted clothes to sell in their thrift stores. This time she could give them something that had never been used.

She congratulated herself on another decision well made by choking down a sip of the Drambuie. It burned a trail down her throat.

Next she pulled a stack of clothing out of her dresser, things she'd bought for her wedding and honeymoon. She dropped her towel and slipped into the white lace bra and panties set. She admired her reflection in the mirror for a moment. This wasn't really her style, not the least bit practical as she normally preferred, but it was so beautiful she was keeping it. A girl deserved a few pretty things. Another sip of the warm liqueur to seal the decision.

Taking the towel off her long damp hair, Cate grabbed the ribbon that had held her grandmother's wedding dress box and tied her auburn curls into a quick ponytail. Then she slipped into the emerald silk pajama set she had thought so sexy when she'd seen it hanging on the mannequin. The elastic waist of the pants hung low, riding on her hips, while the camisole top barely brushed her waistline. She'd hunted a long time for a set to fit like this. At not quite five foot four, she found everything was usually too long for her.

So maybe she could stand to lose another ten pounds like Richard said, but just maybe he should see her like this. Not that he would get to. One more little sip. It went down much more smoothly this time.

Cate turned to the dressing table and searched through her jewelry box, choosing the diamond and yellow gold earrings her father had given her for her college graduation. Normally she never wore anything but her plain silver hoops, but simple diamonds would be appropriate for a wedding. *If there were going to be a wedding. Which there isn't.* Cate was having a difficult time getting the little studs into her ears. Her sense of balance seemed just a bit off.

She glanced at the small emerald eternity band lying on her dresser and placed it on her right hand. It had been a birthday gift from her grandmother. Their shared birthstone. She took just one more little sip and stopped to refill her glass.

Next she reached for the long-sleeved silk Asian-style jacket that went with the pajama set, but stopped as her eyes lit on the bag she'd tossed to the bed when she'd first come home. It held her little treasure, the pendant she'd found in the antiques store today before she'd gone to see Richard.

Nope, not going to think about that scene again.

Instead she'd try on the necklace to see if it looked as good on her as it had lying on the velvet cloth in the store.

Cate held the necklace up and admired it as the light sparkled off the multifaceted emerald. Well, of course it couldn't be a real emerald, even if light did fairly dance off the jewel. Nobody sold those for ten dollars. Still, the gold setting and chain looked ancient. It was so beautiful it had to be the best bargain she'd ever found. It was the perfect "something old" for her wedding. *If I were having a wedding.* Which now, of course, she wasn't.

With some difficulty, Cate fastened the chain around her neck, and stood back to admire her reflection in the mirror.

"Not bad."

The pendant felt unusually warm against her skin, causing a tingling sensation that spread to her neck and shoulders. Or was that the drink?

She pulled the ribbon from her hair, allowing her natural curls to fan out, and lifted her glass in salute to her reflection.

"Here's to you, Richard. Just look what you almost . . ." She stopped suddenly when she noticed an odd green glow behind her reflected in the mirror.

"What the . . . ?"

Cate turned to see a large sphere of emerald green light forming in the middle of her bedroom, pulsing and growing larger. Even more startling than the unusual glow was the man who gradually materialized in the center of the sphere—he was incredible.

Or maybe she was drunk.

Or actually having that nervous breakdown she'd contemplated earlier. *Do drunks having nervous breakdowns suffer from hallucinations about incredibly handsome men showing up in their bedrooms?*

"Oh my God. What are you doing in my . . . who are . . . how did you get in here?" Cate demanded, slamming her full wineglass down onto the dressing table and jerking the chair out in front of her. The little chair wouldn't do much to stop someone his size, but somehow it made her feel better.

He straightened, pausing for a moment, just staring at her before he spoke. "I am Connor MacKiernan. I've crossed time seeking yer assistance, milady. Only you can help me."

He had the most wonderful Scottish brogue. Cate leaned toward him for a moment and then shook her head to clear it.

"Right." Stall for time and this hallucination would probably go away. "Through time." Oh my, he was gorgeous, and with that accent . . . !

But one of them must be crazy.

He was dressed like an ancient Scots warrior, boldly standing there with his legs apart and his hands on his hips, in a bubble of green light, in her bedroom, for crying out loud.

Connor cocked an eyebrow and tilted his head questioningly. "I am no used to begging, but if you require it, I will do so. We've no much time."

"Oh, great. Just great. I have Braveheart-slash-Conan standing in my bedroom, and he's in a big hurry." She blew out her breath in irritation. "What do you want with me? Why am I the only one who can help you . . . to do what?" Cate put her hands on her hips, mirroring his stance. Hadn't someone said you should take the offensive in these situations? She almost laughed out loud when she realized that chances were extremely high no one had ever encountered a situation quite like this one.

"Although some do call me brave, I'm no Conan. I told you, my name is Connor. Connor MacKiernan."

He looked a little annoyed now.

Annoying him might not be such a good thing; he was a really big man. Big and gorgeous.

Is that a knife sticking out of his boot?

"Are you no listening to me, woman? This is important and we hae precious little time." He shouted the last.

While gaping at him, she'd missed part of what he'd said. "Sorry. I'm sorry. I'm not in the habit of having strange men—strange men with weapons, I might add—pop into my bedroom." She stared pointedly at his leg.

That is definitely a knife sticking out of his boot.

"No, you're no the one who needs to apologize." At least he had the good grace to look embarrassed. "I'd no thought of how, or where, I might appear to you." He tilted his head in a slight bow and then, raising his head, he pointed to the emerald necklace she wore. "It's the jewel, milady. It's led me to you as the one to help me save my sister. The Fae magic sent me here to fetch you."

She should be completely freaked out. But he seemed so sincere. *Well, wouldn't all homicidal maniacs, or even simple hallucinations for that matter, seem sincere?*

She could hardly believe it when she heard herself ask, "Save your sister, huh? What exactly does this magic want me to do?"

"You must come home with me, to marry me. Then I'll return you here. No one will even know yer gone."

When Cate laughed, he looked offended.

"Sorry. It's just that, as you can see"—she waved her arm unsteadily around to encompass the disarray in the room—"I've just been dealing with preparations for a wedding." *Is that green circle shrinking around him?* "I still don't get it. Why would you need me to marry you? You don't even know me."

"It's verra complicated."

No mistake, he really did look embarrassed now, and it made him seem much younger, almost vulnerable, as he ducked his head.

"I must marry if I'm to protect my sister. It's no a real marriage. Well, it is, but because it will be in my time, it's no real for you. You'll stay just long enough to marry me and then return to yer own time. Once I hae fulfilled the condition of marriage, I will be free to remain with my family, to protect my sister." He narrowed his eyes. "I will no allow anything to happen to you, lass, if it's fear holding you back."

"I'm not afraid." Well, that was a lie, but it made her feel better to say it. "Where, or should I say when, is your home?" Yes, the nervous breakdown hallucination theory was firming up as the front-runner now.

"Sithean Fardach. Scotland. The year of our Lord, 1272." For the first time, Connor appeared to study his surroundings. "It's a fair distant time for you?"

Cate laughed again. "Actually, 'fair distant' would pretty much be an understatement." *Now what?* She looked around the room. The glass she had set on the dressing table had fallen over. But instead of spilling, the warm caramel-colored liqueur was suspended in the air, never touching the ground.

"Did you do that? No, wait. Obviously you did. How did you do that?" She pointed at the suspended liquid.

"I canna explain. I dinna understand it all." He shrugged. "It's the Fae magic. Time has stopped here, allowing me to come for you. When you return, no matter how long yer in my time, you will be right here, right now—that's all I ken about it. We must hurry, please."

The green sphere is definitely growing smaller. And he didn't look to her like a man who said *please* often.

What did she have to lose? Chances were, she'd wake up in the morning, probably with a huge headache, and be quite amused by her hallucination.

And if not? If he's real?

Hadn't she just been told today—twice, in fact, by both Richard and her brother—that she needed to be more adventurous? What could be more adventurous than a quick visit to thirteenth-century Scotland? Accompanied by what had to be the most gorgeous man she had ever seen. A man who needed her help.

Connor held out his hand. "We must hurry. Time canna wait forever, no even for the magic."

Cate grabbed her pajama jacket and put it on, jammed her feet into the well-worn woven-grass flip-flops Jesse had brought her from his last trip to Thailand, and started toward Connor. She stopped at the last minute, grabbing her grandmother's wedding dress.

"Can I wear this to be married in?" She held the dress

clutched to her, eyeing him defiantly. If he said no, she wouldn't go.

"You can wear whatever you want, lass, I dinna care, but if yer coming, it must be now."

The sphere was pulsing again.

Making up her mind, she picked up the ribbon she'd pulled from her hair and tied it around the dress to form a small bundle. Taking Connor's hand, she stepped into the glow.

He drew her close, putting both arms around her as the sphere closed in on them. Tingles raced through her body. When he looked down at her, Cate was mesmerized by the intensity in his blue eyes.

"I swear, lass, on my honor, I'll no allow any harm to come to you. I'll protect you with my life. And when it's finished, I'll see you safely returned home."

The strength of his determination radiated from him. She was still captivated by the look in his eyes when he lowered his head toward her, slowly, almost as if against his own will. It took her by surprise when his lips met hers, her own eyes fluttering shut. Electricity arced through Cate's body at the simple touch as a multitude of colored lights lit the world around her.

The feel of his soft lips and strong arms and the look in his eyes as he made his promise were the last things she thought of as the lights winked out.

CHAPTER 3

In those final few moments between sleeping and waking, Cate experienced two distinct thoughts: the first involved plunging into a pair of blue eyes so electrifying she felt light-headed, and the second was that someone had left the water running.

She awakened fully indeed to find herself face-to-face with a pair of extraordinary blue eyes—just not the ones she'd been so thoroughly enjoying a few moments before. The water, however, was still running somewhere.

"So you're with us at last. Welcome, lassie, I'm exceedingly pleased to hae you here. We've so much to do." A lovely blonde woman took Cate's arm to assist her and sat watching her expectantly.

"Where am I?" Cate asked, looking around uncertainly. She was outside, sitting on the ground in a forest next to a pool of water, complete with waterfall. At least that explained the running water. This couldn't be possible. Last night had been a dream, hadn't it?

"Weel, I've no traveled through time myself, of

course, but considering how Connor felt when he awoke, I'm guessing you'll be a bit disoriented for while." The blonde stood and reached a hand down to Cate. "Try standing, lass—see if it disna help a bit. Moving around seemed to help Connor."

"Connor?" She rose unsteadily to her feet. "Oh, the big guy in the green light." The one who'd made her stomach do crazy somersaults when he put his arms around her. The one who'd made her forget to breathe when he'd kissed her. "Where is he?"

"He's gone hunting with Duncan. Having no idea when you'd awake, I thought to start the morning meal, so I sent them off." The woman brought a small bucket of water over from the fire. "Here. This is nice and warm. We'll get you up and ready. We should be able to finish everything before they return." She stood with her hands on her hips and smiled pleasantly down at Cate. "It's occurred to me, lass, that I dinna even know what you're called. I'm Rosalyn MacKiernan, Connor's aunt."

"Cate. Well, Caitlyn actually. Caitlyn Coryell. But everyone just calls me Cate."

Whenever she was nervous, Cate couldn't seem to restrain what came bubbling out of her mouth, and she hated it, so she stopped herself by splashing the warm water on her face. It did make her feel better, a little more in control. She reached up to push her hair out of her face. It was curling everywhere, a testament to the humidity in this place. For a fact, she wasn't in Colorado anymore. Now she knew how Dorothy must have felt.

"Weel, Cate, we must hurry if we're to finish the things that need done before the men return. Are you ready? Is there anything I can get for you before we start?" Rosalyn pulled a small velvet pouch from the leather bags piled on the ground.

"Before we start . . . what, exactly?" Maybe she needed to let this lady know that nothing was making any sense here.

"You agreed to help Connor, aye, to save his sister so she might find the fate of her own heart?" At Cate's nod, she continued. "We need thank our Fae Folk for their assistance and"—Rosalyn paused as if deciding on what to tell her—"to tie up the loose ends of the magic so we can proceed."

She took Cate's hand and led her around to the far side of the pool. There, by a tree literally covered in small pieces of cloth, Rosalyn opened the little pouch and pulled out a strip of material, handing it to Cate.

"Simply dip the cloth into the water, and thank the Faeries for yer safe journey. Then tie it on the tree, just like all the other bits there."

"What is the place?" Cate looked around thoughtfully. It was beautiful here, everything lush and green. It filled her with an unaccustomed sense of peace. But it certainly wasn't any place she recognized.

"This is the home of my mothers." Rosalyn looked around with obvious pride.

"Your mothers. How many 'mothers' do you have?"

"A multitude, child."

Rosalyn's musical laughter floated over the water, and Cate took the time to really study the woman. She was tall and willowy, at least half a foot taller than Cate, with light blonde hair pulled loosely into a bun at the nape of her neck. Beautiful would be a mild descriptor for this woman, who might be somewhere in her late thirties by Cate's guess. Most striking of all were her eyes, a study in blue intensity. Very like Connor's eyes.

Cate pushed her own hair out of her face again and made a quick decision. Real or a dream, she was going to make the best of this. What else was there to do?

After kneeling to dip the piece of cloth in the water, she tore it into two narrower strips and used one to tie back her hair out of her way.

"You need to speak to them, as if you actually see them."

But before Cate could utter a word, Rosalyn held up a hand to stop her. "Oh, and ask their blessing and aid for the rest of our . . . task."

Cate stood and faced the water, but Rosalyn again stopped her.

"Oh, and as we're dealing with the Fae"—she smiled sweetly at Cate—"it would no hurt to ask them to grant you true love. They like that." She nodded reassuringly.

"Ha!" Cate looked at the older woman, who was startled by her outburst. "True love? I'm not at all sure I believe in true love." Of course if anyone had asked her yesterday, she would have said she didn't believe in Faeries or time travel either. "But I do believe this, if it does exist, you can't force it to happen or just wish it into being."

"Oh, weel, you may hae the right of it, of course." Rosalyn looked down at the water, a mischievous smile forming on her lips. "But the Faeries, you ken? They believe, and it's them we're asking for help. So you see? Though they've their own way of doing things, we'd be best off to keep them happy." She shrugged.

Cate stepped to the edge of the water and cleared her throat. "Faeries? It's me, Caitlyn Coryell."

She really had never felt quite so foolish in her entire life, but Rosalyn sat there clutching her hands together, smiling and nodding encouragement.

"I want to thank you, all of you, for getting me here safely. And if you don't mind, could you send me home again just as safely? As soon as I'm married and we deal with saving Connor's sister so that she can . . . " *What was it Rosalyn had said?* "Find the fate of her own heart." She turned to Rosalyn. "Is that it?"

"If you're determined you'll no include the true love, I guess it'll hae to do." The woman sighed deeply before continuing. "All that's left is for you tie the strip to the tree."

The smile that had graced Rosalyn's face was gone, replaced with a sad little tightening around her eyes that made Cate feel unaccountably guilty.

Cate looped the strip around a low branch, feeling the burden of responsibility for the other woman's sorrow. "Oh, all right," she said, almost to herself. Turning back to the water, she called loudly, "Faeries? If we could just toss my finding true love into the mix, I'd be really grateful. Thank you very much."

She finished tying the cloth to the limb, shaking her head at her own behavior. Honestly. This had to be the most ridiculous thing she'd ever done. If she didn't count climbing into that green sphere last night, that is. But when she turned back to Rosalyn, she was surprised to find the woman looking at her with tears in her eyes.

"What? Did I do something wrong?"

Rosalyn smiled and shrugged her shoulders. "No. You did everything perfectly. It's just so happy I am." A conspiratorial smile replaced the tears. "You've pleased the Faeries and that pleases me. They're my family, you see." She nodded toward the water.

When Cate looked confused, Rosalyn put an arm around her shoulders and continued, "Let's get settled by the fire, and I'll tell you the Legend of the Faerie Glen and all about my family here."

It was done.

Rosalyn hid her excitement as she glanced at the young woman walking next to her. She was a wee thing, this Cate, but the Faerie magic had chosen her, so there was no doubt. She must be the one. She'd already demonstrated a good heart, easily agreeing to do as Rosalyn needed her to do, even though it was apparent she'd not wanted to.

When Connor had first awakened, Rosalyn had some brief concern as he'd taken one look at the woman lying in his arms and moved away from her quickly, as if he couldn't bear her touch. He'd been more than agreeable to go with Duncan, leaving it to her to deal with the lass.

Which had worked right into Rosalyn's plans.

Everything was going as she'd wanted. She hoped it would continue that way. Not that she really worried about the mortals. The Faerie magic was much stronger than any of them, so she no longer needed to worry about Mairi's fate.

No, it was the Fae themselves that concerned her. Oh, they'd grant their power, and fulfill the wishes and needs expressed in the ritual at the Clootie Well, so long as you met their conditions and passed their tests. It was just that they were a perverse race, always insisting on giving you what *they* thought you needed in the way *they* thought you needed it.

She smiled at Cate as they sat. There was something special about this young woman, she could feel it.

"Long, long ago on a beautiful spring day," she began her story, pushing aside all concern about the Fae. It would do no good to fret on it. They were all committed now.

It was done.

Rosalyn had prepared a kettle of oatmeal by the time the two men returned. The four of them sat around the fire quietly, as if no one knew exactly what to say.

Cate, lost in her own thoughts mulling over the fantastic fairy tale Rosalyn had told her, had barely done more than nod when she'd been "formally" introduced to the two men. She wanted to automatically dismiss the whole thing as ancient superstition, but, in all fairness, she was here, in the middle of this forest, and she had to have gotten here somehow.

Sitting here now, the three of them sneaking quick glances at her, she realized she had no idea what their plan to save Connor's sister required of her. Other than getting married, of course.

Well, no time like the present.

"So. Could one of you tell me exactly what it is you'd like me to do while I'm here?"

To her surprise, both men jumped when she spoke. Duncan almost dropped his bowl, and had to juggle a bit to keep it from spilling.

"Dinna you tell her, Aunt? I'd thought you wanted time with her to talk." Connor turned that piercing blue gaze on his aunt, arching his eyebrow.

"Weel, not exactly, nephew." Rosalyn fluttered her hands in an agitated manner. "We had to get her settled and all once she finally waked. Odds and ends to put in order, you ken? Besides"—she shrugged—"I thought it might be better for you to give her all the details."

A palpable tension filled the air.

Connor rose, dumped his drink into the fire and, setting the cup down, began to pace. Finally he stopped and looked directly at Cate. "My aunt is trying to save me embarrassment. But you'll hae need to hear it all if you're to help us."

He certainly had her attention now. In truth, he'd had it when he'd stood up. The man was tall. He was well over six feet. His brown hair hung in waves to his shoulders and curled a bit toward his face. He wore a tiny braid on one side that was currently tucked behind his ear. And he moved with a fluid masculine grace, all power and confidence.

His aunt wanted to save him embarrassment? Cate wondered just what it might take to embarrass a man like this.

"Seven years ago, I returned home to find my betrothed marrying another man." Connor exchanged a quick look with his aunt. "I was verra angry, and I may hae been a bit rash at the time." Duncan snorted and Connor stopped to glare at him. "Weel, what's done is done." He shrugged, and returned to pacing. "I went to the chapel—"

"Stomped up, right in the middle of the ceremony, yelling at the top of his lungs is more like it," Rosalyn interrupted.

"Verra weel. I stomped up. Then I made an oath before God—"

"And everyone else in the entire village." Duncan interrupted this time.

"And everyone else," Connor irritably acknowledged before continuing, "that as women were all deceitful and untrustworthy, I would marry none whose feet trod the land that day."

"A verra dramatic young man." Rosalyn and Duncan nodded to one another.

"Enough." Connor was clearly uncomfortable with their additions to his story. "Which brings us to now. My uncle is set to force wee Mairi to wed the MacPherson. The old MacPherson. Mairi disna want to. I can only hae say over her if I stay here and she lives under my roof and protection. But I'm in the king's service, to be sent where and when he pleases. He's agreed to release me only if I marry. So, you can see the problem and why yer needed." He leaned against a large tree and poked at the ground with the toe of his boot, while the others nodded in agreement.

"Actually, no, I still don't see why you needed me." Cate was baffled. "You're an attractive man."

Connor's mouth dropped open, while Rosalyn smiled and Duncan began to cough, as if to hide a laugh.

"Seriously. I'm sure there are plenty of women around here who would be more than happy to marry you. I don't understand why you needed to hunt through time for me."

"I made a vow." He spoke to her slowly, as if she were dull-witted. "My honor demands that I dinna break that vow. There is no woman in this land I can marry." Connor shrugged. "Not that I'd want to anyway. I'd no hae any of them."

"So, you're going to . . . what? Tell everyone that you swept me through time to come marry you?"

"No." Three voices rang through the glen simultaneously.

"Good Christ, no, woman. You'll no speak of that to anyone." Connor strode over to where she sat and knelt down beside her, taking her upper arm in his hand.

His touch sent shivers through her whole body, vividly bringing back the memory of the last time he'd touched her, in the sphere of green light.

"You ken that? No one must know about any of this." He swept his arm around to encompass the area where they sat.

"Let her be, Connor, you're frightening her. She's quivering," Rosalyn reprimanded.

He let go of her arm quickly, as if he'd been burned, and sat back on his haunches, but remained very close, a closed expression on his face as his aunt continued.

"There are those who dinna . . ."—Rosalyn paused to carefully consider her words—". . . appreciate my gifts. We would no want to upset them unnecessarily."

Cate thought about that for a minute. If this were in fact thirteenth-century Scotland, witchcraft would be looked on rather harshly. That could be very bad for all of them.

"We'll tell them you've been sent as a gift from Outremer." Connor picked up where his aunt left off. "The daughter of a nobleman whose life I saved in battle during the last Crusade. Of course, I hae no choice but to marry you." He shrugged his shoulders. "It's the only honorable thing to do."

He looked quite proud of himself.

"I can see the male ego hasn't changed in the last seven hundred years," Cate murmured, as Rosalyn chuckled softly. "So, you vowed to marry no woman here. Why didn't you just bring a wife home with you when you returned to Scotland?"

Connor's expression hardened. "Those here can assume I renounced the women of *this* land if they choose. When I vowed no woman, I meant *no* woman. There's none anywhere I'd wed. By using the magic, I may wed, but I have no wife. I've no desire to be shackled to any such devious creature."

"And once we're married, how do you explain it when I'm suddenly not here anymore?"

"We'll tell everyone that we've received word of yer mother's ill health and I've sent you home to be with her for a time." Connor's expression changed back to a satisfied little smirk. "A gift you may be, but even I'm no so hard a man I'd keep you from attending yer poor mother's bedside."

"So, I'm to be a *gift*." Cate emphasized the word with distaste and sighed deeply. "From the Holy Land. Fine. But understand, all of you, I don't lie well." *Is that skepticism in Connor's eyes?* "I'm serious. I'll have to stay as close to the truth as possible, or everyone will know something's wrong. And how am I supposed to convince them I'm Arabic? I don't speak the language, I don't know the customs, and I certainly don't look the part."

"Many a good Christian knight has remained in the Holy Land after the Crusades, raising a family and making a life for himself. I fought side by side with men such as those. You could easily be the daughter of one such as that. Besides, there's none here who'll know. And it'll go far to explain yer verra strange speech and manner." Connor raised an eyebrow in that superior expression she was starting to associate with him. "And yer even stranger clothing." All three of them nodded in agreement.

For the first time, Cate glanced down. She was still wearing her silk pajamas. Her face reddened as the heat spread down her neck. At least she'd thought to put the jacket on.

"We can say her ship hit storms and her things were lost at sea. That will explain why she has nothing else with her." The men nodded as Rosalyn picked up the story.

"Wait a second. I did have something with me. Where's my dress?" Cate suddenly remembered grabbing her grandmother's wedding gown at the last minute.

"Yer dress?" Rosalyn had begun cleaning her cooking utensils. "Oh, yer lacy thing? I've packed that in my bags. It'll be safe there until we reach Dun Ard."

"That doesn't sound like where you told me your home was last night." Cate looked toward Connor, who had picked up several bags and was heading away from their circle.

"Because it's no my home," he responded gruffly over his shoulder as he stalked away.

"Dun Ard is my brother, Artair's home. He's the laird now." Rosalyn briefly frowned at Duncan, who made a rude noise at her statement. "It's where Mairi and I live, and where we'll need to take you to announce that Connor's to be married. You'll stay there until the wedding." She stopped gathering items long enough to pat Cate's arm reassuringly. "Connor must hae mentioned Sithean Fardach, aye?" At Cate's agreeing nod, she continued. "That's where Connor stays when he's here. It's our ancestral home, where he grew up. The old castle is only a few miles from the new."

"Why aren't we staying at Connor's home? It would seem the less I'm around other people, the better off we'd be."

"An unmarried lass staying in the home of the man she's to wed would set tongues wagging. Besides, Artair isna going to be well pleased at Connor's marriage. We need him to believe you to be the real thing. So, Dun Ard it is, I'm afraid."

Cate rose to help Rosalyn gather the rest of the cooking items and put out the fire.

"Where have the men gone now?" she asked, looking around.

"It's time we're on our way. They've gone to get the horses. Late as it is, we'll likely be an additional night on the road." Rosalyn stopped abruptly when she glanced at Cate.

"Horses?" Cate squeaked, going deathly pale.

Oh, God, please not horses.

CHAPTER 4

The woman is insane.

Standing there in the clearing dressed in her strange trewes, with her hands on her hips and her green eyes flashing, she looked to Connor like one of the Fae Folk in whose glen she stood. Perhaps he was insane as well.

How did she think to get anywhere if she wouldn't get on the horse? Surely she didn't expect a fancy cart, although she was obviously the daughter of great wealth; he'd seen the strange, fine furnishings in her bedchamber.

The memory of being in this woman's bedchamber flowed through him like a flooding river. When he'd first seen her, standing by the bed with her hair curling around her bare shoulders, he'd momentarily forgotten why he was even there. She made him think of fire and wild things. She'd raised her arms, exposing flashes of bare stomach, and, well, it wouldn't do at all to think on this now.

He shifted uncomfortably on his horse.

"No." Cate firmly stood her ground. "No, no, no. I don't . . . there is no way. I can't ride on that horse by myself." She looked down for a moment, and when she lifted her head, her emerald eyes blazed. "I'm afraid of them, okay? There it is. I fell off one when I was little and I've never ridden since. I'm sorry, but I just can't." Her arms dropped limply to her sides.

The acknowledgment caught him off guard, bringing with it an unexpected sympathy for her. A fearful woman was something he could deal with, no different from a skittish horse. He needed only to move slowly, speak softly and take charge. She was, after all, his responsibility. He'd sworn to protect her from all harm.

Cate backed away as he edged his mount closer to her. Suddenly, in a single movement, he turned his horse, leaned down and swept her onto the saddle in front of him. She squirmed, breathing rapidly and clutching at his arms.

He pressed his mouth close her ear. "Dinna fash yerself, lassie." He spoke softly, as he might to a frightened animal. "Dinna I tell you I'd no let anything harm you? You'll ride here with me. I'll no let you fall. You can trust me."

Connor held her tightly as her breathing slowed, and she gradually leaned back against him. There was still tension in her body, but at least he didn't worry now that she'd wiggle herself off the horse.

The four of them rode in silence for quite some time. The feel of Cate's hair against his chin and her back stiff against his chest served as a constant distraction. He reminded himself that he held her here only to fulfill his duty. *Was it only duty that caused you to kiss the lass,* his conscience prickled? *And so soon after swearing to see to her protection?* It was no more than a momentary weakness brought on by the Fae magic, never to be repeated, he assured himself.

He straightened, pulling himself back from her a bit. She adjusted in his grip, her head once again resting on his chest, the scent of her filling his nostrils.

She smelled of exotic fruits like those he'd tasted while on crusade in Outremer. He glanced down. Her hair was tied back with what appeared to be a strip of cloth from his own plaid. It was as if it marked her as belonging to him somehow.

Connor shook his head, and tried to concentrate on the task at hand. They had a long way to go before nightfall.

Cate had never been so grateful in her entire life for the opportunity to just stand on her own two feet. Every muscle in her body ached—whether from bouncing on that giant horse all day or from trying to maintain her distance within Connor's embrace, she wasn't sure.

The man certainly had a presence. One that, if she wasn't careful, could easily lull her into a sense of security and belonging that didn't exist.

She helped Rosalyn as much as possible in setting up their campsite for the night. Now she was simply watching as rabbits the men had brought back earlier roasted over the fire. Hungry as she was, even that smelled delicious. Rabbit was certainly not something that had ever been on her menu back home, but it was likely just one of the many differences she should expect to encounter in this place.

I'm actually in the thirteenth century. It boggled her mind whenever she allowed herself to think about it.

What she needed was time to herself. Time away from all this, away from him, to process what was happening to her, to adjust.

"I'm going to walk down to the water. I'll be back in a little while." The stream was not too far from where they had chosen to camp.

"Do you hae need for one of us to accompany you?" It was the first Connor had spoken to her since he'd helped her off the horse when they'd arrived at this spot.

"No." She spoke more sharply than she'd intended in her haste. She attempted to soften it. "But thanks anyway."

"Weel, stay close. Mind now, do as I say. Yer to go no farther than the water." He barely looked at her as he gave the order and resumed his conversation with Duncan, dismissing her like a child.

It was the second time in two days a man had treated her like that.

"Men."

Cate stomped through the lush forest growth. Hard to imagine she had ever thought a "take control" attitude was attractive in a man. She'd known this one for less than twenty-four hours and already he acted as if he had the right to tell her what to do. Here he had just popped in, totally disrupted her life, planted the most electrifying kiss she'd ever had on her, made her think of nothing but him and then completely ignored her until he chose to give more orders.

"Classic male behavior."

Mumbling to herself, she rounded a large group of boulders and approached the water's edge. She knelt down, and after unbuttoning her jacket, dipped her hands in the water and splashed it over her face and neck.

The icy water cooled her face but not her temper. She was still fuming over Connor's attitude when she started to rise and unexpectedly found herself face-to-face with a huge, hairy, drooling beast.

She did the only rational thing she could think to do. She screamed.

Sword drawn, Connor raced toward the stream. Adrenaline flooded his body as his imagination conjured myriad dangers confronting the helpless woman in his care. What had he been thinking to let her wander off alone? The fact that her very presence distracted him from rational thought was no excuse. Her safety was his responsibility and his alone.

As he rounded the boulders, a most curious sight halted him in his tracks. Cate, on her back, pinned to the ground by an enormous dog. He couldn't immediately decide which was more amazing—Cate's giggling or the huge animal happily licking her face.

"Beast," he shouted. "Dinna maul the wee lassie."

The dog perked up his ears and ran to Connor, who ruffled his fur while the dog nuzzled his hand.

"I see you've met my companion. Yer no afraid of dogs, then?"

Cate sat up and brushed herself off. "I love dogs. I'm sorry I screamed. I just didn't realize that brute was a dog when I first saw him." She gave an embarrassed laugh. "Lord, he's the biggest wolfhound I've ever seen."

Connor leaned down, offering a hand to help her to her feet. The blush covering her face and neck was most attractive, especially as it crept down the skin now bared by her jacket's opening. The question of just how much of her skin might be covered by the warm pink color floated through his mind. He quickly let go of her and rubbed his hands together nervously.

"Beast disna usually take to strangers." Connor shook his head as they started back to camp. "I hae seen him chew upon someone on first meeting, but never carry on like he was. Are you in any way hurt?"

"No, he was very gentle. Well, after he knocked me down, that is." Cate smiled up at him. "Beast. Is that his name?"

"Aye, it's what I call him." She looked so young and trusting when she smiled at him like that. Naught but a woman's deceptive mask, he reminded himself. "It's what he is. He usually stays outside the camp when I'm with others."

He took her arm to help her over a downed limb, and somehow maintained that contact all the way back to the clearing, with Beast following closely at her heels.

The wolfhound remained at Cate's side. During the evening meal, Connor ignored her slipping bits of food to the creature as they ate. By the end of the meal, it appeared that Beast was completely captivated by their guest.

* * *

"Right here? On the ground. Out in the open?" She should have expected as much. It was, after all, the thirteenth century. It wasn't as if there were hotels along the road. "Not even a tent?"

All three of her traveling companions stared at her as if she'd lost her mind.

"It's time we sleep. You'll hae to make do. It appears there's no grand inns along our route, milady." Connor's mocking tone matched the haughty look he gave her now as he threw what appeared to be a bundle of blankets at her feet.

Both Rosalyn and Duncan took similar-looking bundles and arranged them on the ground a short distance from the banked fire, quietly climbing into their individual covers. Connor, his own bundle tucked under his arm, turned his back and walked a distance away from her.

She picked up the bundle he'd tossed to her and followed. "I don't expect grand inns." Though an inn of any sort would be more welcome than sleeping out in the open wilderness.

He didn't respond, or even bother to look at her, as he arranged his own bedding and lay down, closing his eyes as if to dismiss her.

"What if it rains?"

"Pull the covers over yer head. The woolens will keep you mostly dry." He still didn't look at her.

"Mostly dry," she repeated. "What about . . . about things out there?" She pointed vaguely into the darkness that surrounded them.

He huffed an impatient breath. "Things? What things?"

"I don't know. Animals. Bears. Whatever big things are

out there." *Bugs. Snakes.* Oh Lord, she hadn't even thought of them until now.

Connor opened his eyes and raised himself up onto one elbow. "Are you afraid, then, lass? Is that it?"

"No." Well, she hadn't been until she started to imagine all the possibilities that actually could be out there in the dark.

He studied her through narrowed eyes, clearly skeptical of her answer before he stood and took the bundle from her arms. He opened it, arranging the blankets on the ground next to his own.

"There. Lie down now and go to sleep. We've an early start tomorrow and a long ride ahead of us. I'll see to any 'things' what creep out of the dark tonight. Dinna you worry." He waited while she looked at the blankets, making up her mind.

Obviously this was her only option. She curled up on the blanket and he pulled a woolen cover over her, then lay down next to her.

Something cold touched her face and she jumped.

"It's only Beast," Connor whispered, but he put his arm protectively across her all the same.

This time it's only Beast, she thought, and scooted closer to him, grateful for the shelter of his arm. Let him think what he wanted; she wasn't really afraid, just being cautious. She would not think about what might be out there. She'd concentrate on going to sleep.

But sleep eluded her for quite some time as her fear of the wild was gradually replaced with a keen awareness of the man lying next to her. She remained awake, listening as his breathing became slow and regular. In sleep, his hold tightened, drawing her closer, and she didn't resist. The strong warmth of him comforted her. Lying in his arms like this, it would be easy to allow herself to imagine him more than he was, to imagine his caress of her meant more than it did. It was impossible not to remember the feel of his arms about her as he'd sworn to protect her from all harm, the look in eyes as he'd lowered his head, the feel of his lips electric against her own.

To her surprise, with Beast curled at her feet and Connor wrapped around her back, even the terrors of the dark forest couldn't prevent her feeling inexplicably safe. As she finally drifted off to sleep, thoughts of a handsome warrior haunted her dreams.

CHAPTER 5

It was growing dark by the time the castle came into sight, sitting as it did on the crest of a small hill. They'd been riding hard for the past hour or so, the men determined to reach their destination before full nightfall.

Cate was exhausted, both from so little sleep the night before and from the exertion of riding for two days. Her legs ached and muscles she didn't even know she had hurt. When she got home, she was never going to ride a horse again. Nothing she could imagine at the moment sounded better than a long hot shower.

Connor shifted the reins, bringing his arm closer around her. The movement brought a wave of memory, of how it felt to lie next to him all night, to be held by him, and she had to admit to herself that her imagination had quickly found something much better than just a shower.

Thinking along those lines, she closed her eyes and visualized a shower with him in it. She relaxed into Connor, allowing herself to get comfortable against his body, when suddenly he straightened in the saddle, tightening his arm around her.

"Riders," Duncan called, not sounding any too pleased as he and Connor quickly sandwiched Rosalyn's horse in between their own two.

"It's only Artair's men, come to escort us in," Rosalyn said as the riders pulled even and turned to surround their small party.

"Greetings, Fergus," she called to the leader of the group.

"Welcome back, milady." Fergus nodded to Connor and Duncan.

It was too dark now to see his face clearly, but Cate felt him and the other riders surveying her with curiosity.

Once they reached the castle, Connor dismounted first, reaching up to lift Cate down. It surprised her when, rather than quickly letting go of her as he had every other time he'd helped her down, he instead tucked her under his arm and drew her toward the entry.

"Yer uncle says I'm to bring you directly to his hall." Fergus seemed uncomfortable, as if expecting an argument.

"Tell my uncle we're tired from our hard journey. I'll join him in the morning."

Fergus held his arm across the door, and Connor's body tensed next to her.

"I'm verra sorry, Connor. Yer uncle says I'm no to take you anywhere but his hall." He shuffled his feet awkwardly.

"We may as weel get this over with, Nephew." Rosalyn leaned over to whisper to him.

"Verra weel, Fergus. Lead on."

In the dimly lit hall, several people sat behind a long table on a raised dais. Seated at the center of the group was a large, stern-looking man whose coloring was similar to Connor's. He must be the uncle. A lovely young woman with shiny black hair was seated on one side of him, while an attractive blond man lounged in the chair on his other side.

Rosalyn stood off to the side observing. Duncan had disappeared completely.

"Uncle." Connor bowed his head slightly in greeting.

"What was so important in Cromarty that you'd no the courtesy to tell me you were going, simply up and left in the middle of the night?" Artair shouted across the table, his reddened face reflecting the intensity of his anger.

"Really, Artair, he's hardly a bairn to ask yer leave. He was only here for a few days, visiting with Mairi." Rosalyn moved to seat herself at the table, motioning to the servant to bring her a drink. "And it was early evening when we left, Brother, no the middle of the night." She actually batted her eyes at the man.

"I'm no asking you, Sister. I'll thank you to keep yer place and let the lad answer for himself." He spoke through gritted teeth, glaring at her.

To Cate's surprise, Rosalyn seemed completely unaffected by him. Just seeing the look on that man's face made *her* flinch. He was clearly angry.

"A messenger brought word that my bride was arriving at the port of Cromarty. I had need to be there to meet her. There was no time to discuss it with anyone." Connor tightened his arm around Cate.

"You had time to discuss it with Rosalyn," Artair challenged with a glare. "I saw no messengers. And what's this about a bride? You said nothing about a bride when we last spoke. Where's she from that she'd arrive at the port in Cromarty?" His glare turned on Cate.

The man looked furious, his face a bright red, his eyes menacing. If not for Connor's arm around her, she would have been backing up.

"The message was mine, no yers, Uncle, so there'd be no need for you to see the messenger. Speaking to Rosalyn was necessary. I could no allow my bride to travel without a chaperone." Although Connor shrugged nonchalantly, the tension remained in his body where he held her next to him. "She's come from Outremer. I saved her father's life in battle and he's sent her to me to repay the debt." He paused only for a moment, scanning the faces of those seated in front of him. "We'll be married right away."

"Married?" Artair shouted. "No without my consent, and you'll no hae that. I forbid it."

The woman at the table gasped. "A heathen? You've brought a filthy little heathen into my home?"

"Anabella." Artair said only her name, without so much as looking in her direction, but it was enough to quiet her.

Connor didn't spare a glance to the woman, his eyes locked on his uncle. "I will wed her, with or without yer blessing. If I have to seek the king's approval over yers, I'll do so, though for the sake of our family, I'd prefer yer consent."

Artair continued to stare at Cate, but his look had turned speculative. His tone changed as well.

"There's no need to involve Alexander in our family affairs. If this one's naught but a heathen's gift for a life debt, lad, you've no need to sully yerself by marrying her. Take her to the old castle and set her up as yer mistress if you like."

Artair elbowed the younger blond man next to him and smiled as if he were well pleased with this new course of action.

"Her father's a wealthy nobleman in his country, Uncle. A man I respect. I would no shame him, or herself, in such a manner."

There was an edge to Connor's voice Cate hadn't heard before. He let go of her then, placing her behind him when he moved forward a few steps.

"We'll marry right away." He rested his hand lightly on the hilt of his sword.

Artair surged from his chair as Connor approached, the two men locking gazes. Tension rippled through the room. The situation had rapidly turned into something quite uncomfortable, something that appeared to be headed toward violence.

These people were nothing like the ones who'd greeted Cate upon her arrival. These people were absolutely hateful. Thank goodness she wasn't really here to marry Connor, or she'd be feeling pretty irritated with this current group.

Above all, Cate hoped that hateful woman up there wasn't Connor's sister. She didn't seem like someone Cate would particularly want to save.

"The filthy heathen's dressed like a common harlot, no a noblewoman, her legs outlined in trews without even the intelligence to look ashamed," Anabella sniped. "I'll no hae a street whore sleeping in my home."

Cate's mouth dropped open in shock. Her rational mind shut down as the exhaustion and irritation coupled. They spoke about her as if she weren't standing right there, as if she couldn't understand the words they said. And the nerve of that awful woman. These pajamas, although, granted, a little horsey at the moment, cost enough to keep that snotty cow in clothing for a year.

Cate fumed, listening without really hearing as they argued among themselves. Everyone was standing now, yelling about "banns" and "honor" and "heathens," pointing at her and carrying on until finally Cate had enough.

Wasn't she supposed to be the daughter of a wealthy nobleman? It was time she started to play her part.

She held up her hand. "That's enough."

No one seemed to notice her, least of all Connor, who had advanced another step toward the podium, his hand wrapped around the hilt of his sword now. The young man next to Artair fingered his sword as well. Things were going downhill quickly.

"I said that's enough," she yelled at the top of her voice. The room went silent at Cate's statement. "I've listened to you people bad-mouth me for as long as I'm going to. Now you can just listen to me for a minute."

Moving forward, she eluded Connor's attempt to grab her arm as she passed him, pitching her voice low to force their attention. "I will not be treated in this manner." She stepped onto the dais and slammed her hands down on the table, leaning toward those standing on the other side. "My name is Caitlyn Coryell, and I am not a heathen, filthy or otherwise." She swept those in front of her with a contemptuous glare before pulling herself up to her full height and looking down her nose at all those assembled, which was no easy task considering that everyone there towered over her, especially Connor's uncle, who stood directly in front of her, his eyes wild with anger.

"I have just traveled farther than most of you can possibly imagine. I am tired, hungry and dirty. I need a room. I need some decent food, and I need a warm bath."

Cate turned to walk out of the hall, emotionally drained after the scene she'd just endured. She stopped as she reached Connor.

"I'm not at all impressed with your family. Where I come from, at the very least we know how to take care of a guest in our home."

Fortunately he took her arm to support her as they walked out of the room. Her palms stung from slamming them on the table and her legs felt almost too weak to support her. Above the babble of voices in her wake, she thought she heard the sound of Rosalyn's laughter.

Cate sagged against Connor, exhaustion and nerves finally catching up with her. His strong arms pulled her close, her head resting against his chest. She felt strangely comforted by the vibration of his deep voice rumbling as he quietly spoke to the older woman who approached them. She didn't care who he spoke to or what they did. She only wanted to close her eyes and sink into the shelter of his protective embrace, where she felt safe.

Within minutes, she was pulled from that haven and escorted upstairs to a room, where, in very short order, she was served a meal of sorts. She'd only just begun to eat when someone else arrived with a large oblong wooden tub, followed by a parade of people carrying buckets of hot water.

The last person in the door was Rosalyn, her arms filled with cloth. She quickly herded all the servants out and closed the door behind them.

"Here are yer drying sheets, lass, and a nightgown you can use. I'll find some things for you to wear by the time yer up on the morrow. They've put you next to my room, so if there's anything you need, you only hae to call out at my door."

Cate looked down at her hands, feeling unaccountably weepy and working hard to blink back the tears. "I'm sorry if I was rude to everyone, Rosalyn. I just couldn't stand it anymore. They were staring at me and talking about me like I wasn't even there, and that woman was just awful."

"Aye, she's a poor excuse for a laird's wife, that Anabella. Dinna fash yerself over her. You dinna say anything they dinna deserve. It's best you remember to deal with that one in a firm manner. You did just fine. Now slip into yer tub while it's warm and then off to bed. Connor's with his uncle as we speak and will hae it all straightened out by the morn. You just rest."

Rosalyn embraced her at the door and left.

Cate undressed and sank into the tub, allowing her body to relax. How uncomfortable this small bath must be for all the tall people she'd seen in this family, but it worked well for her. The water was warm and the soap smelled of crisp, clean lavender. Her biggest challenge for the next few minutes would be to stay awake until she finished.

The encounter downstairs played through her mind and she flushed with embarrassment at the audacity of her actions. Nobody she knew would believe it of her.

Then she thought of Connor. He'd looked like an ancient warrior standing there, his hand resting on the hilt of his sword. Well, of course that's what he was, after all, so he should look the part.

She smiled, still thinking about him as she dunked her hair and scrubbed, feeling much better when she'd finished.

After climbing out of the water and wrapping herself in the drying sheet, she rinsed out her clothing and hung it on chairs in front of the cheerful little fire. The nightgown was much too long, but after standing on the cold stone floor, she felt good tucking her feet into the length of it when she slipped into bed.

Just before fading into an exhausted sleep, her thoughts were filled with images of Connor, fierce and strong, standing in the hall, mingling with her feelings of safety and comfort as he'd held her in his arms. The same feeling she'd had last night as he held her in the forest. Threading through it all was the memory of his kiss, the feel of him lightly touching her lips with his own. It was a heady mixture.

CHAPTER 6

V isions of extraordinary blue eyes once again filled her
dreams, but on this particular night she also enjoyed visions of equally extraordinary strong arms.

Upon waking, Cate stretched, only to find her feet
blocked by a heavy, solid object.

"Beast, how did you get in here?" she asked the huge
dog, sitting up to fondly scratch his head.

"I let him in. Dinna you hear him whimpering
through the night outside yer door? It's fair odd, though.
He's never come in the castle when Connor stayed here
before."

Cate jumped, swiveling her head around to discover
a young woman sitting in one of the chairs by the fire.
She looked like a younger version of Rosalyn, her pale
blonde hair hanging in a long, thick braid pulled over her
shoulder.

The young woman rose and moved to the bed, shoving Beast aside so she could perch herself in his place, all
the while eyeing Cate speculatively.

"I'm Mairi." She lifted her feet, which were bare, to

tuck them under her where she sat. "And yer the one to be my new sister?"

So this was Connor's sister. Yes, she had his blue eyes.

"Hello, Mairi. I'm Cate." Unsure about proper medieval protocol for meeting future in-laws while you were still in bed, Cate leaned forward and extended her hand.

"I'm no going to kiss yer hand," Mairi said derisively. "They warned me you act like royalty."

Cate's hand dropped to her lap. Apparently teenagers were pretty much the same in every century.

"I didn't plan on your kissing it." At Mairi's look of doubt, she continued. "Where I come from, we shake hands with one another as a civilized form of pleasant greeting. I'm sorry, but I don't know what you do here."

Mairi's eyes lit up. "So it's true. You do come from the Outremer. What else do you do there? What's it like to live in the Holy Land? Oh, I'd so love to see anywhere so verra different, to travel and hae some adventures as you must hae had. You must tell me all about yerself." She drew up her knees, her arms hugging tightly around them, eagerly poised for Cate's answer.

Other than the clothing, this suddenly had the feel of a slumber party. All that was missing was an adult to quiet them down.

As if on cue, a quick knock sounded and the door opened, revealing Rosalyn, once again carrying an armful of cloth.

"Mairi. What are you doing in here, lass?" She scolded, but with a smile in her eyes.

Mairi sat up straight. "I wanted to see her for myself. I never thought to have a sister. Connor said he'd no marry, ever." She paused, casting a sly glance at her aunt. "I wanted to see for myself what the 'foreign hussy princess' was like." Her eyes twinkled.

"Och, Mairi. I dinna think Anabella would hae spoken to you already about this." Rosalyn shook her head in disgust.

"No, Auntie, it was Florie who told me." She turned to Cate. "Florie's a maidservant, but she tells me everything. I like her verra much." Then turning back to her aunt, "She says Anabella was in a fair fit last eve'n." A broad smile covered her face. "That alone is enough to hae many here look kindly upon you, Cate. Dinna let that hateful woman get the better of you." She turned back to her aunt. "Florie says Artair was even worse, screaming that he'd no hae his plans set aside for the foreign hussy."

Rosalyn shook her head. "No, I dinna suppose he'll give up easily."

Mairi snorted and leaned back on her elbows. "It isna like it matters, Aunt. He's no match for the power of the Fae, now is he? And he, of all people, should ken that well. He is, after all, yer own brother."

"He seemed awfully angry last night," Cate ventured.

"Aye," Rosalyn acknowledged. "But he'll come round to his senses. In the meantime, we'll just make the best of it, but keep our eyes and ears open."

"That's exactly why I'm here. To tell you all I've heard." Mairi smiled sheepishly. "Well, that and to see my new sister for myself."

"It's just as weel yer here, child. We've much to do today. We'll have Cate try on the shifts and then you can take them down to Beitris for the girls to alter." Rosalyn turned to stare critically at Cate, who had climbed out of bed. "I'm sure they'll all be much too long."

"Aye." Mairi nodded in agreement. "She's a wee thing, no mistake."

Cate sighed. Just her luck; of all the places to be whisked off to, she had ended up in the land of fearless Amazon women. These ladies were almost as tall as Connor. A mental picture of him standing in the hall, looking dangerous, defying his uncle last night crept into her thoughts unbidden. First her dreams, now this. Everything seemed to make her think of him. The familiar warmth spread up her face.

"Oh no, Cate, dinna feel badly. It's no trouble to alter these things."

She was grateful that Mairi had misunderstood the source of the blush.

The three of them began to sort through the garments, creating a pile to be altered. They finally found one dress and shift that, with a belt and some fancy tucking, Cate could wear today. She insisted on wearing her own underwear since they didn't seem to have anything comparable to it in this time.

Mairi left with an armful of things for the seamstress while Rosalyn began to braid Cate's hair.

"You know, I enjoy playing dress-up as much as the next woman, but isn't it a waste of time to have all that clothing altered? I mean, I'm really only here for a day or two."

Rosalyn's hands stilled, and suspicion began to form in the pit of Cate's stomach when there was no reply.

"Isn't that right? Rosalyn?" She turned, but the older woman nervously avoided meeting her eyes. "Oh Lord. Now what?"

"Weel, lass, just a small thing we'd no counted on. The banns must be read. And the surrounding crofters invited."

When Cate started to speak, Rosalyn stopped her by grasping her head and turning it back around to finish her hair. "We'll go down and meet with Connor in a bit. He can explain it all to you then. He's worked out all the details and already set things in motion."

"How long?" No sense in dragging this out. She wanted to know.

"No so long. Just enough time for the banns to be read, you see. Artair is insisting on following the old tradition, and like it or no, he is the laird. Following that, there's the invite to the villagers and crofters, and then you have the wedding." She was making it sound deceptively easy and pleasant.

"So what are we talking here? Three, four days?"

That might not be so bad. Considering what passed for meals here, what she could really use was a quick trip to Taco Bell, but a couple of extra days would be bearable. It just might help with that little ten-pound problem she'd been fighting.

Still, Mairi must have carried away eight or nine garments and as many sets of sleeve covers to be altered. Suspicion surged back again when Rosalyn didn't answer.

"Rosalyn?"

"Oh, verra weel." She sounded annoyed as she tied off the end of Cate's braid with the same little strip of cloth

Cate had used earlier. "The banns must be posted at the church door every Sunday for three weeks."

"Three weeks," Cate yelped as she turned. "I can't stay here for three weeks."

"Weel, you canna go back until you've married. You put the condition on it yerself at the Clootie Well, when you spoke to the Fae, dinna you remember? You asked to be sent back safely after you'd finished yer task. The magic will no work until that time."

"Oh, no." Not three weeks in this place. "No, no, no." She stood and paced. There had to be some way out of this. This wasn't at all what she'd agreed to.

"Where's Connor?"

Connor was unprepared for the small bundle of fury that burst through the door into the solar, where he waited. She might look the part of a proper lady, dressed as she was in a blue gown, with bits of a white shift peeking out at arm and neck. But the resemblance stopped the instant she opened her mouth.

"Three weeks?" Cate hissed at him as she entered the room. "What happened to 'Come home with me and I'll bring you right back,' " Cate fumed, pacing back and forth, coming to stand in front of him, one hand on her hip, the pointer finger of her other hand poking his chest. "You lied to me," she accused, eyes blazing.

"Leave us. And shut the door." The command was low and menacing. No one spoke to him in that manner.

Duncan edged from the room immediately, but Rosalyn remained in the doorway.

"It's no proper for the two of you to be alone in here," she began reasonably, but she didn't get to finish.

"Out," Connor bellowed, and Rosalyn slammed the door behind her.

He looked down at Cate. She glared up at him.

"I dinna lie. Ever."

"Right. All men are so honest." Her voice dripped with sarcasm. "Then what was all that 'I'll bring you right back, no one will even know you're gone' crap? I'm not staying here for three weeks, Connor, I won't do it." She'd poked his chest again to emphasize her last words.

He captured her hand, flattening it against his chest. It trembled there next to his pounding heart. For some reason, it was vastly important to him that she should believe what he told her.

"I'm no all men. I'm just me, and I dinna lie. I told you when it was done, I'd see you returned home, and so I shall. It's no done until we marry. We canna marry until the banns are posted on the church door three Sundays in a row." He shrugged. "Artair insists on following the old custom."

"Old custom? Okay, well then, what about handfasting? I read that you guys always did that. That's an old custom here. Couldn't we just handfast, tell them it's done and you get your sister? Why can't we just do that now and be finished with it?"

Well read or not, the woman had a good deal to learn about the old customs. He'd start her education now.

"Och, aye, handfasting is an old custom, lass. But after a year, we're either of us free of it if we choose. The king isna going to release me for such as that." He shook his head. "Unless you want to stay with me for the year? If we renew for the second year, he mayhaps consider then."

Her look of panic didn't appear feigned.

"I dinna think you would like that so much." He used his free hand to lift her chin, allowing him to look her squarely in the eyes. "Four weeks. Three Sundays for the banns, and then the wedding. I must insist on this from you, but I'll ask no more. It will be done by then and I'll see you home. It's only four weeks, Cate, and it means the safety of my family and Mairi's future. I canna see her given to a man she disna love." That alone would mean the end of his family.

The fight drained out of her; she bowed her head. She didn't try to pull her hand free, and he didn't release it. When she raised her head to meet his gaze, he saw the unshed tears pooled in her eyes.

"Yer no going to bubble on me, are you, lass?" Tears were foreign to him, one of the female tricks he would not bow to. He took her chin in his free hand again and stared at her intently. She must understand what was at stake here.

She took a deep breath, and the Cate he was coming to know returned.

"Okay. Four weeks. I can do this for four weeks. But that's it. Absolutely, positively no more than four weeks."

"It's a bargain then. Four weeks. The first of the banns will be posted on the morrow. We'll attend the service together to make sure."

Suddenly aware that he still held her trembling hand, he released her, walking to the other side of the room that seemed even smaller now, putting distance between them.

Cate cupped the hand he had released, rubbing it with her thumb.

"Did I hurt you, lass?" He thought he'd held her gently.

"What?" She seemed distracted. "No, I'm fine. I just . . . I'm fine." She seemed to notice then what she was doing with her hands and quickly put them behind her.

Ah, there was that lovely pink color spreading up her neck and across her cheeks again. He had to admit, he rather enjoyed seeing her do that.

He cleared his throat, waiting for her to look up again. "There will be a gathering tonight, in celebration of our betrothal."

"Celebration? I certainly wouldn't expect any of your family to be celebrating your betrothal to a filthy little heathen like me."

"They were no too welcoming last night, were they?" Connor shook his head. "But once the women left, we arrived at a compromise, though my uncle is none too pleased with the idea of my wedding." It was why the man insisted on following the old customs, to buy time. Of course, it would do him no good. The wedding would take place and Connor would be released from the king's service, freeing him to watch over Mairi.

"The celebration is part of that compromise." As Artair insisted on following the old customs, Connor insisted they all be followed. The man wanted to buy time? He could pay for it with the goods from his larder, feeding the people who came.

"Well, in any event, I'm sorry for being rude to them. I was tired, and they were . . . not what I expected."

"It's a small matter. You hae no call to apologize. Yer words made all of us stop and think." He walked back over to where she stood and extended his elbow. "For now, may I escort you around the holdings, so you can see where everything is? It's what I'd planned before our wee discussion."

"I'd like that." She took the arm he presented and in return offered a shy smile.

His lower stomach clenched at that look. There was something so innocent about this woman that it completely disarmed him. It was only with effort he reminded himself that all women used their wiles to force men to their will.

And that Connor MacKiernan would never be tricked by a woman's wiles again.

CHAPTER 7

You must calm yerself, Father." Blane reached out toward the older man, letting his hand drop under his father's glare.

Artair stared at his older son. Could he not understand the fine line they walked? "Calm myself?" he hissed. "I canna afford to be calm. I must find a way to stop him from wedding that foreign harlot." *Have to think. Have to think.* His brain raced, the pain building once again in the center of his forehead. *Not now. Not now.*

"It willna matter. We'll come up with another way, Father. I've never been fond of the idea of giving Mairi to the MacPherson."

"No," Artair yelled. "The deal has been struck. I canna change that now." Blane, the son who would one day be laird in his footsteps, should be held responsible for this, too. Why must he always be the one to handle all this pressure? "You, yer the one who stands to lose everything when Connor challenges me for the lairdship."

Blane glared at him with accusing eyes—always with the accusing eyes.

"Connor has told you many a time he's no interested in taking the clan from you, Father."

"Ha! So he says. You canna believe yer enemy, son. Never believe yer enemy." And Connor was the enemy, he didn't doubt that for a moment. "First he plans to ruin me with the MacPherson by keeping Mairi from him, then, when I have no allies, he'll mount a war to take everything." *Everything. I'll lose everything.* After all he'd done for his ungrateful nephew. Now his son. Blane should help him, should deal with his cousin. "You, you should do something."

"What would you hae me do, Father?"

"Prevent the marriage. If he disna marry, he'll hae to return to the king's service, and all will be well. I've bought you time, lad. They canna wed for at least four weeks. Stop the wedding in any way you can."

"As you wish, Father." Blane ducked his head in a quick bow and turned, leaving Artair alone.

For now, he'd play along. Let Connor think he'd won. Wait until their guard was lowered. See what Blane could accomplish.

If his son wasn't successful, there were always other options.

CHAPTER 8

A nxiety was eating away at Cate. She'd been dressed and ready for at least half an hour, waiting to go down to the betrothal celebration. At this point, she almost wished she had agreed to go with Mairi to Anabella's solar to wait for Connor, but the thought of facing that woman without Connor at her side had been more than she wanted to deal with. This waiting, however, was turning out to be almost as bad.

Nervously patting her hair, she wondered for at least the tenth time if she hadn't made a big mistake. Rosalyn and Mairi had wanted to put her hair up in braided coils. She'd refused, telling them there was no way she was going to a medieval party wearing a Princess Leia hairstyle. She really needed to work harder at monitoring what came out of her mouth.

Cate chose instead to let her hair hang loose, pulling back just the sides from her face and tying it in place with her only hair ornament, the little strip of cloth she'd used since her first day here.

The hairstyle discussion had been bad enough, but the

idea of wearing that little hat with the goofy chin strap they'd brought was where she drew the line. Anyway, since she was from a foreign land, more foreign than most of them could guess, everyone would just have to accept her doing things a little differently.

What she wouldn't give for a mirror. The linen shift next to her skin felt odd. For this outfit she had finally agreed to forgo her bra, an undergarment that endlessly fascinated the curious Mairi. On reflection, it had been a good decision. The emerald green overdress laced up in such a way that she felt as if her breasts in the linen shift were being served up on platter. The bra straps would have shown, no mistake about it, as both the dress and the shift fell wide on her shoulders.

Once again, Cate anxiously ran her hands down the front of the overdress, feeling the heavy embroidered patterns that covered the bodice and skirt of the soft wool frock. She tried to tell herself that it wasn't Connor's opinion of the way she looked that concerned her, but rather what all those people she'd met last night might think. Deep down, though, even she wasn't buying that argument. She wanted to look good for him.

"So stupid, Cate. He's just a man."

He was like all men, interested in her only for what she could do for him. In his case, his only concern was to marry her to save his sister. Admittedly a noble cause but still totally his cause. She, Cate, meant nothing; was completely interchangeable. She could be any woman in the world. Well, any woman who hadn't been alive seven years ago when Connor had his temper tantrum, at least.

Lost in thought, Cate jumped at the sound of a light

tap on her door. One last time she smoothed her dress and hair before answering the knock. When she did, what she saw standing there left her speechless.

"Good eve'n." Connor lifted his head from a courtly bow and stood, simply staring at her.

He was magnificent; she could think of no other description. His hair fell softly about his face, emphasizing his strong features and fascinating eyes. Her fingers itched to touch the tiny braid at the side of his face, to tuck it behind his ear. He was wearing a crisp linen shirt, laced just to his throat, and over that a plaid, wrapped about him as usual, but this one was obviously newer than the one she'd seen him in before, with more vibrant colors. A large emerald pin held the plaid at his shoulder.

Her eyes dropped to his legs, strongly muscled, covered in fine dark hair above the soft leather boots he wore. Unbidden, the old question about what a Scotsman wore under his kilt came to mind.

He cleared his throat, smiling at her as if he'd read her thoughts.

That horribly embarrassing blush crept up her throat and onto her face, accompanied by an overwhelming need to say something, anything, to fill the silence.

"I hope you didn't mind coming to my room to meet me. I mean, I suppose it's not really proper for you to be in my bedroom. Your sister offered me the use of your aunt's solar, but I didn't feel comfortable with that, not with your aunt and all."

Clamping her mouth shut to cease the flow of nervous babble took effort and she had to consciously stop her hands from smoothing the skirt yet again.

"I've been in yer bedchamber before, remember?" That half smile again, the one that made her heart skip a beat. "I dinna realize Rosalyn had a solar here. I'd thought she just kept a small room." He tilted his head and looked at her questioningly, arching that eyebrow.

"No, I meant your aunt Anabella's solar."

His eyes hardened immediately, and his whole body stiffened. "That woman's no my aunt. She's my uncle's wife, no more."

He shut her out. Just like that. Anger flowed from him like a living thing.

Flustered, unable to imagine what had gone wrong so quickly, Cate could only think of escape. "Well, I guess we should go down. I'm ready," she said, anxious to move beyond whatever it was she had done.

"No, yer no ready yet." He shook his head and brushed past her, entering her room as she looked about in confusion.

It must be her hair. She should have listened to Rosalyn.

"Ah, here we are." He moved across the room, stopping at the table beside her bed where he picked up the pendant that had guided him to her in the beginning. "Yer no wearing yer betrothal gift."

He walked behind her and gently lifted her hair. Cate was unable to resist when he raised her hand, placing it on her head to hold her hair out of the way as he draped the chain around her throat, fastening the clasp at the back of her neck.

"Now yer ready." He moved his hands to her bare shoulders, resting them lightly there.

Her body responded as one huge sensory receptor. She could feel the weight of his hands on her shoulders and the brush of his breath on the top of her head. Even the hard metal of the pendant felt unusually warm where it touched her skin.

Cate slowly lowered her arm as Connor, still behind her with one hand burning into her shoulder, reached around her to lightly touch a finger to the stone where it hung nestled just above her breasts.

Her breath caught in her throat.

His hand remained there for a moment before he spoke. "This will serve notice to everyone tonight of who and what you are." His voice was low and husky.

"And what am I?" She couldn't believe how breathless she sounded.

His eyes sparkled dangerously as he moved to her side. "The betrothed of Connor MacKiernan."

He touched the jewel he wore pinned over his heart and she realized that it matched the stone she wore exactly.

She gratefully took the elbow he extended, allowing him to escort her down to the great hall below. There had been a moment, with him close to her, his hand on the jewel at her throat, when she'd thought he might kiss her again, but the moment had passed.

Her own fingers lifted to touch the pendant at her neck. Betrothal gift, he'd called it. There was no corner antiques store here where he could have accidentally found such a set. They would have been made by special request. It occurred to her that the necklace looked old even here in its own time, as did the matching pin he wore. She suspected they had their own story.

Sneaking a glance at the handsome profile of the man who walked with her, she wondered if he might one day share that story with her, especially now that she felt she was somehow a part of it.

The music had been playing for hours, it seemed to Cate, while serving people brought course after course of food, much of which she couldn't identify. Some of it was even fairly tasty. Her only real complaint with the meal was directed at the drink. As best she could tell, these people drank alcohol with every meal from the moment they woke up to the time they went to bed. So far, she had managed to get them to bring her water with her meals, although they looked at her as if she were insane when she asked for it.

Tonight, however, everyone was busy, running back and forth with food, and she was left with the choice of ale or spiced wine. She had finally given in and had a bit of the spiced wine, but it tasted harshly bitter, and while it helped quench her thirst, it didn't sit well on her nervous stomach. Nor did it cool her down. If anything, she felt even hotter. With all the bodies and the large fire, it was quite warm in the great hall, and her lovely wool dress, which had seemed just right in her room, now felt exceedingly uncomfortable. Beads of perspiration slowly rolled down her bodice and she could feel a headache starting.

Cate sat at the large table on the dais tonight, Connor on her left and Rosalyn on her right. Artair and Anabella, who she'd thankfully managed to avoid so far this evening, were seated farther down the large table, at the center.

Long tables were placed all about the hall, filled with laughing, talking people, who she assumed must live in or around the castle. Duncan had been at one of those tables when they had first entered.

People milled about, speaking to one another between courses, snatches of conversation drifting all around her. She was uncomfortably aware of the curious stares directed her way and knew many of the conversations were no doubt about her.

Cate felt an irrational disappointment that Connor had not spoken to her since they'd been seated. He had, in fact, acted as if she weren't even there. It was all the more confusing since he'd seemed quite attentive when he'd come to her room to collect her. That had ended the moment they entered the hall.

It shouldn't matter to her in the least. But it did. Worse yet, she wasn't sure whether she was more upset by his lack of attention or by her response to it.

At this moment, Connor appeared deeply involved in a discussion with the young man on his left, who Rosalyn had told her was his cousin Lyall. Rosalyn herself had risen and moved down from the dais, where she was speaking to Duncan, her hand resting lightly on his forearm. Even Mairi was nowhere to be seen.

Cate's dress was too hot, she wanted some water and she felt abandoned. All these strangers were staring at her and talking about her. In some small, still logical part of her brain, Cate recognized that she was working herself into an emotional state. Although she had no explanation for her intense feelings, she didn't seem to be able to do anything to stop them.

This was so unlike her. She had to calm down. She could barely breathe in here.

She remembered a large balcony off this hall from earlier today when Connor had taken her on a tour of the grounds, and thought to make her way there now. Knowing no one would miss her if she escaped to grab a breath of air, she quietly rose and made her way to the side exit.

She walked to the end of the balcony and leaned far out over the railing, inhaling deeply in the moist, cool evening. She could smell the green forest that lurked just beyond the faint circle of light cast by the torches. Although she could still hear muted strains of the music from inside, here it felt cool, quiet and peaceful. It was exactly what she'd needed.

Cate had just begun to relax when she felt a hand at her waist. Startled, she whirled around to find herself facing the blond man who had sat next to Artair last night.

He immediately removed his hand and, backing away, held the hand up as if to stop her from protesting.

"I'd no wanted to alarm you, Cousin, but I feared yer falling over the rail." His smile didn't quite reach his eyes.

"Cousin?" She moved forward, away from the railing, yet not toward this man. There was something about him that made her uncomfortable.

"Blane MacKiernan." He bowed his head slightly, watching her all the while. "Eldest son of Artair, laird of the MacKiernan. If you were to marry Connor, you would be my cousin."

In the dim light he watched her closely as if he were attempting to assess her reaction to him.

"When," she corrected. "When I marry Connor. Not if."

He flashed that humorless smile again. "From yer speech in the hall last night, you seem an unusually intelligent woman." He paused, once again seeming to evaluate her. "I have a proposition I think you'll find sensible."

"What do you mean, a proposition?" Cate asked. She knew she sounded suspicious, but the last proposition she'd listened to had landed her in the Middle Ages for a four-week tour of duty.

"I would propose that instead of marrying my cousin, you entertain my own suit for marriage." He watched her closely over the rim of his goblet as he took a long drink.

"What?" She forced a small laugh. "Surely you're joking. Wouldn't that be a terribly unkind thing to do to your own cousin?"

Blane shrugged. "He's a grown man, he'd survive it." The cold smile was back. "He survived Anabella's rejection of him." He took another drink from the goblet he held.

"Anabella?" Anabella was the betrothed who had married another man? That certainly explained a few things. "She rejected him for his own uncle?"

"You dinna ken that? Granted, she's a spoiled bitch with a terrible temperament, but she's no stupid. My father is the MacKiernan, laird of the clan. He could provide her with everything she wanted. Connor's but a warrior. What could he ever hope to give her? A crumbling castle with no wealth? She made the sensible choice." He took another drink. "The same kind of choice I'm now offering to you."

"How could your father do that to his own nephew? Didn't he realize that she was supposed to marry Connor?" There had to be a reasonable explanation for that sort of behavior.

"Of course he did. Everyone did." He shrugged again. "But my father is the laird. He wanted a young, beautiful, willing wife. Anabella was eager to be that."

Blane's callous attitude appalled her.

"Forgive my confusion, but I still don't understand why you'd want to marry me. Why would you make such an offer to someone you don't even know?" This had certainly been her week for weird marriage proposals.

"I canna believe you dinna ken yer own worth." That smile again, still not reaching his eyes. Moving closer to her, he tossed his goblet over the edge of the balcony and took her upper arms in his hands. "Yer a desirable woman, a mixture of untamed beauty and intelligence. I'm no aware of any man who could resist that." As he lowered his head to hers, Cate placed her hands on his chest and shoved, freeing herself to move backward, up against the rail.

He was an attractive man, tall, blond and well built. Many women would be drawn to his sensuous features. He radiated an air of self-assurance. But there was something lingering behind his eyes that made her uncomfortable, something arrogant and intimidating, perhaps even devious.

He reminded her of someone else. Of Richard. Other than basic build and blond hair, they didn't look that much alike, but they certainly shared an attitude. And they both had that look.

It suddenly struck her that she hadn't thought of Richard even once since she'd been here, and did so now only when confronted with this man who made her so uncomfortable, who made her skin crawl when he had his hands on her. Dealing with this man would require caution.

"Well, of course I'm very flattered by your most interesting offer, but I'm afraid I'm unable to accept." She tried for a smile, but couldn't quite manage one.

"No a sensible choice," he chided as he edged closer to her. "Dinna think Connor will ever be laird of the MacKiernan. That will be mine." The smile was back. "He may hae spent his early life believing that to be his path, but it's no his fate. When his father died, my father became laird, and it's I who'll follow him."

Cate's curiosity got the best of her.

"So, Connor's father was the laird at one time? I thought that sort of thing passed from father to son."

"The lairdship passes from strength to strength, as it should. Connor was but a bairn at the time." His face took on the assessing look again. "So you see, I am the sensible choice. I'll be able to give you a life he never will."

"Well, that's all very interesting, Blane, but really it has no bearing on my decision. I'm not marrying Connor because of his title or what he can give me."

"Surely it's no yer father's life debt? He's a world away from here. He'll never ken what happens to you. You hae to make the best life for yerself."

Obviously he didn't easily accept rejection. She needed an irrefutable reason that even this stubborn man would acknowledge. Something like love? Since men didn't understand it, they certainly couldn't argue with it.

Cate took a deep breath and let it out slowly to calm her racing heart. "Perhaps I can help you understand why my choice can't be changed. You see, my arrival here wasn't the first time I'd seen Connor. The first time I saw him, I was standing in my bedroom." She had his attention now. "From that first moment, from the first time I heard his voice, it was clear he was the only man I'd follow to this place to marry. It was my own decision, not my father's, that I come here to wed him. My father would never force a marriage on me that I didn't want. He's the kind of man who would do everything in his power to secure for me any man of my choosing."

Technically every word of it was the truth. She smiled now, quite pleased with herself.

Until she saw the anger behind Blane's smile. Cate scooted back against the railing as far as possible and began to nervously finger the pendant around her neck.

Blane's eyes locked on the movement of her hand, his smile never faltering.

"You do realize that Connor will never love you? He's no capable of that emotion, no for any woman. He may marry you, but it'll be a poor, cold life."

She shrugged indifferently. "It doesn't matter how he feels about me. I make my own decisions based on my own feelings."

"You make yer decisions poorly then. Yer a prime example of why women should no be allowed to think for themselves. Love is no a reason to wed. Marriage is a business transaction, pure and simple. Each of the parties has something the other wants."

He reached out and grasped the pendant, allowing the back of his hand to rest against her breast, as he lowered his head toward her again.

Cate shoved against his chest, but this time he didn't budge, and with her back against the balcony railing, she had nowhere to run.

Connor felt her absence the instant she stood to leave.

When he'd first gone to meet her this evening, there had been a moment there in her bedchamber where he'd almost lost control, almost fallen into the trap of thinking of her as belonging to him.

When she'd stood in the doorway, her hair flowing about her as it had that first time he'd seen her, he could have sworn it was desire he saw in her eyes. Then, with his hands on her bare shoulders, feeling the heat of her body, the trembling beneath his fingers, his mind had wandered briefly and he'd wondered what it was he might see in the depths of those eyes if he lifted her to the bed and stayed there with her.

He'd come to his senses. It had taken considerable effort, but he made sure he didn't make that mistake again throughout the evening. He'd kept his distance. He'd remained unaffected by her.

Until he felt her leave.

She'd slipped out the door to the balcony and then, shortly after, his cousin had followed her. When moments later he followed as well, it was only to see to her safety, or so he told himself.

He slipped silently into the shadows of the dimly lit balcony, stopping to pick up a cloak he found lying on one of the tables near the door.

Now he was growing increasingly agitated watching as she flirted with Blane, going so far as to place her hands on his cousin's chest. He took a deep breath. It didn't matter to him what she did. His only concern was that she honor her pledge to aid him in saving his sister. Once that was done, she could return to her own time and seek the company of as many men as she pleased. That was, after all, what women did.

Keeping to the shadows, he edged closer to the couple on the balcony. From there he could listen to the faithless wench. Only in the interest of making sure she kept her pledge of course, or so he told himself.

This close he could hear her words and, even in the dim light of the balcony, he could easily see her expression. From this vantage, the scenario was entirely different.

Backed against the rail as she was, Cate reminded him of a frightened doe as Blane took her pendant into his hands and obviously moved to kiss her.

She hadn't been caressing Blane's chest; she was trying to push him away.

The realization staggered him. It took every ounce of Connor's self-control not to spring out and smash his fist into his cousin's pretty face.

"I'm no interrupting, am I?" he asked as he slowly stepped into the pool of light.

Relief flooded Cate's face. "Connor." She started toward him, but stopped immediately since Blane still held the pendant.

"Blane?" He looked pointedly at his cousin's hand, lingering on the jewel.

"Ah, good eve'n, Cousin. I was just admiring yer . . . fine gift to yer lovely betrothed. Did you realize the stone is an exact match for her eyes?" Smiling, he allowed the jewel to slide from his hands as he backed away.

"Aye, Cousin." Connor gritted his teeth. "I'd noted the match. I could no hae missed it." He turned his back to Blane. "I'd hae joined you earlier, Caty, but I wanted to get a cloak for you. I ken how easily you get chilled."

He didn't miss the grateful look on her face as he pulled her against him and draped the wrap around her. She trembled in his arms, and he once again fought back the urge to do physical damage to his cousin.

"Come, lass, we'll get you back into the warmth of the hall now."

"Wasnae that yer mother's jewel?" Blane still smiled, but his narrowed eyes gave him a calculating look. "I'd no hae thought you'd put something belonging to yer mother on a woman of yer own."

Blane was attempting to provoke him, but he refused to be drawn into a fight here with his uncle's men so close by. There was Cate to think of now. He had, after all, promised to see to her safety.

"What's done is done, Blane. I'll no discuss my mother or my betrothed with you." Once again, he fought back the urge to vent his rage on the man, instead moving Cate past his cousin, before pausing at the door to turn back. Blane was his kin, his flesh and blood. He'd grant him this one warning. "My thanks to you, Cousin."

Blane's face momentarily revealed his surprise. "For what?"

"Why, for watching over my wee Caty, of course. Without you here to look over her in my absence, someone may hae thought to take advantage of her." He glared at his cousin, waiting until the other man looked guiltily away. "I would hate to ruin the celebration for my lady by forcing her to see me kill someone simply because that man thought to put his hands on what's mine. And she is mine." He knew Blane understood when his cousin paled.

"As always, it's my pleasure to be of assistance to you, Cousin." Blane bowed his head slightly in acknowledgment, but did not meet his eyes.

"You do realize he wasn't watching over me, don't you?" Cate asked in a whisper as they closed the door.

"Aye, lass, I ken the truth of the matter." He walked her through the hall and toward the stairs to the upper chambers, his arm still wrapped protectively around her. "He'll no bother you again. Blane was ever the braggart, but he kens how it stands between us now. You hae no need to fash yerself over him." He'd see to that.

"Where are you taking me?"

She looked up at him with those amazingly innocent eyes, and, for just a moment, he was filled with an overpowering need to hold her close.

Instead he moved away, placing a bit of distance between them. He wasn't a fool and he wasn't about to act the part of one again. Her rejecting Blane had nothing to do with any feelings she might have for him. She was simply waiting until she could go home, nothing more.

This attraction to her now was nothing more than his having denied himself the pleasure of dealing with his cousin as he would have preferred. His body sought some physical release. Nothing more.

"It's late and we've an early morning. The church service starts promptly. You want to see the banns posted, aye?" When she nodded her agreement, he gave her a little push up the stairs. "I'll go find Mairi and send her up to keep you company. Go on now." *Is that disappointment in her eyes?*

She went up a few of the stairs and then turned, quickly coming back down, stopping when she was just high enough to be face-to-face with him.

"Thanks for being my knight in shining armor."

Before he could guess her intent, she leaned forward and, resting her hands on either side of his face, placed a soft kiss on his lips.

"And for rescuing me from the horrible blond dragon."

Then, smiling brightly, she disappeared upstairs, stopping only to toss the cloak back down to him.

The cloak floated around his head and fell to the floor. He was entirely too stunned to notice anything other than the feel of her hands lingering on his face where she'd held him captive.

CHAPTER 9

It had been entirely worth any amount of embarrassment she might suffer tomorrow.

Cate fell back onto her bed, arms clasped tightly around her middle, smiling in satisfaction. The look on Connor's face had been priceless. He was always so in control, so arrogant and above what was happening around him. It was thrilling to know she could rattle him just a bit.

Now she could hardly wait for Mairi to arrive so she could attempt to find out more from the girl. If what Blane had told her was true, it was no wonder that Connor didn't trust his uncle to watch over his sister.

Thinking of Blane sent a shiver through her. That man had seriously frightened her tonight. But then Connor had shown up, just like the knight in shining armor she'd claimed him to be before she'd kissed him.

Not that she could really consider what she'd done on the stairs tonight to be a real kiss. That had been no more than an impulsive indulgence on her part, with absolutely no participation from him at all. Perhaps if she hadn't run away so quickly . . . Perhaps he'd have kissed her again as he did the night he'd first come to her? She couldn't help but wonder as she brought her fingers to rest on her lips. For a man so strong and rugged, his mouth had been amazingly soft.

Lost in that particular daydream, she didn't notice the knock at her door until the pounding became frantic.

"What is wrong with me," she mumbled to herself as she got up to answer the knock. Fantasizing about Connor was a bad idea. Hadn't she very nearly made a horrible mistake by letting herself imagine Richard to be more than he actually was? No, she had learned her lesson. She wouldn't make that kind of error again.

Mairi stood at the door holding a decanter of the spiced wine that had flowed so freely at dinner. Cate found even the smell of it distasteful. Mairi, on the other hand, apparently had a real fondness for the drink. It made her quite talkative, which fit Cate's needs nicely.

"Yer sure you dinna want any?" the girl asked as she plopped herself down on the fur in front of the fire.

"No thanks. I don't see how you can drink that stuff." Cate made the appropriate nasty face, and Mairi laughed, stretching her bare feet to the fire.

"Why have I never seen you in shoes? Don't you have any?" Cate, already in her nightgown, asked as she joined her companion on the floor in front of the fire.

The girl gave her an indignant stare. "Of course I hae shoes, a whole pile of them. Weel, I hae three pair." She then leaned over and whispered conspiratorially, "I dinna wear them because it makes Anabella furious to see my bare feet. So I never wear slippers. I'm actually quite used to it now." She sat back up with a satisfied grin, wiggling her toes.

"I take it you don't like her?"

"I despise the harlot." Mairi leaned back against the chair before she continued. "I do everything in my power to make her life miserable."

She arched an eyebrow in a way that made Cate think instantly of Connor.

"She humiliated my brother, you ken? Marrying my uncle instead of Connor the way she did." She turned to the fire and spat. "And him? Weel, he deserves no better than the likes of her. Truly that was the finest thing she ever did for Connor, though he canna accept the truth of it. She never loved him. She loves herself and her pretty clothes and being the lady of the manor." Mairi tilted her head slightly, staring at her bare feet for a moment before turning an assessing gaze on Cate. "That's all Connor needs, you ken? Just someone to love him."

A change of subject was required—quickly, before Mairi could go for the obvious question. The one Cate couldn't answer.

"Mairi, tell me more about the old customs. I understand that the banns are to post public notice of the marriage so that if there's any reason you shouldn't get married someone has a chance to speak up. But what happens after that?"

"By the old customs, after the third posting of the banns, the prospective bride and groom ride out to the surrounding countryside. They personally invite the people to come to the churchyard for the wedding and then to the castle after for the celebration. It can take a full day or more to ride to all the outlying areas." She nodded wisely.

"Ride out. As in, riding on a horse?"

Mairi nodded her assent.

"Why don't they just send messengers? Wouldn't that be faster?"

Not to mention much safer for those prospective brides who happened to hate horses with a passion.

"Weel, that might be faster, but it's no the way it's done. You see, the riding-out is the groom's chance to show off his choice of bride to his people, so they can see what a fine job he's done of catching himself a beautiful and accomplished woman."

"Accomplished?" That didn't sound promising.

"Aye. Like how she speaks and looks, how she behaves toward his people, how weel she sits her horse, things like that. It's all about a man's pride, you ken?"

"What if she can't, oh, let's say, sit a horse? What does that do to the process?" Cate groaned inwardly, anticipating the answer she knew was coming.

"Weel, that would be an embarrassment for the groom, would it no?" Mairi chuckled to herself.

It was obviously time for another change of subject. "How old are you, Mairi?"

"I'll be eighteen end of the month. That's when my dear, loving uncle plans to marry me off." She shook her head. "He's such a fool."

The girl's response took Cate by surprise. "I wasn't sure you knew that. You don't seem at all concerned about having to marry someone you don't love."

"Love?" Mairi snorted her disbelief. "I canna even tolerate the presence of the old goat my uncle thinks to give me to. He's a filthy, lecherous old thing who, the maids say, beats his women. He's gone through three wives already."The girl nodded for emphasis before taking another drink from her cup.

"That's horrible. Aren't you terrified? What if you actually have to go through with this wedding?"

Mairi smiled, and from her expression Cate almost expected the girl to reach over and give her a pat on the head.

"It willna happen, so I've nothing to fear. Neither Connor nor Rosalyn will allow it. Between them and Duncan and my cousin Lyall, I've nothing to worry about. They've always protected me. They all ken the necessity of allowing me to make that decision for myself."

"But women here are given in marriage against their will all the time, usually when they're much younger than you are now." Cate had studied her history. She knew that to be a fact. She would be too terrified for words in this girl's place.

"Och, aye. But it's different with us, you ken? Rosalyn told you the legend, aye?" When Cate nodded, Mairi continued. "I've no got the power. That goes only from mother to daughter, more's the pity." She gave Cate a wicked smile. "There's them I'd give a lesson to if I did hae it. The Faerie blessing is on my father's side. So, though I dinna get the power, I still hae the blood of the Fae, so I'm still entitled to the protection of the blessing. According to the legend, there's only one true love for each of us and, as a daughter of the Fae, the blessing grants me the right to find my own true love."

"Then why is your uncle so set on forcing you into a marriage you don't want?"

"Because he's a fool, as I said. He'd never try to do anything like that to Rosalyn, you ken? But because I'm the daughter of a son, rather than the daughter of a daughter, he thinks he's immune to the curse." She shrugged. "Besides, he owes the MacPherson a great deal of money, so he thinks to pay his debt using me, poor excuse for a man that he is. And poor excuse for a woman I'd be to let him get by with it."

Suddenly her eyes widened and she slapped her hand over her mouth. "Och, Cate, I'm so sorry. I dinna mean to say that yer at fault for yer father's sending you to Connor to pay his life debt. Oh, Rosalyn's right, I blether on entirely too much."

She looked absolutely stricken with guilt, one huge tear rolling down her cheek.

Cate already felt close to this spirited young woman. She couldn't allow her to think she'd said something wrong, especially over a situation that didn't really exist. It wasn't Mairi's fault that she hadn't been told the whole story.

She reached out and took Mairi's hands in her own.

"You don't have any reason to be upset. It's not like you think. My father didn't really send me here. I came of my own free will, do you understand? I'm here because I chose to be here with Connor. My father's a wonderful man. He'd never, ever consider forcing me to do something I didn't want to do." She laughed then. "And even if he did, my brothers wouldn't allow it."

"You hae brothers back home? Tell me about them." Mairi freed one of her hands to swipe at her face.

"I guess you could say they're just typical older brothers. They make me so angry sometimes. All three of them can be so very irritating, always thinking they can tell me what to do; always thinking they know what's best for me, just because they're older."

"Och, aye." Mairi nodded. "Like Connor."

"But they love me fiercely. I know they'd do anything to protect me and keep me happy."

Mairi nodded again. "Just like Connor."

Exactly, Cate realized. She should have recognized earlier why she'd bonded with Mairi so quickly. They might be from entirely different worlds, but they had a lot in common. They'd both been sheltered from the real world by their families and they both faced marrying men they didn't love. The only difference was Cate had been able to save herself from that fate. Now she had the opportunity to save Mairi as well.

"I had three brothers, just as you do," Mairi said suddenly, her eyes again filling with tears.

"What happened to the others?"

"The oldest, Dougal, was in the battle where my father was killed. We lost him there as weel." She again wiped her eyes with the back of her hand. "Kenneth was hunting and fell from his horse a couple of years later. They said he broke his neck and died as soon as he hit the ground."

"I'm so sorry, Mairi. Were they a lot like Connor?"

"I canna say. I wasnae born until the month after my father and Dougal died. I dinna even really remember much about Kenneth, just bits of a tall boy laughing, leaning down to pick me up and throw me high in the air."

She sat up straight before continuing. "Connor says they were strong and true, both of them, so it must be. I light a candle for them on the anniversary of their birth each year. It would be just too sorrowful knowing they died with no one to remember and honor them." She sighed. "No long after Kenneth's death, my uncle sent Connor away to school. Connor was furious. I was just a wee thing but I remember that weel." She shrugged. "Then the following year my mother died."

"With Connor gone so much, you've really had no one but Rosalyn." Cate couldn't imagine not having her brothers with her all the time she was growing up. Just the thought was horrible. "Not that she isn't lovely."

"I could never repay Rosalyn for all she's done for me. She's been wonderful to me, more of a mother than an aunt. But there's also my cousin Lyall. He's been my friend and protector in Connor's absence. He's older— only a year or two younger than Connor—but he disna like Anabella any better than I do. He says she's naught more to him than his father's wife, and that he thinks Connor's the luckiest man alive to hae escaped that one. He's always there when I hae need of him. He disna approve of my being wedded to the MacPherson any more than Connor does." Mairi picked up her wine, once again nodding wisely.

"So, Lyall is Blane's brother. Are they at all alike?" If so, she'd want to try to avoid him, too. She remembered Rosalyn's having pointed him out to her as he sat next to Connor. In fact, she would have noticed him anyway. He looked very much like Connor, though not quite as tall or muscular.

"No at all; perhaps because he's the younger son. I think he's more like Connor. Blane, now." She shook her head in disgust. "Cut from the same arrogant cloth as his father, that one is. Does whatever his father tells him. And he drinks too much. It's a fair shame he'll be the next laird."

It was quiet in the room as she took another sip from her cup.

"It's Connor who should be laird, you ken? It fell to my brother Kenneth, but my uncle was acting for him until he turned eighteen. Then, when Kenneth died, Artair took it all." She leaned toward Cate and continued in a whisper. "It's why they hate Connor. They fear him, you ken? Each time he comes home, stronger and more valuable to the king, they fear he'll take it all away from them."

"Will he? I mean, once he's settled down here, will he seek his rightful place?" Was that his real reason for wanting to be married?

Mairi shook her head sadly. "I hope yer no thinking to wed my brother to become the laird's wife. It will no happen even though my uncle and cousin fear it. They're such fools. They canna even see he disna want what they hae. He disna want the responsibility of all the people. He says he has his hands full just looking after me and Rosalyn. He will never challenge our uncle. That would mean war, and Connor says he's seen too much of the death of battle to bring it to his own doorstep and those he loves. Och, my poor brother. He's suffered such burdens."

Cate's heart ached for both the young woman sitting with her and for the man they discussed. She knew it made no sense, but she wanted to make sure that she didn't add to those burdens he already carried.

When the idea hit, she thought it perfect.

"Mairi, do you ride well? Horses, I mean."

"Of course I do." She gave Cate a suspicious look. "Dinna you?"

"Not only do I not ride well, I don't ride at all. Horses scare me to death." She took a deep breath, pausing only for a moment so she wouldn't lose her courage. "Do you think you could teach me? Before the riding-out thing, I mean? Could you teach me in secret, as a surprise for Connor? I wouldn't want to shame him in front of all his people."

"Mayhaps." Mairi eyed her speculatively. "Does Connor know?"

"Of course he knows I can't ride."

"No, I dinna mean that. Does he know yer father dinna send you here? That you came because you love him?"

Cate stared at her, speechless. How could she possibly respond to that?

CHAPTER 10

Cate awoke thinking, not for the first time since she'd been here, that she would gladly hand over a thousand dollars for a cup of coffee. Or a chocolate bar. Or even a cup of good old Scottish breakfast tea. Trouble was, the Scottish wouldn't have breakfast tea for a couple hundred years yet. Or any other form of caffeine that she could find.

She frowned. Caffeine headaches were the worst. Next time she was going to get stranded in the Middle Ages, she'd remember to bring along provisions. The instant she got home, she fully intended to head straight to her favorite corner Starbucks and indulge in a grande—no, a venti—coffee Frappuccino. With extra whipped cream. Calorie count be damned.

Stretching, she bumped her foot into her constant bed companion, Beast. He licked her toes, then turned over to go back to sleep. The dog had slept in her bed every night since she'd been here, and spent every day with her as well. On one of the rare occasions when Connor spoke to her, he grumbled that she'd already ruined the dog, softened him up so that he'd no longer be a fit companion for a warrior.

Anabella said much worse. Of course, Anabella's dislike of the creature was only one of the reasons Cate let him sleep in her bed every night. There was something very comforting about having your own private guard dog that just happened to be the size of a small horse—a small horse with very large teeth.

As she dressed and started her day, she thought about her time here. The last two weeks had settled into a fairly predictable routine. Meals, such as they were, were taken in the great hall with the entire family, which Cate quickly learned included all the soldiers and workers who inhabited the castle as well as the actual family members.

She could count on what she now secretly thought of as Anabella's Snipe of the Day being served up sometime during the midday meal, usually when the number of observers was largest. She always had something hateful to say. The woman seriously tried Cate's patience.

Blane still made her uncomfortable. He hadn't so much as spoken to her again, but she'd frequently feel a nagging little prickle on the back of her neck only to look up and find him watching her.

Artair ignored her completely. She figured that after the first night's perusal of her unsuitability to be in his family, he didn't consider her worth his notice again.

Connor, when he was around, was polite but distant. She assumed that quick kiss on the stairs had rattled him more than she'd planned. He seemed to work at keeping his distance, spending hours in the lists practicing his swordsmanship. In the long run, that made things easier for her. She couldn't explain to herself why she felt so out of control around him, and she didn't really want to try.

Cate spent her days with either Rosalyn or Mairi, the former keeping her out of trouble and the latter showing her new ways to get into it. Growing up without either a mother or a best girlfriend, she was enjoying their company immensely, in spite of the hardships they took for granted as everyday life.

Mairi had quickly become her favorite companion. One day they had wandered out to the forest under the pretense of gathering herbs, but had actually spent the time wading in a small stream running through it, playing like children. Cate had told Mairi how women where she came from frequently went without shoes, even decorating their toes with paint and jewelry. Mairi was so delighted with the idea that Cate had given her the birthstone ring she wore to try on her toe. It fit perfectly. They decided Mairi should keep it and wear it proudly. After all, Anabella would certainly notice and be appalled.

The most exciting times were those when she and Mairi had stolen into the trees behind the lists to watch Connor practice his swordsmanship. Good Lord, the man was amazing. None of those he worked out with could ever match him. And when he'd stripped off his shirt, tossing it aside, Cate was convinced her heart had actually stopped beating. Mairi had giggled so hard, Cate was terrified they'd be caught, but they'd managed to escape unnoticed.

Each day, when they were sure Connor was occupied in the lists, she and Mairi would sneak away for her riding lesson. She'd made great progress. Well, great progress for her at least. She could sit on the horse by herself now without freaking out, and yesterday had even managed a bit of forward motion.

Judging from the activity in the courtyard and the men moving toward the lists, she had just enough time to grab a bite from the kitchens before finding Mairi for today's lesson.

"Come on, boy." She patted Beast as they headed through the great hall toward the kitchens. "I bet we'll find something for you, too."

"So now you converse with a beast."

Just her luck. Anabella was in the room, seated at a table with several ladies.

"We canna really expect much more of her, you ken?" The woman spoke to those around her, but obviously intended that Cate hear.

Her audience watched eagerly for any reaction, some not bothering to hide their giggles.

"She comes from a land of filthy heathens and disna know any better. She even allows the vile creature to sleep with her, in her bed."

"Better than what you sleep with," Cate muttered to herself.

"What's that?" Anabella questioned sharply.

"Only good morning. Sorry I can't stay and visit. I'm just headed to the kitchen for a bite." As if they had any interest at all in visiting with her.

"If you dinna laze in bed till such a late hour, you'd be able to take the morning bread with everyone." Again the muffled laughter.

Cate had been down early before. Anabella was no where to be found. Mostly it was the men, preparing for their day in the lists or the fields. They hadn't seemed particularly comfortable with her company, so she hadn't seen a need to return.

"And you'll no be taking that great dirty beast into my kitchen."

"Very well." Cate led Beast back into the entry and opened the door, waiting for him to go outside. "Just for bit, boy. I'll bring you something good." She ruffled his fur and reentered the great hall. She made it almost all the way to the back exit before Anabella spoke again.

"Disgusting creatures such as that do not belong in the kitchen . . . but at least the dog is staying out." The laughter wasn't muffled this time.

Cate continued through the doorway, her back stiff, her face red. She wouldn't give Anabella the satisfaction of acknowledging she'd heard. But as she reached for one of the hard rolls from the basket, she realized she no longer had any appetite.

She headed out the back door of the kitchen. There was no way she was walking back through those women. She'd go find Mairi and face the horses instead. Even a horse was preferable to Anabella.

Her mind still on her latest embarrassment, Cate was intent on finding Mairi so they could begin today's lesson. She came to an abrupt halt when she discovered Blane waiting in the stables instead of the girl she sought. Mairi, arriving just after her, didn't seem any happier to see him than Cate felt.

"What are you doing here? Come to spy on us?" Mairi accused.

"Och, Mairi. Ever the hellion. Hae you taken to corrupting wee Caitlyn then?" He gave his cousin a disdainful look, taking a bite from the apple he held before tossing it away. "And here I came to help you, lassie."

"And what kind of help would that be yer offering, Blane?" Mairi stood with her hands on her hips, a skeptical look on her face.

"Father's sent Lyall on an errand. Before he left, he asked that I come in his place today so you wouldn't be disappointed." He spoke to Mairi, but his heated gaze was on Cate.

Mairi paused, caught for a moment in indecision. "Verra weel, Blane, but yer to tell no one. No a single soul. Do you promise?"

"I promise." He favored them with a deep bow. "I am at yer service, fair maidens."

Mairi sighed. "It was to be a surprise for you, Cate. I planned to have Lyall here to help us, but now we'll hae to make do with him." She gestured her head toward Blane, wrinkling her nose. "I thought we'd look for a meadow today. You can gain some comfort there with a long, slow walk."

When Cate started to shake her head, Mairi held up a hand to stop her. "You'll no ever learn to ride inside this stable. We need to get you into the open. Blane can lead the horses down and we'll meet him there. Yer running out of time. If you truly want to do this, we hae to do it now."

"Fine, we'll do it your way." Cate sighed.

Mairi was right. Just managing to climb onto the back of the horse and sit there wasn't going to be enough. She just wished she didn't have to do this with Blane around.

The sound of metal on metal rang loud in Connor's ears; the feel of the steel reverberated in his hand as he deflected his opponent's parry. This he understood; this he was comfortable with; this required no real thought, only the physical response that was second nature to him.

He glanced behind him, toward the trees, wondering if he'd catch a glimpse of the woman who hid there each day to watch him at practice.

It had surprised him the first time he'd noticed his sister and Cate sneaking about the edge of the lists, but now he'd come to expect the daily surreptitious visits. Though he chose to keep his distance from the woman until they were wed and he could send her safely home, even he would admit it was no blow to his pride to know that she admired him at practice each day. What warrior wouldn't appreciate that?

He dodged a strike from his opponent, the blow just missing his arm. That was sloppy of him. His concentration wasn't what it should be today, some little detail nagging at his senses. He narrowed his attention back to the work at hand for the next few thrusts. The men here weren't of the caliber he was used to for practice, and soon his attention wandered again.

Where were the girls? Their absence today struck him as odd. Either Mairi and Cate were getting much better at hiding, which he very much doubted, or they simply weren't coming.

As he finished off the last of the men who'd waited to practice today, he noticed Beast standing by the entrance to the lists. Another oddity. The creature hadn't left Cate's side for days.

He leaned down and grabbed the shirt he'd tossed to the ground earlier, using it to wipe the sweat from his face before heading into the shed to clean his weapon.

"Connor!" Duncan jogged toward him.

Not a good sign. His old friend rarely moved faster than necessary, and certainly didn't run anymore, unless in battle.

"I'm thinking we hae a wee problem." Duncan, his hands on his hips, huffed a bit to catch his breath.

Connor knew without asking the problem would be Cate.

An hour after they'd left the stable, they met at the spot Blane had suggested. It had been a long walk through the forest, farther than she'd been since her arrival, but even Cate had to admit it was the perfect place. They were in a lovely rolling meadow that looked to stretch forever. It was surrounded on three sides by forest, and certainly far enough from the castle that no one would know where they were or what they were doing.

Almost immediately Cate realized she had a problem. "I can't do this here."

The other two stared at her blankly from the backs of their horses.

"I can't get on the horse here. I've got nothing to climb on." She wouldn't have to ride today, she thought, and it wouldn't even be her fault.

Laughing, Blane dismounted and strode toward her. Reaching her side, he easily lifted her to the horse's back, allowing his hands to linger at her waist even after she'd gained her seat. He then remounted, placing his horse on one side of her while Mairi took a position on the other side.

They silently followed the stream that meandered through the meadow for miles, often with Blane leading the way. Though they'd gone slowly, Cate was exhausted. The muscles in her legs trembled from gripping so tightly to the horse. Her fingers were cramping from the death grip she'd held on the reins for the past few hours.

She was, however, proud of herself. She'd actually ridden all alone, and quite a distance at that. Maybe she would be able to do this after all.

"That's far enough, dinna you think, Mairi?" Blane broke the silence, pulling up his horse. "She's looking a bit worn, and we still hae to go back."

"Yer right. Come on, Cate, let's turn back now. We've been out for a good long while. You've done just lovely today."

"Perhaps it'd be best if we let the horses and the riders rest for a wee bit, ladies. Here." Blane took Cate's reins from her hands and led her horse closer to the trees, while Mairi followed. "There's shade here. It will be more comfortable for you."

Mairi dismounted and walked her horse back over to the stream. Scooping water with her hands, she splashed it over her face.

Cate flinched at the touch of Blane's hand on her leg. "Would you like me to lift you down, Caitlyn?"

She jerked her leg to move it out from under his touch. "No. I think I'll just stay where I am." She forced herself to make eye contact with him. "Thanks anyway."

He stood looking at her for a moment. "Yer choice." He lowered his voice so only she could hear. "It seems yer ever the one to be making poor choices." With a shake of his head, he stalked off toward the stream.

The chill of the evening coming on hadn't been so noticeable before Cate moved out of the fading sunlight. She flexed her fingers. When she finally did come down off this horse, she was going to be in a world of hurt. Already she felt cold and achy all over. The only thing she wanted less than to be sitting on this stupid horse was to have that man's hands on her again.

Cate was still trying to decide exactly what it was about him she disliked so very much, there being so many options to choose from, when she heard a thudding noise in the trees beside her. As she turned to investigate the noise, she felt a sharp stinging blow just below her right shoulder blade.

"Ouch," she yelped. "What was . . . ?"

Before she could finish, there came another, softer smacking sound, this time from behind her.

Her horse cried out in terror and reared onto his hind legs. She grabbed for his mane, just as his front legs hit the ground in full gallop. Her reins dangling loosely, she leaned forward and held on for dear life until the horse suddenly reared up again, smacking her face into his neck, causing her to lose her hold.

The horse's feet slammed back to the ground and he again bolted. Cate flew through the air. As the ground came rushing up to meet her, she remembered how bad it had hurt the last time she'd done this.

Connor grimaced. Sitting silently on his horse just at the edge of the forest, he could barely believe his eyes.

"It appears yer snitch had the right of it. There they are."

Hadn't she a brain in her head? What in the name of all the saints was Cate doing on a horse this far from the castle and with Blane?

"Aye." Duncan reined his horse up even with Connor. "And Mairi's with them, just as Hendri said she'd be."

Duncan had been suspicious when he'd seen the girls sneaking out of the stable. The boy had been more than happy to share the information he'd overheard when Duncan had slipped him the shiny copper.

He'd brought the information directly to Connor, who fumed silently now as he watched the scene in the meadow beyond. The woman had no sense at all, sitting there on that horse, her legs bared from the knees down. If she were really his betrothed, if this weren't just some horrible farce, he'd ride down there now, throw her over his shoulder and take her home with him where she belonged. Did she have no idea of how dangerous it could be out here unprotected as she was?

He was, in fact, considering doing exactly that when Beast hunkered down and began to growl.

"Do you see anything?"

It was a bad sign. He trusted Beast's instincts. They had saved him more than once. Connor stood in his stirrups to look around, turning quickly at the sound of

Cate's scream, just in time to see her horse rear and gallop away.

"Good Christ, she's no got her reins." Duncan started forward, but Connor was already flying ahead of him at a dead run.

Connor fought down an overpowering need to retch as he vaulted from his horse and knelt beside her crumpled body. Don't let her die, he prayed, please don't let this happen again. He didn't think he could live with another failure. He should have been with her just has he should have been with his mother all those years ago. This was his fault.

He had gone out of his way to avoid her since the night of their betrothal celebration. Being near her stirred feelings he didn't know how to deal with, made him want things he had no right to. Still, he should never have left her alone. She was his responsibility. He had brought her here. Self-recriminations filled his thoughts, threatening to overwhelm him.

He shook his head to clear his mind. He couldn't afford to think about it now. He had to know what he was dealing with here, just how badly she was hurt.

Gently rolling her onto her back, he saw first the blood seeping from a cut on her forehead, dark against the copper of her hair. His stomach knotted. Hair that had escaped from her braid curled around her face. He lightly brushed it back out of the way.

There was blood on her cheek where she'd scraped the ground, but that didn't look serious. Tenderly he touched her pale cheek where the skin was scraped raw, sliding his hand down to her neck. Relief washed through him as he touched her pulse beating strong and steady there.

He was slowly moving his hands down her arms, checking for other injuries when Mairi and Blane reached them. Mairi was holding on to her side, gasping for air.

"Is it bad, Connor?" She began to sob, but he couldn't take the time to comfort her now. "It's all my fault. She wasnae ready. I should hae seen it. What hae I done to her?" She fell to her knees beside Cate, head in her hands.

They needed a cart. Without knowing how badly she was injured, he wouldn't risk putting her on a horse and they were a good two hours' ride from the castle.

"Blane." Standing there as he was, staring into the forest, the man was of less use in a crisis than the wailing girl at his side.

"Blane!" The shout drew his cousin's attention. "Ride to the castle. Bring us a cart. And blankets."

Finally spurred into action, Blane sprinted to his horse and galloped away without a word.

It was early evening and they had only an hour or so of daylight left at best. The temperature had already begun to drop. Taking Cate's hand, he rubbed it briskly between his own.

"Just open yer eyes for me, Caty. Just let me see yer still here with me."

Reaching over to his sister, he grabbed the tail of her shift and ripped away a swath of the soft material to use for Cate's wounds, quickly tearing it into smaller pieces.

His movement drew Mairi from her stupor. She jumped up and ran to her horse, easily pulling herself onto his back.

"I'm going, too. That stupid fool will no even think to

bring Rosalyn. She'll ken what to do for Cate. I'll fetch her here."

Before he could do anything to stop her, she was gone, leaving a cloud of dust in her wake just as Duncan arrived, Cate's errant animal in tow.

"It's no a good idea, her going off alone like that." Duncan sat on his horse, watching the small figure disappearing in the distance for a moment before he looked down. "Is there anything I can do for the wee lass?"

"No. She's alive, but I dinna even ken how badly hurt she is. Go after Mairi. Keep watch over her for me." He blotted at the wound on Cate's head with the cloth in his hand.

"Here, laddie." Duncan tossed a silver flask down to Connor as he started past. "This will help with cleaning her wounds. And when she wakes, a few swallows of that will ease her pain." The old warrior grinned. "Many's the time it's eased mine."

Giving his friend a grateful nod, Connor dampened the cloth with a few drops of the whisky. As he turned back to clean the wound on her head, he found her staring up at him.

She smiled weakly, "You're always here to rescue me, aren't you? Every time I need you, there you are."

Her comment lanced through him, bringing a sharp pang of guilt. No, he hadn't been there when she'd needed him.

She moaned and closed her eyes as she tried to sit up, but he held her down with a firm hand.

"Dinna move around, Caty. I've no decided what you may hae broken yet."

The gash on her forehead wasn't deep and the bleeding had nearly stopped, but a large discolored bump was forming. He blotted at it with the whisky-soaked rag. Her breath hissed as she sucked it in and her eyes flew open.

"Good Lord, Connor. What do you think you're doing to me? She jerked her head, and but for his firm hold would have moved away.

"I'm cleaning the gash on yer head so yer no down with the fever tomorrow. Then I'll check to see what you may hae broken."

She'd closed her eyes again.

After pouring whisky onto another cloth, he noted with disgust that his hands shook as he lightly blotted the scrape on her cheek.

She hissed softly again and slapped at his hands.

"Weel, I guess you've no broken yer arms." Dropping the cloth, he began to methodically move his hands down Cate's body, feeling for anything amiss.

"Don't do that. It hurts. Nothing's broken." She slapped at his hands again as he tried to keep her from sitting up. "Stop pushing and poking at me, Connor."

Deciding that allowing her to sit would do less harm than fighting to keep her down, he assisted her to a sitting position.

She narrowed her eyes and glared at him. "I'm a healthy woman. I don't smoke or drink. I take vitamins. I get my minimum daily requirements of calcium every single day. It would be highly unlikely that I would have broken anything. Oh, ouch." She wrapped her arms around herself and leaned over. "But everything hurts." She groaned and closed her eyes again. "I hate these freakin' horses."

She was ever saying things that made no sense to him, so he couldn't depend on that to determine whether or not she might have suffered serious injury to her head. It didn't look so bad now, but it worried him greatly. You could never tell with head wounds. He'd seen it many times after a battle; strong warriors with what appeared to be a minor bump on their head would go to sleep and never wake up. And she was no strong warrior. He would need to keep her awake.

He silently resumed his inspection of her, feeling her legs and then moving to her back. Her dress was torn from her shoulder and the skin cut and oozing blood where she'd obviously made impact when she'd landed. A large bruise was already forming on the fair skin around the laceration. Although this cut was deeper than the other, the slow loss of blood would seem to indicate that there was no need to stitch or, God forbid, to cauterize the wound. He would need to clean it right away to prevent the fever that so often accompanied wounds.

He smiled wryly. Based on her earlier responses, he didn't think she was going to like that.

"Ouch. I mean it, Connor. Quit poking me. My bruises have bruises," she complained.

He smiled in spite of himself and held out the flask to her. "Here. This will help the pain."

She groaned through gritted teeth as she turned around to glare at him. "I'll make you a deal. How about that?"

"Anything you want, Caty darlin', just drink the damn whisky." She was the most stubborn woman he had ever met.

"Well, there's only one thing in this place that I hate

more than your nasty whisky"—she made an awful face and shivered—"and that's your nasty horses. Promise me that, no matter what, I never have to get on a horse by myself again; that anytime I ever have to go anywhere on a horse it will be on your horse, with you holding me on it tightly. Promise me that, Connor MacKiernan—swear to it on your honor—and I'll drink whatever you want me to."

He'd have been willing to promise her almost anything. To have her request turn out to be something he'd already determined to make happen anyway made him want to laugh out loud. At this very moment, he wanted nothing more than to hold her in his arms, where he could keep her safe.

Instead he placed his hand over his heart and adopted the most solemn look he could manage.

"I promise. I vow it on my honor." He shoved the flask into her hand. "Now drink," he ordered firmly.

She tilted the flask up and immediately began to gasp and cough. "Oh Lord, that tastes worse than Cody's Drambuie."

He pushed the flask back to her mouth. After the second drink, her eyes were watering.

He encouraged her to take yet another.

"You may be surprised to learn that the liquid gold in that flask yer so quick to spurn is a highly valued item in this land. I myself am quite fond of it."

Her look of disgust brought a smile to his face.

A few minutes later, when she screamed as he cleaned her shoulder with that same liquid gold, he wished he had saved a bit of it for himself.

CHAPTER 11

Thankfully she had been right. Connor could find nothing broken. His main task now was to keep Cate from going to sleep.

"How much longer do we have to wait here?"

Weariness was evident in her voice. Whether from the head wound or from the whisky, he couldn't be sure.

"As best I can tell, another couple of hours should bring them back." It would be full dark before then. Fortunately it looked as though they'd have a goodly moon to guide them tonight.

"This is ridiculous, this just sitting here."

He had never seen her sulky before. With her braid coming down and tendrils of hair curling around her face, she looked quite young.

"I'm cold, Connor." She frowned up at him. "I'm cold and I'm hungry and I hurt everywhere. I just want to sink into a big tub of really hot water. I want to go home. I want to go home right now."

"A fortnight, Caty. Just a fortnight more and you'll be free to go home."

He didn't look at her. He couldn't. Just the thought of her leaving caused a strange tightening in his chest. He'd concentrate instead on what he could do to keep her warm until the cart arrived.

"No." She barked at him, stopping him in his tracks. "Not my home. Home here. You already know I haven't broken anything. Why can't we just get on that huge monster horse of yours and go now? Why do we have to just sit here?"

"It's yer comfort I'm thinking of, lass. The cart will be easier for you."

"Ha. Like bouncing around in a great wooden wagon for a couple of hours is going to be more comfortable than being held by . . . " She suddenly stopped talking and stared wide-eyed at him.

Shaking her head, she continued quietly. "I just want to go, Connor. I don't want to sit here anymore."

Now that he was sure she had no broken bones, there really was no reason to continue to wait. He felt the brief sting of annoyance at his own lack of action. Only with her did he act so foolishly. They would just take it slow and easy. Somewhere along the way, they would meet up with Blane and the others coming back from the castle.

Without another word, he tied her horse's lead to his saddle and, lifting her easily, climbed on his own mount, nestling her securely into his embrace.

* * *

The rhythmic plodding of their ride was lulling her to sleep. He repeatedly jostled her awake as she drifted off, but he needed to do more. If he could just get her to talk, that should keep her awake. But what to talk about?

Well, there was that one little thing that had been nagging at the back of his mind recently.

He cleared his throat, working up to the question.

"The night I brought you here, you said you were preparing for a wedding. Whose wedding?"

He held his breath while waiting for her response, not understanding why the answer was so important to him, only that it was.

"Mine." She shrugged.

Of course, he should have realized that. It explained why she had been so distressed at having to remain here longer. She had a life, a man waiting for her. He had never even thought to ask, his concerns for his sister outweighing anything else.

They rode quietly for a time as he considered the idea of her marrying. An irrational anger built toward the unknown man waiting for Cate in her own time.

"Is it this Cody that you'll marry?" His voice shattered the silence of the night and she jumped.

"Cody?" She sounded sleepy and confused.

"You mentioned him earlier tonight. You said something about his Drambuie." He hoped he didn't sound as irritable to her as he did to himself.

"No, Cody's my brother." She sighed. "I have three of them. Brothers." Her slurred words gave testament to the effects of the whisky.

"Then who is the man yer marrying?" Impatience made his words sharper than he'd intended.

"Richard." She yawned and put her arms around his waist. "But I'm not marrying him."

"Yer making no sense, lass. You say this Richard is the man yer to marry, but yer no marrying him?" He was bewildered, but strangely relieved.

"I am engaged to be married to Richard." She pulled her arm away from him and held her hand up in front of his face. "See? There's my engagement ring." The small stone reflected the bright moonlight as she waved her hand back and forth before lowering it once again to his waist. "But I'm not going to marry him."

"That wee stone was his betrothal gift to you?" When she nodded, he considered for a moment. "It's no so large as the gift I gave you, is it?"

"No, Connor, it's not. Yours is much larger." She began to giggle, and he waited patiently until she finally recovered.

"Is that why yer no marrying him then? Because he's poor?" He waited anxiously for her answer.

"No. In fact, he's pretty successful. He makes a lot of money. He has a nice house, nice clothes, nice Porsche." She looked up at him and shook her head. "Don't even ask—it's kind of like a cart in my time but a lot more comfortable, and, trust me, Richard has a really expensive one. No, I'm not marrying Richard because I don't love him." She laid her head against his chest. "And I don't want to talk about Richard anymore. Thinking about him just makes me angry."

"Was he bad to you then? Did he hurt you?" His hands

clenched on the reins, causing the horse to balk. He consciously relaxed his grip.

"The only thing he hurt was my feelings. He made me think he loved me, but he didn't. It's just as well. I know now that I never really loved him anyway. It doesn't matter." She sighed deeply.

She might say it didn't matter, but her sigh made him think otherwise. Richard must be a great fool to trifle with this woman's heart in such a manner. Connor smiled grimly as he thought of how he might enjoy the opportunity to meet this Richard.

She was relaxing, drifting off to sleep again. "What is this Drambuie you spoke of, and why did you hae yer brother's?" Anything to keep her talking.

"You know, it's actually kind of funny you don't know what that is since it was invented right here in Scotland. No, wait, I guess it really isn't. It won't be invented for a couple hundred years. I read about it on the bottle. Bonnie Prince Charlie and all." She shook her head and sighed. "God, I hope I'm not screwing up some space-time continuum by telling you stuff. This is so weird. Anyway, it wasn't my brother's. Okay, technically I guess it was but he gave it to me. For my birthday. When I turned twenty-one."

All this time she'd been here and he knew so very little about the woman he held in his arms. "How old are you then? One and twenty?"

"No." She giggled again. "In fact, since I won't even be born for something like seven hundred years, I guess I'm a huge negative number right now." Followed by another wave of giggles.

He gave her a stern look and arched his eyebrow. "Dinna try my patience, lass."

She giggled again. "That look is so you, Connor. But you can't intimidate me."

She tightened her arms around him, causing a tingle that traveled down to his toes and back again, pooling somewhere just below his waist.

"I'm twenty-four. My birthday was last month." She grinned up at him, "Last month my time, that is, not your time." Another wave of giggles.

Some people should not drink.

"Tell me about yer brothers."

"Well, there are three of them. They're all older than me. Cass is the oldest, then there's Cody, and then Jesse. Jess is my best friend. See, my dad has this thing about the Old West." She looked up at him and rolled her eyes. "I'm not even going to try to explain what that is. Dad's always been fascinated by what he thinks are the misunderstood characters of that period of history. My poor brothers each got named after whichever one he was interested in at the time. When I was born, my mother put her foot down and insisted on naming me herself." She giggled again. "Good thing, too, or I'd be Belle Starr. To this day my dad still reads everything he can get his hands on about the Old West. He always says they had their own code of ethics that's worth remembering." She abruptly quit talking.

"Tell me more about yer family."

"I don't want to talk about them anymore. It makes me sad to think about home. They're so far away." Her voice trailed off so that he could barely hear the last. "I miss my family," she whispered.

He glanced down to find her staring intently up at him. "What is it?"

She removed her arms from his waist, shifting her weight until she leaned back against him. Another jolt of sensation shot through his body, and he found himself suddenly needing to concentrate just to breathe normally.

She sighed deeply. "Thinking about my family and all. My dad always says that honesty is the most treasured virtue we have, but also the most fragile. So, now I'm feeling guilty, Connor. I wasn't completely honest with you when I forced that bargain back there." She shook her head and continued to stare down at her hands clasped in front of her. "I mean, I really do hate horses and I don't ever want to get on one by myself again. But that's not the only reason I wanted your promise to let me ride with you."

She shifted again, and turning to look up at him, she placed her hand on his chest, causing him a whole new wave of breathing difficulties.

"More than anything else, I think I just wanted an excuse to be here like this, close to you with your arms around me. You agreed to what I asked without a single question, even though I failed you." She sniffled. "I'm so sorry I let you down, Connor. I really thought I could do it. I was so sure I could learn to ride in time. I honestly did try. I didn't want to humiliate you in front of all your people. You have to believe me. I'm so sorry."

He stopped the horse to give her his full attention, looking down at her upturned face. Deep emerald pools, brimming with tears stared back at him.

"I dinna ken what yer talking about, Cate. You've no done anything to humiliate me."

"Not yet, but I will next week." Tears began to roll slowly down both cheeks now. "Mairi told me how when we do that riding-out thing, all the people will judge you on the bride you've chosen. And I won't even be able to ride on a horse by myself. They'll think I'm not accomplished or whatever, and you'll be humiliated for getting stuck with somebody like me who can't do any of the things your wife should be able to do."

She patted his chest, right over the spot where his heart tightened, her tears flowing freely now.

"I'm sorry I let you down. I so wanted to be able to surprise you by learning how to ride, to make you proud of me."

"Yer daft." He took her upper arms in his hands and gave her a little shake. "I dinna care if you can ride. It's of no importance to me." The hopeful light in her eyes caused him to go on when he would have stopped. "I much prefer to hae you right here next to me, where I can feel you close, where I'm sure yer safe. I'm no a man to be embarrassed by riding out with a beautiful lass in my arms."

He released her then, and being mindful of her bandaged shoulder, slid his hands up to caress her face. Using the pads of his thumbs, he wiped the tears from her cheeks.

The wise thing would be to remove his hands from her now and continue on toward the castle. But he wasn't feeling like a wise man tonight.

Her eyes widened and then fluttered shut as he lowered his mouth to hers. Her arms went around his neck as her soft lips opened with only the slightest encouragement from him. She tasted of fine whisky and something indescribable that could only be Cate. He didn't think he'd ever get enough of her.

As he pulled her closer, meshing their bodies tightly together, the distinct rattle of wood and harness sounded in the distance.

Damn. His cousin had always had such bad timing.

CHAPTER 12

Cate stretched in the wooden tub, leaning back to rinse her hair one last time.

Arriving here last night seemed all a blur. She'd been so exhausted she'd slept the entire day away. She might still be sleeping if Rosalyn hadn't tempted her out of bed with the lure of a hot bath.

She looked out the window to see that the sun had already set. With the fire burning cheerfully next to her, she hadn't noticed before. Rosalyn would be back soon to look over all her cuts and scrapes.

She stretched again, sighing contentedly. It had been the most perfect evening of her life.

Well, if you left out the falling-off-the-horse part. And the cuts and bruises. And the part where she'd made a total idiot of herself. She laughed out loud at her own foolishness.

It was the kiss that had been perfect.

The first one he'd given her, the one in the magic bubble, paled in comparison. And since that night on the stairs, she had wondered what a real kiss from Connor, a kiss of passion, might be like, but her imagination hadn't done the man justice. Even thinking of it now sent unfamiliar tingles to her toes and flooded her face with heat.

She'd been kissed before. Still, to be completely honest, she couldn't exactly think of herself as an experienced woman. Richard was the only other man who'd ever kissed her. By comparison, his kiss had been more of an insistent pawing and groping that had left her wanting to escape more often than not.

If she had doubted in the least her decision to call off her marriage to Richard before, she had no doubts now. He had never made her feel like this. Like she was floating. Like she wanted to dance and sing. Like she never wanted it to end.

But it would end.

She would be going home soon.

The thought struck like a bucket of cold water. In two weeks she would leave here and never see Connor again. She'd be far away, back in her own world. And he knew that as well as she did. He'd been the one who brought it up last night. He had reminded her it was only two more weeks.

Abruptly the water in which she sat seemed uncomfortably cool and the wooden tub pressed painfully against her injured shoulder. She felt like such an idiot. Just because some man had the ability to kiss her until her stomach dropped to her feet didn't mean she could start making rash assumptions about him or his intentions. After all, Richard had probably made that little receptionist's stomach drop, too. Although she seriously doubted it.

She must remember that Connor was only a man. And like all men, last night he was just . . . What had Richard called it? Oh yeah: "seeking his relief." Like Richard, his only real interest in her was in what she could do for him. In his case, he simply needed a wife. Once the wedding was over, he'd be only too happy to see her gone. When she hopped into her green bubble transport, he could get back to his real life. After all, he'd been quite clear from the start: he had no desire for a wife.

The whole Richard experience should have been more than enough to teach her that the happy-ever-after love she used to dream about just didn't exist. When was she going to learn?

Still, she couldn't help thinking of how he'd held her close to his body, refusing to move her to the cart when the others had found them. How he'd carried her up to her bed when they'd finally reached the castle, and the way he'd looked at her as he'd tenderly traced her cheek with his thumb before he left her in his aunt's care. Thinking of those things, she couldn't prevent the little surge her heart took.

"Oh, just stop it," she said out loud.

"What?"

Rosalyn was standing just inside her door, her arms full of drying sheets and salves she'd brought. Lost in her own thoughts as she had been, Cate hadn't even heard her enter.

"Oh, not you, Rosalyn. I'm sorry. I'm just talking to myself again."

Rosalyn arched an eyebrow, but thankfully didn't pursue the matter.

"Here, wrap up in this and let me hae a look at what you've done to yerself."

Clucking like a mother hen, she informed Cate that the bump on her forehead and the scratches on her face should disappear in a few days. After inspecting and treating the cut and bruise on her shoulder, Rosalyn pronounced her exceptionally lucky and rose to leave, but Cate stopped her.

"I'm pretty sure I landed on this shoulder first, and then my face." She smiled wryly as she watched the other woman try to hide her own smile. "I know, not very graceful. It was such a stupid accident. I still don't understand exactly how it happened. But anyway, there's another spot, on the other side of my back below my shoulder blade, that really hurts. Could you look at it for me?"

Cate dropped her covering lower to allow Rosalyn better access. "I don't see how I could have bruised that side of my back when I fell." She stopped as she heard the other woman's sharp intake of breath.

"What? What is it?" Once again she found herself wishing for a mirror.

"What's this?" Rosalyn ran her hand softly over Cate's shoulder blade, above the injury Cate wanted her to see.

"Oh that. That's not what I mean, Rosalyn. Do you see anything just below there?"

"Aye, lass, I see the injury below." She continued to trace the pattern on Cate's shoulder blade. "But what's this?"

"That's just my birthmark. It's always been there. I know it's weird when you first see it. The first time I caught sight of it, I was climbing out of a bathtub and I glanced back into the mirror. I must have been about four or five. I was sure I was bleeding. I ran down the hall of our house, completely naked, screaming for my dad." She chuckled at the memory. "My brothers still find ways to tease me about that. Cass, that's my oldest brother, says that if you squint your eyes and turn your head just right, that birthmark looks like a flower. Considering where it is, I've never been able to get that kind of a perspective on it."

"It's a verra unusual Faerie mark." Rosalyn continued to lightly trace the shape with her index finger.

Cate smiled over her shoulder. "You sound just like my granny. When I was little and I'd complain about how ugly it looked, she'd call it my 'Faerie kiss.' As I got older, I learned they're not unusual at all. Lots of people have birthmarks. Mine's fairly common, in fact. Both my mother and my granny had similar marks."

"Of course," Rosalyn murmured. "Passed from mother to daughter."

"I don't know that it's genetic. But I do know it's really not an uncommon thing at all. Of course, I never wear anything with a back low enough for it to show. I even used to hunt for bathing suits that would cover it. I'm just grateful it's on my shoulder blade and not my face."

"Aye, it's verra dark against yer pale skin. As you say, like blood. I've never seen one so dark." Rosalyn moved her hand lower, causing Cate to wince as she touched the spot that hurt.

"Ouch. That's it. I can't quite reach my hand around to it. What do you think it is?"

"It's no so serious. You've a swelling here with a small cut in the center. Quite bruised as weel. But thanks to this, you hae a wealth of colors on yer back now to go with yer Faerie kiss." She smiled at Cate as she started to the door. "From the looks of that on yer back, if I dinna ken the truth of it, I'd think you and Mairi had been throwing stones at one another, along with all yer other wee bairn games."

Rosalyn's laughter floated back to Cate as the woman made her way down the hall.

"Wee bairn" games, was it? Well, what could she expect? She and Mairi had certainly done a few foolish things in the past couple of weeks, but throwing rocks at each other hadn't been one of them.

There was, however, something about the whole idea of rock throwing that nagged at the back of Cate's thoughts, eating away at her peace of mind as she got dressed. It was that same feeling she had when she'd forgotten something important, like whether or nor she'd turned off the oven or unplugged her curling iron.

It was still worrying away at her as she dressed and braided her hair, and even later, when after she'd eaten, Mairi peeked around her door. Bouncing across the room to her favorite spot on the rug, the younger woman took a seat and stretched out her legs, bare feet near the fire.

"Rosalyn told us at eve'n meal that you were recovering quickly. Anabella felt sure you were pretending just to get sympathy." Mairi grinned.

"I'm not sorry to have missed that." Cate had no doubt that Anabella would have something hateful to say.

"It's the best part of being indisposed and having my meals brought to me." She grinned in return.

"You look no worse for the ordeal. Weel, other than those nasty marks on yer face, but they'll heal. I, on the other hand, must have lost a good ten years. I was so frightened when I saw you on the ground. Even Connor's lecture was no so scary as that." Eyes wide, she shook her head.

"Connor's lecture? He was yelling at you? For what?" It was hard to imagine Mairi standing still for a lecture from anyone.

"No so much yelling. He disna actually yell at me. But he was in a mighty fury that I'd take you out riding without him being told. He was still listing all the dangers I'd no been wise enough to consider when Rosalyn came down from seeing to yer broken body." She chuckled as Cate rolled her eyes. "I was fair relieved he dinna take dinner with us, him in his foul mood."

"He didn't come to the hall to eat?" Though he'd avoided her steadfastly for the past two weeks, he'd still taken every meal with them.

"No. When Rosalyn first joined us outside the hall, coming straight from you as she had, she was in a fine merry spirit. When she found him scolding me she told him he needed to practice self-control and then something about remembering how the Fae always answered yer pleas, but in a manner of their own choosing." Mairi leaned back on her elbows, shaking her head. "He had a fair fit at that, his face going all red, and he stormed out. Rosalyn just laughed and went into the hall." She shrugged her shoulders. "Honestly, Cate, I've no understanding of men, and no patience to gain it. They act the part of fools or wee bairns in overgrown bodies, with their posturing and fighting. They start with throwing stones at one another and end with swords."

"Yeah, I'm right there with you." She joined Mairi on the rug, the two of them sitting in companionable silence, both lost in their own thoughts.

Unexpectedly that elusive little worry at the back of her mind popped up, front and center. No wonder, the stone thing bothered her.

"Mairi, did you notice anything unusual when my horse bolted yesterday?"

"You mean other than yer flying through the air and smashing into the ground, looking for the world like a rag puppet?" The girl had a way with description.

Cate rolled her eyes again. "I'm serious, Mairi. Did you hear anything from over where I was? Before the horse bolted?"

"No, I was splashing a bit in the water, and then Blane came over, annoying me, trying to strike a conversation. He'd no be quiet and leave me be."

Cate jumped up. "I need your help. Will you stay here and make sure no one comes looking for me?"

Mairi stood up, looking bewildered. "Of course you can hae my help. What are you doing? What's wrong?"

"Don't ask me now. If I'm right, I'll tell you all about it when I get back." At her friend's look of disappointment she added, "I'll tell you all about it when I get back, even if I'm not right. Deal?"

"If you'll no let me go with you, it'll hae to do," Mairi groused as she accompanied her friend to the door.

* * *

Cate crept downstairs and out through the courtyard, trying to keep to the shadows so no one would see her. Briefly she considered going to find Connor first, but discarded the idea. She wasn't ready to explain to anyone what she suspected. Not until she had some proof to back up her suspicion.

A fine stinging mist fell from the night sky, and the cold of it was a shock to her. She wished she'd worn more than the thin shift and overdress she had on. If only she'd brought a cloak. She had remembered a candle, but realized as she made her way quietly through the dark that she had no idea how she'd light it when she reached her destination, the stables. She could really use a good flashlight about now.

Once inside, all she would need to do was find the horse she'd ridden yesterday. Momentarily she considered going back as she envisioned dealing with the horse again, but gathering her resolve, she continued on.

If she was right, she was about to find her proof. The horse she rode yesterday was going to have the same mark on his rear end that she had on her back. She remembered having heard a noise just before her horse went wild, like something hitting the tree beside her. Like maybe a stone?

She was soaked to the skin by the time she reached the stables and starting to shiver. She'd need to hurry with this and get back to her room. As she entered the dark stable, her eyes were immediately drawn to the soft glow coming from a connected room. She assumed that must be where the stableboy slept, and she prayed he wasn't there now. Creeping nearer the door, she was re-lieved to find the little room empty except for a small rumpled cot and a cheerful little fire.

Leaning close to the fire, she lit her candle. It was a temptation to linger near the warmth, but the boy would no doubt return before long. She didn't want to be caught snooping and have to explain what she was doing.

Cupping her hand around the candle to prevent the light from going out, she started down the first narrow aisle between the stalls. If she remembered correctly, the horse she'd been riding was kept back here.

Cate found the stall she was seeking on her second try. Fortunately the beast was standing with his rear end toward her, munching away on his oats. He looked enor-mous in this light. Holding her candle high, keeping a wary eye on his hind legs, she leaned in and gently ran her hand across his flank.

The horse swung his head up to look back at her as her hand skimmed the first bump. He whinnied and stamped his front foot when she touched the second.

That was good enough for her. She'd found the proof she'd come looking for. Now she just had to figure out what it meant and what to do about it.

Connor sat high on the battlements overlooking the courtyard, seeking solace in a pitcher of ale. He regretted immensely his high tolerance to the stuff. He would gladly welcome the respite from his thoughts that being down-on-his-face drunk might bring. The fine cold mist only added to the weight of his mood.

The woman was driving him insane in a way no other

ever had. He had spent the last fortnight avoiding her as much as possible, spending long hours in the lists driving his body to exhaustion, all to prevent what he had then allowed to happen last night. He was such a fool.

He was sworn to protect her, but in order to do that he had to be near her, and it seemed as though he could no longer be near her and keep his hands off her. She turned that alluring green gaze upon him and his innards came to life. She placed her tiny hand upon his chest and his brain ceased to function. For the first time since childhood, he was unsure of what to do.

He wondered if Rosalyn had guessed, if that was what she had referred to with her cryptic words about the Fae. Was she trying to tell him this was the price he had to pay for seeking the help of his Faerie ancestors? He had spent the past seven years mastering his emotions. Self-control was always his now. He wouldn't allow it to desert him because of a woman.

He must keep in mind who and what Cate was. In spite of the irrational possessiveness he felt every time he came near her, he'd do well to remember that she wasn't his. Even now she wore another man's betrothal gift, the man who would claim her when she went home.

That bastard, Richard.

She might say she wouldn't marry him, that she valued love over wealth and power, but she was only a woman like any other, and when she returned home, she'd seek the wealth and power. She still wore the man's ring, didn't she?

He'd do well to remember when he wed her on the steps of the church, it would mean nothing to her but a task completed so that she could go home. And go home she would, in less than a fortnight now.

To Richard.

It would be Richard who spent his days drowning in the green pools of her eyes, indulging in the softness of her lips. He hated the man for his expensive cart, for having his mark upon Cate, but most of all for waiting patiently seven hundred years in the future.

"I thought I'd find you here." Connor started as Duncan sat down beside him.

"It's no a good idea to be creeping up on a man in the dark of the night, Duncan." He made no effort to keep the irritation from his voice.

"I dinna creep. I fair stomped." Duncan took a drink from the tankard he held. "And I'd thank you no to snap at me. I'm no the one yer angry with."

"My apologies, old friend. Yer absolutely right." Connor sighed deeply. "It's my own self who disgusts me this night."

After all these years, all they'd been through together, he owed Duncan honesty at the very least.

"Aye. But you hae no need to apologize to me. I ken it's a fair mess yer twisted into by our wee lassie." Duncan calmly took another drink.

Connor's head snapped around to stare at him. "And just what 'wee lassie' might you be speaking of?"

"Dinna try to deny it to me, lad. I've learned yer ways since you were a wee bairn in changing cloths." Duncan snorted. "You sit alone in the dark with yer sour face, biting at any who's foolish enough to come near you. There's no a doubt in my mind who the root of yer problem is, only what you plan to do about her."

"There's naught needs to be done. Within the fortnight, the marriage will be accomplished and she'll return home. I'll be free to look after Mairi." He turned to the older man. "The plan is as it was from the beginning. No changes."

They sat together in silence, staring out over the darkened courtyard for a few moments.

"Hae you thought to ask yer woman to stay here with you then?" Duncan asked it quietly, gently, as if to soften the magnitude of the question.

"She'd hae no reason to stay. She's no my woman. There's a wealthy man who waits for her in her own time. Richard." He forced down the urge to spit to rid his mouth of the nasty taste left by saying the man's name. He took another drink instead. "The ring she wears is his betrothal gift to her."

"It's only a wee bauble, that." Duncan said thoughtfully. "No much for a wealthy man."

"Aye."

"And this man, this Richard, he's a verra far distance away from her now, is he no?"

"Aye, a verra far distance." Connor nodded his head slowly.

Surely Duncan must understand. Women might all be deceitful in matters of the heart, but he could never be. His honor would never allow it.

"I'd no steal another man's woman." It came out hard, cold.

"I dinna think you would. I'm only saying a thing that's given freely canna be stolen."

"She's given me nothing, Duncan."

"As you say, but I could no help but notice the way she clung to you last night. And the way you looked at her."

Connor stiffened. "She was hurt. I'm responsible for her safety, and I failed to protect her. I have a role to play, and I play it. It's that and nothing more. I've no desire to be tied to any woman."

Silence stretched out, the two men once again staring into the night, each lost in his own thoughts, until Duncan abruptly nudged Connor's arm with his now empty tankard.

"Weel, laddie, since yer doing naught but playing a role, it looks like it just might be time for the next act to begin." He pointed down to the edge of the courtyard. "Isna that yer lassie there, creeping along in the dark?"

Connor stood and cursed.

What could she be up to this time? She moved slowly across the courtyard, attempting to keep to the shadows.

"Christ. She's no even wearing a cloak. She'll be soaked to the skin and down with a fever next."

The woman was a plague to his peace of mind. With no thought to her own safety, she merrily traipsed from one predicament to the next.

He'd a mind to just let her go. Or throw her over his shoulder and carry her off. Or tie her up and toss her into his room, where he could keep an eye on her. His mind raged with frustration.

She disappeared into the stables.

A man would have to stay with her twenty-four hours a day to keep one such as her out of trouble.

Cursing again, he threw down his tankard and trotted off to the stairs.

Cate was nearing the exit now, moving slowly away from the animals toward the large stable doors, when her candle went out.

She gasped as she felt a breath on her neck, only seconds before a torch sprang to life, dimly lighting the area around her. She turned.

Blane, only a few feet away, was fitting a torch into a holder. He started toward her and she slowly backed away, realizing she was only steps from the wall.

"I saw a light moving through the dark. I would no hae expected to find you here." He looked predatory in this light.

"My candle went out." She could think of nothing else to say.

He was close enough now to reach out and touch her, which he did, running the pad of his thumb over the scratch on her face. She jerked her head away and edged closer to the wall.

"Aye, it did. I blew it out. Dinna anyone ever tell you fire is dangerous in a stable?" He moved closer and once again ran his thumb over her cheek. "But perhaps danger is another of the poor choices you make."

He'd been drinking. This close, his breath reeked of alcohol. Again he moved his thumb over her cheek.

"If you were my woman, I'd no let this happen to you."

"You were there with me yesterday, and yet this happened." Logically she knew she shouldn't argue with him, but she said it anyway.

"Aye. Because yer no my woman."

He lowered his eyes and it suddenly occurred to her that the wet linen shift covering her breasts left little to the imagination. Obviously he realized it as well. She crossed her arms in front of her and he smiled, his teeth gleaming in the torchlight, the predatory look more pronounced than before.

"My offer's still open if yer interested yet. Sometimes the choices we make are not necessarily what we want, only the better of two poor options. You might find the benefits of belonging to me more pleasant in the long run than the alternative."

Her mouth went dry as his hand slid from her face to her neck. She nervously bit at her lower lip, a move she instantly regretted as his eyes fastened on her mouth and he licked his lips.

She weighed her options. Her back was, literally, to the wall. He was a big man. Not as tall or as muscular as Connor certainly, but he still towered over her. He'd been drinking, apparently quite a bit, but she doubted even that would give her the leverage she needed to defeat him in a contest of strength, if it came to that.

Which left her with her wits as her only weapon. And as stupid as she'd been to come out here in the dark alone, she was feeling sorely underarmed and outmanned.

"Well, since my decision hasn't changed, I really do need to get going. I'm sure Mairi's waiting for me and I don't want her to worry."

"I canna believe Mairi has any thought as to where you are, wee Caitlyn."

He took her braid into his hand, staring down at it. He slid his fingers down her hair, jerking off the small strip of cloth she tied there, crushing it in his hand.

Real panic engulfed her as his other hand tugged at the laces that held her dress closed over her shift. For the first time in her life, Cate regretted not having learned even one of the martial arts moves Jesse was always trying to teach her. She could certainly use one of them now.

She tried to push him away, but he pressed up against her body, crushing her back into the wall, his breath in her ear when he spoke.

"Is it a rendezvous yer here for then? I wonder who it is you might be thinking to meet so late at night in a dark stable? I wonder what you might be planning to meet him for? Perhaps he's no coming and we should start without him."

His mouth came down harshly over hers, his teeth grinding into her lips when she heard the deep baritone response to his question.

"That would be me she's waiting for, and I'm no one to take kindly to her starting anything without me."

Blane eased slightly away from her, allowing her just enough room to see Connor standing at the edge of the torchlight. His hair was dripping, the small side braid plastered to his cheek. His wet shirt molded to the chest muscles that flexed as he deliberately laid his hand on the hilt of his sword. But it was his eyes that held Cate's attention, glittering with intent.

She'd thought earlier that Blane looked predatory. Connor looked absolutely feral.

Slowly moving to her side, Blane let her laces slide through his fingers and she released the breath she hadn't realized she'd been holding. He continued to move slowly away from her until he was nearly a yard distant.

Connor hadn't moved at all.

He and Blane stared at one another, locked in some primal battle of wills.

"Sorry, Cousin." Blane bowed his head slightly, a little off-balance, though never breaking eye contact with Connor. He held up the little strip of cloth he'd taken from Cate's hair. "Should I assume this to be yer territory marker then? It is yer plaid, is it no?"

Connor's eyes continued to glitter dangerously, but his voice was low and even when he spoke. "Aye, Cousin. I'd think you'd hae recognized it sooner. It marks her as mine. But you were already aware of that, were you no? This is ground we've covered before."

Cate ran the back of her hand over her mouth, tasting blood where her lip had been cut. She heard a pathetic whimper and was shocked to realize it had come from her.

Connor strode to her side then, turning his back on Blane. He gently took her laces and tied them with shaking hands. He pulled her hand from her mouth and looked at the blood smeared there, his face losing all expression. His eyes hardened as he turned and moved toward his cousin.

They stared at one another for a brief moment.

Connor leaned over and picked up the strip of plaid from the floor where Blane had dropped it. He straightened and, without warning, swung his arm, connecting the back of his hand to Blane's mouth with a sickening thud. Blane flew back against the stall nearest to where he'd been, sliding slowly to the hay-strewn floor. He brought his hand up to his mouth, where blood trickled from the corner. He shook his head and glowered at Connor but said nothing.

Connor's voice was low and lethal as he leaned down over Blane. "Consider that yer last warning, Cousin. Cate belongs to me. I'll no kill you this time because yer in yer cups, and I'm thinking you've no idea what you've done." He paused and breathed deeply as if he were fighting for control when he spoke. "But mark my words. If you ever touch her again, you'll take yer last breath at my hand."

Connor stalked across the courtyard, dragging Cate along beside him. She was forced to run to keep up with his stride, but he didn't care. White-hot fury slashed through his entire being. It filled him, consumed him, leaving space for only one other emotion. An emotion with which he had no experience.

Fear.

Fear for what had almost happened to her. Fear for what could yet happen to her.

The mist had turned to a steady falling rain, but Connor didn't feel the cold. He was impervious to everything around him until Cate stumbled and would have fallen but for the grip he kept on her arm. He stopped.

Turning his face up to the heavens, he breathed deeply, raggedly, fighting desperately to regain some vestige of control over his raging emotions. His eyes closed, the rain washing over his face, his mind continued to replay the same scenes over and over. Blane's hands on Cate; her dress hanging open, exposing the soaked shift she wore underneath; the heart-wrenching sound of her whimper; the blood he'd seen when he'd lowered her hand from her mouth. Her blood.

He opened his eyes and gazed down at her. Her face, too, was turned skyward, eyes closed, allowing the rain to wash down over her. Her hair, completely loosened now, hung in clumps about her shoulders. The raindrops joined in her lashes and rolled down her cheeks in small rivulets of water. She looked delicate and fragile. His stomach clenched as the unfamiliar fear rolled over him once more.

"Yer going back to yer room and yer staying there." He forced the words through gritted teeth.

"No." She breathed the word wearily, keeping her eyes closed. "I don't want to go to my room now. I need to talk to you."

"You'll do as I say." He yelled it at her, grabbing her other arm and giving her a small shake.

Her eyes flew open. "I'll do no such thing. I told you I need to——"

"You will." He cut her off.

The fear receded, leaving a cold calm behind. He knew what he had to do now.

"You'll do exactly what I say. You'll stay in yer room. You'll go out only with an escort. I'll no risk harm to you again so long as yer here, Cate. I canna."

Her eyes blazed with rebellion as she opened her mouth to respond.

He'd allow no discussion. Crushing her to him, he covered her mouth with his. He intended to punish her for her defiance, but the moment their lips met, he could think of nothing but her softness and his need for her. He ravished her mouth, pouring his soul into the kiss.

Forcing himself to pull back, he looked down at her. Her lips were softly parted, her eyes glazed.

Seeing her that way, he decided to follow one of his urges from earlier in the evening. He gathered her up in his arms, tossed her over his shoulder and headed toward the castle.

He smiled triumphantly, knowing the shock would guarantee her silence. It did.

At least for the first few moments.

"Put me down this very instant," Cate hissed into the back she hung against, emphasizing her demand by smacking her hand into him. She might as well have been smacking the stone walls around her.

One minute she'd been trying to get her wits about her to tell Connor what she'd discovered, the next he was kissing her senseless. And then, without even allowing her time to recover, he'd slung her over his back like a bag of dirty laundry, hauling her off through the darkened castle halls.

"Be quiet," he growled, tightening his grip around her legs.

They came to a stop and she realized they had reached her room. He slammed the door open and stomped inside, dumping her unceremoniously onto her bed.

"What's going on?" Mairi jumped up from her spot by the fire. "What are you—"

"Out." He pointed at the door without taking his eyes from Cate's.

"But what—"

"Out," he bellowed, and Mairi ran from the room.

"Look, Connor, I don't know what you think you're doing but—"

He didn't allow her to finish. "I canna stand guard on you twenty-four hours a day, woman, and since you've no the good sense to watch out for yerself, I'll no allow you to blunder into harm again. I'll hear nothing from you on this. Yer confined to this room. You'll go nowhere without Duncan or myself in attendance."

His eyes glittered with emotion as he looked down at her; his breathing was ragged and she didn't think it was from the exertion of carrying her. That he was furious, there was little doubt.

"I need to talk to you about—"

"I've nothing I want to hear from you. There are forces at work here you obviously choose to ignore. I'll no allow you to put yerself in that danger."

Forces at work? That was what she was trying to tell him. "Exactly. That's why we need to discuss—"

"There will be no discussion on this point. You'll do as I say, and you'll give me no grief on it, or I swear I'll bind you to that bed."

"What?" Who did he think he was? She stood up, facing him. "You have no right to treat me like this."

"I hae every right. I'm sworn to protect you and I'm going to do exactly that, in spite of you, it seems."

"You can't just order me around, lock me in here and expect me to stand for it."

They glared at one another, toe-to-toe, for perhaps the longest moment of Cate's life. Without warning, he leaned down and swept her off her feet. One hand behind her head and one arm beneath her knees, he lifted her, bringing her face close to his own.

"I dinna expect you to stand for it," he whispered, his breath warm on her face before he crushed his lips to hers, sapping the fight out of her with the explosiveness of his kiss.

She thought to push at him, but instead found her traitorous arms reaching to twine about his neck. They'd barely found their destination when she felt herself flying through the air, once again tossed to the bed.

Connor reached the door in two long strides. "What I do expect is that you stay in that bed tonight, and remain in this room as yer told." He walked out and slammed the door behind him.

The pillow Cate angrily threw after him bounced quietly off the closed door, landing on the floor with a small poof, doing nothing to soothe her frustration.

CHAPTER 13

Aye, she rejected my offer again." Holding the wet cloth to his face, Blane paced across the room before turning to glare at his father. "But I dinna doubt I could hae had her if Connor had no arrived."

The jeering sound of derision from his father inflamed him. He threw the cloth to the floor. The effects of the whisky were gone, too quickly, as always, leaving him to face this without any protection for his raw nerves.

"She weakened, Father. I sensed it. I could hae changed her mind."

"It disna matter. You dinna want her anyway." The old man tapped his finger thoughtfully against chin. "We'll simply hae to remove her. It's the only way."

"No. You'll no do her any harm. You said I could do this my way." Blane stopped his pacing. He had to do something, think of something before it was too late. "I've changed my mind, anyway. I want her now."

"Because she belongs to Connor? Because he wants her?" Artair's eyes glittered with a greedy intensity.

"Perhaps. Just as you once coveted what was his." He paused for only a heartbeat. "As you coveted what was his father's."

"Dinna provoke me," Artair screamed at him, a fevered look about him. "I'm laird here." He leaned toward Blane. "He canna stay. He must not. We hae to find a way to send him back to his king. Too much depends on his leaving. I'll no lose everything now." He returned to tapping his finger on his chin, the movement turning random and erratic.

"Challenge him for the wench if you want her so badly." The hard voice came from the shadows.

"No." Both men simultaneously replied.

"It would no work." Blane answered quickly.

He'd always suspected he was no physical match for his cousin. After tonight, he knew it to be true. Even sober, he'd have no chance of defeating the man.

"We canna risk bringing the king down on our heads by doing injury to Connor. It must be done in another way, the marriage stopped somehow. I'll hae to think on this." Artair drew himself up, gathering his courage. Glancing to the shadows, he lowered his voice almost to a whisper. "And there's Rosalyn's protection of him to consider."

"Then remove her as well." The voice in the shadows held no mercy.

"Never. Have you lost yer wits?" Artair's eyes glittered now with fear. He turned to Blane. "Yer way has not worked. After this latest encounter with yer cousin, it mayhaps be best if you dinna draw his attention for a few days. For now, go to the MacPherson. Assure him he'll have his payment for our debt by month's end."

"Yer debt, Father," he corrected. "I'll assure him of payment on yer debt." Blane hated the MacPherson almost as much as he hated his father. With a mocking bow, he turned and left.

"You must never, ever speak of harming Rosalyn again. Dinna even think on it. You know the legend. It would be the end of us." Artair had the air of a man half crazed as he ran from the room.

From the shadows, a bitterly mocking comment echoed down the hall after the laird: "Would that the gods deliver me from superstitious fools and cowards."

CHAPTER 14

Cate hadn't seen Connor since he'd unceremoniously dumped her in this room four nights ago, laying down the law like some overbearing caveman.

He'd refused to talk to her then and he'd refused to talk to her since, even though she'd repeatedly sent Mairi and Rosalyn to ask him to come to her. It seemed as though once he'd made up his mind, he wouldn't discuss, he wouldn't compromise, he wouldn't even listen. Now he was refusing to speak to the other women as well.

Compared to him, her brothers stacked up pathetically short in their teasing attempts to make her life miserable. Good thing they'd all never meet.

Even when it had occurred to her that first night that Beast had been missing since her accident, she'd finally had to resort to bribing Duncan into delivering that message to him.

Duncan. He infuriated her as well. Every time she opened her door, there he was, hounding her every move. She grimaced. And in order to get her message about Beast delivered, she'd had to promise not to try to elude him or make his job more difficult. He'd completely refused to allow her to leave the castle, even to set foot in the courtyard, threatening to toss her over his shoulder as Connor had if she didn't "behave like a good lass." The last two days he hadn't even allowed her to leave her room.

Seriously. These men were way out of hand.

"Damn them both. I hate being treated like a runaway child." She threw herself down on the bed, staring up at the canopy above.

Then, to compound matters, she'd learned from Mairi that Connor had moved his things from the barracks where he'd been staying with Duncan into the room next door to hers, presumably to make sure she didn't sneak out of her room at night.

And that was by far the worst thing of all.

Because when she was absolutely, brutally honest with herself, she acknowledged that lying here at night knowing he was in the room next door, wondering what he was doing and why he wouldn't even speak to her, was the most frustrating part of the past four days.

She'd even stooped to pressing her ear against the wall that separated their rooms last night in hopes of hearing something, anything, that might make her feel she'd had contact with him. But there had been nothing, no sound at all from his room. Or at least nothing that carried through the thick stone.

After he'd rescued her in the stable, she'd known he was beyond furious with her. But then, in the courtyard, the way he'd kissed her. Never in her entire life had she experienced anything to compare with that. Afterward she'd thought just maybe . . .

"Stupid, stupid, stupid." She pounded her fists on the pillow above her head.

What was wrong with her? This whole trip-through-time thing must have scrambled her brains. She hadn't been able to control her emotions in the least since she'd been here. All that awful, arrogant Neanderthal had to do was look at her and her heart started pounding, her hands shook, and she wanted . . . well, whatever it was she wanted, it sure as heck wasn't happening.

She needed to clear her mind, to unwind and stop thinking about him. Cate breathed slowly and concentrated on relaxing. She would let her mind go blank and roam free.

Deep breath in, deep breath out, just like in the yoga class.

But when she closed her eyes, she saw only Connor. Connor taking her hand, Connor in the rain looking down at her, his eyes filled with anger and pain, Connor pulling her close to kiss her.

"Aarrgghh," she growled, sitting up in a huff, slamming her fists into the mattress. She'd never been any good at that mindfulness relaxation crap.

Cate looked over at the table next to her bed. There was the pendant that had first brought him to her. It sat like a great unblinking eye staring at her from its nest on the crumpled strip of plaid she'd used in her hair since her first day here. Connor had tossed it down on the bed next to her when he'd tossed her there.

They all saw it as Connor's territorial marker, did they? It'd be a dark day in hell before she put that back in her hair again.

She stood and began to pace, turning her consideration to another of her great frustrations over the past few days, the mystery of the stone bruises.

She had tried to discuss it with Connor, first on the night when she'd discovered them and again later. She'd attempted to get him to come talk to her so she could bring up the subject of the marks on the horse, but he wasn't talking—or listening—to anything.

She hesitated to say anything to Mairi or Rosalyn. If someone had intentionally spooked her horse, as she believed, then she didn't want that same someone coming after either of her friends. They would be safer if she kept them in the dark. If she told either of them, they might try to hunt for clues on their own. Worse yet, they might find the person, and then what would happen?

She was still pacing, trying to manipulate the limited number of mental puzzle pieces into some sort of reasonable picture, when she heard raised voices in the hallway. She threw open the door to find Duncan blocking Mairi's access to the room.

"Yer no listening to me, lassie. She's no going anywhere until Connor returns."

Watching them now brought to mind the old saying about the immovable object meeting the irresistible force.

"That's what I'm trying to tell you, Duncan, you big oaf," Mairi yelled at him. "He's back. He's back with Beast and . . ." She caught sight of Cate standing behind

Duncan. "Cate, you hae to come with me. Beast has been hurt. Connor's just ridden in with the poor creature hanging over his horse."

Her heart in her throat, Cate attempted to push past Duncan, only to find her way firmly blocked.

"Damn it, Duncan, move. This is serious. I have to go." She pushed at him again, trying to slip past his massive frame.

"Aye, lassie, it may be serious, but yer no going anywhere. And I'll thank you to remember yer promise. Connor says yer to stay put, so stay put you will." He started pulling her door closed.

"Mairi. Go find out for me what's going on." The door slammed in her face.

Pacing the floor and waiting for news, Cate would never have believed an hour could go by so slowly.

"But you're sure he's going to be all right?" Cate asked again, and once again Mairi nodded her head affirmatively.

The two of them sat on the floor of Cate's room, eating dinner in front of the fireplace. At least Duncan had allowed her company tonight.

"Connor went looking for him right after you were finally able to get Duncan to listen to you."

They both shook their heads, exchanging a "men-are-so-dense" look.

"He's been gone the last two days, tracking Beast. Connor says that the arrow still being in his leg kept him from losing too much blood. He'd already tended the poor creature's wounds before he got him back to the castle, and now the dog is resting in Connor's room. Duncan will watch over him."

Cate snorted. "How's he supposed to watch over Beast when he's busy playing prison guard outside my door all day?"

"He's not now. They're all three of them keeping watch over you from Connor's room. Connor and Duncan hae been in there since before I came up with yer dinner." She narrowed her eyes speculatively. "From what little I heard"—a small guilty smile played around her lips—"before they noticed me, you ken? They're planning yer riding out."

Connor had been gone for two days. Now he was back in the castle. Right next door, and she hadn't even known.

Irritating, arrogant, bossy, aggravating man.

Fine. She was almost looking forward to the riding-out just so she would have the uninterrupted opportunity to give him a piece of her mind.

Mairi was still talking. "There Anabella was, carrying on about yer making life so difficult for everyone taking all yer meals in yer room." She leaned back against the nearest chair and chuckled. "I only wish you could hae seen her face when Rosalyn told her how much you had missed yer pleasant dinners together with her."

Both women grinned.

"I'm beginning to think your aunt Rosalyn has a wicked sense of humor."

"Aye. She does say she finds her greatest joy in the simple things."

They both giggled over that.

"So, have I missed anything else?"

"Och, aye. I must be going daft. I canna believe I almost forgot the most wonderful thing of all." Mairi's eyes shone with excitement. "The king himself will be attending yer wedding. Lyall returned just this midday with the news. I suppose that's the errand my uncle sent him on, though I've no yet had the chance to talk to him alone. I was in the hall when he arrived. At first everyone was so concerned because of his bandaged arm, but then he told us about the king, and everyone started talking all at once. Anabella's already in a fair state about it, worrying how she's going to impress the king, I imagine."

"I wouldn't think the king would make a habit of attending too many weddings. Does he?"

"It's that much he thinks of Connor that he's coming." Mairi tilted her head to the side. "I've heard talk that Connor saved the king's life once, but I've never been able to get him to tell me anything about it. He never wants to talk to me about what happened when he's been off in the king's service. Some of it must be awful for him, I ken that. But I know he must talk to Lyall. They spend hours together in the lists when he comes home." She sighed and shook her head. "Sometimes I feel verra left out."

Cate understood exactly how she felt. Regardless of how involved she might be in the family business, she was never included in the discussions of tactics or the actual operations. And they never talked about it when they came home, at least not to her.

It seemed she was constantly finding similarities between herself and Mairi, between Connor and the men in her family. Once again it occurred to her how little men had really changed in the centuries between her time and this.

Listening to her friend now, she realized that women hadn't changed so much either. Stick Mairi in a pair of jeans and a T-shirt, and she'd fit right into any group of young women walking down the street in Denver. She glanced at Mairi's bare feet, the emerald ring sparkling on her toe, and revised that thought. Better make that any group of young women in Boulder.

Mairi sighed deeply. "I'm even thinking of wearing shoes for the wedding. I hate to give Anabella the satisfaction, but I'd no want to embarrass Connor in front of the king." An attractive blush stained the girl's cheeks. "I've never seen a king before."

"Well, that makes two of us," Cate murmured thoughtfully.

Life just continued to get stranger and stranger. To think, Richard had been so impressed because a couple of congressmen and a senator were supposed to come to her wedding back home. Here, because of Connor, not her, she was getting married in front of King Alexander III of Scotland.

"Were you able to follow the tracks at all?" Duncan sat on a stool by the fireplace.

Connor shook his head. "The rains had ruined much of what was there, most of the area turned to mud. Once they veered into the stream, I lost them, as they'd intended. I checked both upstream and down, but didn't find where they'd come out." He leaned back in the hard chair he'd pulled close to the open doorway. From this spot he could see both Cate's door and the hallway, and ensure that no one could overhear their conversation. "I should hae noticed Beast's absence earlier. If I'd gotten to him sooner, perhaps I would have found more evidence."

Found more, perhaps, but at what price? He would have been gone when Cate blundered into the stables. Even after four days he hadn't been able to rid himself of the uncomfortable prickle of fear and the overriding anger that accompanied it.

"So you learned precious little." Duncan shook his head, reaching down to stroke the dog sleeping next to him.

"I learned we were right to suspect treachery. Someone was in those woods. I dinna ken how, but I'm sure they were responsible for Cate's accident. I only need the proof to tie it together. And there's no doubt they thought to kill Beast when he found them."

"They?"

"Aye. I found tracks for at least two separate mounts."

"I thought yer uncle was being too accommodating to this whole setup. What do we do now?"

"We hae to think of what they may do before they do it and be ready."

His uncle. Artair was behind it, he was sure, though he had no proof. He'd known when the older man gave in on the wedding with nothing more than a demand for following the old customs it was merely a bid to buy time.

He hated this. It was like the kind of political intrigue that permeated the king's court, the one thing he detested about being in Alexander's private service. Give him a battle on an open field facing a known opponent any day.

"What about taking the women and going home?" Duncan leaned toward him. "We could protect them at Sithean Fardach, no worry. I dinna like being here, lad. There's too many people about. Too many unknowns."

The old warrior was right, but that plan carried its own dangers.

"We've been over this, Duncan, weighed the risks. Staying here, keeping my future bride under the protection of my family, is the proper thing to do." Protection? That was a joke.

Duncan snorted derisively. "As if you've ever had a care to doing what they deem proper."

"If we escape to Sithean Fardach now, they'll be watching, their network of spies stationed outside by the time of the wedding. It will be much harder to convince them we've sent Cate home directly after. If we can just hold out until the wedding, we have the luxury of time before they're in place. Then, after she's gone, we can tell them all that her father sent an escort for her. No one will be the wiser, and we'll have Mairi and Rosalyn safely tucked away, out of their reach."

He didn't like the plan any better than Duncan did, but it was the only logical course of action for now. Unless they came after her again. Another attempt and he'd be out of options. He'd not allow her to come to harm.

"And the riding-out? You'll still chance that?"

"Aye, I've no choice." He smiled grimly at his friend. "But I've an idea to make it safer. They'll ken we're to do this so we'll hae to be on our sharpest guard the whole time."

"We?" Duncan frowned in confusion.

"Aye."

With one last glance down the hallway to ensure their privacy, Connor launched into his plan. They'd keep to the old customs as his uncle demanded. He simply planned to add to them a bit.

CHAPTER 15

Final banns were posted and the wedding ceremony was just five days off. Today was the day Cate and Connor would ride out to the surrounding countryside to personally invite each and every person to attend the wedding and celebration.

She had, at most, a week left here.

Cate had been up for hours, unable to sleep, anxious about what the day would bring.

After changing her outfit twice, she was once again dressed in the lovely green overdress she'd worn for her betrothal party. Putting it on, she had thought longingly about how much better she would feel facing this ride dressed in a pair of her favorite jeans.

Glancing across the room, she caught sight of her grandmother's wedding dress. Last night, when Rosalyn knocked on her door, she was delighted to find the older woman holding the dress that meant so much to her. It had been packed away since her arrival.

Cate had untied the ribbon holding the dress in a crumpled bundle and carefully stretched it over a chair, smoothing it down to encourage the wrinkles out before the wedding.

She walked over to it now, running her hand over the old lace. Her grandmother had been a wonderful woman, strong and unafraid to make the decisions necessary to control her own life. She wouldn't have let any of these people intimidate her.

"Why can't I be more like you, Granny?"

She still hadn't seen Connor since the night he'd confined her to her room, effectively putting her under house arrest. She was nervous about spending the day alone with him, but more than that, she was determined. Especially after her conversation with Mairi last night.

Mairi finally had the opportunity to spend part of the afternoon with her cousin Lyall. And somewhere in their discussion about his adventure, the king coming, and everything that had happened in his absence, he'd apologized for leaving her in the lurch the day he was supposed to meet them for the riding lesson. It appeared he had never asked Blane to take his place that day. Mairi had barely given it more than a mention, but it had certainly captured Cate's attention.

Blane had lied to them. More important, why had he lied to them?

Although Cate didn't have an answer to that question, when she added it to the marks on the horse that matched the one on her back, everything seemed just a little too suspicious to be coincidence.

When she was a girl, Cate's favorite heroine had been Nancy Drew. She'd read every single one of those books, and she knew how to spot a mystery a mile off. Not that she'd ever been involved in any of her own, but still, even she could tell something was going on around here.

Blane was her number one suspect.

She didn't like him and she didn't trust him. Now she was sure she had more reason than ever to suspect him of . . . well, something. She hadn't quite put it all together yet, but she was determined to share her suspicions with Connor. He couldn't possibly ignore her through an entire day of their being alone together like they would be today.

Alone together, riding.

Would he remember his promise to her? Her face flamed and her heartbeat accelerated at the thought of being held by him as they rode through the countryside. She took a deep breath to prepare herself.

When the knock sounded at her door, she quickly ran her hands down her skirt, more to dry her sweaty palms than to straighten her dress.

Cate was surprised to find Duncan waiting at the door to collect her, but not nearly so surprised as she was when she reached the courtyard and found the large group of people already assembled there. It seemed she and Connor were to have an entourage for their little outing.

Not at all what she'd expected based on what she'd been told about this particular custom.

Rosalyn, Mairi, Lyall and Fergus, the guardsman who'd escorted them upon their arrival at Dun Ard, were all waiting on horseback along with Connor, who nodded to her, but didn't speak. Duncan's mount was waiting as well.

She studied Connor's face briefly before descending the stairs, but could determine nothing, his expression completely closed to her.

When she reached the courtyard, just as he had that first time in the forest, he drew his mount near her. Reaching down, he swept her up into his arms. She couldn't prevent a little gasp as he swung her up, and for just a moment something flickered there in his eyes before he closed himself off again.

While it appeared the discussion she planned would have to wait, at least he hadn't forgotten his promise about allowing her to ride only with him.

The sun was high overhead. They'd ridden for hours, and Cate had lost count of the number of people they'd spoken to. Every stop was more of the same. People came out and stared up at her with unabashed curiosity. A smiling Connor introduced her to each person and then issued the official invitation to attend their wedding and the celebration that would follow. Then they left, off to seek the next group of people.

And each time they left, the smile Connor had worn was left behind as well.

It was painfully obvious to Cate that this must be a distasteful duty to him. He hadn't spoken directly to her even once and only smiled when approaching the various crofters to play out their little charade. During the early hours, while the others had visited with one another as they journeyed, he rode in silence, looking everywhere but at her, holding himself stiff as if to avoid contact with her body.

In response, Cate had done her best to keep her distance, too, holding her back rigid, not allowing herself to relax into him. The few times she tired and let down her guard, his whole body had tensed and she'd corrected her position immediately.

Finally even Cate had been fooled by his performance when they stopped at the last crofter's house and a small boy there asked Connor if something was wrong with his lady's legs that she had to ride on his horse.

The adults had smiled uncomfortably and looked embarrassed, his mother pulling him in front of her and quickly placing a hand over his mouth while his father apologized. Connor laughed and ran his hand over Cate's shin where her dress left it exposed by her sitting on the horse. He told the child that "his wee Caty" had the finest legs in all of Scotland and that she rode where she was by his choice, so he could keep her near his heart. Then he'd winked at the little boy and, leaning down confided that he would understand someday when he found his own lady.

Everyone had laughed and bid farewell, and all the while Cate's heart pounded double time in her chest. Yet as soon as they had ridden away from the family, she'd glanced back at Connor's face to find the hard look had returned to his eyes and he ignored her, once more scanning the horizon.

It had all been an act to him and nothing more. But to her it was the final straw of the day.

Reluctantly she acknowledged to herself that his behavior toward her hurt, but she determined that she wouldn't let him see it. She had her pride to think of.

Back in her world, Richard may have made a fool of her, but she wouldn't make that mistake here in this time. She wouldn't let that happen to her again.

Even though it chafed that pride now to speak to him, she had to ask him for a rest stop. She couldn't sit here next to him for another minute knowing how much he wanted to be rid of her, not without everyone finding out just what a fool she really was. The pressure from the tears was already building behind her eyes, her throat closing off. She had to escape, if only for a short time.

Cate cleared her throat, hoping her voice wouldn't give her away. "I need to get down."

Connor flinched when she spoke. "What?"

He sounded gruff and annoyed to her overly sensitive ears.

"Down." She hadn't meant to yell. She breathed deeply, desperately seeking to gain control. "I need down. Now. I need to stop."

She couldn't look at him, but at least she'd managed the whole thing without bursting into tears.

"Verra weel." He sighed against the top of her head and turned to the others, pointing. "There's a place just there, a break in the forest by the stream, that will do fine for a meal stop."

"Thank the saints," Lyall muttered. "I'm fair hungry enough to eat the sacks we carry the food in."

The others laughed at the young man's grumbles while he grinned amiably. There was general visiting again as they stopped and dismounted.

Cate felt as if it took forever to reach the chosen location just a few yards away. As soon as Connor lifted her off the horse, she raised her skirts and ran. She wasn't sure where she planned to go, but she needed to get away, into the trees, away from all the eyes, away from him. She heard him call her name, but she kept going. She thought she might have heard him curse, but she was too far away to be sure.

She stopped downstream and leaned over. Placing her hands on her thighs, hanging her head low, she simply breathed, gasping for air. She couldn't be sure any longer if she needed to cry or throw up.

It hurt. His total rejection of her caused actual physical pain. This felt worse than when she'd walked into Richard's office and found him with his receptionist.

She kneeled down by the stream and splashed a handful of water on her face just before Connor burst through the underbrush into the clearing.

"Dinna ever, ever run away from me like that again." He was scowling fiercely as he grabbed her arm and pulled her to her feet. "What were you thinking to run off like that? Anything could hae happened to you." He was breathing hard.

Grateful that the water on her face hid the tears, she shook her arm free of his grasp.

"I had to . . . " She stopped.

What could she possibly tell him? That she was stupid enough to think that she might have meant something to him? That it hurt so bad she couldn't breathe, couldn't think when she realized she didn't?

"I felt sick."

The excuse sounded lame to her ears, but for a moment she imagined concern reflected in his eyes. Then it was gone.

"Yer better now?" Back to the gruff, annoyed Connor.

She nodded, not yet sure of her ability to speak.

"Then you'll come back, join us to eat?" He had his hand on his sword, looking around, everywhere but at her.

She nodded again and they walked back to where the others waited.

"I told you to leave her be," Mairi complained when they reached the makeshift picnic.

Cate took the bread and cheese the girl handed her and walked away from the others. She sat with her back against a rock, watching the water flowing swiftly away down the stream.

It was a good thing she was going home soon. She was completely losing her mind here. Her reaction to this man was absolutely, totally preposterous. She'd known him for less than a month. She couldn't, wouldn't, feel anything for him. In another week, she'd never see him again, unless it was in a history book somewhere.

Her stomach clenched at the thought. When she returned home, he would have been dead for over seven hundred years. It would be as if none of this had ever happened, as if he weren't real.

This was insane.

She was insane.

He was the only one who was acting sensibly. She couldn't possibly care for a man who wouldn't even exist in a few days. She had to collect her wits and be sensible as well.

She had accepted the logic but was still trying to control her emotions when Connor and Lyall sat down a few feet from her, deeply involved in discussion.

"How many times are you going to make me speak of this? I hae no interest in replacing yer father. He's laird of the MacKiernan."

"But, Connor, he's gaming away everything. It's become a sickness with him. One of many. It's why he plans to give wee Mairi to the MacPherson. He owes the man that much more than he can pay. He fears the MacPherson will ride against him." Lyall spoke quietly, urgently. "The people would follow you gladly if you'd only bring yer men here to throw him out. You can see for yerself how they greet you today. They remember how it was when yer father was laird."

"No, Lyall. I've told you before, I'll no do it. After my marriage, I'm content to settle at Sithean Fardach and make my life there. I'll keep Mairi safe with me and yer father will just have to find another way to pay off his debt to the MacPherson. It's no my concern. Dinna hound me with this again. Artair is the laird."

"But you've no sworn fealty to him, Connor. Everyone knows that."

"My loyalty is to my king and no one else. I'll swear to no other man. It disna change a thing. I'll no challenge Artair and bring death and destruction to our land. I've seen what happens to the people when there's a struggle for power. I'll no be a part of it." Connor stood and threw the remains of his lunch into the water. "We've stopped long enough. We hae to get on the road or we'll no make it back before dark sets in."

They mounted and started off again, but this time Cate had other things on her mind to distract her from feeling sorry for herself.

It was starting to make some kind of sense now. If Lyall, who was obviously close to Connor, still thought there might be a chance that he would attempt to reclaim his rightful place as laird, it would only follow that his uncle and Blane, who never talked to him at all, would think the same thing.

Of course, it still didn't explain what someone would hope to gain by spooking her horse. Or Blane's actions toward her for that matter.

Where was Nancy Drew when you really needed her?

They had ridden for perhaps another thirty minutes when Cate spotted a small boy approaching, running hard. She clutched at Connor's sleeve, but he had already seen the child. He urged their horse to a gallop to meet him.

"What is it, lad? What's happened?" The boy's eyes were large and he was gasping for air. He looked no more than six or seven years old.

"It's my mum, sir. It's her time and she sent me to fetch help."

Duncan had reached them now. He leaned down and lifted the struggling boy up behind him. "Where do you live, lad? Show us the way."

"No. You canna take me back. My mum says I'm to find someone to take me to the MacKiernan. She says she needs Lady Rosalyn."

Rosalyn pulled her horse forward, next to where Duncan was trying to restrain the struggling boy.

"Be still, child. I'm Rosalyn. Who's yer mother that she'd send for me?"

"Grizel Maxwell, milady. My mum says Lady Rosalyn has given her promise to come when she called."

His eyes were enormous brown saucers. Cate could feel the fear in him from where she sat.

"Och," Rosalyn groaned. "No wonder." She turned to the others. "Grizel's the midwife in this area. She's no one to ask for help, and she's lost her last two babes. After the last time, I chastised her for no sending for me. Mairi." Reaching for the boy and placing him on her own horse, she called for her niece. "We're closer to the old castle than to Dun Ard. Yer likely the only one who can find my potions and herbs there. They're in my tower, in the little solar. Ride to the castle, lass, and bring them back to me quick as you can. If you cut cross-country, it'll be much faster. Grizel lives just around the next bend in the road. Go quickly now and hurry back to me."

Mairi took off without a backward glance, looking for all the world like a wild creature taken flight. Connor yelled her name, but she didn't turn her head.

"Dinna fash yerself, Cousin. I'll go with her to make sure she's safe." Lyall wheeled his horse from the road and galloped away after her.

Rosalyn turned back to the boy. "And what is yer name, lad?" She was stroking his head and he seemed to be calming.

"I'm Donald." He looked at Connor. "Are you the MacKiernan?"

"No." Connor nearly yelled it, but as the boy cringed,

he gentled his voice. "No. That would be my uncle. I'm Connor MacKiernan."

"The mighty knight MacKiernan?" The boy was wonder-struck, his mouth hanging open in awe. "My da tells stories about yer battles, he does. They're my favorite tales. When I grow up, I want to be a knight just like you and fight for our king."

Cate smiled at the look on Connor's face. He was actually blushing. This was something she'd never expected to see in him.

"Weel, Donald, you hae done yer parents proud this day, fetching help for yer mother." Rosalyn spoke soothingly to the boy as they neared his home. "Is she all alone?"

"No, milady, my da's with her, but she says he's worthless to her at this point in the process."

Rosalyn ducked her head, but not before Cate saw the broad grin on her face.

"Just wait until my da sees who I'm bringing home." His face glowing with hero worship, the boy was still staring at Connor, who shifted uncomfortably in his saddle.

Modesty? Cate was surprised at finding yet another facet to the man.

When they arrived at the small house, Rosalyn held up her hand to prevent them from dismounting.

"You'll none of you do me any good here, and likely only cause the lady more discomfort at having such guests when she canna greet you properly. After Donald's brought his father out, go and finish yer rounds. I'll return when I can."

Rosalyn entered the small cottage, holding the little boy's hand.

The others stayed where they were until Donald returned with his father. Ian Maxwell's eyes shone almost as brightly as his son's when he was introduced to the mighty knight MacKiernan.

Connor ordered Fergus to remain at the Maxwell home to watch over Rosalyn. Cate was once again surprised by his actions when she realized he must have noticed how little the Maxwell family had—he also left all their remaining provisions.

CHAPTER 16

Only a complete idiot would miss a perfect opportunity like this. Although Cate had spent the better part of the day feeling like a fool, she refused to be an idiot as well.

They had visited several more families after leaving the Maxwell home. There were just the three of them now. Duncan and Connor held their horses to a walk, riding side by side, the clip-clop of hooves the only sound disturbing the silence.

They'd just left another small home, and Duncan said it would be quite a ride before they reached another. The sun was low on the horizon.

It was obvious to Cate that Connor wasn't going to start a conversation with her, so if she were ever going to work on her mystery, there was no time like the present.

"Connor?" She smiled when he jumped, but didn't turn to look at him. "There's something important I've been wanting to discuss with you for some time now."

"Aye. So I've been told. Repeatedly. I wondered how long it might take you." His whole body was rigid against her back.

"Do you even have any idea what I wanted to talk to you about?"

Arrogant, bossy, aggravating man.

"It disna matter." He paused to take a deep breath. "Being kept in yer room, I'd imagine."

"You know, Connor, your people skills leave a lot to be desired."

The room thing was a whole different conversation from what she had in mind right now, and she wouldn't let that distract her.

"No, what I've been wanting to talk to you about all this time is what happened when I went riding with Mairi and Blane." Against her back, Connor stiffened at the mention of his cousin's name. She kept going anyway. "I don't think it was an accident at all. I think someone intentionally frightened my horse. As a matter of fact, I even have proof."

The men exchanged a look. They pulled their horses off the path and Connor dismounted. Duncan circled the area watchfully before joining them and dismounting himself. The two men stood together looking up at her. Waiting.

She crossed her arms and looked down at them from her seat high on the back of the horse. So, they thought to continue to treat her like a child? Thought to play stubborn Scotsmen with her, did they? Well, she had Scots' blood, too. Eight or nine generations back, maybe, but nevertheless, she could be just as stubborn as they could. She arched an eyebrow in perfect imitation of the man who watched her.

"Och, Connor, take her down off that animal before

we all get gray and wrinkled. She's no going to tell us anything from her perch up there."

Bless Duncan for giving in first.

The minute her feet touched the ground, Cate turned her back on Connor.

"Just lower the neck of my dress. I want to show you something."

She heard a strangled sound and turned to find his face quite red. Duncan chuckled silently.

"It's no proper." He finally managed to grind out through his teeth.

"Oh, for crying out loud." She turned her back to him again. "Okay, then, just run your hand down my back, right under my shoulder blade." She waited.

Nothing.

She turned to glare at him. "Just. Do. It." She turned her back again.

Nothing.

"Fine. Duncan, you do it."

"No. I'll do it."

She'd swear it sounded as if Connor actually growled.

Duncan's shoulders shook, his face turned away in an attempt to hide his laughter.

Connor's fingers slid tentatively down her back.

"Farther to the right. There. Ow! Right there. Do you feel that?"

His fingers were directly over the still swollen spot. She had refused to allow Rosalyn to put any more of her wonderful salves on the wound. It was, after all, her evidence.

"It's a welt. I'd imagine you have them all over yer

body after the fall you took." He sounded odd, distracted.

"See this?" She turned, tugging at her shift to expose her injured shoulder.

He raised his hand toward the spot and then dropped it to his side.

"This is where I landed first. Right on this shoulder. And then here." She pointed to the almost healed spot on her forehead.

"And then here." She pointed to the cheek that was now injury free. "What do you notice about all those spots? Where they are? What they have in common?"

He simply stared at her for a moment.

"They're all on the same side, where you fell." He said it quietly, thoughtfully.

"Bingo. But not that bump on my back. It's on the other side. The side I *didn't* land on. And more important, there are two matching bumps on my horse's rear end."

"What?"

Now both men looked interested.

"Just before my horse bolted, I heard a noise, like something hitting the tree beside me. I turned to look for what it might be and—wham—something smacked into my back. Right where the welt is. Directly after that, I heard another sound, and the horse screamed and reared up. I'm pretty sure he reared again a bit later, but since I was doing a head dive right after that, I kind of lost track." She shrugged. "That next evening, Rosalyn made a remark about this bump on my back looking like Mairi and I had been throwing stones at each other, and that's when it finally dawned on me. That's the sound I'd heard.

A stone hitting the tree, a stone hitting me, and at least one hitting my horse. When I went to the stables that night, I found the same exact marks on the horse I'd been riding." She paused. "Right before I found Blane."

Take that, Nancy Drew.

"So that's what you were doing in the stables?" Connor's eyes narrowed in warning. "You went there to look for marks on the horse? You went alone, even when you thought someone might be trying to hurt you?" His eyes glinted dangerously.

"Yes." She held up her hand to stop him. "And before you say another word, just let me say that I realize now that it was really stupid of me to go traipsing off in the dark by myself. I should have found you and told you then. But I didn't because at the time I thought it would be better not to say anything until I had proof. I'm sorry. I was wrong to do that. You have every right to be angry with me." She held the apologetic look as long as she could, then grinned.

"But I was right, and I found the marks on the horse to prove it. Somebody intentionally spooked my horse."

She looked expectantly from one to the other of the men. They exchanged that look again, but neither of them said anything. And they didn't seem particularly surprised.

"There's something else, isn't there?"

There must be. Her brothers always got like this when they were keeping something from her. What else could possibly have . . . ?

"Beast." Her eyes glowed triumphantly. "That's it, isn't it? Mairi said he had an arrow in him when you found him. Somebody shot him with an arrow. Was he there? When I got tossed off that horse, was Beast there?"

"Aye. He went off after . . ." Duncan started.

"Duncan." Connor stopped him with a hand to his shoulder. "I dinna think—"

"Don't you even try to leave me out of this now." Cate's eyes flashed as she moved closer to Connor, one hand on her hip, one finger poking his chest. "Don't you think I'd be a lot better off knowing exactly what I'm up against rather than waltzing around here thinking everything is just fine?"

Connor captured her hand, trapping it against his chest. "You hae a bad habit of doing that, lass. I dinna appreciate being treated like bread dough to be poked down."

Duncan, shaking his head, moved away from them, trailing his horse behind him, but Cate paid him little heed.

"Well, I don't appreciate being treated like a mushroom."

He stared at her blankly.

"You know, kept in the dark and fed . . . never mind. It's an old saying." She glared up at him. "At least where I come from it's an old saying."

Connor still had her hand pinned to his chest. He stared at the ground as if considering her request for more information.

Cate stared at their hands, hers clasped tightly in his. His heart beat rapidly under her fingertips. His face was hard, his eyes closed now, his lips pressed together tightly, his jaw clenched as if the thoughts he grappled with pained him.

She'd wanted to help by telling him what she knew, but it seemed from his reaction that she'd only given him more to worry about. She had become the burden she had sought to avoid.

"I'm so sorry. I only thought to help." She lifted her free hand, tracing with her finger the line of his jaw down to his lips, wishing she could do something to ease his worry.

At her movement, his eyes opened wide in shock and then narrowed. He groaned before crushing her to him, lowering his mouth to hers. She sank into him, eagerly opening her mouth to allow him access just as they heard the first *whoosh-thud,* followed quickly by a second.

In the instant between the two sounds, Cate found herself flat on her back with Connor on top of her, one large hand under her head cushioning the fall.

"Did you see where it came from?" he hissed at Duncan, who was also on the ground, several feet away across the clearing.

"No. But I hae a good idea of direction. I'll check," he whispered as he inched away.

"What . . . ?"

Connor's free hand came down over her mouth, pushing her head back down. Unable to do anything else, she looked up. Two arrows stuck out of the tree trunk above where they lay. Her stomach clenched as she realized the arrows had hit right where she'd been standing.

Apparently giving in to your baser instincts occasionally could save your life. Not to mention get you kissed.

In spite of her fear, she smiled against the callused roughness of his palm, still clamped over her mouth to keep her quiet.

He made a shushing noise, almost absently, without ever taking his eyes from the forest around them. They waited, not moving, as long minutes passed by.

She looked up at him, watching him scan the area for danger. She inhaled the scent of him, so close. All her earlier efforts at finding sensibility completely abandoned her.

Cate closed her eyes and, bit by bit, physical awareness of him flooded her senses. Part of his weight was supported on his elbows because, although he lay fully on her, she could still breathe. His chest brushed lightly against her breasts, which suddenly felt much too large for the dress she wore. From the waist down, she and Connor were firmly tangled together, one of her legs caught between his thighs. She attempted to shift her leg slightly, hoping to make their position less uncomfortable for him, and his muscles tightened around her thigh.

Her mouth went dry. She unconsciously tried to lick her lips only to find the tip of her tongue brushing against the hand he still held there.

He groaned and she opened her eyes to find him staring directly down at her, his face only inches from hers, his hair draping down to caress the sides of her face.

Breathing wasn't so easy anymore. She wanted him to kiss her again more than she wanted anything in the world.

"I canna find any sign of him."

Connor flinched and she very nearly screamed when Duncan hunkered down next to them.

"It's drawing dark. What do you want to do?" Duncan spoke in hushed tones, as if someone might be out there even now. Listening.

Connor moved to a crouch beside her and her body trembled at the cool night air replacing the warmth of his weight. Cate rolled to her side, pulling her legs up. She closed her eyes and concentrated on each breath.

In. Out. In. Out.

"Stay here. Dinna move." He leaned over her, his harsh whisper stirring against her ear.

Didn't he know she wasn't capable of movement right now? She opened her eyes and watched the two men advance stealthily toward the horses. He moved like the panther she'd admired as a child when she'd visited the zoo.

"Come on, Caty. We hae to go." Connor helped her up and lifted her onto the horse.

This time she snuggled fully back against him, craving his touch.

He stiffened only for an instant and then pulled her close. Enveloping her in his arms, he whispered in her ear. "Dinna be frightened, lass. I mean to see you safe."

"Do we take this road back to Dun Ard? Whoever it was could still be waiting." Duncan scanned the area as if he could see through the gathering dark. "I'd give a full cask of ale to have Beast here tonight," he mumbled.

"Aye, weel, as Lyall said, Beast was in no fit shape to be traveling this far with us today. But it would hae been a boon to hae him." Like Duncan, he looked about, peering into the darkness. "We'll no take the road. As you say, anyone could be waiting. If we go through the forest it's no too far to Sithean Fardach."

"You've decided then." Duncan nodded slowly. "Travel will be slow through the forest in the dark. On the other hand, everyone is aware that we'd no planned to go there today." Duncan seemed to be considering the idea.

"Aye. So no one would expect it."

Duncan laughed, slapping his leg. "Yer in luck, Caty, lass. Sithean Fardach's steward has hoarded away casks of the finest heather ale to be found anywhere in Scotland." He sighed. "Aye, it's truly a pleasure to be going home again."

CHAPTER 17

❧

They met with no further incident on their journey to Connor's home, but the men remained tense and vigilant as Cate now recognized they had been all day. She rested her head against Connor's chest the entire way, his strong heartbeat a comfort as he held her tightly to him.

The land began to rise steeply. Sithean Fardach sat at the very top of a large hill. It looked like something created for a movie set, and Cate wondered briefly if it still existed in her time. Smaller in overall size than Dun Ard, it was a great square building with round towers at each corner. The entire structure was surrounded by a massive wall.

Cate realized just how massive the wall actually was as they started through the arch. They entered a tunnel at least ten feet long, which accounted for the thickness of the wall.

"The portcullis is open on both ends." Duncan spoke uneasily.

"Aye. They'd no reason to hae it closed. See to it, Duncan. I want the gates and drawbars in place. No one in or out. I'll speak to Niall."

"Consider it done. I'll see you inside." Duncan grinned and hopped off his horse, heading back to the entrance archway.

They continued across the courtyard, stopping at the foot of some very impressive wooden stairs, which led to large entryway doors that appeared to go into the second story of the castle. When they reached the foot of the stairs, Connor dismounted and lifted Cate to the ground as a man hurried down the stairs toward them.

"Welcome home, lad." The man threw his arms around Connor, slapping him on the back. He tilted his head toward Cate. "Is this yer lassie then? Margaret will be in a mighty fury. She'd no expected you until after the wedding." He chuckled.

"Aye, Niall, this is my Cate." He turned to her, his hand still on the older man's shoulder. "Cate, this is my steward, Niall. He keeps the castle running for me."

Niall laughed. "Dinna say that in front of my Margaret. She's the one who does all the work." He turned back to Connor. "Mairi dinna tell us you'd be coming when she was here earlier for Rosalyn's healing basket."

"She dinna ken we'd be this way tonight. I've left Duncan at the wall to close the gates. I want them to stay closed until we've had a chance to discuss a few things."

The older man sobered immediately. "I'll send help down to him." He turned and yelled, "Ewan!"

A young man appeared from another building in the courtyard, running in their direction.

"Father?" He noticed them then, his face breaking into a grin. "Connor. You've returned."

"Down to the gates with you, lad. Give Duncan a

hand while I get these two inside to yer mother." Niall smiled fondly at the young man as he ran off in the direction of the gates.

Margaret was waiting just inside the door. After greeting Connor, she immediately began to fuss.

"Och, laddie, they told me you weren't to come home until after the wedding. I've done nothing to prepare yer chamber yet." She started away and then stopped, turning to glare at them. "And you'll no hae given this poor lass anything to eat either, hae you? Just look at her. Janet," she called before turning back to Cate. "Out late in the dark and cold, no food. Men. No a sensible thought among them." She continued to grumble, taking charge of Cate and sitting her down at a small table near a roaring fire.

Soon Cate had a warm blanket wrapped around her shoulders and a small plate of bread, cheese and cold meat sitting on the table next to her. Margaret left her to her meal, muttering about preparing a proper chamber for the "wee lassie."

The men disappeared as soon as Margaret had taken charge, but now they returned, Duncan with them. Margaret bustled in with additional plates for them such as the one she'd brought to Cate.

Cate listened absently as they chatted about the people they had met that day, with Margaret and Niall asking specific questions about friends they hadn't seen for a while. When Margaret asked about the wedding and their unexpected arrival tonight, Niall sent her out for more ale, and turned the discussion to the animals and some problem they'd had with their pens. Cate could almost think the men were avoiding the discussion.

After a time, Cate noticed Janet, who she had learned was Margaret and Niall's daughter, nodding off on her stool by the fire. She tugged at Connor's sleeve to bring it to his attention.

"It's late and we've been thoughtless to keep you from yer beds so long. You go on to sleep. I'll show Cate to her bedchamber." When the older woman started to protest, he stopped her. "Dinna fret, I can find my way about my own home, Margaret. Go on, now, see to yer own family."

She smiled and patted his arm. "You are my own family, lad." Then she yawned and followed her husband as he carried their daughter away.

Connor seemed to genuinely like these people. It was the most relaxed Cate had ever seen him.

"They seem very nice."

"Aye. They're hard workers, too." He took her arm to assist her as they started up a small spiral staircase at the back of the hall. "Unlike Dun Ard, we don't have many servants. It's just Niall and Margaret and their children. It works fine for us. Duncan and I help when we're here." He sounded defensive.

"Everything seems lovely. It doesn't look as though you need anyone else here."

The first door they passed was slightly ajar. Cate peeked in as they passed. A small fire burned with chairs gathered in front of it. She also saw a desk in the room before they continued up the stairs.

They stopped at the very top of the stairs, where an enormous wooden door opened into a large curved room. Cate realized she was in one of the round towers she'd seen from the outside. The walls were hung with tapestries, and centered on one side of the room was a massive four-poster canopied bed, complete with curtains that were tied back at each poster. The floors were covered in a multitude of rugs of various kinds so that no stone showed through at all.

"Wow. This is gorgeous."

Connor looked up from where he was lighting the fire. "Do you like it then?"

"Very much. I haven't seen anything like this since I've been here. Or before, for that matter."

Her room at Dun Ard had been nice, but much smaller, and nothing like this. Certainly at home there was nothing like this.

"It was my grandparents' room at one time. The things here are verra old. I dinna want to change any of them." Connor rose and started toward the door. "If you need me for anything, I'll be in the room directly below."

"Wait." She didn't want him to go yet. "Do you have . . . is there anything here I can sleep in?"

He looked pointedly toward the bed.

"To wear, I mean. Like nightclothes."

Connor glanced around the room, a rather helpless expression on his face. "I'll go wake Margaret. I should hae thought."

"No. Wait. Don't bother them for just this. We can find something, I'm sure. What about . . . a shirt?" At his look of confusion, she continued. "Do you have an extra shirt? That would work just fine."

"Aye." He walked to a trunk at the foot of the bed and, having opened it, removed a shirt and handed it to

Cate. "It'll no be long enough, though." A small grin played about his mouth.

"Trust me, it'll be longer than some of the stuff I wear back home.

He looked surprised at that, then shrugged and walked back to the door. Opening it, he stopped. "Cate?"

"Yes?"

"I wanted to tell you . . . I only kept you in yer room so you'd be safe. It was the only thing I could think of to do. I'm sorry if it angered you." He spoke with his back to her, never turning to face her.

"It's okay. I understand why you did it. I'm not angry now. But I would like to know: Are you planning to keep me confined to that room for the rest of the time I'm here? Once we get back there, I mean?"

"No. You'll no be confined to that room again. Good night, Cate." He turned only slightly as he walked out and closed the door. She could have sworn he was smiling.

Connor was still smiling as he entered the solar below. This had been his favorite room growing up. It was in this room his father had sat at his desk and gone over accounts. It was in this room that he and his brothers had learned to read Greek and Latin. It was in this room that his mother had sat by the fire to work on her mending in the evenings while his older brother had played music.

He walked over to that fireplace now and, squatting down, lit his candle from the fire. He looked around. It was a wonderful room, cozy and full of pleasant memories. There just wasn't anyplace to sleep.

Of course he could have gone to a bedchamber in one of the other towers, but he couldn't bear the idea of being that far away from Cate. The gates were down and the drawbars set. No one was getting in here without his knowledge. Still, it was his duty to protect the woman, and in order to do that he must remain near her.

He pulled a chair close to the fire and arranged another across from that, for his feet. He placed a stool in between the two chairs. That should do. Much better than some of the places he'd slept in the last several years.

Sitting down, he pulled off his boots and shirt and, best as possible, attempted to get comfortable in the makeshift bed. He leaned over and blew out the candle sitting on the table next to him.

Staring at the fire, he smiled again, thinking of Cate. If he didn't know better, he might think she hadn't wanted him to leave her. Perhaps she was just uncomfortable in new surroundings.

He wasn't sure why he had apologized for doing what needed to be done, but it had seemed to make her happy. Especially when she learned that she wouldn't be kept in that room any longer. Her response might change when she found out he didn't intend to let her go back to Dun Ard at all.

After finding Beast, he'd suspected that someone was trying to harm her, and now he had proof. Someone thought to prevent his marriage. That someone was, more than likely, his uncle. Regardless of the reason, there was no way he was going to allow anyone another opportunity at her. Today on the road had convinced him of that.

Tomorrow he'd send Duncan to fetch Mairi. Cate should have someone to keep her company here prior to the wedding. It might not suffice for propriety's sake having only another maiden to stay with her, but no one would question his choice of Mairi. It was apparent to everyone the women had become great friends.

He'd also get word to Rosalyn to come directly here when she finished at the Maxwells'. Again, it would be the only sensible thing to do. They would need an adult female to properly chaperone the girls.

That done, he would have all the women he cared for and needed to protect under his roof and, more important, behind his gates. And it would be accomplished without any fuss or show, just a simple "temporary" arrangement that would become permanent. He'd deal with whoever watched later. He should have done this long ago. He was sure Rosalyn would approve. Mairi would think of it as a great adventure.

And Cate? How would Cate react to the impropriety of living in his home before they married?

Closing his eyes, he tried to imagine which of her many expressions he'd be treated to when he told her she wasn't leaving Sithean Fardach until the wedding. But the only one that came to mind was the way she had looked lying under him on the ground today, her eyes the soft inviting green of the forest that surrounded them.

That memory made him think of her upstairs right now wearing only his shirt. Now there was a vision to make a man smile.

His body stirred to life, wanting her in a way that surprised him. He shifted to find a more comfortable position.

It was going to be a long, restless night.

Cate tossed her dress and shift over the chair by the fire. She slipped into the shirt, breathing deeply as she passed it over her head. It smelled of Connor. She smiled.

The ends of the sleeves went far beyond the tips of her fingers.

He had long, strong arms.

The lacing up the front of the shirt opened to below her breasts, but she tied it shut.

He also had a large, well-muscled chest.

Looking down, she saw that the tail of the shirt hit just above her knees. And Connor had thought it would be too short. Well, it was too short considering the yards and yards of material the women wore here.

She found a pitcher of water sitting on a long table positioned against a far wall. There was a bowl there and some soap. She picked up the soap and sniffed. Unlike the lavender soap she'd been given at Dun Ard, this smelled of lemon and mint. Interesting. If she remembered her history, they wouldn't have ready access to lemons in this part of the world for a couple hundred years, so it had to be something else. An herb of some sort? She'd have to remember to ask Margaret tomorrow. For now she headed to bed.

It was one of the largest beds she'd ever seen. The curtains hanging around it felt like heavy velvet. Once those curtains were untied and pulled closed around the bed, this would certainly be a cozy place to spend the long winter nights. Pulling back the covers, she climbed in and snuggled down. She breathed deeply, sniffing the covers next to her nose. Lemon and mint and leather. They smelled of Connor, too.

She closed her eyes and shivered thinking of him. What was she going to do about him? No other man had ever made her feel this way.

This whole thing was supposed to be a strictly business kind of deal, nothing more than a quick little adventure. She was only here to help him out and then zip back home. He'd been very clear about everything up front, giving no false impressions as to what he expected from her. Get married, save the sister, go home.

So, how come somewhere along the way it had started to get so personal? Obviously she couldn't be serious about someone like him. He was overbearing and arrogant, both personality traits she'd firmly marked off her list after Richard. On top of that, Connor gave her orders like he had a right to, like there was no tomorrow. And in a way there wasn't. This time next week he wouldn't even exist anymore.

But oh, Lordy, the man could curl her toes with his kiss. She smiled and snuggled against the pillow. It also smelled of Connor.

Her eyes flew open and she sat up. The pillow smelled of Connor. The covers and the soap smelled of Connor. He'd reached into the trunk in this very room and pulled out one of his shirts.

She crawled out of bed and struggled to lift the lid on the trunk. She picked up another shirt off the top and sniffed it. Connor. She put it back and closed the lid,

looking around. This may well have been his grandparents' bedroom at one time, but now it was his bedroom.

"And that," she said softly to herself, looking at the
massive piece of furniture she'd just crawled out of, "that
is his bed."

He said he'd be in the room directly below. But they
had passed that room on the way up and it had looked
like some kind of sitting room.

So her knight in shining armor, the man who'd saved
her butt more times than she'd care to admit since she'd
been here, had given up this wonderful bed and was even
now trying to curl that luscious big body into a cold chair
downstairs.

"Well, damn." She'd always had an overdeveloped
sense of guilt.

After she pulled a blanket off the bed and grabbed one
of the pillows, she started for the door. It seemed to be
the least she could do.

Connor woke to the sound of cloth rustling.

The room was dark save for the flicker coming from
the fireplace. He'd been too good a warrior for too long
a time to give himself away, however. He noiselessly
moved his hand to the dirk by his side and waited.

He inhaled deeply. It was Cate. He hadn't spent the
entire day smelling that intoxicating scent not to recognize it now. What was she up to this time?

Opening his eyes to the smallest of slits, he watched
her pad silently toward him, her arms filled with something. Silently until she apparently connected with one of
the chairs closer to the door.

"Damn," she hissed, hopping just a bit. She tossed something on the ground and then moved closer to him.

He worked to keep a grin off his face, closing his eyes tightly as she approached nearer.

"Connor?" It was barely a whisper.

He thought for just an instant about answering her, but decided instead to find out what she planned to do. He responded with a mild snore.

"Oh, good." Followed by, "Oh, my." She breathed the words, very close to him now.

He felt a light flutter against the bare skin of his legs and chest and realized with a jolt that she had placed a cover over him. Her hair lightly brushed against his face as she tucked the cover around his shoulders.

She was moving away, so he chanced another quick peek. She was leaning over to pick up whatever she had tossed to the floor.

The sight of her bare legs, exposed to her thigh as she leaned over, hardened his body to the point of physical pain. Thank God she'd covered him with the blanket, or surely she would have noticed.

She turned toward him and he closed his eyes tightly again. She was very close now, one knee propped on the chair, trying to tuck a pillow behind his head without waking him.

He couldn't resist a small touch. He groaned and turned, allowing his arm to move across her bare leg, his hand open against her thigh, effectively trapping her there. The skin was even softer than it had looked and it took everything he had not to pull her under him.

"Holy shit." She barely breathed the sound, freezing in place for a long second. Then she reached down and slowly lifted his hand, laying it across his chest before she moved away.

He snored lightly again and felt her move close once more. Her hair brushed against his bare shoulder this time and, surprisingly, her lips touched his forehead.

"Pleasant dreams, my sweet knight," she whispered. Then she moved away.

Again he opened his eyes the barest minimum to watch her tiptoe out.

Oh, he'd have pleasant dreams this night, no doubt.

CHAPTER 18

The sun shone in the open window and the fire was freshly rebuilt when Cate opened her eyes and stretched in the huge bed, inhaling deeply. She loved that smell. She'd had a wonderful sleep and the best dreams. She stretched again and sat up. Slipping out of bed, she washed and dressed quickly, and headed down the stairs.

She stopped briefly outside the room below hers, but the door was closed. Standing quietly, she held her breath, but she heard no sounds from the other side. Disappointed, she continued on down the stairs. The hall where they'd eaten last night was deserted, too.

She looked around, trying to decide what to do, when she heard someone enter. Janet watched her from the other side of the hall.

"Can I get something for you, Lady Cate?" The girl curtsied.

No, that didn't feel right at all.

"Good morning, Janet. It's just Cate. Where is everyone?"

The girl's eyes were round with surprise. "The men are out working, milady. My mum and I were in the kitchen."

Cate approached the girl and took her hand. "Will you show me where the kitchen is?"

They walked through a door she hadn't noticed before at the back of the hall and into a kitchen area. The smell of baking bread came from a room beyond that. Margaret was standing by a large kettle hung over an open fireplace that took up almost the entire side of one wall.

The older woman glanced up as they walked in and looked flustered. "Janet. Why ever would you bring our lady back here?"

Cate laughed. "Please, Margaret. It's not Janet's fault. I asked her to bring me to the kitchen." She closed her eyes and sniffed loudly. "Ummmmmm. It smells wonderful. I hope it's not a bother to have me in here."

Margaret smiled then, her expression relaxing. "Thank you, Lady Cate. It's no a bother. This whole castle will be yers to direct in a few short days, so yer welcome to go wherever you please. Would you like me to prepare yer morning plate?"

"I'd really be pleased if you'd both just call me Cate. The whole 'Lady' thing makes me uncomfortable." She smiled hopefully at them.

To her surprise, Margaret laughed. "Weel, Connor warned me you'd not be what I'd expect, being a foreigner and all. And I'm pleased to say he was right. I'd say he's done a fair job for himself, would you no agree, Janet?"

The young girl giggled, and picked up a spoon to help her mother with the cooking. Margaret moved to a table, where she began cutting up peaches and tossing them into a pot.

"Are those fresh peaches?" What a stupid question. She could smell them from across the room. "May I have one?"

Cate hadn't seen fresh fruit since she'd been here. Everything had been stewed to a pulp. She sat on a stool in the corner, eating the peach, more contented than she'd been for days, knowing this feeling wouldn't last for long. Soon they'd have to leave to get back to Dun Ard.

"Do you know where Connor is?"

"He went out early with the other men. He said they'd be back by noon meal."

"Really? Well, I guess I have some time on my hands then. Is there anything I can do to help you?"

Janet dropped her spoon, and both of them turned to look at Cate with their mouths slightly ajar. Margaret recovered first.

"Not a thing, my dear. Why don't you explore a bit? Get to know yer new home. The gardens are out just through that door, if yer interested."

"Oh. Gardens. As in vegetables?"

Margaret nodded. "Aye. And Lady Rosalyn's herbs as well."

"Cool. I mean, that would be just lovely. Thank you."

Cate jumped off her stool and hurried through the door. This was great. She'd explore on her own and discover what they grew that made Connor smell the way he did.

* * *

Lemon balm.

It grew in one corner of the herb garden. That explained the scent in the soap. And on Connor. Mint was growing there as well, along with rosemary, chamomile and parsley, just to name a few.

She stopped to pick a few leaves, crushing them in her palm to release their aroma. If she were only staying here instead of at Dun Ard, she might not get her morning caffeine, but she would certainly be able to have a lovely cup of herb tea, and that would be almost as good.

The garden area had been carved out of the hillside and surrounded by a rock wall. A little stream bubbled in at the very back and flowed along the edge of the wall and out again. Near the water, someone had placed a small rock bench under the shade of a tree, and it was here that Cate spent the next hour. The morning sun, coupled with the smells of the growing herbs, relaxed her completely.

She leaned back against the trunk of the tree and sniffed the lemon balm and mint she held crushed in her hand. The aroma brought sharp memories of Connor. Of how he'd looked with the firelight glinting off his bare chest last night. It had taken all her willpower to cover those magnificent muscles with a blanket rather than her hands. The man had a body that inspired her to daydreams as well as night dreams.

Eventually her curiosity got the better of her and she went back into the kitchen. Margaret sent her off to explore again, and after looking through the main hall and the rooms on that level, she headed out the main entrance to the great wooden staircase that would lead her down to the courtyard.

From the landing at the top of the stairs, she spotted him immediately.

"Yer lady's looking for you, Connor." Ewan grinned and gestured his head up toward the main entrance of the castle.

Connor straightened and wiped perspiration from his face with the back of his hand. They'd been repairing the fencing for the horses since early in the morning. He had hoped the hard work would help him get his mind off Cate.

It hadn't.

At least out here, he'd thought, he could avoid the coming confrontation about his decision to stay at Sithean Fardach. He had already made up his mind, and why he would even give thought to her reaction to his decision was beyond him at this point. Her safety was the only consideration. She'd been angry with him for the last week. Another few days shouldn't matter. But for some reason it did. So he had avoided her.

And now, there she was. She stood at the top of the landing, pulling her hair back from her face where the gentle wind blew it all around. That same gentle breeze also billowed her skirts, exposing just the slightest bit of lower leg.

The memory of watching her in his room last night slammed into him, filling him once again with need.

She'd seen him now, looking in her direction. She waved a greeting and was immediately running down the stairs, headed toward him. Nothing to be done for it. He'd have to face her soon enough with the news that he was keeping her here until the wedding. If her sense of propriety was offended, so be it. He might as well get it over with.

Wiping his hands on his plaid, he walked toward her. She looked happy this morning. He supposed that would be changing soon.

"Good morning, Connor. You have a lovely home. I've just been enjoying the gardens."

"Cate." He nodded. "I'm pleased you like it." He paused and looked down at his feet. "I was planning to come look for you as soon as I cleaned up a bit."

"Are we going to be leaving soon?"

He couldn't quite meet her eyes. "Weel, that's along the lines of what I was planning to come talk to you about, you see." He took her arm and began walking her to the other side of the courtyard. Cate rarely took things quietly. No point in exposing Ewan to the disagreement that was to come. "I've had another thought about that."

She stopped, forcing him to stop or drag her along. "And just what thought might that be?"

Connor sighed deeply. "Someone's attempted to hurt you at least twice that we know of. At my uncle's home, I canna be sure of who is around or what is happening. It's too large and there are too many people. Here I can close the gates and I know exactly who is in and who is out." He looked up hopefully and waited.

"Okay. And . . . what?" Her brow was furrowed, the smile gone.

"I dinna hae any proof of who is trying to harm you, Cate. I dinna want to risk being around so many strangers when any of them could be the one, you ken?"

"No. I don't. What exactly are you trying to tell me?"

Hands on her hips now. Bad sign. She'd have that poking finger out soon.

"I sent Duncan out at first light to Dun Ard. He's gone to collect yer things and Mairi to keep you company." He clasped his hands behind his back, taking the pose he would strike when giving orders to his men. "Yer staying here until the wedding, and that's final. I'll hae no argument from you about it." He looked over her head. He was ready.

Or so he thought.

Her body hit him full force, her arms around his neck. He almost fell over from the shock of it, throwing his arms around her only at the last minute to gain his balance. She kissed him on the cheek, grinning wildly.

"Oh, Connor, that's the best news." She hugged him again. "Thank you so much." She jumped down, lifted her skirts and started to run back toward the stairs.

"Wait. Where are you off to?"

"Tea." She yelled at him, laughing over her shoulder. "I'm off to make some tea."

He shook his head in astonishment. The woman never ceased to surprise him.

CHAPTER 19

Tomorrow she would be Caitlyn MacKiernan. It gave her goose bumps thinking about it, and not just because her bathwater was cooling quickly. Cate MacKiernan. It sounded pretty good. Too bad it wouldn't last long.

Sighing, she reached for the razor and soap from the table next to the tub. At her request, Mairi had swiped the razor for her from Connor's things. Cate smiled. Poor Mairi. As if she hadn't been able to get into enough trouble all on her own, now Cate had introduced her to petty thievery. Technically it would only be petty borrowing. She would sneak it back to him in the morning. After all, she couldn't have the groom showing up unshaven.

She frowned at the razor in her hand. It really was nothing more than a thin knife blade. In fact, she might have been better off borrowing that knife Connor always had sticking out of his boot. It would probably have been just as safe as this thing. Janet's eyes had gone huge when she saw it lying on the table as she'd helped with the bath, and she hadn't even known what Cate was planning. No wonder Mairi had thought the whole idea crazy. Mairi may have been right this time, but she was going through with it anyway.

She wrapped up in her drying sheet and propped her leg on the side of the tub. There just didn't seem to be any easy way to do this. Her underarms were finished with only one tiny little cut, even though it had taken forever. She had soaped the lovely lemon-scented bar all over her leg and started the first swipe up when she heard the noises in the stairway outside her door. Footsteps and Beast's bark.

"Cate." Followed by pounding on her door. "Open this door immediately."

"Go away, Connor, I'm bathing." What was he thinking, pounding on her door and yelling like that?

"Open this door or I'll break it down." He sounded furious. Or frightened.

"Go away, Connor. I'm finishing my bath, for crying out loud," she yelled back.

How was she supposed to concentrate on finishing this if he kept carrying on out there? Break down the door. The stupid door wasn't even locked. She'd just started another swipe up her leg when the door burst open, spilling him into the room, Beast right on top of him. She would have laughed if she hadn't slipped with the razor at that point. Instead she hissed in pain. Razor cuts always stung.

"What do you think yer doing?" He looked as frantic as he sounded, sprinting over to grab her wrist.

"I'm shaving my legs, thank you very much. What does it look like I'm doing?" She jerked her wrist away from him.

"What? Yer doing what?" He couldn't seem to stop staring at her leg. "Yer bleeding."

He reached toward her leg and she slapped his hand.

"Damn right I am. You try working with one of these things when people are bursting into your room and see if you don't cut yourself, too."

Now he just looked angry. "What do you think yer doing to yerself?"

"I told you, I'm shaving my legs." She tried to sound patient, which she wasn't feeling. "It's a process using a sharp thing"—she waved the razor at him—"to take the hair off your legs." She pointed at her leg and then stood up, putting her hands on her hips. "Preferably accomplished in private."

"Good Christ, yer wearing nothing but a drying sheet." A dull red covered his face and neck. He started toward her, but stopped quickly and turned his back to her.

"Well of course. I told you I was bathing. What did you expect I'd be wearing?"

He paused for a moment, breathing deeply. "I dinna think about what you might be wearing. When I heard Janet talking to her mother, I only thought . . . " His voice trailed off. "Why are you doing that?"

"Shaving? Because I don't want hairy legs for my wedding." She frowned at him.

Men were so clueless.

He snorted, and shaking his head, he walked as far as the doorway.

"That's my razor, is it no?" He kept his back turned.

"It is. But I'll return it in plenty of time for you to try

this same process on your face tomorrow. Minus people bursting into your room, of course." She hoped the sarcasm wasn't lost on him.

"Aye. Weel, see that you do." He pushed Beast through the door and then calmly walked out, closing the door behind him.

"Now what do you suppose that was all about?" Cate muttered as she finished her leg. It briefly crossed her mind that there was always the option to return the razor tonight and ask.

Connor stood on the landing outside Cate's door feeling foolish.

"This is what happens when you spend too much time around women," he said sagely to Beast as they made their way back down the stairs. "Yer mind warps until you can't think straight. That's what they do to a man."

When he'd walked past the bakery and heard Janet hysterically telling her mother about the razor Cate had hidden by her bath and how she feared her new lady would do herself harm, he hadn't even taken the time to consider the implications. Hadn't taken into account the dramatic nature of a wee lassie such as Janet.

No, he had simply raced upstairs without a sane thought in his head, determined to protect his lady from herself.

Instead he'd very nearly ended up having to protect her from him.

When he'd realized she wore nothing but a cloth, her legs glistening with the moisture of her bath, his mouth had dried, and with every fiber of his being he had wanted nothing more than to sweep the damn cloth away and take her to the floor.

He'd managed to turn and walk away with his dignity intact, but just barely. Now his body coursed with an unfulfilled need and anger at his own actions.

He needed to work this off.

"Duncan!" he yelled, crossing the great hall and throwing open the door. A few hours in the lists with a worthy opponent and he'd be good as new.

Everything was ready. Cate's wedding dress, still draped over the back of a chair, was almost completely wrinkle-free. Mairi and Rosalyn were working on the floral garland she would wear in her hair. They had retired to Rosalyn's tower, telling her she couldn't see it tonight. That she should go to sleep early and get plenty of rest because tomorrow would be a long, busy day.

The only problem with that whole scenario was that she was wide awake. And really, really nervous. A girl didn't get married every day.

"See, this is why they invented bachelorette parties," she mumbled to herself, flopping back on the bed for the hundredth time. She sighed deeply.

"This is never going to work, so I might as well just give it up."

She climbed out of bed and began preparing another pot of chamomile tea to relax herself. Not that the first one had helped.

Four days ago, when she learned she was going to stay at Sithean Fardach, she had found a small kettle to keep in her room and gathered the herbs she liked best. Evening tea had become one of her favorite parts of the day since then.

Sitting on the floor in front of the fire, waiting for her water to boil, she briefly wondered if they had bachelor parties now. More specifically, she wondered if Connor was having one. It would actually be pretty simple to tell. She could just slip downstairs and listen at his door.

He'd continued to stay in the room below, but after she'd threatened to boycott his room and sleep on the stair landing with Beast, he had moved some bedding into the salon. He might be sleeping on the floor, but at least it looked pretty comfortable. She'd checked when he was out practicing his swordsmanship. It was hard enough knowing she slept in his bed without thinking of him on those uncomfortable chairs. He had obviously been miserable that first night, with all the groaning and tossing and flinging his arms about.

Cate put the herbs into the water she'd just removed from the fire, crushing them a bit and stirring in honey before she put a cover on top. The smell of chamomile and mint floated around her. She sat back down and stretched her now shaven legs toward the fire. Not a bad job for her first time with that ancient razor thing, but she'd certainly never speak ill of a plastic safety razor again.

She had continued to wear Connor's shirt to bed each night, even though Mairi had brought all her things from Dun Ard, including her nightgown. But the shirt still smelled of him and there was something comforting about that.

Comforting and yet very scary.

Being around Connor felt almost too comfortable now. In the last few days, they had seen each other constantly. He would show up behind her when she least expected it and seemed to derive great joy from catching her unawares, although he always pretended to be oblivious. His eyes twinkled when he smiled. And he had smiled a lot the last few days.

It was scary as well. Just watching him walk across the courtyard caused her heart to perform outrageous flip-flops. When he put a hand on her shoulder, instead of the flip-flops, her heart felt as if it completely stopped for an instant. She'd decide to avoid him for a day only to find herself hunting all over the castle just to catch a glimpse of him or hear his voice.

This was a completely new experience for her. He was a completely new experience for her. And in a day or two, the experience would be over.

She'd never see him again.

In the final analysis, that was the scariest part of all. Those were the thoughts that haunted her when she was alone. Could she handle never seeing Connor again? How did she really feel about him; was it just attraction or was it something more?

The only thing she was sure of was that she wouldn't find the answers to those questions sitting in this room by herself.

Tossing on her cloak, she grabbed her pot of tea and Connor's razor. On the landing, she stepped over Beast's snoring body and headed down the stairs.

Cate made her way slowly down the narrow stairway. The torches were far enough apart that the lighting was very dim here. She stood in front of Connor's door trying to make up her mind. There was no sound from inside.

She very nearly turned and went back to her room. But if she did that, she'd spend the rest of her life wondering, questioning.

Taking a deep cleansing breath, she tapped lightly on the door. When there was no answer, she tapped again, a little harder. She was just turning to leave when the door opened.

"Cate? Is something wrong?" He was standing there in only his plaid. He leaned out to look both directions into the stairway.

"No. I'm sorry. Did I wake you?" He didn't appear to have been sleeping. He looked . . . rumpled, handsome, with only the drape of his plaid covering one shoulder.

"No. I canna seem to sleep this night. But yer knock was so light, I wasnae sure I really heard it." He leaned against the frame of the door.

They stood for a moment, just looking at one another. Cate broke the silence.

"Well, I can't sleep either. So I came to return your razor." She handed it to him.

He chuckled. "Good. I'll hae need of that on the morrow." He rubbed his hand across his cheek and chin.

She'd never seen a five o'clock shadow look so sexy.

"And what's that in yer pot? More shaving items?" He grinned at her.

She grinned in return. "No. It's my special herb tea. I was hoping you'd invite me in so we could share it. Do you know what a bachelor party is?"

"I canna say I've heard of such a party." He looked at

her speculatively, not moving out of the doorway. "You'd no want to be ruining yer reputation, now would you, Caty, by coming into my room in the middle of the night?" The grin he wore was sexy and inviting in spite of his words.

"Well, I figured that since I'll be an old married woman in a few hours, maybe my reputation could take it. What do you think?"

He searched her eyes and then stepped back, sweeping his arm out in invitation.

"Do you have a cup? My hands were full so I couldn't carry mine down." Cate walked in and headed toward the fireplace. His bedding was laid out there and she seated herself on it.

"Only this." He picked up a tankard from the table as he passed and drained the contents. He walked to where she sat and handed her the mug.

"Come on." She patted the area next to her. "Sit down with me and try my tea. We'll visit a bit, and have our own bachelor party, which is really nothing more than a way for the bride and groom to pass the evening before their wedding."

He stood for a moment longer as if debating his next action. Eventually he sat beside her as she poured the tea into his tankard.

"I hope whatever you had in here doesn't leave a bad taste."

He grinned again. "Seasoning. Like as not it'll make those bits of weed you use taste better." He took the tankard and tried a small taste. "This is no so bad." There was surprise in his voice.

"That's right. Even you'll have to admit it's pretty good. And it's supposed to help you relax." She took the tankard from him and took a sip. She could taste the "seasoning" the whisky had left behind. Fortunately it was faint.

"Has it helped you to relax this night?"

"No more than that seasoning you had in this mug appears to have helped you." She smiled at him. "But at least you look more relaxed than you did in my room this afternoon. What was that all about?" She took a sip of tea and handed the cup to him.

He shrugged carelessly and looked into the fire. "Nothing of any importance. I am sorry if I frightened you when I rushed into yer room. I hope the cut's no serious. How is it now?" He lifted the vessel to his lips for a drink.

"It's fine. See for yourself." Pulling back the cloak, Cate extended her leg.

When he choked, she knew it had nothing to do with the tea. She pounded on his back.

"You've nothing on yer legs, lass." He gasped between coughs. "What the hell are you wearing under that cloak?"

"Your shirt. And I have as much on my legs as you have on yours. In fact, I'm wearing a bit more than you are. I'm not the one sitting around naked from the waist up." She arched an eyebrow at him.

"Thank God," he breathed, looking nervous. "And I'm no naked. I hae my plaid over my shoulder." Now he sounded offended. "Would you prefer I put my shirt on then?"

She tipped her head and considered. "No. I'd prefer you just sit where you are." There was no way she would willingly have him cover that magnificent chest. Let him think what he would.

Now it was his turn to arch an eyebrow. "Brazen hussy tonight, are you?"

"No. I'm just trying for complete honesty tonight. Somehow that seems like the right thing to do, since we're getting married tomorrow and all."

Connor paused a moment, studying her before he responded. "Verra weel. To complete honesty between us then." He picked up the tankard and saluted her with it.

"It's weird, isn't it? Thinking about getting married tomorrow, I mean?"

"Aye. Verra strange."

"Well, you already know what I'm wearing now, so I guess I don't need this anymore." She shrugged the cloak off her shoulders, allowing it to pool behind her. "It's too hot in here for that, anyway." Rising to a kneel, she strained more of the tea into their tankard.

When she turned, Connor was staring at her through narrowed eyes, head tilted to one side.

"What? What are you thinking? Right this minute. And remember, we agreed on the whole honesty thing." She smiled at him.

"I was thinking what an unusual woman you are." He continued to stare at her, stretching out his legs toward the fire, leaning back on his elbows.

"Thank you, I think." Cate stretched her legs out toward the fire as well, leaning back on her elbows next to him. She giggled.

"Yer turn, lass. What are you thinking right now?"

"You won't like it."

"Remember 'the whole honesty thing,' " he echoed her words. "I answered when you asked."

"I was just thinking how odd it is to be in a place where the men wear shorter skirts than the women do." She giggled again when he sat up straight, looking offended.

"I dinna wear a skirt. This is a plaid. And yer no wearing a skirt at all. Only a shirt."

"Whatever. I knew you wouldn't like it. Tell you what." She sat up. "I'm feeling charitable. You get two questions to make up for that since you didn't like my answer. How's that?"

"Verra weel. I'll agree to that. Let me think. I wouldna want to waste one of my valuable questions."

She was beginning to get uncomfortable under his scrutiny by the time he finally spoke again.

"The dress you brought with you, the one you plan to wear tomorrow? Is this the dress you'll wear when you marry that Richard?"

His eyes were guarded. She could read no expression there at all.

"First of all, I've already told you. I'm not marrying Richard. Second of all, that dress was my grandmother's. She wore it when she married my grandfather. Then my mother wore it when she and my father were married. There's no way I'd ever get married now in any other dress."

"So, when you were planning to marry Richard, that was the dress you were going to wear?"

"No." She turned to him then. "See, you have to understand. That's part of the reason I'm not marrying Richard. He didn't like that dress, didn't think it was good enough. He said it wasn't stylish, didn't fit who we needed to be. He'd already picked out a different dress for our wedding."

"So yer not marrying him because he didn't like yer grandmother's dress?" He looked confused now.

"No. I'm not marrying Richard because he didn't love me enough to let me to wear the dress that made me happy. Because how I looked was more important to him than how I felt. There are lots of other reasons I'm not marrying him, but that pretty much sums up our relationship."

They sat quietly for a while, passing the tea back and forth.

"I hae my second question now." Connor finally broke the silence.

Cate turned to look at him. His eyes were dancing, twinkling in the firelight. He looked like a mischievous little boy. She smiled. "I'm ready, I think."

"I dinna ken what you were saying to me this afternoon. Weel, in all honesty, since we're being honest tonight, there are many times when I dinna ken the half of what yer talking about. But the whole idea of not wanting to get married with hairy legs confused me." His eyes were still twinkling above an amused little smile.

"In my time, many women find it more attractive to remove the hair from their legs and their underarms." She stopped when both his eyebrows rose. "Yes, underarms, too."

"Women find this attractive?"

"Yes, well, mostly because we assume men find it attractive."

"So, you remove yer hair because the men in yer time find it attractive. What about it do they find attractive?" His voice was low and soft.

She couldn't break eye contact with him now if she tried. Looking into those eyes, she was having difficulty thinking of words. "Smooth. Because of the way it feels smooth, I guess."

"Smooth?" It was just the one eyebrow raised, framing heated blue eyes, eyes she felt she might melt in.

She reached over and took his hand, laying his palm down on her leg, just above her knee. Then, still holding her hand on top of his, she ran his hand down her leg and back up. "Smooth. See?" Her leg was on fire under his hand. His fingers flexed on her knee.

"Aye." His breathing sounded a bit heavy. "And in yer time, do many of the men go about feeling yer smooth legs?" His voice was still low, but came out rough now.

"Only if I were to let them." She could float in those eyes.

Eyes that narrowed now as he smiled, a slow, predatory smile. His hand began to slide up her leg, under the tail of the shirt, as he leaned over her and took her lips with his own. She was drowning in the sensation of him and it felt wonderful.

Her own hands were busy discovering the contours of his back as his continued its journey up her leg, now on her outer thigh, reaching the satin barrier of her lacy panties. His hand slid past that, across her bottom and up her back, pulling her to him. She moved her arms to his neck, pushing the plaid from his shoulder before her fingers traveled up, weaving into his soft hair. His tongue slid insistently between her accommodating lips. He ravished her mouth, his tongue dancing with hers.

She wanted this moment to continue forever. She wanted more.

He moved over her, freeing his other hand to start a journey of its own, never interrupting the kiss that was consuming her body and soul. The hand behind her back moved up to cradle her head, supporting her as he deepened the kiss. His other hand lightly skimmed her stomach, upward until it reached the swell of her breast.

Her breasts throbbed, demanding his touch. When at last his thumb played over her hardened nipple she gasped, arching her neck, giving him access to her throat. He moved down her neck, kissing, nipping, tasting, until he met the laces of the shirt she wore.

She wanted to cry out when he moved his hands from her body until he slowly, very slowly, began to loosen the laces, unthreading them until he held one long string in his hand.

She lost track of what happened to the lace as he lowered his head to the deep, open V of the shirt, his fingers drawing back the cloth that had so recently impeded his way. His hair trailed over her breasts as his warm, moist mouth slid over her heated skin until at last he reached the breast his hand had so recently deserted.

Once, twice his tongue flicked over the sensitive nipple, his breath on the moistened tip sending waves of desire shooting straight to her core.

His hands glided down her waist, again reaching the lacy barrier she wore. One hand slid to the small of her back, while the other continued down, pressing it's way under the material, resting for a moment on the smooth skin there before continuing on, pausing only to caress the mound of curls just below.

His mouth closed over her breast, gently sucking her in, the pressure driving her wild with want. She moaned and he pulled again, taking more of her into his mouth.

The hand that had stilled moved on, lower, as if searching for the center of her need. When one lone finger moved lower still, parting the curls, she gasped, every nerve ending in her body alive.

His hands sent electrifying pulses radiating out all over her. She clasped his head to her breast and rocked against the hand he'd pressed into her.

"Oh God, Connor, please," she moaned, not knowing what she wanted of him, only that she wanted more, that she wanted him as much as she knew he wanted her. She could feel his need pressed against her leg.

He stilled. His rapid breaths felt cold against her heated skin, and when he pulled back from her, she felt the loss intensely. She opened her eyes to find him staring down at her, his breathing ragged.

Then he smiled. A wonderful, bewitching smile that made her want nothing so much as his mouth on her again.

"Yer the most beautiful woman I hae ever held, wee Caty. And if I dinna pull away from you now, I'll no be able to. Then, on the morrow, you'll no want to marry me. And marry me you must."

Her own breathing was a ragged match for his. There was nothing she could say. If she opened her mouth now, it would be to beg him not to stop.

He moved off her, rising to a crouch next to her, and sliding one arm under her legs and the other behind her back, he gathered her in his arms and stood. He didn't take his eyes from hers as he carried her to her bedchamber. There, he kicked opened the door and carried her to the bed. He paused, holding her for a moment, as if his determination wavered. She still couldn't speak, could barely breathe.

"When I've returned you to yer home and you think back on this time, know that resisting yer body was the hardest thing I've ever done. It's my sworn duty to protect you from harm, and that's what I'll do now." Then he kissed her gently on the forehead and, after laying her on the bed, walked out the door and shut it behind him.

Cate simply lay there, trembling, looking up at the canopy above her, feeling her heart pound throughout her body.

One thing was for sure: she had an answer to her questions.

What was it Jesse had said? Love sneaks up when you least expect it. Well, she sure hadn't expected it here. Not in this time. Not with this man whose devotion to duty outweighed everything else.

All she could say was, these magic-manipulating Faeries had either really bad timing or a terrifically sick sense of humor.

CHAPTER 20

The morning broke to reveal a gray, misty sky. Unable to sleep, Cate watched it arrive. She felt as gloomy as the view out her window.

While last night had called for a bachelor party, this morning screamed for a pity party. Somewhere along the way, life had taken a decidedly unfair twist. Not that she had ever expected a fairness guarantee, but her current situation was really on the far edge of just-so-not-right.

In a few hours she would marry the man she loved. The same man who did not, would not, love her in return. Oh, he desired her, she didn't doubt that, but love wasn't in his equation. He was all about honor and duty and sending her home, as he'd reminded her last night. He'd been honest from the beginning—he had no wish to be stuck with any woman. And even if she could somehow come to terms with all that, could accept loving someone who would never love her in return, it wouldn't matter because she was going to be whisked away, never to see him again.

She sighed deeply, sitting up on the edge of the bed.

Some days weren't worth getting up for. A smile flitted across her face as she thought of the T-shirt she wore to bed at home with that very sentiment emblazoned across the front of it. What would Connor think if he could see her wearing that particular shirt? It barely covered her bottom.

Embers still smoldered in the fireplace, and with only a little effort, she was able to coax new flames. She set her pot of water over them to boil and waited. Her kettle had been left behind in Connor's room downstairs, so she put her herbs and honey directly into her cup. When the water boiled, she poured some into her cup and the remainder into the bowl on the table to use for washing her face.

The soap burned her cheeks and neck, instantly bringing to mind the dark stubble that covered Connor's face last night, and how wonderful it had felt moving across her skin. Chills ran up and down her body.

"I am never going to get finished by the time Rosalyn and Mairi arrive if I don't stop mooning over that man."

She'd just finished washing her face when the first knock sounded at her door.

It was Mairi, carrying the garland she and Rosalyn had finished making the night before. They had woven ivory ribbons together with heather and lavender and some lovely white flowers Cate couldn't immediately identify. It would be tied around her head, allowing the ribbons to trail down her back.

Rosalyn arrived shortly after Mairi. Together they helped Cate into her wedding dress, all the while marveling at the design and the material. The underdress was an antique ivory satin, sleeveless, with an empire waist.

The neckline plunged in the front. The whole was covered with an antique ivory lace, which squared across the neckline, creating a discreet peek-a-boo effect. Tiny pearl buttons ran down the back. They also ran the length of the lace sleeves from the elbow to the wrist.

It was a dress she would never have been able to get into by herself. As the dress slid over her hips, Cate noted absently that she must have lost that extra ten pounds after all. The dress smoothed down, fitting like a dream.

"I hae never seen such a gown." Mairi spoke admiringly, reaching out to touch the sleeve. "These tiny bits upon the sleeves are beautiful."

"Aye, she's a fair bonny bride." Rosalyn nodded, placing the garland on her head and beginning to weave small locks of Cate's hair around the garland to help hold it in place.

"Oh, wait." Tugging the garland out of her hair, Cate ran to her bed, searching frantically under her pillows until she found what she wanted.

"Here." She held out the worn little strip of cloth from Connor's plaid. Mairi had gathered it up with all the other things from her room at Dun Ard when she brought them here.

"I'd like to weave this around the flowers in the front before we put it on. Do you think we can do that? So that it will plainly show?"

Rosalyn nodded in satisfaction. "Aye, lass. I'm sure we can manage that."

The garland securely in place, Mairi picked up the necklace from the table and started to lift Cate's hair.

"No. You can't put that on me."

"But you must wear yer betrothal gift for the wedding." Mairi's shocked tone was echoed in her face.

Cate's eyes twinkled. "Oh, I plan to wear it for the wedding, all right. It's just that I prefer to have someone else assist me in putting it on. Someone very masculine." She grinned and Mairi threw her arms around Cate, kissing her cheek.

"I'm so happy yer to be my sister. Yer exactly what my brother needs to brighten the whole rest of his life." Mairi hugged her again and started out the door ahead of them.

Cate exchanged a look with Rosalyn before heading out herself. The whole rest of his life? Only if his life was limited to just one day. Of course, in a way, it was. When she returned home, he would be . . .

I will not cry. It would be her mantra today.

She had always wanted a sister, a built-in someone to be her best friend. Now she was this close to having one she liked so much, and she'd only get to keep her for a matter of hours.

Within the space of the next twenty-four hours, she expected to lose a best friend and the man of her dreams.

In spite of her mantra, the threat of tears rose in her throat as she descended the stairs.

Connor was so handsome standing there she could barely breathe at the sight of him.

He stood in the main hall, fidgeting with the emerald pin at his shoulder. When he looked up and smiled helplessly at her, she was momentarily stopped in her tracks. Had she thought he was merely handsome before? The man was truly magnificent.

Cate hurried over to him, reaching up to adjust the pin over his heart.

"Your turn now. I'd like you to help me with this, please." She handed the necklace to him.

He held it in a shaking hand, staring at it for a moment before moving behind her to position it around her throat. She was aware of the heat from the jewel the moment it touched her skin.

"I'd ask a moment alone with my bride, if you all dinna mind." He said it quietly, moving to stand in front of Cate.

Everyone left the hall, going out onto the great front stairway and down to the courtyard.

He ran his finger along the cloth woven into the front of her garland and, meeting her gaze, arched an eyebrow.

She chuckled at the familiar haughty expression.

"Yes. I decided today would be a most appropriate time to wear your territory marker again." She backed up and did a little twirl for him. "What do you think? Do I look all right?"

His face was serious, solemn as he moved close. Taking her hands in his, he gazed into her eyes.

"I meant my words last night, wee Caty. Yer a beautiful woman and you make a beautiful bride. And aye, the dress, though most unusual, suits the unusual woman who wears it." He lifted her hand, searching her eyes. "I hae a boon to ask of you on our wedding day. Will you grant it?"

"Whatever you want, Connor. You only have to ask." She meant it with her whole heart.

"Although this is no real, it's the only wedding day I'll ever hae." He gripped her hand tightly. "Selfish though it may be, I canna stand the thought of marrying a woman who wears another man's betrothal gift. Will you remove it for me, Caty? Just for this day."

Richard's ring. She hadn't even thought about it. The tears she'd held at bay all morning began to roll slowly down her cheeks now. For a woman who never cried, it seemed to be all she could do since she'd been here. She slipped her hands from his grip and pulled the ring from her finger, holding it out to him.

He held it in the palm of his hand, looking down at it for a moment before he dropped it into the little leather pouch he wore hanging from his waist. Placing his hands tenderly on either side of her face, he wiped her tears away with his thumbs.

"Thank you." He said it quietly, softly. "I'd no intended to cause you pain. I'll guard it for you weel and return it on the morrow." He stared at her with sad eyes.

Before he could remove his hands, she placed her own over them, holding him there. "My tears aren't for the ring, Connor. They're just . . . because." She shrugged.

How could she ever face telling him that her tears were for him? Tears she couldn't stop because he believed this wedding wasn't real, because soon she'd leave him forever, because she loved him and he didn't love her. She sighed deeply and let go of his hands to wipe at her face. Her cheeks were still raw and the salty tears burned.

He extended his arm to her. "Yer face seems a wee bit chafed this morning. Did you try shaving that as weel as yer legs?"

She took his arm, grateful to him for changing the subject to give her time to compose herself.

"No, I did not. But I do believe shaving was involved. Had one of us shaved his face last night, mine wouldn't be so sensitive this morning."

His eyes widened as the meaning of her words gradually registered with him and a dull red color spread up his neck and face. Then he laughed and continued to chuckle to himself as they descended the great stairs to begin their journey to be married.

A large crowd surrounded the church when they arrived. Cate recognized Connor's family, and a few of the people from Dun Ard, but for the most part, the people blended together in a sea of faces as she and Connor approached the minister waiting for them outside the church. Her heart beat so loudly she was surprised the clergyman couldn't hear it from where he stood.

The wedding ceremony took place outside on the steps at the door of the chapel. The mist cleared and the sun shone brightly, burning away the gray clouds. The ceremony itself was a blur. For the most part, she only remembered staring into Connor's eyes the entire time.

Except for the rings. Cate knew that wedding rings weren't part and parcel of medieval weddings, so she hadn't expected them to be part of hers. But they were.

Connor gently lifted her hand and placed a heavy gold ring upon her finger. Turning her hand over, he laid a larger gold band in the center of her palm. He then extended his hand and waited for her to place that ring upon his finger. She did so with trembling hands. The look on his face at that moment would stay in her memory forever.

He smiled at her then, gripping her hand tightly

through the rest of the ceremony, which was over before she knew it. Yelling and cheering erupted all around them as they turned and went to find his horse.

When Connor suddenly dropped to his knee, she immediately knew the man in front of them must be King Alexander III. She did her best curtsy and bowed her head, but couldn't resist a peek up to see the man.

The king pulled Connor to his feet; dragging him close and clasping him in a great hug, he pounded him on the back. He was shorter than Connor and much younger than she had expected, his looks made even younger by a broad smile and his dark hair falling just short of his shoulders.

"Weel done, MacKiernan. Verra weel done. She's lovely."

"Thank you, yer highness." Connor bowed his head.

"Let's have a look." Taking her hand in one of his, Alexander lifted her chin with his forefinger and, with great enthusiasm, loudly pronounced her a "bonnie wee lassie fit for his own brave knight" to everyone present.

To which the crowd cheered wildly again.

The king turned back, still holding Cate's hand, which he passed over to Connor.

"No doubt she'll give you many a braw lad." He then laughed. "And since I've also no doubt you'll no want to return to my service with this one waiting at yer hearth, I'll expect you to raise a new batch of MacKiernan warriors to serve my son, Alexander."

Everyone shouted and laughed as the king once again slapped Connor on the back and made his way through the crowd, surrounded by the attendants who accompanied him.

Connor lifted Cate up onto his horse and settled her close to him as they joined in the large procession of people all heading up the hill toward Dun Ard. He held her clasped tightly to him, but said nothing as they rode.

The music of the pipers and flutes and drummers floated down to them before they actually reached the castle. Long tables of food were set out in the courtyard, already filling with the villagers and crofters who were joining them for the day of celebration. People who were dancing in the open spaces between the tables lifted their cups in toast to the couple as they passed by. They stopped often to receive the greetings and good wishes of the people gathered there.

Still more musicians played inside the castle. The king, rather than Artair, sat at the center of the long table on the dais this day. Artair was seated on one side of the king and Connor was placed on the other, with Cate next to him.

She was unable to locate Rosalyn, but did notice Blane sitting a few chairs down from his father. As before, he watched her with an intensity she found unnerving. The one time their eyes met, he bowed his head slightly and lifted his cup in acknowledgment. Cate quickly looked away.

Lyall came up from one of the tables below the dais where he was seated, bowing low over her hand before kissing it. He offered congratulations to Connor, who'd risen from his seat when Lyall had taken her hand. They hugged and pounded on each other's backs. It was such a classic demonstration of testosterone-filled goodwill, Cate almost expected to see high fives.

Lyall had been looking for Mairi and wondered if they knew where she was. Only then did it occur to Cate that she hadn't seen the girl since their arrival at the church for the wedding ceremony. Connor mumbled something about her having run off to find shoes. Cate hoped the king hadn't seen her shoeless yet or her new sister would be most upset.

Even in the midst of so many strangers, there were several men who caught Cate's attention as they hovered near the dais. These were large men, with hard eyes. They reminded her of the men who worked with her brothers. Many of them were introduced to her as they stopped to exchange quiet greetings with Connor. She could easily imagine him being one of their number. More than likely, they were the king's bodyguards. And, more than likely, if this were anyone else's wedding, Connor would have been one of those milling about the dais keeping watch over his king.

Connor felt himself on full alert, unable to relax even for a moment. After so many years, he felt almost vulnerable without Duncan at his back, but his old friend had his own task to accomplish this day. Still, there were others here, men he trusted and could depend on if need be.

He constantly scanned the crowds, wondering if they'd make another attempt on Cate's life today. He'd not allow her out of his sight for even a moment. He'd not make it easy for them.

She sat next to him, quietly picking at the food on her plate.

It had cost him dearly, chipped away at his pride, to

ask her to remove the ring she wore. Richard's ring. Even now he felt the weight of it in his sporran.

When she'd taken it off and handed it to him, her tears had only confirmed what he should have remembered all along. She belonged to another man, a man of wealth and power that she'd chosen. Just like his mother, just like Anabella.

And what they had very nearly shared last night did nothing to change that. He had regained control of his traitorous body in time. Now they were wed. Very soon she'd be gone; no more Cate, no more temptation. He had only to keep her safe until then and his duty to her would be fulfilled.

The festivities lasted late into the evening hours and Cate was feeling the effects of having had so little sleep the prior night by the time Artair approached them.

Connor stood and nodded his head in greeting. "Uncle."

"Nephew. I think it's past time yer bride met some of my guests."

The older man held his hand out toward her, but Connor inserted himself between them and took her hand himself, assisting her to stand.

"She'll go nowhere this day without me in attendance."

"Nowhere?" Anabella had approached unnoticed, and now clutched at Artair's arm, favoring them with her sickly sweet smile. As usual, her tone was belittling. "Surely you'll allow her some privacy, Connor. No even to the garderobe without you?"

"Nowhere," he responded firmly. "No even the

garderobe without me." Connor smiled, although his eyes narrowed and there was no humor in his look. "No on this day."

He turned to his uncle, Cate's arm securely tucked into his own. "Lead the way, Uncle. We'll meet yer guests together."

"Verra weel, if you insist." Artair didn't seem particularly pleased. His eyes glittered strangely.

Artair led them to an enormous man Cate had noticed earlier in the evening, sitting at a table near the dais. He had long, wild red hair that appeared to tangle with his long red beard. Both were streaked liberally with gray. Ale dribbled down that beard now to join food left there at some earlier time. The smell of unwashed bodies hit Cate hard as they approached.

The man slammed his tankard to the table when he looked up and saw them. "High time you brought the wench to me for inspection. Give the MacPherson a kiss, lassie," he shouted to the accompanying hoots and laughter at his table. He reached for Cate, but was stopped by a strong hand on his wrist.

"I think no, MacPherson. No one will be putting a hand on my bride this day but me, and certainly she'll be kissing no one else."

Connor's eyes held the same dangerous glint as those of the men roaming behind the table on the dais, one of whom joined them even now.

"Is this a friend of yers then, MacKiernan?" The man who'd been introduced to Cate as Robert leaned into their group and smiled, a hard tight look that made Cate shiver.

Still holding the large man's wrist, Connor made introductions. "This is the MacPherson, laird of the Clan MacPherson. And this is Robert MacQuarrie, one of the king's guardsmen and a man I do call friend." He let the wrist go, pushing Cate behind him, and smiled in a way that reminded Cate of a bullfighter waving the red flag.

The MacPherson jerked his hand away, his face purpled with rage. He stood, knocking several plates from the table in the process of hefting his bulk. He turned to Artair, who shrank from the man's fury.

"We're done with yer festivities, MacKiernan. Dinna forget what you owe me. I'll give you to her birthday and no a moment longer. Then I come to claim it. Or take it out of yer hide." He spit at Artair's feet and stomped out.

The majority of the men at the table rose and left with him, all grumbling and pushing their way through the hall with unnecessary roughness. Artair stared after them for a moment, as if stunned, and then hurried away in the opposite direction.

Robert chuckled. "Weel, that should save some damage to the pantry, losing that group."

Connor smiled, a genuine smile this time, placing his hand on the other man's shoulder. "I dinna need yer help, Robbie, you ken? But I was glad to hae it all the same."

"Aye, weel. I ken you did no need me, but Alexander worries like a mother hen at times. What's a man to do? I go where my king sends me."

Both men laughed at some shared joke. Robert bowed to Cate and backed away.

"That was the MacPherson? That fat, disgusting old man is the one Artair wants to give Mairi to?" She couldn't even begin to comprehend.

"Aye, that's the man. But dinna fash yerself over it. That will no be happening now, thanks to you. Artair will hae to find some way to pay his debts other than with my sister."

He pulled her close then and whispered in her ear, his breath sending shivers all over her body. "We should try to make our escape now. Everyone will be busy with what's just happened and we may have a chance to sneak away if they're distracted by the fuss the MacPhersons are making as they go." He looked grim as they started out the door.

"I don't understand. Why would we need to sneak away?"

"Och, Christ, it's too late," he murmured, tightening his grip on her as he looked out the door. "I'm sorry, Caty, I'd hoped to save you this." He uttered the last just as a laughing, cheering crowd of people mobbed them.

Both of them were lifted bodily off the ground, carried outside and tossed into the back of a straw-filled cart. Connor's horse was tied to the back and people, some on horseback, some on foot, swarmed around the cart as it started through the courtyard. Another cart, carrying musicians, followed lending accompaniment to the crowd, many of whom were singing, all of whom were in high spirits.

"What's going on here? Where are they taking us?" Cate was forced to yell to make herself heard over the noise.

The cart rolled over a particularly large rut and she was thrown face-first into his lap.

"Here, here. None of that, lassie. You'll wait till we get you to the castle," an old man yelled from the back of a horse riding next to the cart. The crowd nearest him roared with laughter.

Connor grinned sheepishly as he helped her to sit up. "They're escorting us to the bedding. The celebration lasts until the marriage is consummated." At her look of horror, he laughed out loud. "Dinna look so terrified, wee Caty. I'd no let them watch."

She stared at him in disbelief. The man was actually laughing, like he was enjoying this insanity as much as all these people.

His laughter faded to a seductive smile and he rose to his knees. Taking her by her arms, he pulled her to him and stared down into her eyes for only a moment before he slanted his lips over hers.

She dissolved into his arms, her concerns melting away. His tongue danced with hers and she could think of nothing but him and the way she knew his hands would feel on her body.

He tightened his hold, one hand sliding under her hair to grasp her neck, deepening the kiss. At his touch, even the raucous sounds of the laughter and the cheering disappeared, blocked from her mind.

In that moment, there was nothing in her world but Connor and his body next to hers.

CHAPTER 21

꒰⌒꒱

Their arrival at Sithean Fardach was unnerving, to say the least.

When Connor had told her the crowd was escorting them to their bedding, he hadn't been exaggerating at all. It appeared these people planned to do exactly that. The boisterous mob carrying them surged into the main hall and up the spiral stairs.

Only at the door to the bedroom did Connor finally take charge of the situation. The bottleneck afforded by the narrow staircase made their escape possible.

At last the two of them were behind closed doors, but the mob still roamed the castle and the courtyard below, musicians playing loudly to accompany the still singing, partying crowd.

Connor locked the door, pushing heavy furniture in front of it to keep any particularly enthusiastic revelers out. He knelt by the fireplace, adding wood to the small fire, trying to drive the chill from the room.

Rising from his position by the fire, he moved to where

she stood and ran his hands up and down her arms in an effort to warm her.

"Yer safe, wee Caty. Dinna be afraid." He pulled her to him, running his hands up and down her back.

"I'm not afraid. Much."

She leaned back to get a good look at his face and almost wished she hadn't. God, the man was gorgeous, even with that imperious look he assumed now, arching his eyebrow as he so frequently did.

"Then yer shivering must be from the cold. Where's yer cloak?" He looked around the room.

"Downstairs. I guess your hands were too full last night to bring it along when you delivered me here."

He looked embarrassed for a moment.

"Weel then, downstairs it'll hae to stay. I'm no opening that door for anything and dealing with that lot again."

Cate nodded in complete agreement.

The wind howled around the shutters and made its way into the room. Even the little flames of the fire danced wildly in response to it.

"I guess I should change out of this gown. It's old and kind of delicate."

"Aye. I suppose that would be for the best." He turned around and looked at the door. "I'll keep my back turned, if you like, but I'm no going out that door." He shuddered and smiled when she laughed.

She looked around the room.

"I have an idea," she said as she walked toward the bed. "Help me untie all these draperies. We can draw them closed and it will make a perfect dressing room."

He gave her a doubtful look but assisted her in closing the curtains about the bed.

Cate thought for a moment, trying to decide what she could change into. Wearing his shirt last night had very nearly gotten her into trouble, so she quickly discarded that idea. Then her eyes lit on her own silk pajamas. Why not? Who knew when she'd be going home? She might as well be dressed for it. Taking them in a bundle, she climbed up into the bed to change.

Her makeshift dressing room quickly revealed its pros and cons. She had her privacy, but it was dark. Very dark.

It was only after she was kneeling in the bed that she realized she couldn't get out of the dress by herself. She might in time make her way through enough of the buttons on the arms to allow her to pull her hands out, but there was no way she'd ever be able to undo the back of her dress. She considered her options for only a moment. She didn't have any.

"Connor?" She poked her head out of the curtains, following it with her body. "I need your help."

He looked up immediately when she called his name. He sat in a chair pulled close to the fire, slowly feeding more wood into the sputtering flames.

"I'm at yer service, milady." He smiled.

She felt the smile to the tips of her toes. Taking a deep breath, she walked over to where he sat and extended an arm.

"I'm stuck in my dress. I can't reach all these buttons to undo them. Would you help me?"

He stood slowly. For just an instant she could have

sworn she saw something flicker behind his eyes before he reached for her wrist and began to work at the buttons. When he finished her second arm, she turned her back and lifted her hair.

Was that a groan? She turned sharply to look at him, but his eyes gave nothing away as he worked studiously at pushing the tiny pearls through the tiny holes.

"If you'd just be still, this would go a bit faster," he grumbled.

When he finished, she held the dress tightly to her and climbed back into the curtained bed. Not only was it dark in the confined space, it had also gotten warm. Very warm. Perspiration dotted her forehead by the time she finished changing into her pajamas. Those old-timers who invented these heavy bed curtains had certainly known what they were doing.

Cate folded her dress and laid it near the far edge of the bed. She attempted to pull the garland from her hair, but it tangled further so she left it there. Propping the pillows alongside the wall behind her, she leaned back against them to wait.

Instantly the dark closed in on her, and her own breathing sounded loud. This wasn't going to work at all.

"Connor?" She poked her head out through the curtains again, this time at the foot of the bed.

He sat, leaning toward the fire, rubbing his hands together. The room felt quite chilled in comparison to the enclosed area of the bed. The rain had returned in full force and was blowing against the shutters, with some of the moisture finding its way into the room.

"Aren't you going to come in here with me? It's certainly drier and much warmer." She held out her hand in invitation.

"This will be fine. You go ahead and try to get some sleep. I'll keep watch over the door." He didn't turn around.

Cate considered her situation briefly. This could be her very last opportunity to spend time with him, to even talk to him. She wasn't going to let it pass by with her in a dark little cave hyperventilating as the walls closed in while he sat out by the fire, cold and uncomfortable.

She climbed out the foot of the bed and padded over to him. Inside the curtains she hadn't thought to put on the jacket that went with her pajamas. She was warm enough. Out here, however, the cold air immediately raised chill bumps on her skin. Cold and damp was not a pleasant combination.

Squatting down beside him, she reached for his hand. This time he did groan when he looked at her. Low in his throat, more exhaled air than true sound.

"Yer going to freeze out here dressed like that. Get back into bed." He tried to make it sound gruff, frowning at her, but he rubbed her hand in between his. "Yer already getting chilled."

"Well, then we'll freeze together. I'm not going back in there alone." When he would have protested, she placed her finger over his lips. "It's dark in there and I don't like being in the dark alone. Come with me. Keep me company. I'm not sleepy anyway." She stood up and tugged at his arm.

He shook his head but allowed her to pull him to his feet, and he followed her to the bed. She crawled in first and he followed, leaving an opening in the curtains at the foot of the bed. The flicker of the firelight dimly illuminated their little cave, giving it a cozy rather than claustrophobic feel. Or maybe it was the company that changed the feel of the space.

She began pulling at the garland again, but he moved her hands and gently unwound her hair until the garland was free. He tossed it to the foot of the bed.

They sat with their backs propped against the wall, several inches separating them, until Cate scooted closer. Connor lifted his arm and she ducked under it, allowing it to rest on her shoulders, leaning her head over against his chest. She held his hand, twisting the ring she'd so recently placed on his finger.

She held up her own hand next to his, and admired the gold bands there in the faint light. Intricate carvings covered their surface. Hers felt warm and heavy on her hand. It felt as if it belonged there.

"These rings are beautiful. Tell me about them."

He reached out and touched the one on her hand, turning it around and around on her finger.

"There's no much to tell. They've been in my family for generations. My grandparents wore them last. They had been passed to Rosalyn. She brought them to me yestereve, saying as she'd hae no need for them, it would honor her if I used them today."

Her curiosity got the best of her. "Why has Rosalyn never married? She's a beautiful woman."

"There hae been those who hae sought her hand, but she's refused them all. She says she waits for her true love to ask." He shrugged and continued to turn the ring.

No wonder the woman had insisted on that bit about true love at the Faerie Glen. She truly believed in it.

"Your grandparents wore these last? I would have expected you to have used your parents' rings."

In the dim light, his face hardened and his lips drew tight. "I'd no put my mother's ring on yer hand."

"Why not? What happened with your mother? What did she do that made you so angry?"

He started to pull his arm away, but she held tightly to his hand.

"Tell me. I know there's something. Blane was trying to upset you with it the night of our betrothal party, out there on the balcony when he mentioned this necklace being your mother's." She touched the jewel at her throat. "What happened?"

He was silent for a moment, his body tense, head bowed. When he spoke his voice was raw with agony. "She betrayed my father's memory. She moved from here to Dun Ard, gave herself to Artair. They sent me away then, to school in Britain, where my mother's people lived. I hated her for that."

In the silence that followed, his free hand clenched into a fist, shaking with the force of the pressure he applied. When he continued, the words were spoken so quietly, Cate needed to strain to hear them.

"Then she died. While I was so far away, unable to watch over her, unable to protect her, she died."

Such horrible, undeserved guilt for a boy to carry into manhood.

"I'm so sorry, Connor."

His body stiffened at her words. "I dinna need yer pity."

"And you don't have it."

He shifted to look at her, a frown on his face.

"I'm serious. I'm sorry you carry that burden, but I don't pity you. At least you remember your mother. I have almost no memories of mine."

He leaned back against the wall again, and Cate waited, the silence again building between them. Her only consolation was that he allowed his hand to remain linked to hers.

"Did you ever ask her why she made the choice she did?" she whispered.

"What?"

"Your mother. Did you ever ask her why?"

He paused for a moment and she thought he might not answer, then he shook his head.

"There was never a time to ask. I tried to talk her out of it. I pleaded, I argued, I forbid it. So they sent me away. But I dinna need to ask why. It would hae been for the power and the wealth. Artair was the laird. My mother had always been the laird's wife. I suppose she could no help herself. Even though she went to him only as his woman, no as his wife. It's the way of women."

Cate continued to hold his hand, stroking the back of it, until gradually the tension in his arm ebbed away. He reached out with his other hand and touched the ring he'd placed on her finger that morning, reminding her it was still there.

"I suppose I should give this back to you now since I don't have any idea when I'll . . . " She didn't think she could even say the words. "I mean, we finished what I came here for. You're married now, the king seems happy, you can stay home and take care of Mairi." She stopped and breathed in deeply. "Do you have any idea when it will happen? When I just won't be here anymore?" Her voice cracked on the last.

Connor tightened his arm around her. "I dinna ken the way it will end." He stopped and breathed deeply, too. "I think I would like it best if you would wear the ring. I'll hae no need of it again. I like the way it looks where it is. Think of it as a keepsake, something to help you remember yer visit here."

They were quiet for a time, simply sitting together in the warmth, holding hands.

Her adventure was at an end; the four weeks she'd thought an eternity, gone in the blink of an eye. She'd done everything she'd agreed to. And more. She'd never expected to become attached to any of these people, and yet they were as much a part of her life now as those back home.

Home. At any moment, she would be transported back to her own life, back to . . . what? What waited for her there? Richard? No. Now that she knew what it was to feel love for someone, she could never settle for less.

Cate glanced up at Connor. He sat with his head back against the pillows she'd propped there, his eyes closed, pinched little lines at their outer edges.

If Mairi was right and there was only one true love for each person, Cate had no doubt that she had found hers and yet she was getting ready to leave him behind. By this time tomorrow, she'd have no more than the heavy ring on her finger and a memory.

Glancing up at Connor one more time, Cate made up her mind. If all she would have was a memory, she might as well make it a memory worth having.

"Connor?" Though she whispered, he started at the sound.

"Aye?"

Unable to easily find the words to ask for what she wanted, she stroked the back of his hand with her finger, avoiding his eyes.

"When I'm gone, I would like to think that you won't forget me right away."

"I dinna think I'll be forgetting you anytime soon."

His voice had an odd catch to it so she risked a quick look at his face. His eyes were electric in the muted light of their man-made cave.

"What I mean is, I know you don't have a very high opinion of women and I don't want you to remember me like that." She was making a mess of this. "Not when I know I'll never forget you."

His eyebrow lifted in question, while his eyes narrowed. "What would you have me remember of you then, Cate?"

She released his hand and rose to her knees. Turning to kneel beside him, she cupped his face in her hands.

"Only this," she said, leaning in to kiss him softly.

His entire body stiffened and he watched her warily, but she was determined not to be deterred at this point.

She broke the kiss, her hands moving up the roughened stubble of his cheeks and into his soft hair.

His hands remained at his side, fisted tightly.

Tucking the little braid behind his ear as she'd longed to do so many times, she leaned into him again, placing a delicate kiss on the ear she'd brushed with her finger.

He still hadn't moved when she ran the tip of her

tongue around the edge of his ear, ending at the lobe, which she gently gripped between her teeth and sucked.

He grasped her upper arms so quickly, she wasn't even sure she'd seen him move.

"You must stop. You've no idea what yer doing," he growled, pushing her back.

When his grip loosened, she rose again to her knees, this time straddling his lap as she moved in closer.

"That's where your wrong, Connor. I know exactly what I'm doing." *More or less.*

Once more she leaned into him, her hands back in his hair, and again she traced the contour of his ear with her tongue, sucking his lobe into her mouth.

It made a tiny sucking sound when he jerked her away, his breathing fast and uneven. Her own breathing seemed a little irregular as she gazed into his eyes.

"I'm sworn, on my honor, to protect you from all harm." The bruising grip he had on her upper arms gradually relaxed until he no more than touched her skin. "Dinna make it impossible for me to protect you from myself."

She leaned back from him. Brushing his hands from her arms, a spark of apprehension lit her body at what she was getting ready to do. She'd never thought of herself as an aggressive woman, certainly not in this arena, but she knew what she wanted now.

Reaching down, she grasped the tail of her camisole and lifted it up and over her head, baring herself to him. She trailed her hand down his cheek once again.

"For this one night, Connor, I don't want you to protect me. I want you to . . ."—she couldn't say love me, wasn't brave enough to admit her feelings to him, so she compromised with herself—". . . make love to me."

He stared at her as if he were frozen as long seconds crawled by and her heart almost stopped. If he rejected her now, she thought she might die of embarrassment.

Then he groaned, and when he gripped her arms this time, it was to drag her body close to his, not to push her away. He buried his face in her breasts, his hands on her back.

"Och, Christ, forgive me," he whispered, his breath hot on her tender skin.

He rolled them then, bringing her body securely under his. Evidence of his need pressed against her stomach as he slanted his mouth over hers, his tongue darting through her unresisting lips to dance with her own.

She fought with the material of his shirt, pulling at it until he lifted his upper body just enough to tug it over his head and toss the linen wildly away. Then he covered her with his body, his bare chest coarse against her sensitive breasts.

He kissed her again, deeply, before leaving her mouth to trail his lips across her cheek and on to her ear in an obvious imitation of what she'd done to him earlier. He lifted her hair and continued down her neck onto her shoulder, kissing, tasting, nipping.

His hands slid down her shoulders onto her chest, and lightly across her breasts. They stilled there at her gasp, his thumbs slowly rubbing small circles around the nipples that tightened until Cate thought they might burst.

She felt the cool air when his hands moved on, sliding to her sides. He gripped tightly and lifted her up in the bed until his lips touched her breast. He held her to him as he kissed his way to one of the recently abandoned nipples, taking it in his mouth, running his tongue around it in the same maddening, circular pattern his thumb had traced.

His hair draped onto her bare chest, feeling like strands of silk to her overly sensitized skin. She buried her hands in it, holding him to her. The coarse stubble of his chin raked a trail as he turned just a little to take the other breast into his mouth.

Gliding from her sides to her back, his hands moved down, encountering the soft, silky material of her pajama bottoms. His thumbs hooked under the elastic and they slid down, his palms sweeping the firm roundness of her bottom.

"Take them off or I tear them off." His words rumbled against her breast. He rose just inches from her body allowing her to kick off the offending pants.

When his body covered hers again, she realized his plaid had disappeared in the process as well, the heat of his skin melding into her own.

He kissed her breastbone and down, delivering little charged pools of sensation in his wake as his tongue darted along the path he took. At her navel he stopped, nibbling at the edge, his tongue circling, entering, and circling again, over and over.

His hands trailed lower, pushing her legs farther apart, then sliding up her thighs until his thumbs rested over the heat of her center. There they began to move, one circling erotically, mesmerizing her as a powerful arousal grew, consuming her with need.

He nibbled his way back up to her breast, once again lavishing his tongue's attention on her nipple.

One finger slid across her fevered skin and entered her, pressing deep, moving in and out, slowly, in harmony with the movement of his thumb, like the ebb and flow of an ancient ocean.

She would have screamed with the staggering sensation his hands wrought, but his mouth covered hers, his tongue dipping in to steal her very breath.

A second finger joined the first, and he swallowed her moan, leaving her mouth to trail his lips down her neck and back across her chin.

His hands left her and her body shuddered at the loss.

"Wait," he whispered near her ear, his breath stirring her hair, damp now with perspiration.

Then she felt him enter her, slowly, stretching her to accommodate him, only a little and then out. Slowly again, in a little farther and then out. One more time, slowly, farther still and out.

"God, Connor, don't stop. Now," she pleaded.

"Now," he echoed, sliding his hands to her hips and driving himself into her.

The sting was instantaneous, and when she gasped he stilled inside her and waited, kissing her neck, her cheeks, her eyes as she panted.

"Should I stop?" His voice was strained, as if he'd forced himself to say the words.

The sound made Cate feel powerful and in answer to his question, she rocked her hips away from him and back, tilting, pressing, taking him deeply into her.

He growled, deep in his throat, or was it a laugh? She

couldn't be sure, swept away as she was on the frenzy of feeling he was building in her again.

When the sensations flooded over her, she held on to his shoulders tightly, digging her fingers in to anchor her against the feelings she thought might sweep her away.

Within seconds, his fingers clamped around her hips, holding her close as he surged into her, his body pulsing in a series of shudders.

They lay together, their breathing ragged, their bodies damp, as Cate considered what she'd just done.

No regrets. When she woke up tomorrow in her own time, she would still be thankful for this particular memory.

After a time, she reluctantly moved from the bed to find her clothing and dress, unwilling to awaken, naked and alone, in her own bedroom. When she returned to his side, Connor pulled her close, and kissed the top of her head.

They lay quietly, snuggled together. Though she fought it, Cate could feel herself drifting off.

"Connor?" She whispered his name one last time.

"Aye?"

"When I'm not here when you wake up in the morning? I mean, when the Faeries do their thing or whatever and I'm gone, I just want you to know that I'm glad I came. That I was here, with you. I wouldn't have missed this time with you for anything in the world."

"Aye, wee Caty. I would no hae missed our time together either."

He leaned down and kissed her forehead, tucking her close under his arm, where she felt protected and safe. Where she wanted to stay.

CHAPTER 22

Connor awoke on his back, a foreign weight on his body. Foreign, but entirely welcome. Cate covered him like a blanket, her head pillowed on his shoulder, her arm across his chest and one shapely leg draped across his thighs. If he shifted his position but a little, the warm, moist center of her would be perfectly positioned over the part of him that had already come to life at the sight of her sleeping there in his bed, at the thought of having her once more.

Instead of shifting, he swallowed hard, took a couple of deep breaths and looked down at her again. In the morning light filtering through the curtains of the bed her face looked peaceful, delicate, beautiful. The small thin strap of the silky garment she wore had slipped down off her shoulder, exposing the creamy whiteness of her skin. Her perfect breast, barely covered, pressed against his chest. The same perfect breast he'd explored so thoroughly last night.

He wouldn't think it possible that he could harden more, but he did, painfully so. And as he did, he once again swiftly considered the whole shifting idea, but discarded it as she stretched against him, opened her eyes and smiled. Suddenly he found himself unable to even think, let alone shift.

"Good morning." Her smile, sleepy and seductive, struck at the center of him. She slid her leg off him and stretched again.

Pins and needles shot through his body. He wanted her more than he wanted his next breath. More than he wanted his next heartbeat. Having her last night had done nothing to slake that need. If anything, it made it worse. No, he couldn't give in to that again. He'd dishonored himself enough.

"Good morning." His voice croaked like a young lad.

"I'm still here." Her eyes opened wide and she sat up quickly in bed, the other strap falling from her shoulder and the top of her little covering started to sag.

He watched her sitting there, holding his breath. If her top fell down, if he saw her right now, naked in front of him, he'd have to take her. He'd have no choice, no control over it. His heart raced, not really sure which option he wanted more.

She put both her hands on his chest and leaned down to his face. "I'm still here. The Faeries didn't take me." She hovered over him, wearing a silly grin.

It almost made up for the vision of heaven he had when he lowered his eyes from her face.

"Good Christ, woman, yer almost completely out of yer clothes. Do something." He could barely get the words out.

She looked down. "Oh."

She tugged the straps high up on her arms as she sat up straight. Now her stomach was exposed, her perfect little belly taunting him with its very nearness. The perfect little belly he longed to revisit with his hands, his mouth.

He made a gurgling noise and sat up, gasping for air.

"You don't wake up so well, do you, Connor?" She rolled off her side of the bed, throwing back the curtains. "I'm still here." She said it with wonder in her voice.

She'd gone daft. Overnight. She'd lost what little sense she'd had. Of course, he should have recognized that last night. Perhaps that would have helped him do as he should have done.

He thought he might be able to stand finally and was just swinging his legs off the bed when she threw back the curtains on his side.

"Why am I still here? I'm supposed to be gone. What happened?" She was leaning over him again, a small frown on her face.

This would never do.

He took her by her shoulders and pushed her back, standing up in the process, although not all the way up. He couldn't quite manage that just yet.

"I dinna hae any idea why yer still here, Cate. But you most certainly are, I can assure you of that."

She seemed to notice his posture now. "Are you okay? Is there something wrong? Can I do anything for you?" She moved closer, putting her arm around him, leaning her face close to his, concern clear in her eyes.

There was most certainly something she could do.

"No, give me just a minute."

He breathed deeply and then straightened, looking down at her. She was lovely in the morning light.

Cate backed up and crossed her arms under her breasts, exposing even more of her flat little stomach, the shiny cloth pulled tight across her breasts. Breasts that would, he remembered from last night, tighten and harden with merely the slightest stroke of his hand. And when he tasted her . . .

He groaned, shaking his head. "Yer killing me, Cate. Put some clothes on."

"What? Oh." She picked her jacket up off the floor and put it on. "Is this better?"

"Aye, it is. Thank you."

She smiled and patted him on the back as she passed, moving over to poke at the fire. "Well, looks like we made it through our wedding night, doesn't it? That should make all your noisy partygoers happy, convinced that we're really married. Maybe we can take down the barricades now."

"Och, Christ, I almost forgot."

He strode back to the bed and stripped the covers away, tossing them to the floor, searching.

"What the hell are you doing? Have you gone crazy?" Cate's eyes were enormous.

There he found what he sought, in the center of the bed—a few small drops of dried blood. He ran his hand across the spot and looked up at her, guilt eating at him. He'd done that, broken his vow to protect her from harm, taken that from her.

He started to pull the cover from the bedding.

"Don't even tell me you're doing what I think you're

doing." She looked incredulous, her mouth slightly open.

The various scenes of what he could do with that mouth passed quickly through his mind before he answered.

"Weel, we could hae let them watch, but this will serve as proof." He'd planned on cutting himself, using his own blood to accomplish his proof. He'd never thought it would come to this.

She froze at his words, turning her back on him. "No. Of course you're right. I never considered they'd want proof. I didn't plan any of . . ." She paused, shaking her head. "I just can't think of why you'd want to show them that." She pointed back at the bed without turning to look at it.

"Because they'll check. For proof of consummation of the marriage." Surely she could understand how it was.

"That's barbaric. I can't believe anyone would intrude on something so personal, so private." Her words were low, strangled as if she forced them out.

"It's no barbaric. It's proof. If we dinna consummate the marriage, we're no married and I'd no be released from my service to the king. Now it's done." He stood and frowned at her.

She kept her back to him, her arms wrapped tightly around her middle. "Good. Now it's done. And now you're free to leave aren't you? You don't have to stay in here with me anymore. You can move that stuff away from the door, and you can leave, can't you?"

"Aye, I can." He didn't understand. Moments ago she was happy and playful. Now she had completely shut off from him.

Had she finally understood that she hadn't gone home as she'd thought she would? More than likely, and she was angry about it. Angry with him for what he'd done to her.

He moved the furniture and opened the door.

"Rosalyn should be back later today. Shall I send her to you when she arrives?" He spoke stiffly, without looking at her.

"Yes, please," she mumbled as she sat down in one of the chairs, her back still turned to him.

If he didn't know better, he'd think she was crying. There was no understanding women. Not any of them. This one least of all. He slammed the door shut behind him.

With luck, there might still be a bottle of Duncan's whisky in the room below.

Connor stood before the fireplace in his favorite room, staring into the ashes left by the fire, which had long since burned out. Even this room, with all its warm memories, gave him no comfort.

He held in his hand the proof he'd deliver to the king's man today. The proof that would free him to take charge of his destiny and that of his sister as well. The proof that had so offended Cate.

Margaret had brought the bedding to him earlier, dropping it in his lap and staring disapprovingly at him until he insisted she speak her mind. And speak her mind she did, telling him in no uncertain terms that she had expected better of him as a new husband on his wedding night. That she'd never thought the young man she'd helped to raise would leave his new bride so unhappy.

"She sits in her chair just staring into the fire. I canna get her to eat, or rise, or even to bathe, and you ken how she loves that. It fair shatters my heart what you've done to that wee lassie," she had scolded. "You'd be best off to go back up there right now and fix things between you, or you'll regret it for all yer days."

There was much about Cate he'd regret all his days. It shamed him that Margaret assumed he'd hurt Cate, but there was no way he could tell her the truth. That Cate mourned because she was still here when she'd expected to be returned to her own time and her family, not because he treated her ill on her wedding night.

He gave a short mocking laugh. It was, in fact, he who suffered, both the shame of having allowed a woman to entice him into breaking a sacred vow and, worse yet, the mental agony of knowing he would make the same choice if given the opportunity again. He could not refuse her; he wanted her too badly for that, no matter how he fought it.

Had Duncan's idea of asking her to stay been the answer to his problem? He wanted her body, there was no doubt about that. One night had done nothing to satisfy that need. He felt possessive of her, wanted to protect her. But could he ever feel more for her—could he ever trust her enough to allow himself to feel more for her? He didn't know if he would ever be able to answer that question.

Insistent knocking interrupted that line of thought, saving him from continuing to battle his inner demons for now. Niall poked his head around the door.

"They've arrived. The king's man is waiting in yer public solar below, as you requested."

"Good. Hae you told Rosalyn that Cate requires her attendance?" He didn't meet the man's eyes. He couldn't face the censure he feared he'd find there.

"Aye. She's on her way up to see our lady even now."

Connor turned, proof in hand, and headed out to face the man waiting in the room below.

Cate continued to sit as she had since Connor left her, huddled in the chair by the fire, her arms clasped around her middle. The tears had ceased long ago. She had none left. And still it hurt. It hurt so badly.

Proof. Last night had been nothing more to him than a way to provide proof of a consummated marriage. The time they spent together, the closeness they'd shared—none of it meant anything to him. It was all a little play for the benefit of his king and some mysterious "they" who were going to come to check, physically check, for crying out loud, whether or not the final act had been completed.

Still, it was her own fault, once again. He'd tried to tell her last night, made clear his feeling about women. Even tried to dissuade her from her rash decision to sleep with him, reminded her that it was his duty to protect her. She'd chosen to ignore it all, so sure she'd never have to face him again.

But she did have to face him again, humiliated as he rooted through the covers searching for his proof, his trophy, exposing it, and what they'd done, to the world.

So now what? Why was she still here? She desperately needed to talk to Rosalyn. She had to figure out what to do next. Rosalyn hadn't returned to the castle—at least, not as of an hour or so ago when Margaret had been in to change the bedding.

That had been truly awful. Margaret hastily changing the covers on the bed, hovering around, trying to get her to eat, sympathetically offering to prepare a hot tub so she could soak her "poor wee" body. And finally, her efficiently whisking away that all-important piece of evidence Connor would need to prove their wedding had ended successfully.

Cate wanted to curl up in a little ball on the bed and wallow in her pain, in her shame, but she didn't know if she'd ever be able to climb back into that bed again. It had seemed such a haven last night, a place separate from the rest of the world, a place where Connor had confided in her and shared his feelings. She had hoped then that he trusted her, cared for her. She'd been foolish enough to ignore everything he'd said, to let herself imagine he might love her.

Only a light tap sounded at her door before Rosalyn entered, drawing Cate from her melancholy thoughts.

"Niall said you wanted to see me? What is it?" she asked, coming into the room.

"I'm still here."

"Aye. Yer still here." Rosalyn continued to give her a questioning look.

"I'm still here. I did everything I was supposed to do. I got married. Connor gets to stay home, Mairi's safe. My task is done. I even wore the necklace all night. Why haven't I popped back to my own time yet?" Cate rose from the chair and walked to meet Rosalyn at the door as she spoke. "I don't understand."

Rosalyn took her hand and guided her back to the chairs, where she sat beside her.

"The necklace has nothing to do with it, Cate. The magic acts on its own. The necklace merely held the magic, pointing the way for Connor to find you. No." She shook her head sadly. "Yer still here because you've no done everything you asked for. It all must be finished before the magic will work."

"But I have. I asked to complete the task, to get married, to save Mairi, to go home safely." Cate shook her head in confusion. "Then I tied the cloth on the tree and . . . " She stopped in midsentence. Her eyes growing large, she slapped her hand over her mouth and groaned. "Oh no." She stood and started to pace. "No, no, it can't be that last bit. Not the true love thing. Don't tell me that's why I'm still here."

"Aye, I'm afraid it is." Rosalyn nodded sympathetically and patted the chair beside her, motioning for Cate to return to her seat.

"Well then, we just have to go back." Cate sat. "Back to your Faerie Glen. You'll just have to talk to them. Explain to them. That's not going to happen. I have to go home. I have to get away from here."

"Going back to the Glen will no help you. I'm afraid it disna work like that. I've no the power to change what was asked for that day."

"Well then, how does it work? You had the power to get me here."

Desperation clouded her mind. There had to be a way. She couldn't stay here, facing Connor every day knowing how he felt about her.

"You must try to understand the way of the magic. My ability is no so strong as some. My mother, for instance, was stronger in the power than I am. We, the daughters of the Glen, are marked from the beginning of our lives. The lighter the mark, the less power we can use. The first time we access the power, we go to the Glen of our mothers and ask to be recognized as a daughter of the Fae. If we hae the mark, the Faeries speak to us and lend us their power. Then we can . . . do things." She shrugged. "It's no so easy to explain. Since the power belongs to the Faeries, and they only lend it to us, it often works in the way they intend, no so much the way we do."

Rosalyn stood and paced, rubbing her hands together. "For any small things I might need, I could do them right here. But for something requiring a great deal of power, like reaching into time, I needed the magic of the Glen, to call on the power of those who live there. That's why we traveled there for me to cast the spell into the jewel."

"So, why wouldn't you be able to draw on that power again if we went back there now?"

Rosalyn stopped pacing and ran her hands up and down her arms. "There is no power strong enough to stop what the two of us hae brought about." She sat down again, taking Cate's hand.

"I still don't understand."

"All the power, the legend, the reason for the power—all of it flows directly from true love. There is only one true love for each of us. Remember the legend I told you? Pol's true love was Rose, and he lost her. It was for his love of her that he blessed all their daughters who carried his blood for the rest of time. He thought to ensure that they would be able to find their own true loves, no to lose them and suffer as he had."

"You told me that. There in the Glen, you told me the Faeries believe in true love." Cate whispered it, in awe.

Rosalyn rubbed Cate's hand between her own.

"Aye, I did, but I hae to tell you now, I did more than that." She took a deep breath before continuing. "When I said the words that would send the jewel into time, I had no idea where or when it would go, but I did ken who it would find. I charged the jewel to find a verra specific woman. The only woman who could heal the wounds of Connor's heart, the only woman destined to be his own true love."

"What?" Cate jerked her hand away and jumped up.

"Aye. And then you completed the ritual by asking for true love and tying a strip of yer true love's clothing to the tree." She shook her head sadly. "I'm sorry, Cate. There's no way to undo what we hae done. There is nothing stronger than the magic of true love."

Cate paced the length of the room. This couldn't be happening. She couldn't be trapped in this time, forever loving a man who couldn't love her in return. She stopped in front of Rosalyn, kneeling at her feet, taking her hands.

"And what if Connor can't love? Is it possible that one of the parties in this true love thing might choose not to participate?"

Rosalyn hesitated. "I canna answer that. It may be. That could explain why so many of us never get our true loves."

"Oh, Rosalyn." Cate dropped her head to the older woman's lap. "Do you have any idea what you've done to me? Connor doesn't love me. He'll never love me. He'll never love anyone. He doesn't trust any woman. He only knows betrayal from women. The only thing he wants in life is to see Mairi find a man of her own choice so he can go back to serving his king."

Rosalyn smoothed her hand over Cate's hair, petting her like a small child.

"He disna ken what he truly wants. His heart has suffered more wounds than his body. Until those wounds are healed, he'll never ken."

"Maybe if we explain it all to him. Maybe somehow that will . . ."

"No." The older woman stopped her. "You canna do that. The magic will no allow you to hear the truth of it until yer heart has made its own decision."

"But I don't understand. You just told me all about it. Why can't we tell Connor?"

"Because, child, yer heart has already made its decision." Rosalyn said it quietly, continuing the soothing strokes on Cate's hair.

"How do you know that?" she whispered, afraid to move, to see the other woman's face.

"I watched it happen. I saw it in yer eyes while you took yer vows in front of the chapel. I see it on yer face each time he touches you. If it were not so, if you had not already accepted the truth of how you feel about him, the magic would no hae allowed me to tell you now."

"What do I do?" Cate whispered still. "I don't know how I can stay here facing him every day knowing he doesn't love me." She lifted her head to look at Rosalyn, the tears she thought all used up returning. "Everything has just been an act for him, his feelings for me nothing more than honoring his oath to protect me. How do I even explain that I'm still here when he wants nothing to do with a wife, when he wants nothing more than to see me gone? It hurts so much."

Dropping her head, she sobbed, while Rosalyn resumed the comforting stroke down her hair.

"Weel, you canna leave. No until his heart allows him to admit he loves you."

"So you're saying, if he ever does fall in love with me, then I get zapped back home? That makes no sense." She spoke without lifting her head.

"Aye. Only then. The Fae make the rules, no us. They hae their reasons for what they do. For now, let's get you cleaned up and dressed. We need to go find yer husband and make him aware that you'll no be leaving us anytime soon." She smiled, and patting Cate's head, stood.

Cate sniffed loudly. "You know, this just continues to get better and better. I'm stuck here, in torment over a man who doesn't love me, and if he ever does love me, I'm instantly gone, and I never see him again. You do realize that those are some seriously sick-assed Faeries that you're related to, don't you?" She sat up, wiping at her eyes.

"Weel, the Fae do hae their own way of dealing with the world and with us."

Rosalyn smiled sweetly, looking for all the world like the proverbial cat that just ate the canary.

CHAPTER 23

꧁ ꧂

Robert MacQuarrie stood with his back to the door when Connor entered the public solar, a testament to the trust he had in Connor. The man turned and swept low in a courtly bow, smiling broadly.

"Robbie. I'd no expected it to be you here."

"Weel, escorting Duncan and yer ladies seemed a goodly task for a man like me. Add to that the chance to see you so soon after yer wedding, and I had no choice but to offer my services for the job."

"I'm in yer debt for looking after my sister. When I learned the MacPherson would be at the celebration, I sent Duncan to take her away someplace safe. I greatly appreciated Alexander's offer to send one of his men to assist in her protection."

Robert shook his head, smiling. "Yer sister is quite a . . . spirited lass."

Connor laughed. "Aye, she is that. I take it she was no too happy with the arrangements?"

"She dinna seem to appreciate missing the wedding celebration. When yer aunt led me to the crofters where

Duncan had taken her, we found he had her locked in a room there and had already assured the Maxwell family that you would replace all the furniture she broke." He grinned again. "I must say, when she kicked me as I hefted her onto my horse, I was fair pleased she'd left her shoes behind somewhere. She was indeed a handful, though a lovely lass."

"Aye, weel, as long as you remembered no to hae yer hands too full of her." Connor frowned at him.

Robert tipped his head in acknowledgment. "Aye, spoken like a true older brother." He laughed, holding up his hands in submission. "I'm no here to fight, no even for someone so lovely as her."

Which reminded Connor just what his friend was here for. He tossed the bedding he carried over to him.

"There. You can take it to Alexander so he can see I've done my job. By that he'll ken I'm no returning to his service."

He felt a twinge of guilt remembering Cate's reaction to what he was doing right now.

Robert held the cover up, then wadded it into a ball and tossed it into the fire, where the flames instantly began to lick through it.

"Alexander disna need to see yer proof. He'll take my word. And yers. And after meeting yer lovely new wife yesterday, he disna expect to see you in his service again. He's pleased to see you settled. We all are. Though, I must say, you dinna look quite so happy as I'd expected after seeing that fine lassie you married." He tilted his head inquiringly.

"She's no so happy with me right now." Connor

shook his head. "I swear I canna figure how her mind works."

"No so happy? Perhaps you dinna do yer job as husband as you should. Would you like me to show you how it's done then?"

At Connor's warning look, his friend laughed, again holding up his hands in surrender.

"I'm only haeing sport at yer expense, friend." He approached Connor and slapped him on the back. "I dinna ken everything there is to about women, but this I do: no man can figure how their minds work." He laughed. "Dinna try so hard. Just relax and enjoy her. You've yer whole lives together to figure her out. And from the looks of her, what a joy that should be." He slapped Connor's back again.

Another twinge. This time it was regret. Regret that his friend was wrong. That he wouldn't have his whole life to figure Cate out. That she could be gone even now as they stood here speaking of her. The thought left him feeling hollow.

"I'm sorry, Robbie. What did you say?" The man was still going on about something.

"Aye now, that's what I would expect from a new husband. Too busy thinking of more pleasant duties to pay attention to an old friend?" He laughed again. "I was telling you that I'll be taking advantage of yer hospitality for a while. Alexander has asked me to remain with you until he returns through this way. He dinna care for the look of the MacPherson, or the threat he poses. He thought you may hae need for some company." He shrugged. "As I said before, I ken you dinna need my help, but I go where my king sends me, and for now, he sends me here."

Connor nodded. "I plan to keep my gates closed to everyone, so I dinna think to need yer help. But yer welcome here all the same."

Unless the Fae had already taken Cate. Or they took her while she stood in the same room with Robbie. That might be difficult to explain to his friend.

That twinge again. Pain this time at the thought of Cate not being there.

"Dinna look so distressed, Connor. I'll promise no to eat my weight in food and I'm sure I'll be a much better practice partner than Duncan so you dinna go soft and lose yer sword arm. And should the MacPherson be foolish enough to come, he'll regret facing two of the king's best."

"Aye. Weel, sooner or later, he'll come. As I said, yer welcome for as long as Alexander chooses to leave you here."

He smiled at his friend. He'd just have to deal with all the other things as they came.

"Though I'm thinking the king's just tired of all the food and drink you use from his stores."

Robert smiled sheepishly. "Could be. Speaking of which, dinna I hear Duncan claim on more than one occasion that yer castle here had some of the verra finest heather ale to be found in all of Scotland? Do you suppose that you and yer lady will be sharing some of that with the likes of me tonight?"

Connor smiled. "Duncan and I both will join you. We'll hae to see about the company of my lady. I'll hae to ask Cate about that."

"Ask me about what?"

Both men turned to find Cate standing in the doorway, Rosalyn at her side.

Connor's heart leaped in his chest. They hadn't taken her yet. She was still here. Of course, what he was feeling was only relief that he wouldn't have to deal with explaining her absence yet.

"Connor? What did you need to ask me?"

When she tilted her head like that, the sunlight coming through the window fairly sparkled off her hair. She looked like a sun-drenched Faerie might.

Robert laughed quietly and caught him in the ribs with a quick elbow. "Honestly, old friend, you have to quit drifting off and pay attention. You'll hae her to yerself soon enough this eve'n." He whispered the last, still chuckling to himself.

Connor's face colored a dull red. He cleared his throat. "Robert will be staying with us for a while. He was just asking if you'd be joining us for heather ale this eve'n."

"Ah yes. The infamous ale Duncan loves so well. I would imagine my company could be arranged." She smiled and came forward, holding her hand out to Robert, who gallantly caught it and placed a kiss lightly on the back.

Connor glowered at his friend and pulled Cate to his side. "He'll be staying until Alexander comes back through this way."

"Well, we certainly seem to have plenty of room here for guests." Placing a hand on Connor's chest, she looked up at him. "When you've finished here, do you think we could have a few minutes alone? I need to speak to you."

"We're quite finished, milady." Robert bowed. "I'll leave him to yer care." He grinned broadly.

"Robert, why don't I get you all settled in a lovely room and show you where everything is." Rosalyn took his arm and led him out, shutting the door behind them.

Connor's heart pounded under Cate's hand, though his face displayed no emotion as he looked at her. Just another thing that had made him such a good warrior. Cate would bet he'd be a great poker player as well. Maybe she'd teach him the game. Just as soon as she figured out how to come up with a decent deck of cards. It appeared she'd certainly have the time.

"Yer still here. I'd thought you might . . . with Robert here and all, you ken? I wasnae sure of how to explain if you were gone. When you go, that is." He stopped. Without warning. Just shut his mouth and looked at her.

She smiled up at him, patting his racing heart. "Well, that's what I have to talk to you about. Let's sit and be comfortable, shall we?"

She took his hand and led him to some large chairs placed near the wall. As Rosalyn had suggested on the way here, she might as well make the best of this since there was no alternative. Of course, "best" could be a very subjective term depending upon how he reacted to her news.

"About that whole explaining-my-disappearance thing? You're not going to have to. It doesn't look like I'm going anywhere for a while."

"No?" His grip tightened on her hand.

But no change in expression. Yeah, this guy would make one seriously dangerous poker player.

"No."

"And why is that?" He still held her hand.

"It seems your aunt and I had a little communication problem that first day in the Faerie Glen. It appears that whatever we said to the Faeries . . ."

"She had you speak to the Fae?" he interrupted, sounding surprised. "That first day? While Duncan and I were hunting?"

"Yes. That's what we were doing while you were gone. She told you. She called it something like finishing up odds and ends. You didn't know?"

He shook his head. "No. It never occurred to me. I should hae guessed."

"Well, anyway, somewhere in those odds and ends we were tying up, one of us, me, said something she shouldn't have. So here I stay for now." She shrugged.

"What did you say? What exactly were the words that are keeping you here?"

She opened her mouth to tell him. *True love*. Nothing came out. She tried again. Nothing. *Rosalyn certainly knows her Faeries*.

"I'm waiting, Cate. What did you say to the Fae?"

"I can't tell you. Seriously. The words just won't come to me. I try, but they won't let me tell you. All I know is, here I am and here I stay for now."

Now the hard part.

"I know you weren't planning on being stuck with a wife, didn't want one at all, in fact. But there's not much I can do about this, so, the ball's in your court."

"Ball's in my . . . I dinna understand you. What are you trying to say to me?" He looked as confused as he sounded.

"Sorry. What I mean to say is that it's up to you now. What do you want to do with me? I can't go home. Tell me what you want me to do."

Something she couldn't readily identify flashed through his eyes before he lowered his head, effectively closing off his thoughts to her. He stared at the hand he still held, twisting the ring on her finger, around and around.

When he raised his head, he once again wore that perfect poker face.

"I swore to protect you until I could take you home. If yer no going home, you'll stay here where I can protect you. It's that simple."

"It's not simple at all. I don't really know how to do anything useful here in this time, Connor. I'll have to learn everything all over again. I don't know what to be, I don't know what to do."

He shook his head. "You dinna need to do anything useful. You'll continue to do the things you've done since you first came. Yer my wife now, aye? That's what you'll be then. It should no be so hard to learn." He patted her hand. "There. Simple. That's all settled then."

He stood and crossed the room to the fire. Leaning down, he shoved more of the wood into the flames and looked back at her over his shoulder.

"Dinna fash yerself, wee Caty. We'll work it all out in time. For now, let's go find Rosalyn and see what she's done with Robert. And you can practice yer wifely duties by helping me with Mairi. She's likely to be in a fine fury with me."

"We'll work it all out in time," he'd said. He was wrong. It wasn't about time. It was about love.

The food in front of her had gone cold, but it didn't matter to Cate. She had no appetite anyway.

She'd watched the men all through dinner, talking and joking, comfortable in one another's company. The three of them—Connor, Duncan and Robert—had obviously shared much together. They sat now, relaxed with mugs of ale in their hands, laughing over some exploit Duncan had recalled.

The calm shattered when young Ewan ran into the hall.

"There's a rider at the gate, Connor. He says he brings a message for you and he'll no leave until you see him."

Connor leaned forward in his chair. "Only one rider? Yer sure of it?"

The boy nodded, his eyes large and serious. "Aye. My da is out there now. I'm to ask if we should admit him."

"It's only one man, lad," Duncan mused. "We can handle that easily. Best to hear what he has to say so we ken what we're up against."

"Bring him in," Connor agreed.

All storytelling ceased as they waited silently for the messenger. The man appeared shortly, wet and dirty from his ride.

"Who are you and what do you want?" Connor spoke without rising from his seat.

The man looked around the hall, his gaze resting contemptuously on Rosalyn before he responded.

"I'll no speak of this in front of the witch."

Connor rose slowly from his chair, his eyes hard upon the man in front of him. "My aunt is no a witch, and I dinna appreciate yer insult of her. You'll apologize now if you wish to leave this hall with yer head intact."

"No," Rosalyn interjected, rising from her chair, drawing all eyes. "There's no need for the man to apologize. I canna be insulted by the ignorant and superstitious. I'll be retiring now anyway." She turned to Cate and Mairi. "Will you ladies join me?"

Silence hung heavy in the hall as the three of them exited. Her curiosity aroused, Cate stopped outside the door, peeking through the narrow opening they'd left.

Connor still stood, frowning at the visitor, who launched into what appeared to be a formal introduction of his purpose.

"I come as a messenger of the Clan MacPherson, personal envoy of Red Dunald, laird of the MacPherson, to deliver his demand to you, Connor MacKiernan."

"And what *demand* might that be?"

"You are instructed to deliver one Mairi MacKiernan, yer sister, to the chapel in the village below, come one week from this Saturday, her to be given over to wed the MacPherson himself on that day." The messenger nodded his head emphatically at the end of his little speech.

Connor calmly seated himself, and took a drink of his ale before answering.

"No."

"What?" The messenger seemed flustered. "That's yer reply to the MacPherson?"

Connor leaned back, propped both his feet on the table, one crossed over the other, and regarded the man for a moment. "My reply is this. First, that being my sister's birthday, I've no intention of taking her anywhere at all. Second, I dinna seem to remember anyone, particularly someone so esteemed as the MacPherson himself, approaching me to ask for my sister's hand. If yer laird has fancy for the lass, perhaps he'd best announce his intent." Connor took another drink from his mug. "At the direction of our laird, the MacKiernan himself, we MacKiernans follow the old customs when it comes to marriage."

The messenger turned on his heel, heading toward the door.

Cate, fearing she'd be caught, started for the stairs, only to have an arm dart out of a doorway and grab her, dragging her inside. A soft hand clamped over her mouth.

"Shh," Rosalyn cautioned. "If yer going to listen in, you hae to learn the nearest hiding places," she whispered.

"No even the common courtesy to let you enjoy yer new wife for few days before he started in." Robert shook his head in disgust.

Connor shrugged. "It was only a matter of time before it began."

"Good thing I'm here." Robert grinned and refilled his mug.

"Aye? 'Cause I dinna remember hearing a word from you to the flustered lad who just left."

"Exactly my point. He had need only to look at me sitting here beside you, and the fear sent him running back to his mighty laird."

Connor shook his head, smiling in spite of himself at his friend's audacity. Still, there was no better man to have at his side in the coming days. He reached for the pitcher of ale only to have Robert whisk it away, withholding it from his reach.

"No, my friend, I dinna think you get any more of this. Duncan and I will finish here while you go upstairs and see to yer new bride."

Robert and Duncan both chuckled as Connor rose and left the room. He stopped outside the door, wondering what awaited him up the spiral stairs.

Cate sat on the floor in front of the fire waiting for *her husband* to arrive. Her hands shook and her stomach pitched, making her glad she hadn't eaten. With what she'd learned from Rosalyn, she had made her decision. Now she had only to see it through.

After leaving the small larder where they'd hid, the women had just parted ways when a thought occurred to Cate. A question for which she needed an answer.

"Why have you never married, Rosalyn? Why have you never found your own true love?"

The woman stopped, her back rigid before she turned. "Oh, I found him. I'm still waiting for him to realize that he loves me."

"How long have you waited?" Cate was caught by the sadness in her new aunt's eyes.

"Almost twenty years now."

"What? Why haven't you done something, said something to him?"

"Now, Cate, did you no say yerself, we canna force true love? If it's meant to be, it will be."

Cate had watched, stunned, as Rosalyn disappeared beyond the entry to her tower.

Twenty years. It would be one thing to search that long, but to have found the right person and do nothing?

Not for her. She wasn't willing to wait patiently for twenty years, or to settle for less than the real thing.

Jesse may have been right that love happened when you least expected it, but she was going to gamble everything on his being wrong about your not being able to make it happen.

Make it happen she would; she only needed to figure out how. And quickly, she thought, listening to the footsteps approaching her door.

Cate looked up at Connor as he entered. She rose to her feet, but didn't move toward him, didn't say a word.

An uncharacteristic knot formed in his stomach—too much ale perhaps; surely not apprehension. He had no reason to be concerned about what went on behind the veil of this woman's eyes.

He strode into the room possessively. It was his bedchamber. Reaching the center of the room, he stopped and drew off his shirt, turning to the woman who was now his wife.

She stood motionless, watching him as if waiting for his next move.

His wife. The words knifed at him.

He deliberately arched an eyebrow and swaggered over to her, determined to demonstrate his bravado.

She didn't resist when he pulled her to him, kissing her face, her neck, her soft, pliable lips. But other than her rapid breathing, she didn't respond either.

He drew back to look down at her. Her eyes, the color of a deep forest glen, should have been warning enough that something was amiss.

He ignored the warning, kissing her neck again. Grasping the ties to her overskirt, he tugged and her hands came up to rest against his bare chest, as if holding him at bay.

"Connor?" she whispered, trembling in his arms now.

"Aye, wee Caty?" he whispered back, not completely sure which of them trembled.

"Do you love me?"

"What?" He drew back from her again. What non-sense was this?

She pulled away from him, her hand trailing down his chest, leaving a trill of sensation in its wake.

"Before we go any further, I have to know where I stand with you." She looked up at him, her eyes dark and serious.

"Where you stand? Yer my wife, are you no? I thought we'd settled this earlier."

She backed up another step and he took one toward her, almost unconsciously, as if stalking his prey.

"Technically. But that's not what I'm asking. Do you

love me?" She took another step back from him, crossing her arms under her breasts.

He stared at her, mute, unable to answer her question.

"Okay." She nodded as if to herself. "If not love, do you trust me?"

"Trust you?" He choked on the words. Trust a woman? He could never have imagined her asking this of him.

"No? Then we'll just have to see how much I can trust you; how much that honor of yours is really worth."

"What?" She questioned his honor? He closed the distance between them in one stride, grabbing her arm, pulling her close enough that she'd feel his breath when he spoke. A move calculated to intimidate. "Explain yerself, woman."

"I can't be your wife, not in that sense. I can't give my body to any man who doesn't love me, doesn't trust me."

"Then what was last night?" The trembling was her, her arms shivering under his fingers.

"Apparently a mistake," she whispered, lowering her head.

He drew her to him, burying his face in the warm curve of her neck until she spoke. Her voice shook, but her words stopped him.

"You swore to protect me from harm. If you take me against my will, you'll be the cause of that harm. So what of your precious honor now?"

He let go of her arms and stepped back, searching her face for her true feelings. He saw only determination. Yet her chin trembled as if she might cry. Fear? That cut deep, the thought that the woman he'd sworn to protect was afraid of him.

He turned and walked away, stopping only to pick up his shirt before leaving the room. His mind raged at the swirl of unfamiliar emotions assaulting him as he descended the stairs. He would not lose control.

"Connor?"

His aunt's sharp voice halted his progress. She stood at the bottom of the staircase, hands clasped behind her back.

"Where do you think yer going?"

She hadn't used that tone with him since he was a small lad and it rankled his raw feelings now.

"To find someplace with no a woman in sight to get very drunk and go to sleep."

"I dinna think so, Nephew. As long as yer friend Robert stays here, you'll do weel to keep up the pretense of haeing a loving wife upstairs. You dinna want the king thinking this is no a real marriage, do you? You've yer sister, yer whole family to be thinking of."

She was right. He wanted to yell at her, push her out of his way and continue on, but she was right. He had no choice.

He turned and went back upstairs, stopping at the closed door. He reached for the knob, then changed his mind, sitting down on the landing. He'd wait for a bit. Give the woman inside time to climb into bed and go to sleep. Then he'd go inside and pull his chair near the fire.

He leaned back against the door, preparing for yet another long night.

CHAPTER 24

Life settled into an uneasy routine of long days and even longer nights.

Cate spent the better part of her days with Mairi or alone in the gardens. Working with the herbs felt familiar to her, almost like being in her own little garden back home. When there was nothing to do, as was frequently the case, she could at least sit in peace and think. A pastime that was not always so peaceful.

The castle had a few books, thanks to the foresight of Connor's parents and grandparents, though they were more along the lines of manuscripts than books. They'd look beautiful under glass in a museum. Some were in Latin, which she had studied at school and might have eventually deciphered. At least one was written in Greek. But the whole lot of them were hand copied in a flowing manuscript that was totally illegible to her.

Connor read them late into the night. Every night. Sitting by the fire in their room, only crawling into bed long after he thought she was asleep. Which of course she wasn't. She was beginning to think she'd never have a peaceful night's sleep again. *Damn those Faeries, anyway.*

The same evening she had informed Connor that she was staying, Rosalyn had pointed out that with Robert in the castle, they'd better figure out a way to share their bedchamber, or it would be pretty difficult to hide the fact that they weren't. So they retired to the same room each evening.

Connor built a large screen for one corner of the room so that she could change her clothes in privacy. Every evening she would slip into her overly long nightgown and climb into bed while he sat by the fire reading. She would pretend to sleep, and hours later he would finally crawl into his side of the huge bed. They kept their distance at all times.

She only hoped he was suffering as much as she was, but she didn't see any real signs of it, other than his looking tired all the time and being a bit grouchy when his friend Robert joked about new husbands who didn't get enough sleep.

It was midafternoon and she had completely exhausted her list of things to do. She had weeded in the gardens until there were no weeds anywhere to be found. Margaret shooed her out of the kitchen every time she even made an appearance. Rosalyn was busy with her needlework, and Cate's only attempt at that had been disastrous. Even Mairi was busy elsewhere.

Early that morning one of the maids from Dun Ard, Florie, had shown up at the outer gate, carrying a message for Mairi from her cousin Lyall, and Cate hadn't seen the two of them since they'd run off to Mairi's chambers.

After standing in the middle of the great hall feeling useless for a while, Cate decided a change of location was in order. She would go outside and feel useless there. At least the scenery would be better.

Cate walked out onto the landing of the great staircase and leaned on the railing. She really loved this spot and thought she might ask Connor to build a bench for her here. She could see far off into the distance, down the hillside and over the entire courtyard from this point.

Best of all, from here she could watch Connor and Robert doing their daily exercise with swords. She never tired of watching him, especially when, like now, he'd gotten warm and removed his shirt. Even from here she could see the muscles rippling under the skin of his back and on his arms.

Cate still had no real plan for making Connor love her. She had begun to think of all this as a game she and Connor played. Neither of them knew the rules or the boundaries, only that the stakes were very high. She sometimes resented the fact that more than likely, Connor didn't even realize he was involved in a contest. And in spite of his unknowing participation, she feared that, ultimately, she was going to lose. She wasn't sure how much longer she'd be able to hold out in the game without making a complete fool of herself. It was only a matter of time before she broke down and threw herself at him. She wanted him that much.

She suspected he wouldn't refuse her, since he did seem to find her physically attractive, but that really wasn't the way she wanted it. He might never love her, but if she could at least earn his trust, life would be good.

Well, as good as life could be without caffeine in any form, and without chocolate, potatoes, tomatoes or chili peppers. The thirteenth century was sorely lacking in Cate's favorite foods. She sighed, and was momentarily lost in a good fantasy about a baked potato smothered in sour cream when she heard Ewan's warning yell.

"Riders approach."

The men below scrambled, hurrying up the stairs to the wall tower where Ewan stood watch.

From where she stood, Cate counted eight horses riding hard. Hiking up her skirts, she raced down the steps and across the courtyard to the wall tower stairs. She climbed those quietly, staying in the shadow of the door, just far enough out to see, but not far enough to attract the attention of the men gathered in front of her.

She immediately recognized Artair and the MacPherson among the riders at the gate. The others were men she didn't remember seeing before.

"Connor MacKiernan." It was one of the men she didn't know. "As you dinna show at the chapel at the appointed time three days ago, we've come to claim Mairi MacKiernan for bride to the MacPherson as granted by the laird of the MacKiernan. Open yer gates and send her out."

Connor propped his leg up on the wall, laying his sword across his knee.

"That's fair odd. I dinna remember having granted permission for my sister to marry. Did I mention such a thing to you, Robert?"

He spoke loudly, for the benefit of those on the horses below rather than those gathered on the wall with him.

"Now that you ask, I dinna remember yer having told me of such a thing. Duncan, did he speak to you of this?" Robert also spoke loudly for the benefit of those below.

"No, I dinna believe he did." Duncan shook his head, scratching his beard. "And I'm sure I would hae remembered such as that."

Connor yelled down to the men below. "I dinna believe I'll be sending Mairi out this day. You can tell the MacPherson he's made a mistake. There's no agreement for him to marry my sister. You must have the wrong MacKiernan lass."

"Be reasonable, Connor. You were aware that I arranged this before yer return. It was settled long ago. Send the girl out. Make this easy on all of us," Artair shouted.

"No, I dinna think so, Uncle. Mairi expresses no desire to wed Red Dunald MacPherson, and she's told you as much. She's no going to marry any man she disna want. You of all people should understand that. She'll remain behind my gates. She's under my protection now." He smiled down at the men, his eyes glinting dangerously.

Robert took a position similar to Connor's, sword across his knee, leaning out a bit to look down on his audience.

"And under mine as weel. And as I'm a representative of the king, that puts her under the protection of King Alexander the Third. I dinna think you'd want to challenge him for her hand, now would you?" He grinned down at the men below and slapped Connor on the back, speaking quietly to his friend. "See, that's how you do it.

Look at that fat one. He's about to have an apoplexy. His face is turning purple." He chuckled.

"Yer a fool, MacKiernan." It was the MacPherson, Red Dunald himself, this time. "Yer laird has ordered it. You hae no choice in the matter. You must obey. Send her out to me now."

"I dinna obey Artair. He's no more my laird than you are, MacPherson. He's my uncle, that's all. I've sworn no fealty here. My only loyalty is to the king." Connor continued to smile down at them, his hand stroking the sword on his knee.

"And you'd best remember that Alexander is loyal to those who've sworn to him. Any aggression against this castle will be looked on as aggression against the king himself." Robert looked at Connor and nodded. "That raised the price for him, did it no?"

He and Connor both chuckled this time.

Cate watched them in fascination. They stood, stripped to the waist, perspiration glistening on their muscles. Hollywood had never gotten it quite right. These men, these warriors, joking and taunting their opponents below seemed to be enjoying themselves. They were a study in elegant leashed violence, just waiting for the moment to burst loose. She shivered, convinced that it would be a fierce thing to witness, repelled and enthralled at the same time.

The MacPherson spoke quietly to Artair before he and his men turned their horses and rode away, leaving Artair below, staring up at the men on the tower walk.

"You'll regret this, you ungrateful cur. I'll see to it that you regret this. After all I've done for you, you'll no ruin everything for me. You'll no have it all back." He screamed at his nephew, shaking his fist in the air before turning his own horse to gallop away.

"Weel, I would no count on being invited for holiday celebrations with yer uncle this year." Robert shook his head.

He and Connor were both laughing as they all turned to leave the wall when they caught sight of Cate.

Connor stopped, placing both hands on his hips, a small scowl on his face, his eyebrow arched as usual. "And what are you doing up here?"

The others continued past her, exchanging winks and smiles as they hurried down the stairs.

Cate tipped her head and looked at him thoughtfully before answering, the seeds of a plan forming in her mind. "Being impressed."

His eyes widened in surprise. "Aye? Impressed were you? Did you no think yer husband could handle the likes of them?"

Her husband. The words momentarily rattled her but she quickly recovered. "Oh, I figured you could handle them. I just didn't know you could look so good doing it." She smiled, strolling over to him.

"Good, eh? If you liked that, you should hae seen me with the Saracens, or even the Norsemen. I could hae truly impressed you with the likes of them. Now those were worthy opponents, not like this bunch." He smiled at her and, putting his arm around her shoulders, walked her down the stairs. As they reached the bottom, she slid her arms around his waist and gave him a little hug.

Again he looked surprised. "What did I do to earn that?"

"Nothing in particular. It's just for being you." There was no point in her adding that it gave her the opportunity to run her hands over the glistening muscles that appealed to her so much.

She started across the courtyard, pleased at the look of confusion on his face.

"Caty?" He caught up with her and twirled her around to face him. "In the future, you'll no be on the tower walk when riders come. I'll no hae you being a target for their archers. You'll just hae to find somewhere else to be impressed with me." He twirled her back around and smacked her on her bottom. "Now off with you, lass. I've work to do." He turned and walked away, laughing.

She stared after him, the seeds of her plan sprouting full bloom. Oh yeah, she'd been going about this all wrong.

CHAPTER 25

Cate sat among the herbs for the better part of the afternoon, contemplating her dilemma, finalizing her plan. She was living with a man she loved with all her heart, and yet she was pretty much as unhappy as she could possibly be since he didn't love her in return. She knew that for a fact because, if he did, she wouldn't be here. Sighing deeply, she rolled her eyes at the absurdity of her situation.

It occurred to her while watching Connor on the wall today that maybe she was approaching this whole thing incorrectly. She was dealing with a warrior. She needed to think of this not as a game, but as a battle.

Being a woman who liked to take into account all her alternatives before acting, she considered what options were available to her.

Her first option was to continue as she had been, waiting and hoping that maybe someday Connor would fall madly in love with her, and the whole time she waited, she'd continue to be miserable. Considering how long Rosalyn had waited in vain for her true love, Connor might never make that leap. And even if he did, she'd be gone and still miserable.

Her second option was to look at this battle thing in a whole new light. Watching those men up there today, laughing and joking in the face of danger, she'd been struck with how they seemed to enjoy themselves. Perhaps that was what she'd never quite grasped in life—the ability to find and take what joy she could.

She had already faced the fact that sooner or later she was going to give herself to this man, so why not do it on her own terms? She might be going to lose this battle, but at least she could go down in a blaze of glory that would leave Connor wondering just who had won the war.

And maybe, just maybe, her brother was wrong and it was the Faeries who had the right of it. Perhaps you really could urge true love along, if you only worked at it.

All things considered, she'd spent way too much of her life just reacting to whatever came along. The time had come to stop letting life happen and start *making* life happen. She was finally ready to take charge and follow a brand-new battle plan.

Cate stepped back and admired her handiwork. It looked pretty good, even if she did say so herself. She'd moved the chairs off to the side of the room and placed a large fur in front of the fireplace. The fire was burning low. She'd scrounged extra candles and had placed them around the room. They added a warm glow to the area. Sitting next to the fur was a bottle of Connor's favorite whisky, a pot of her tea and two large cups. The book he was currently reading was waiting there on the fur as well, an important part of her plan.

Finally she'd changed into her silk pajamas. Connor seemed to have something of a fascination with the little top.

She smiled at the thought. If physical attraction was the best weapon in her arsenal at the moment, she'd just have to make use of it.

Battle lines were drawn, awaiting only the firing of the opening shot. She smiled broadly as she heard his step outside the door.

"If I'm going to lose anyway, I might as well enjoy doing it," she murmured.

"Who were you speaking . . . what hae you done in here?" Connor stopped just inside the door, looking around.

"Just a little rearranging. I thought, if you didn't mind, perhaps you'd be willing to help me learn to decipher the writing in your books." She nodded toward the book on the floor. "I'm an educated woman in my world. It's very frustrating not being able to even read here simply because of the style of the writing." She smiled at him, hoping for an innocent look.

"Aye, weel, if that's what you'd like, of course I'll try to help you." He rubbed his hands down his plaid, and slowly moved toward the fire. "You've moved the chairs?"

"I did. I thought it would be easier if we sat on the floor. That way I can follow along while you're holding the book rather than having to lean across the chair arms to see."

He stood by the fire, rubbing his hands together. "You've added some candles."

"Well, the writing is already difficult for me to read. No point having it dark as well."

He looked down at the whisky and then back to her with the familiar arched eyebrow. "And this?"

Cate sighed deeply for effect.

"Well, Connor, you're not the most patient man in the world. So, if I go more slowly than you expect, perhaps a small drink will help to calm you." She smiled brightly again.

He smiled back now, narrowing his eyes. "And what yer wearing?"

"Well, if I'm going to be sitting on the floor, pants are the most discreet thing I could possibly wear. And these are the only pants I have."

The man had the truly suspicious nature of a successful warrior. Time to up the offensive with her next weapon.

"Are you going to question absolutely everything I've arranged? If you don't want to help me, just tell me and I'll forget the whole thing." She crossed her arms under her breasts and backed away from him. A small pout was her crowning touch.

He swiftly came across the room, bringing his hand to rest on her shoulder. "No, no. I dinna mean to upset you. I'd be pleased to work with you on the book. I was just . . . surprised by yer request." He shrugged his shoulders and led her over to the fur. "Hae a seat and we'll get started."

Sitting down next to him, she poured whisky into his

cup and tea into hers while he opened the book to the spot where he'd left off the night before.

"What exactly do you want me to do?" He favored her with his now familiar arched eyebrow.

She started at his question, blushing at the first thought that raced through her mind, a thought that didn't involve the book he held at all. It had much more to do with his lips. And hands. And . . .

"Um, well, for a start, why don't you go over the individual letters so I can begin to recognize them. The writing is quite different from what I'm used to."

She moved to her knees and scooted slightly behind him so that, kneeling, she could look over his shoulder. She could also lightly touch her body to his back in the process. Her heart pounded so hard at the contact, she wondered if he noticed it.

"Are you sure you can see from there?" When he turned to look at her, their faces almost touched, and he quickly leaned away, into the book. "Perhaps I'd best start over from the beginning," he mumbled, flipping to the first page.

"The beginning would be good," she acknowledged.

They spent the next ten minutes with him pointing out the individual letters in each word on the pages before them, Connor appearing to concentrate diligently on each one.

Time to advance the lines a bit.

Cate leaned into him, raising her arms to take down her braid.

"Perhaps we've done enough for tonight and you should get yer rest." He closed the book and stood.

No, that wasn't at all what she wanted.

"Connor?" She placed her hand on his thigh to stop him.

He froze.

"Could I ask for a small favor?"

"Aye." His voice sounded a bit strained. "I'll do what I can."

"Would you rub my shoulders? My muscles are all knotted. I don't think I'd ever be able to get to sleep like this."

She let her hand slide slowly down his leg before lifting it to gather her hair on top of her head. She waited.

"Aye. I can do that if it will help you."

He waited for a moment before rejoining her on the fur. Then he reached over and, picking up his cup, drained it. He rubbed his hands together nervously before placing them on her shoulders.

"It is somewhat warm in here," he muttered.

"It certainly is. Oh, just a second." She dropped her hair and turned to flash him a quick smile. "This will make it so much better." She pulled her jacket off over her head and tossed it away, following up with a deep, satisfied sigh.

"There now." She piled her hair up again, turned her back to him and waited.

His breathing sounded a little fast as he lightly placed his hands back on her shoulders and very gently pressed. "Is this what you wanted?" His voice was as unsteady as his hands.

She dropped her head forward, letting go of her hair so it fell over his fingers. Then she moaned.

"Harder, Connor. Much harder." She intentionally used the breathiest voice she could manage, hoping she wasn't going too far.

With a strangled sound he abruptly stood. "I canna do this."

Her moment of truth had come; time for her to pull out all the stops and aggressively pursue what she wanted. She'd already determined to do whatever it took.

She turned and rose to her knees in front of him, angling her shoulder so that one of her camisole straps slid down onto her arm. "I don't understand. What's wrong?"

Breathing hard, he looked down at her with tortured eyes. "Dinna you ken what yer doing to me? I'm only a man. You've made it clear to me, I'm no to touch you. What is it you want from me?"

Locking her eyes on his, she placed her hands on his knees and slowly began to slide them up, under his plaid, allowing herself to savor the feel of his muscles tensing under her fingers.

"Everything," she whispered. "All of you."

He sank to his knees and, grasping her upper arms, he pulled her to him. "Are you sure you ken what yer doing?" His voice was husky with need.

Cate smiled slowly, leaning into him. "No. I have no idea what I'm doing. The only thing I'm sure of is that I want you."

He let go of her arms, his breathing ragged. "If I dinna leave now, I'll no be able to . . . I dinna think . . ."

She stopped him with a finger to his lips. "Exactly. Don't think anymore. Just do." She slid her arms around his neck, her hands twining in his hair as she brought her mouth up to his.

His arms wrapped around her, carrying her to her back on the fur beneath him. She slid one hand down to drag the plaid from his shoulder and tugged at the laces on his shirt with the other. Pulling back from her to his knees, he drew the shirt off over his head.

At Cate's sharp intake of breath he smiled brashly, his teeth gleaming in the firelight. "Do you like that then?"

Running her hands across the muscles of his chest, she answered breathlessly. "Oh yes. Very much." She grinned up at him. "I think you may have found that new way to impress me."

Eyes narrowing, his smile turned blatantly seductive. "I've no even begun to impress you yet, lass. But I will. My turn now." Sliding his hands up her sides, he slipped her camisole off over her head, growling as he gazed at her. "I canna tell you how long I've wanted to do that."

"What else do you want to do?" She could only whisper, every nerve ending in her body screaming for his hands to be on her.

"This." He covered her body with his, kissing her mouth, making his way down to her throat, kissing, lightly nipping as he relentlessly moved lower.

The sensations of his bare chest moving against her breasts whet her appetite for more. Soon his hand replaced his chest, his fingers kneading, circling, inflaming her. And when she thought it could get no better, his mouth replaced his hand, his tongue teasing her nipple into a hard little mound.

She moaned, low and needy.

And he pulled back from her.

She didn't think she could live through it if he quit now. She could barely think, barely speak, but she had to.

"No. Don't stop." She opened her eyes to find that brash, confident smile she loved.

"I'm no stopping. I dinna believe I could stop now even if you asked it of me." He gave her a heart-melting grin. "I plan to impress you as no other man ever has."

"You're well on your way to it." She wasn't lying. The last time they'd done this, she'd been completely inexperienced and it had been accomplished in near darkness. Now in the glow of the fireplace, the light cast by the candles reflected off the hard muscled planes of his body. She found the sight of him almost as arousing as his touch.

Almost.

She kicked off her pajama bottoms and he grinned.

Leaning over her, he lifted her arms above her head and, holding them there, kissed her again, long and slow, his tongue dancing in and out of her mouth. She met him thrust for thrust.

He ran his fingers down her arms, along her sides to her stomach, just under the elastic of her panties.

"Does this scrap of lace you wear serve some purpose?"

She could only nod.

His fingers continued to run back and forth just under the cloth, slowly, erotically. She could think of nothing but his hand, what he was doing, the sensations pooling just below where his fingers lingered.

He laughed, sliding the lace down her legs and tossing

them away. Then he stood and she watched in the flickering light of the fire as he unwound his plaid, dropping it to the floor.

So now she'd seen for herself what was under those plaids. And if he was at all representative, it was probably a good thing they kept everyone in suspense. Otherwise they'd be beating back hoards of women at the airports all over Scotland. She grinned up at him.

"Are you still impressed then?" A confident smile this time.

"Very much so."

"Weel, if you liked that, just wait till you see what comes next."

He breathed harshly as he moved over her, that slow, seductive smile sending arousal tingling through her whole body.

"As I recall, it only gets better."

"Oh, aye, wee Caty, I promise you. Much, much better."

Her skin was so soft it gave him pleasure just to stroke it. And her smell, like a field of flowers. He buried his nose in the curve of her neck and breathed her in, relishing the moment.

Whatever had caused her to change her mind, he prayed it never ended. He'd do whatever he could to see to that.

He kissed his way down her neck and lower, stopping to worship at each of her breasts, enjoying the feel of her soft little hands stroking his back, fluttering at his shoulders before gliding up to comb through his hair. He'd never guessed having fingernails trailing lightly against his scalp could be so stimulating.

He slid his hands down to her waist, marveling at how delicate she felt in his grip. With his thumbs, he brushed lower, onto her stomach, pleased when he felt her muscles quiver at his touch. He kissed her breastbone and lower, allowing his tongue to linger against her sweet, fragrant skin, reveling in her soft intake of breath when he reached her navel, once again dipping and swirling, nibbling his way around the edge.

Down over the smooth, firm skin of her bottom he slid his hands, extending his fingers, reaching her thighs, spreading them, running his palms up, around, and into the curls that drew his attention.

His thumb circled, searching. When she gasped, hips undulating in unison with his movement, he felt as masterful as he ever had in battle, knowing he'd found his mark.

He held her close when her body shuddered and she called out his name, inflaming his own arousal.

"Now, Connor, now," she pleaded breathlessly, a request he was more than ready to fulfill.

Again he spread her thighs, this time to center himself against her, moving slowly into the familiar warm haven he had visited only once before. His hands grasped her hips, whether to pull her close or to anchor himself he wasn't sure, didn't care any longer.

Her tight heat surrounded him, inch by inch, as he fought to slow his response, to prolong the intense pleasure of this experience.

"Now, Connor, now," she cried, locking her legs behind him, tilting her hips into him.

"Now," he echoed, surging into her, again and again, over and over, carried on a wave of overpowering passion.

As he felt her body stiffen and convulse around him, he slowed, holding her tightly to him until his own imminent release forced him to plunge one last time into the welcoming paradise that was Cate, his body throbbing, pulsing, leaving him exhausted and weak.

Until he looked into the eyes of the woman who lay under his body. They shone with a satisfaction he knew he had put there.

He rolled to his back, pulling her with him. She snuggled into him, her soft, aromatic hair under his chin, her warm, slick body molded to his.

At that moment, he wanted to roar as he would on the field of battle. His woman was well impressed and he felt victorious.

CHAPTER 26

Cate lay in his arms marveling at the man. When Connor promised better, he certainly delivered.

Deciding to go for the joy in life had been the best choice she'd ever made. She'd had no idea she could feel like this. Even if he could never bring himself to truly love her, she thought, she just might be able to live with this. It might not be love, but it was very, very good.

Lifting her head from his chest, she looked up at his face and grinned when she saw his eyebrow arch, that slow smile forming on his lips again.

"Do you think you might be up to haeing me impress you again then?" His hands under her arms, he slowly slid her body up his until their mouths were almost in contact.

"Well, I can certainly feel that you're up for it again." She giggled until he pulled her down, filling her senses with another of his mind-numbing kisses.

"Wow," she whispered when he let her go.

"I take it that's good?" He had the look of a man who knew the excellence of his own performance.

"Good enough that I'm willing to give you another shot at it."

She grinned at him again, moving her hand down his body until her fingers wrapped around what she sought.

He sucked in his breath, his eyes darkening.

"Aye, wee Caty, I'm fair ready to impress you again. Now. I canna wait."

In one powerful move, he flipped her to her back, sliding his knee between her legs to push them open as he covered her mouth with his own.

This was heaven.

She'd just wrapped her leg around his back when the pounding started.

"Get the bloody hell away from my door." He moved away from her face only long enough to yell, smiling as he returned to plunder her mouth.

"Connor, you must come." It was Margaret outside the door, sounding frantic. "You must hurry. It's Lyall at the gate, and Niall says he's hurt."

"Och, Christ," he moaned as he pulled away from her, resting his forehead on hers for a moment before rising and grabbing his plaid. "Dinna you move from that spot." His eyes had that dangerous glint as he headed out the door.

The instant he was gone, Cate jumped from the bed and retrieved her own clothing, shoving her arms into the little jacket. As she ran out the door, she nearly fell over Beast, who stood panting on the stair landing. "Okay, boy, come with me if you want, but for crying out loud, stay out from under my feet." Horses, even in dog form, seemed to plague her here.

* * *

The courtyard was a bustle of activity, the dark pierced only in spots by light from the torches at the bottom and top of the stairs and the one Niall held. Robert pulled Lyall down from his horse. The young man appeared exhausted, nearly falling from his mount into Robert's arms. He grabbed for Connor, pleading frantically for help.

Racing down the stairs, Cate was knocked aside as Beast bolted past her, snarling and growling. She grabbed the railing to stop herself from falling.

"Beast!" Connor yelled, not taking his eyes from Lyall. "Ewan. Take Beast to the cellar and leave him there. He must hae got the scent of whoever was following Lyall. I canna deal with him now."

As Cate approached more closely, she saw blood trickling from the corner of Lyall's mouth, and cuts above his eye.

"Calm yerself, Lyall. Slow down and take a deep breath." Connor was supporting his cousin's weight, moving him toward the stairs to take him inside. "What are you trying to tell me about Mairi?"

"He has her. Even now he rides, most likely to the MacPherson. I could no stop him. I tried. We hae to go now if we're to save her." His head sagged against Connor, and Robert slipped under his other arm, helping to support his weight.

"Duncan. Go to Mairi's rooms. See that she's there." Connor continued toward the stairs. He scowled at Cate when he noticed her.

"Did I no tell you to stay where you were, woman?" A small smile played about his lips, even as he struggled with the weight of his cousin, when she snorted and raised an eyebrow in imitation of an expression he used often.

"Verra weel. Make yerself useful then. Find Rosalyn to help the lad."

She took off running up the stairs, meeting Rosalyn just inside the door. The woman was dressed only in her nightgown, looking very distressed, clutching her healing basket tightly to her. That alone frightened Cate more than anything else tonight. Rosalyn was never afraid.

They followed as the men lifted Lyall onto a chair in the great hall. Margaret appeared with a bucket of warm water.

Rosalyn's hand shook as she dabbed at Lyall's forehead. "I've a bad feeling, Connor. Something's verra wrong. I dinna ken what it is, but I've no felt this for many, many years."

Tension sparked in the look that passed between Connor and his aunt. He placed a hand on her shoulder and would have spoken, but Duncan burst into the hall yelling.

"She's gone. I searched the whole of the tower. Her bed's no been touched."

Lyall lifted his head. "Aye, I tried to tell you." He groaned and Rosalyn put a cup of whisky to his lips.

"What's happened to Mairi? Who has my sister?" Connor's eyes blazed with fury.

"It's Blane. He sent Florie with a message earlier, as if it were from me, telling her to meet me, that I needed her to come right away. That I was in trouble and needed her help. I found Florie weeping in the stables, and she told me the whole story. She dinna want to do it, but she was afraid of what would happen to her if she dinna obey."

Connor stepped back and exchanged a hard look with Duncan, who left the hall at a run.

"Where are they now?"

"I'm no positive, but I'm thinking he heads to the MacPherson." He shook his head. "I found them on the road and I tried to stop him. You must believe me. His men jumped me and left me there. When I came to my senses, I rode here as fast as I could."

"How many men does he travel with?" Robert had the look of a man already planning strategy.

"Six, maybe eight. I dinna think there's more, but I'm no sure. We hae to hurry." He attempted to stand, but fell back to the chair.

"Easy, Lyall. Just give yerself a wee bit to gain yer strength." Rosalyn brushed back his hair, frowning down at him, confusion evident in her expression.

"Yer going nowhere but to bed. Niall, you and Ewan see that he gets some rest." Connor restrained his cousin with a hand to his shoulder. "Yer no good to us this way, lad. We'll find her and bring her home. Robert's a fine tracker. Duncan's getting the horses even now."

He was off and running up the stairs toward their chamber before Cate could even rise from her seat.

She found him there, putting on his shirt and boots, gathering his sword and knives.

"What are you going to do?" She asked it quietly.

"I'm going to bring my sister home."

"You do realize it was probably Blane behind all those

things that happened to me before the wedding, don't you? The fall, the arrows, all that?"

"Aye. I suspected him and his father of that. And more. It's why I brought you here." His eyes were filled with pain when he looked at her. "Here I could keep you safe, all of you. But only so long as you stayed within the walls. I dinna ken why she would go out without speaking to me first."

Cate went to him, putting her arms around his waist and clutching him close to her. The pain caused by fear for his sister was as tangible to her as her own fear for his safety.

"He's dangerous, Connor. Promise me you'll be careful. I couldn't bear it if anything were to happen to you."

His arms went around her then. Hugging her tightly to him, he kissed the top of her head.

"Dinna fash yerself, wee Caty. He's no so dangerous as I am."

He smiled at her, running his fingers down the side of her face before he put her away from him and went to the door.

"I dinna want to hae to think over yer safety as well when I'm gone. Promise me you'll no leave the castle, that you'll no even go out on the grounds until I return."

"I promise. Don't worry about me. Just concentrate on what you have to do. Get Mairi and come back to me. Safely." She smiled up at him bravely.

"Aye, I will." His eyes gleamed for a moment. "And when I do, we'll finish what we started. That's my promise to you." He turned and ran down the stairs.

She stood at the window, watching as he mounted and rode away, until she could see him no longer. After tossing off her jacket and climbing into bed, Cate pulled his pillow close, breathing in his scent. It would be a long time before she would be able to sleep. For years she had watched as her father and brothers had boarded planes headed off to danger, and yet it had never frightened her as Connor's leaving did. Just another downside to this whole true love thing she was going to have to learn to deal with.

The sky was just coloring with first light when Cate finally dozed off. She slept fitfully, her dreams filled with horrible visions of men fighting with swords, of them attacking Connor, of his body limp on the ground.

When the pounding first woke her, she wasn't sure where she was. Groggily she crawled from the bed and crossed to the door.

"What is it?"

"You must hurry, Cate. It's Connor. He's been hurt."

Throwing open the door, she pushed Lyall aside and started to run down the stairs, only to be stopped as his arm snaked around her, pulling her up short. She grabbed at his hand, but quickly let go when she felt the blade at her throat. She was wide awake now.

He pulled her close, chuckling into her ear.

"My mistake. I meant to say that he *will* be hurt when he returns, no that he already is." His breath against the side of her face sent chills of fear through her. "Walk quietly down the stairs for me now, like a good lass."

"I don't understand. What are you doing?"

"Of course you dinna understand. Yer but a woman and a foreign one at that." He pulled her to a stop at the foot of the stairs. "I hae to admit, however, seeing you dressed as you are, I'm beginning to think Blane may not hae been so far off the mark in wanting you for himself. I may need to rethink that portion of my plan."

He laughed and yelled for Niall.

The older man came running, skidding to a stop as he rounded the corner into the hall and saw the knife at Cate's throat.

"Aye, Niall. I see you recognize the lady's predicament. Very wise of you to stop there. You'll go out to the gates and raise them now. My men are awaiting entry even as we speak. Oh, and should you think to do anything less than what I ask, you'd best ken that young Ewan lies on the floor of my room, trussed up like a bird for the table." He smiled, his eyes glittering wildly. "No to mention how messy this lady's future would be."

When Niall continued to stand, his eyes wide with fear, Lyall screamed "Go," and the man ran.

"What do you hope to accomplish with this?" Keep him talking. Her father had always told the boys to keep their enemies talking.

"It's all part of the plan. Dinna fear, Cate, you'll be right at the front to see it all. Yer a verra important part of it now, though yer arrival did vex me at the start. I've overcome that and realize this will be even better. Just as soon as everyone is in their proper place, we can begin. Ah." He looked up as the main doors opened. "Here are some of my men now."

Four large men entered the hall, two of them dragging

Blane between them. He had obviously been beaten and was barely conscious.

Cate gasped at the sight of him and started forward only to feel the knife pressed to her throat.

"No, no, no. You must be still and behave yerself. We hae much for you to do yet." He spoke quietly into her ear, chuckling as he did so. Then he turned and yelled orders to the men. "The entrance to the old dungeon is in the cellar below this hall. Throw him there. And the old man who opened the gates as weel. You'll find a woman and lass in the kitchens. Bring them out to the courtyard. Oh, and, Malcolm, take another man with you up to the chamber in that tower to the left. Bring my aunt down to join us in the courtyard."

Lyall pushed Cate toward the doors. As they passed Blane, he lifted his head and smiled sadly. "I never wanted any harm to come to you. I thought I could save you from this, but I failed. I'm sorry."

"You could no even save yerself, Brother. Always the weak link. Always the one to feel sorry for anyone who might get hurt. Many's the time I told Father we'd hae to watch out for yer cowardice. And now look at you. You wouldn't have been half the laird I'll be. You were never worthy of being the first son. It always should have been me. Get him out of here." Lyall pushed her forward.

When the men dragging Blane opened the door to the cellars below, Beast burst out, snarling, heading straight for Lyall. One of the men grabbed a chair and smashed it over the dog's head, and he dropped to the floor, motionless.

"Beast!" Cate gasped.

He lay so still. She wanted to reach out, to check him, but didn't dare. Now she realized it was Lyall he'd been going for earlier. They should have trusted the poor dog.

"I hate that disgusting creature." Lyall stopped to prod at the body with his foot. "He almost took my arm off that day in the forest. If not for my archer, I'd hae worse than the scars I do." He grinned, looking pleased with himself. "Throw the body in the dungeon with Blane. It should make his stay more interesting."

Again he pushed Cate toward the door.

"Where are you taking me?"

"We hae to get to the tower wall. Yer loving husband will be returning shortly. When he disna find a trail to follow, he'll grow suspicious. But it will be too late." He sang softly in her ear, "Too late, too late."

"Blane didn't have Mairi at all, did he? Where is she? What have you done with her?"

"No, Blane had nothing to do with Mairi's disappearance, though he made an excellent decoy, dinna you think? And he did provide me with my disguise when he attacked me after he discovered what I was doing." He laughed grimly. "Though I had not planned on quite that much realism, I suppose it did make me all the more convincing when I arrived. Even you seemed distressed by my act." With the arm that held her, he gave a little squeeze. "I expect Mairi's at Dun Ard by now, safely locked in her room, waiting for her groom to come claim her."

"But you care for Mairi. You've always been good to her. How could you even think of letting that horrible old man have her?"

This couldn't be happening. Her head was spinning.

"I hae been good to her, hae I no? Mairi's great fun. A good diversion from the daily cares. She's amused me for years. Best of all, she's provided me with an easy way to keep track of Connor's activities. Ah weel, now she'll amuse the MacPherson. That horrible old man as you call him will make a powerful ally when I'm laird of the MacKiernan."

"When you're laird? That's what this is all about? You're doing this simply to be laird?"

"There's nothing simple about what I do, my dear. I'm second son of the MacKiernan. There would be nothing for me but what crumbs Blane might choose to toss my way. Think you I'd be satisfied with a warrior's life like Connor? I dinna think so. No, I'll remove all the obstacles and take my rightful place at the head of the clan, where I belong."

He began humming in her ear.

They reached the tower wall and stood near the edge of the walk. Cate's stomach felt sick as she saw the horses approaching. She could think of nothing to do, no way to warn Connor. She knew the instant he spotted her there, when he drew his sword.

"Good," Lyall yelled down to him. "I'll need you all to follow my cousin's lead. Draw yer weapons. Oh, and you can toss them to the ground as weel. Then I'll let you enter."

"And why would I choose to throw away my weapons, Lyall?" Connor had laid the sword across his lap.

"Perhaps you dinna see the dirk I hold to this lovely wee neck. I'll hae no choice but to slice it open and let her bleed over the side of yer wall if you dinna do as I say."

He giggled and Cate feared for an instant that he planned to do exactly that as she felt the sting of the blade pressed tightly against her skin.

Connor cursed and threw his sword to the ground. Duncan and Robert did the same.

"And yer small weapons, Cousin. Every single one of them. Then climb down off yer horses and we'll let you inside."

He removed the knife, rubbing at the spot where it had been with his thumb. From the burn, Cate knew he had drawn blood that last time.

She could hear the gates being opened as Lyall slowly walked her back down the stairs, his thumb and fingers tight about her throat, the knife in his other hand at her side. He was humming again.

When they emerged into the courtyard, she saw Connor, Robert and Duncan on their knees, arms pulled behind them, tied with rope. Lyall's men were looping the rope from their hands up around their necks, rendering them virtually unable to move.

Rosalyn, still in her nightgown, stood only a few feet away, the man named Malcolm holding tightly to her arm.

"Lyall."

She called to him sharply and he turned to look at her, not releasing his hold on Cate's throat.

"Yer man is hurting my arm. It's yer duty to see to my protection, is it no?"

He laughed, softly at first, then harder.

"No, Aunt, it's no my duty. I dinna ever accept that old superstition. But be grateful. Yer better off than this one."

He shook Cate a bit by her neck causing her to gasp

for air, stumbling as they continued forward, closer to Conner.

"At least yer no bleeding." He laughed again. "I hae finally delivered my own self from all the superstitious fools and cowards," he yelled at no one in particular. "I dinna need the gods."

Connor's eyes blazed with fury when he jerked his head up, the rope binding his neck. He glanced quickly at Cate before speaking, as if to assure himself she was unharmed.

"Yer father's no going to take kindly to yer treatment of Rosalyn."

"Ah weel, it's no so much a matter of what my father will think anymore. It's a verra sad time at Dun Ard, you see." He shook his head as if saddened, and then brightened. "Or it will be later today when the people there discover the terrible accident my father had riding home from yer castle yesterday." He smiled maliciously. "Strange, but it's verra similar to the accident he arranged for yer brother, Kenneth, all those years ago. Fate, do you think?" He shook his head. "Poor Anabella will find herself a widow before the day grows much later. And her with no bairns." He made a tsking sound. "Her position at Dun Ard will be tenuous at best."

"And Blane? We dinna find any tracks that would indicate he's on his way to the MacPherson with my sister. Has he had an accident as weel?" Connor's voice was harsh, his eyes hard.

"Och, no. My men did a fine job of disguising their tracks, did they no? I'm paying them extra for that. How many times did you circle around before you realized?"

He smiled, running the knife lightly against Cate's skin, tracing the line of her camisole strap. "As for Blane, he's enjoying the comforts of yer own dungeon, such as they are, even as we speak."

"The dungeon? That's been closed off since my father's time."

"Aye. But I've reopened it." He laughed again, a high cackling sound.

"Then what hae you done with Mairi?" Connor appeared calmer now, as if the warrior had taken over, replacing the man.

"Safe and sound. Locked in her room at Dun Ard. Awaiting the arrival of her anxious groom. Although I imagine she's no too happy." He giggled.

"The king will deal with you harshly for this." Robert spoke for the first time, and was rewarded with having his head jerked back by the man holding his ropes.

"Oh, I think not. I think yer king will be ready to reward me when he hears how I was forced to kill my own brother to avenge Connor's death. Or perhaps Connor will kill Blane, and I can avenge his death. I haven't decided which I prefer yet. For now, you'll all rot in the same dungeon together. I hae plenty of time to decide."

"Why would anyone believe I'd harm Blane?"

"Everyone recognizes yer right to challenge for the position of laird. And with my father dead, what better time?"

"I told you, and everyone else, I'd no interest in being laird."

"Oh, aye, you did. Over and over. It would hae been so much easier for me if you just would hae fought him. All yer deaths could be so easily disguised in bloody big battle, but you'd no do that. Too damn much honor. Always making my plans more difficult, you were. Just when I think yer gone for good, and perhaps I'll no hae to deal with you any longer, you drag her in and find a way to get married."

He shook Cate by her neck, again causing her to gasp for air.

"Leave her be," Connor yelled, straining against the ropes.

"Oh, I dinna think so. In fact, I think her part in my plan has just changed." He smiled broadly as Connor struggled helplessly against his ropes. "I think, before this day is over, she'll willingly come to me, for the same reason yer mother came to my father."

Connor froze, his eyes blazing with hatred.

"No." His voice was low, almost a growl. "Cate will no betray me."

"No, she'll no betray you," Lyall agreed pleasantly. "She'll come to me to save yer life. Just as yer mother went to my father to save yer life. To save you from Kenneth's fate. To guarantee you were sent away to her family. To keep you safe."

He pulled Cate close to him, his face only inches from hers. "What would you be willing to do to hae me spare Connor's life, eh?"

The man was truly insane. She had no doubts. His eyes glittered inches from her face as his hand tightened on her throat, the other rubbing the knife he held across her stomach.

"Anything. I'll do anything you ask if you'll just let him live."

"No," Connor screamed, raging against the ropes. "You canna do this to her. Cate." He turned his gaze to her, pleading. "You dinna hae to do this for me."

Laughing, Lyall released her, allowing her to run to Connor, to kneel by him, to place her hands on his face.

"I can't let him hurt you. Don't you understand? I love you, Connor. More than anything. I'll love you for as long as I live. Even if you'll never love me in return, I'll do anything to save you. Whatever it takes."

The anguish on his face bore into her soul before he closed his eyes. He groaned and opened them again, passion smoldering there, passion for her. She could feel it.

"Yer wrong, wee Caty," he whispered. "I could not see it before, would not, but it's right here in front of me. I ken the truth of it only now when it's too late. I'll go to my grave loving you. Please, for me, dinna let him do this to you." His eyes were begging her now.

"Oh, Connor." She threw her arms around him only to be roughly jerked back by Lyall, who shoved her across to the man holding Rosalyn.

"Keep her there until I've finished." He laughed, a mean hateful sound. "I begin to see the attraction in taking another man's woman." He walked to Connor and, drawing back his foot, kicked him in the face, knocking him to the ground. "I've often thought I'd enjoy that." He laughed again. "I do."

"Stop. Stop it. I'll do whatever you want, just let him be." Cate struggled to pull free of Malcolm's grip.

"Oh, I've no doubt you'll do whatever I want. We'll get to that in due time." He continued to laugh, backhanding

Connor to the ground this time after the guardsmen had hauled him back to his knees.

Cate collapsed to the ground, watching through tears while Lyall continued to punish Connor. Watching the horror through a prism of tears that blurred her vision until she could hardly see. Watching through a green, shimmering prism of light.

Only when she heard Rosalyn calling her name did she begin to realize what was happening.

"No," she whispered.

Time had stopped. Everyone in the courtyard was frozen in place, Connor on the ground, relief clear in his expression as he looked toward Cate, blood trailing down from a cut on his face; Lyall, his hand drawn back to inflict another punishing blow.

Only Rosalyn standing just outside the pulsing sphere spoke to her.

"Remember what I told you. The darker the mark, the stronger the power." She placed her hand, fingers spread, against the sphere. "My power brought you here. Yer own can bring you back if it's what you choose."

Rosalyn turned and ripped her nightgown from her shoulder, exposing her back. Through the pulsing green light, Cate plainly saw the faint marking on Rosalyn's shoulder blade.

When she squinted her eyes and turned her head just right, it looked like a flower.

Then the lights went out.

CHAPTER 27

Cate awoke on the floor of her own bedroom, a wet, sticky spot under her hand. She lifted it to her face and sniffed. Drambuie. The liquid from her overturned glass hadn't even had a chance to dry. Although she had spent almost two months in the past, she had only been gone from here for a few minutes.

She rose to her feet, wondering if it had all been a dream, a nightmare. Looking in the mirror, she saw the blood smeared on her throat. Her hand flew to the spot. Pulling it away, she looked at the traces of blood there, smeared across her palm, her fingers, and the heavy gold band she wore.

"He's real. Thank God, he's real." She shivered, fighting the urge to give in to hysterics. She had to do something, to save him. But what?

"Whatever it takes." She said it out loud, firming her resolve. That was what she'd sworn to him. That was what she meant. But how?

She walked to the bathroom and picked up the washcloth lying there, still damp from the shower she had taken so long ago. No, less than an hour ago. After she washed the blood from her neck and hands, she pulled bandages and antibiotic gel from her cupboard and tended to her neck.

How could she save him? There wouldn't be time.

Turning her back to the mirror, she looked over her shoulder at her reflection. Her birthmark was an exact duplicate of the one Rosalyn bore, except where the older woman's was pale, her own was a deep, dark red. She smiled.

How could she have forgotten? It wasn't about time. It was about love.

She had all the time she needed. She just had to map out a strategy, arrange for reinforcements and locate a couple of Faeries. No problem.

She strode to her living room. Picking up the portable telephone, she glanced at the clock. It was time to put that twenty-four-hour research department at Coryell Enterprises to work. She punched in the number.

"Peter Hale."

She was in luck; he was her favorite researcher. Peter was a major über-geek, but he never missed a detail and that was exactly what she wanted now.

"It's Cate. I have a top priority for you."

"Ms. Coryell. It's kind of late. How soon do you need it?"

"I need it yesterday, Peter."

"Gotcha. Fire away."

"I need research in Scotland. Find me two castles, one called Dun Ard, the other Sithean Fardach. They'll be within a few miles of each other. Somewhere a couple days' horseback ride south of Cromarty. They would have been in use sometime around the thirteenth century. I need names, dates, history, the complete workup from around 1270 forward. Everything you can find. That's enough to get you started. I'll be in the office first thing in the morning with some names from that time period I want researched.

"Whoa. Thirteenth-century Scotland. Could be tough. We dealing with terrorists or crazies?"

"Something like that. You get me a lot, you get it quick and I'll see to it you get a bonus."

"No worries. Anything else for now?"

"Yeah. If you can find someplace in that same area that has Faerie legends associated with it and some trees covered in little pieces of cloth, that bonus will make Christmas look like pocket change."

"Awesome. I'm already on it, boss lady." The line went dead.

She immediately dialed again. Five rings, just like the last time she'd dialed this number. She smiled as she heard the sleepy voice on the other end.

"Yeah? Talk to me."

Jesse never woke well.

"It's me."

"How many times are you going to wake me up tonight? You have something else you don't really want to talk about or have you come to your senses and decided to dump that creep?"

"It's a real long story. I'm having plane tickets delivered to your hotel tomorrow for you and the guys. Use them. I'll be waiting for you at the airport on the other end."

"What's up? New assignment?"

He was wide awake now, all business.

"Sort of. Let's just say I'm getting ready to treat you to the adventure of a lifetime, big brother. I'll explain everything when you get there."

She hung up and laughed. She knew Jesse. A true adventure junkie, he'd never get back to sleep now.

Cate leaned over and dug through the drawer of the table where the telephone sat. One crumpled Hershey's Nugget was all she could find. She unwrapped and popped it in her mouth in one quick move.

"Oh yeah, baby. SPECIAL DARK chocolate with almonds." She sighed. "Starbucks will have to wait for later."

She'd just started to dial another number when the doorbell rang. The unfamiliar sound jangled her nerves and she laughed at herself as she walked over to answer the door, still holding the telephone.

Richard waited at the door, looking exceedingly well groomed in his tuxedo. And exceedingly irritated as he pointed the cell phone in his hand at her.

"I've been trying to call you since I left the condo to make sure you're ready, but your line's been busy. We're going to be late to the dinner as it is." He seemed to actually see her for the first time. "And you're not ready." He shook his head and his eyes narrowed. "Although this is a good look for you. A very good look." His eyes trailed appreciatively down her body and back up again before meeting hers. "Is this your way of apologizing for our little misunderstanding this afternoon?"

He reached for her but recoiled at her loud guffaw of laughter.

"Yeah, like that's going to happen." She didn't have the time or inclination to argue with him right now. She held up her phone to show him. "I'm dealing with a situation. You're going to have to do dinner without me."

"These are important people, Cate. You understand their impact on my career."

"What I'm dealing with is more important than pushing your career. We'll talk tomorrow."

She shook her head in disgust and slammed the door. He could stand there and make a scene on her front porch or he could go meet his important people, she didn't care which he chose to do. Knowing Richard, he was already in the car.

Tomorrow she'd deal with their future together, or rather, their lack of a future together. He was not going to be happy that she couldn't return his ring yet.

She punched the telephone's ON button and dialed again. The answer took longer this time, but finally came.

"Yeah?"

"Daddy? It's Cate. We need to talk about Mom's family." A pause. "Oh yeah, you could say something unusual happened."

She smiled and curled up on the sofa, getting comfortable for a long, informative, way overdue chat.

The airport in Inverness had been congested and the girl at the car rental desk a nightmare, but those had been nothing compared to dealing with her brothers' skepticism. Even though their father had hit some of the high spots for them on the plane trip from Madrid, they were still having a hard time accepting her whole story.

Even now, careening down the wrong side of the road in their small van, she occasionally caught one of her brothers staring at her like she needed to be committed. After the longest week of her life, she wasn't completely sure they were wrong. At least she could identify with how their clients felt now. And once they reached the coordinates Peter had given her for a likely Faerie Glen location, she'd know for sure whether or not to hunt up a local psychiatrist.

They had spent the last couple of days scouting their location. Dun Ard still existed, although greatly changed. It was now serving as an upscale hotel and hunting lodge. Her father, Cody and Cass were already registered there as guests.

She had wanted to weep at the site where Sithean Fardach had stood so proudly. Only a fenced-off pile of rubble remained, posted with danger signs to warn off trespassers. It was just as well. Even if she had been able to get near the old dungeon entrance, she wouldn't have had the courage to check for bones anyway.

Cate took a deep breath to clear her mind as her father pulled off the road to park. They would have to hike the remaining two miles back into the forest from here. This was as close as they could take the van. Getting out, she nervously wiped her hands down the front of her jeans. Doing so caused the wide gold band on her left had to slide up and down, its weight a reassurance and solid reminder of what was at stake.

No one spoke as they hiked back through the forest, the lush green foliage gradually growing denser and more tangled until at last they broke through into a clearing.

Cate hoped Peter was happy with his bonus. He'd certainly earned it.

The glen had changed very little. The waterfall still tumbled merrily into the deep green water of the pool. The biggest difference was the trees. Not only had they grown larger, now many of them surrounding the pool sported limbs covered in bits of cloth, each bit representing someone's dream. It was a staggering realization.

"Okay, guys. This is it. Just move over to the edge of the clearing there and try to make sure no one else wanders in. I don't want to get hauled off to a Scottish funny farm because someone catches me standing here half naked, talking to invisible Faeries."

She grinned at her brothers, rolling her eyes when Jesse indicated that she might want to consider a quick trip to that farm when this was over. Her father gave her a hug and then joined his sons, fanning out around the perimeter of the area, stationing themselves with their backs to the water.

Cate walked to the pool and took a deep breath, letting it out slowly. It was her moment of truth.

"Hey, Faeries. Remember me? Caitlyn Rose MacKiernan?" Her bravado wavered for only an instant. If this didn't work, she knew at least three men who would tease her unmercifully. And one who would die, seven-hundred-and-thirty-some-odd years in the past.

She stripped off her T-shirt and turned her back to the water. "See this? I'm here for my formal introduction to the family."

Standing in her bra, she waited for only a few seconds before shivers ran up and down her body. It felt like a finger softly tracing the pattern on her back. She turned and confronted the shimmering image of a woman with long blond hair tossing about in a nonexistent wind.

"Hi." Not the most clever of greetings, but the best she could come up with at the moment.

"Welcome, Daughter of the Glen." The voice was ethereal. She heard it only in her mind, but it was real enough nonetheless. "How may I assist you? Do you wish to borrow our power for some task?"

"Yes and no."

Cate had never expected a Faerie to look surprised, but this one did. Cate grinned at her.

"I need to borrow power, but not from you. There's too much I don't know. I'm here to see the source. I want to meet my . . . grandfather, Pol." He was sort of her grandfather, give or take twenty or thirty generations.

"It is not done. He never comes."

Cate turned and, reaching over her shoulder, pointed to her birthmark. "See this? I've seen two others of these, but none as dark as mine. From what I understand, even my mother's was lighter. I've been led to believe that the darker this is, the stronger my Fae bloodline is." She turned back toward the water, facing the now obviously agitated Faerie. "I need to speak to my grandfather. I need his help. Without it, the man I love is dead."

The water in the center of the pool began to bubble at her words. The Faerie in front of her shimmered away, casting an apprehensive look over her shoulder. From the center of the pool, the form of a man rose and shimmered closer to her.

He was tall, with the long, lean build of an athlete

who competed hard, a runner or a cyclist maybe. His pale blond hair curled down onto his shoulders, framing tilted eyes of emerald green. Eyes Cate recognized. Eyes she saw every day in her mirror. Her eyes.

"You're my ancestor, Pol?"

"I am Pol." He tilted his head, studying her quizzically. "In all these many years, none of my daughters has ever requested my presence."

"Maybe none of them was as desperate as I am." Cate shrugged. "I'm here to ask your guidance. The man I love is going to die if I can't get to him."

Pol lifted his hand and a gentle breeze wafted through the glen, causing Cate's hair to flutter about her shoulders. He gazed intently into her eyes.

"I understand. I see it in your thoughts. You believe this man to be your true love. How much do you love him?"

She didn't even have to think about the question.

"More than anything. More than life itself."

He studied her thoughtfully. "Do you love him enough to die for him?"

There was no sound in the glen. No birds, no wind in the trees. It was as if Nature herself held her breath waiting for Cate's answer.

She considered and chose to take the gamble of answering honestly.

"No, Grandfather. Dying would be the coward's way out and would do nothing to save him. I love him too much for that. I love him enough to fight for him, to live for him."

Silent moments stretched out as Pol looked into her eyes, seeking the truth of her heart, looked with eyes that saw right through her to her very soul. Then he laughed, a musical sound that captured the wonder and mirth of life itself. The sound echoed through the glen, bouncing off the trees and the water, enfolding Cate in its warmth.

His smile was beautiful, raising goose bumps on her skin.

"You are indeed strong in my blood, Daughter, stronger than any in many centuries. Take my power. Do with it as you will, within the limits of the Fae. Find your true love and save him."

A tingling sensation started in her toes, like tiny butterfly wings brushing over her skin. It traveled up to her head, to the very roots of her hair.

"That's it?"

Pol smiled and began to shimmer. "That's it."

"That's not it. I need to know why."

"Why what, daughter?"

"If your blessing was to ensure that your daughters found and kept true love, why did it allow mine to be taken from me?" The question that had haunted her for so long.

"The key to your answer lies in the words *true love*. It's easy to say you love someone, to speak the meaningless words. I see in your heart that you've spoken them to another, though you didn't mean them."

Cate nodded. She had said those words to Richard.

"Ah! But to prove it? That requires you to move beyond yourself. To reach deep into your heart and call on that love to give you the necessary strength to do that which you think you cannot do. My blessing requires that proof. You think yourself powerless, afraid, unable to control your own life, yet to prove your love, you must bravely take control."

Pol floated away from her, shimmering again, his form becoming transparent.

"Wait. I still have questions you need to answer."

"What questions could you possibly have?"

She was incredulous.

"How do I go back? I don't have the pendant. I don't know any spells or special words. I don't want to be asleep when I get there like I have been both times I've time-traveled. How do I save Connor? What do I do? You know, a few little things like that."

That lovely laugh again, tinkling through her mind, warming her all over.

"You don't need a pendant or spells. Use whatever words you will. You have the power of the Fae, the power of my daughters, my power. It was Fae magic that allowed you to travel the first time, not the necklace. The jewel was merely the vessel that held the magic. You are the holder of the magic now. If you don't want to sleep, don't. And as far as saving your beloved, you already know what to do. You have these men here with you, these men who protect you even now. Your thoughts told me they have experience in saving people."

Pol continued to shimmer, moving toward the center of the pool. "What do you do? As you told your beloved, Daughter, you do whatever it takes. Just remember this: you cannot change the outcome of history. You can only alter the circumstances."

He shimmered over the bubbling waters and faded from sight. The waters calmed.

"Never a straight answer. And to think, just two short months ago I couldn't have imagined Faeries to be such aggravating creatures," she mumbled, pulling on her T-shirt. Fleetingly, she heard laughter in the air.

"Are we just going to stand around here all day while you talk to yourself over there or what?" Jesse had squatted down, his back still turned to her.

"Didn't you hear him?"

Her brother turned now. "Hear who? I only heard you, Tinkerbell."

Cody snickered, putting his hand over his mouth, pretending to rub his nose but still looking guilty. "Sorry, Caty." He turned to Jesse. "Tinkerbell? Good one, man."

"Never mind." Cate shook her head. "Let's get out of here."

"Did you get what you needed here?" Clint Coryell looked at her questioningly.

She could always count on her dad to cut to the chase.

"Yep. I sure did."

They started their hike back to their parked van.

"We'll go in just as we planned. Tomorrow morning you'll drop Jess and me at Sithean Fardach and you guys will depart from Dun Ard. Dad will coordinate control issues from this end."

Jesse spoke up. "I'm still not completely on board with your coming along, Cate. We're experienced in going in and extracting hostages. You've never done anything like this. Can't you just wiggle your nose or something and send the three of us without your having to be there?"

Cody and Cass mumbled their agreement.

It was progress. At least they weren't questioning the weird factor anymore, just her competence.

"No. We've been over and over this. It's not a nose-wiggling deal. I only left a couple of things back there that came from this time, and using them as a beacon is the only way I can figure to do this."

"Besides," Clint interjected. "This is going to be a whole new ball game for you boys, too. Cate at least has some experience in this . . . terrain, so to speak."

"Exactly. Cody and Cass won't need me. They're going to target on my birthstone ring. I'm sure Mairi's still wearing it. You find yourselves a gorgeous, tall blonde with my ring on her toe and you got the right girl."

Her brothers exchanged a look.

"Whatever. You'll arrive where it is and she'll be there. You just explain who you are and get her out. The most you should have to deal with are a couple of guards." She turned to Jesse. "It's not going to be that simple with Connor. We'll have to find him, and there are the others with him we'll need to help as well. We'll zero in on Richard's engagement ring."

Jesse snorted. "Somehow I don't think that creep would appreciate the irony of his ring saving your new husband." He grinned. "But I'd sure like to be the one to tell him about it."

"I'm sure you're right. The ring should still be in Connor's sporran. I don't think he had it with him the night he went out to find Mairi. That means it's proba-bly still in our bedroom, but it could be anywhere. You'd have to find your way from wherever it is to the dungeon and then pick out the right man. You need me for that."

"I've always worked pretty damn well from maps. I never had to take a client in."

"Yeah, well, you're not getting a map. And I'm not a client. So you just better plan on doing some good on-the-job training, because I'm going with you."

"God, I hate it when she goes all stubborn like this." Jesse grumbled all the way back to the van.

Cate paced back and forth in front of the rubble that had been Sithean Fardach, too nervous to sit down.

"I still think you should have gone for the Lara Croft look." Jesse lounged on the ground, his head pillowed on the backpack he would carry.

"I'll keep that in mind for the next time. This is fine." Her jeans were comfortable and the turtleneck was necessary, though bulky and itchy. Her only concession to looks had been her hair. She wore a thin braid down one side of her face, tucked behind her ear. Like Connor's. "I don't need leather to do this."

"Hey, I make this leather look good. Besides, this stuff is quiet, soft and gives me the flexibility to kick ass when I need it." He grinned at her. "I should be getting paid to do their commercials."

She rolled her eyes. "Is it time yet?"

"Almost. I told you I'd let you know when we hit 0900 on the dot. Relax. You remember the stuff I showed you how to do?"

"I can't relax. And yes, I think I do. I guess we'll find out if I need it."

"You better. Just remember to watch me when the time comes. You going to be okay?"

"Yeah. It's just that this is so important. He's so important. I don't want anything to go wrong."

"Don't worry. I won't let anything go wrong. I understand what he means to you. Hey, I'm looking forward to meeting him. Must be something pretty special."

"He is." Cate placed a hand over her nervous stomach. This had to work.

Jess looked down at his watch. "Okay, baby sister. It's go time."

Clearing her mind, Cate closed her eyes.

"By the power of the Fae, I send two men in search of my ring and the woman who wears it. Find her and return immediately." She peeked at Jesse and shrugged. "Oh, and they'll stay awake. Go now."

"Not very poetic. Do you think it worked?"

"Yeah, it did. I could see them in my mind. Amazing."

Cody and Cass had looked pretty surprised when the sphere surrounded them.

Jesse stood and pulled his backpack over his shoulder.

"Ready to rock and roll." He grinned at her, taking her hand.

She closed her eyes again. "Take us to Richard's ring. No sleeping. Do it now."

The words were barely out of her mouth when the green sphere surrounded them. The look on Jesse's face was worth the trip. The lights didn't go out this time, but they certainly performed one hell of a show.

CHAPTER 28

When the lights stopped flashing, it was dark. Very dark. And it smelled of horses. Cate groaned. Just her luck.

As her eyes adjusted to the light, or lack of it, she could see that they were in the stables. Conner's sporran hung from a peg on the wall. Cate rummaged through it and found the ring, slipping it in her pocket.

"Ready?" Jesse barely made a sound as he breathed the question.

At Cate's nod, he started toward the doors just ahead, pulling her along with him.

"Remember, you stay behind me all the way."

As they reached the door, it flew open, propelled by one of the men working for Lyall. In a single motion, Jesse shoved Cate to the wall with his arm and struck at the man with his feet, bringing him down. Instantly he was on top of the guard and then there was silence. Jesse wasn't even breathing hard.

"Give me that rope," he whispered.

"Is he . . . I mean, did you . . . ?" She couldn't bring

herself to ask the whole question, not sure she really wanted to know what she'd just seen her brother do.

"Kill him? Would I be asking for a rope to tie up a dead guy? Use your brains and hand me the damn rope," he hissed.

"Are we just going to leave him here? Tied up?"

"Look, Caty. I don't want to have to deal with this guy again, and I can't kill him. For all I know, if I did, somebody real important in the future, like, I don't know, the president or something, could just cease to exist. Who knows what weird shit we could cause if we kill someone who isn't supposed to die." He shook his head and rolled his eyes. "Dad was right. This thing isn't just business as usual."

They peeked through the doors, scanning the courtyard. Two men stood at the bottom of the stairs to the entryway. Two more were at the top.

Jesse pointed to a low wall at the back tower. "What's on the other side of that?"

"Gardens. And a back entrance to the castle, through the kitchen." Cate grinned. "Am I earning my keep yet?"

Her brother rolled his eyes again, adding a quiet snort for good measure. "We'll go in that way. Stay behind me and stay low."

They moved quietly out the door and, keeping to the shadows near the walls, they slowly made their way to the garden wall. Once there, Jesse climbed to the top and then lowered a rope he'd taken from his backpack down to her. She smiled when she saw he'd even made a loop in the bottom so she could just insert her foot and hold on while he pulled her up.

Noises from the kitchen gave them momentary pause until they saw it was only Margaret and Janet preparing a meal to feed the men who held them captive. No guards were in the kitchen.

"Margaret," Cate whispered to get her attention.

The older woman turned and, in her surprise, dropped the spoon she was holding. She ran to Cate, enfolding her in a hug.

"What are you doing here? How did you ever get away from those awful men?"

"We're here to free Connor and the others."

Margaret gasped as Jesse entered the kitchen, and Cate took her hand.

"Don't be afraid. This is my brother, Jesse. He's here to help me. Where are the guards? Will they be able to see us when we go out to the cellar door?"

"Aye, they would. But you dinna need to go that way. There's an entrance through here from the bakery to the cellar as weel." Margaret wiped her eyes with her apron. "They were fair harsh on the men before taking them down. I dinna believe they hae any guards in the cellar, though. No need for them." Fresh tears rolled down her cheeks. "My poor Niall's down there. And they've got my Ewan in the hall, acting as a servant for them. Most of the guards are there in the hall, eating or sleeping, drinking everything they can find. A few are outside." She used the apron to wipe at her eyes again. "Poor Rosalyn is tied to a chair in the hall, forced to watch them and listen to their nasty insults. That horrible Lyall left her there."

"Isn't he the guy with the knife who left that little calling card on your throat?" Jesse's eyes glittered dangerously. "I want to know where that guy is. I want to have a little chat with him before we go." He smiled unpleasantly.

"Lyall's in yer bedchamber, milady."

Jesse looked to Cate and she nodded. "I can lead you there. After we find my husband." She grinned. It felt so good to say those words. "Don't worry, Margaret. We're going to get them all out safely. I promise." She patted the woman's hand.

Cate and Jesse hurried through the arches into the heated area where the ovens were housed. They easily found the door to the cellar and descended the stairs.

"The lady was right. No guards. Where's the dungeon entrance?" Jesse pulled matches from his backpack and brought the torch on the wall to life.

"Somewhere in this cellar." She didn't need the light to show her Jesse's face. She could feel the irritation radiating off him.

"Oh, you need me. I'm the only one who knows where to go." His whispered falsetto might have been funny under other circumstances.

She glared at him. "Be quiet. The hall, where there *are* guards, is directly above us."

They moved into the room.

"Shhh. Listen."

A low moan. That would be the dungeon. She just hoped it wouldn't be Connor.

"We're looking for some type of hole in the floor."

They worked their way around the large cellar room until they heard the sound again. It came from a grate in the floor, only a few feet away.

Bending down, Cate tried to see something in the

blackness of the pit below, but gave up quickly. "Connor? Are you down there?"

"Cate?" Only one word, yet carrying a wealth of skepticism and hope combined. "What are you doing here?"

She grabbed Jesse's arm and whispered frantically. "That's him. We have to get him out. Do something."

Jesse scanned the floor but could find no ladder or rope. "I don't see anything to climb up with. How did they plan to get these guys out?"

"They dinna plan to get us out. They plan to leave us here. Who do you hae with you, Caty?"

Connor was moving below them. Others were stirring as well.

"It's okay, Connor. It's my brother, Jesse. We'll figure something out. Just hold on. Who's down there with you?"

"Duncan, Robert, Niall and Blane. Duncan's no doing so well, though. I think they may hae broke his rib."

"Now, now. Dinna be telling yer lassie that. I'll be fine. But if you could hae a drop of that fine ale waiting when I climb out, I would appreciate it."

Duncan sounded so hopeful, Cate had to smile. And he was right. She knew that he, at least, would be fine. The packet of Peter's research still sitting on the backseat of the van flashed through her thoughts.

Using the rope they'd brought with them, they gradually got all the men up from the pit. Blane was the second man out. He once again attempted to apologize, but Cate stopped him.

"Don't. I owe you as much of an apology as you owe me. I totally misjudged you. We'll call it even."

"Connor and I had a similar conversation. Right after he dropped in on me. I regret the things I put you through, but I had hoped that I could stop this. I did all that I could. Perhaps not all that I should hae. But all that I could. That's my burden to live with. I appreciate yer understanding."

He limped over to sit by the wall, leaning back and closing his eyes.

Connor, as Cate expected, waited until the others had been helped out. As Jesse and Robert pulled him through the opening, Cate threw her arms around his neck.

He pulled her tightly to him.

"You should no hae come back. Yer no safe here." He glared at Jesse. "I would hae expected yer brother to see to yer safety first."

Jesse snorted. "You're supposed to be her husband. You should know how damn stubborn she is. You think you could have stopped her from coming?"

"Aye, I'm her husband. And aye, I could hae stopped her." He ducked his head and grinned. "Weel, I could hae tried."

Reaching around Cate, he gave his hand to Jesse. "I'm pleased to hae you as family, Jesse." He looked around, arching his eyebrow. "You dinna happen to bring any weapons, did you now?"

"As a matter of fact I did." Jesse crouched to the floor and opened his backpack, removing a roll of cloth. He released the ties and unrolled it, spreading it across the floor. Neatly stored in individual pockets, a variety of knives gleamed from its entire length.

"You guys comfortable with knives?"

Robert laughed as he reached for one. "I'm starting to like some of yer relations, MacKiernan." He whistled as he drew one of the knives from its holder. "This lad has good taste in weapons. I've never seen the like of this before." His teeth gleamed wickedly in the torchlight. "Can I hae more than one?"

"Take what you need, guys."

Jesse stood and began to fill them in on the locations of the guards and hostages. When he mentioned Rosalyn's position in the hall, Duncan growled and picked up another knife, groaning as he did so.

"Let me have a look at those ribs."

Jesse pulled a medical kit from his backpack. After inspecting Duncan's chest, he tore open a white package and wound an elastic bandage around the older man's ribs.

"What cure is this?" Duncan asked suspiciously.

"It won't cure you, but it will take some of the pressure off. Rest is the only thing for you now. It feels to me like they're just bruised, not actually broken. Oh, and swallow this."

He handed Duncan an ibuprofen, which the older man eyed for a moment before shrugging and popping it in his mouth.

"Do you think leaving an elastic bandage in thirteenth-century Scotland is a wise thing to do?" Cate didn't want to think of the possible repercussions if some twenty-first-century archaeologist dug this up.

"Hey, in this humidity, that thing will rot long before anyone could ever find it. Besides, I've had bruised ribs before and they hurt like a mother." He gave her a sheepish grin.

Once everyone was equipped, Robert took the lead toward the door heading to the Great Hall. Connor stopped, holding Cate back until the others had moved away.

"Yer not going up there with us. You head back to the kitchen. Stay with Margaret. I dinna want to think about harm finding you again." His eyes glowed with warning.

"Don't you think I'd be better off with you and Jess around to protect me?"

"No. I think you'd be better off far away from here. But since you dinna follow that path, I'll hae to settle for this. You go back through the other door and stay in the kitchen until I come to claim you. It's no open for discussion." He twirled her around and, with a light smack on her bottom, pushed her forward. One eyebrow lifted. "This will no take long." He winked and turned to follow the others.

Cate headed toward the kitchen. She had to find a way to get into that hall with them. She was supposed to be there.

Creeping to the top of the stairs, she put her ear to the door and listened. Nothing. That should be good. She turned the knob and the door shot forward, spilling Cate to her knees. She lifted her head and stared up into a pair of glittering brown eyes. Wild eyes. Lyall's eyes.

"Oh, that's lovely. Welcome back, wee Cate." Lyall grinned madly as he reached down and grabbed her arm, pulling her to her feet. "I dinna ken where you've been, but I was sure I'd find you."

Three of his guards were with him, including the one named Malcolm.

Her problem of how to get into the hall was solved. Now she only had to worry about getting out again.

Connor was already planning what he'd do as they went through the door ahead when her brother took his arm to pull him aside.

"Before we go through that door, there's something you need to understand, Connor. I'll help all I can when we get in there, but I'm limited in what I can do. Not my time and all that stuff, you know? You can kill whoever you need to because it's your time. But I whack somebody and suddenly the next seven centuries are seriously messed up."

"Verra weel, I ken the problem." He started to move forward.

"No, I don't think you do." Jesse grabbed his arm again to stop him. "I want the bastard that tried to slit my sister's throat. I can't kill him, but I can mess him up. I just want to make sure you're there to finish him off."

Connor grinned wickedly. "You dinna need to fash yerself over him, Jesse. He'll no leave this place alive. To my mind, he was dead the minute I saw him on the tower wall with his filthy hands on my Caty. It was only a matter of when."

"I'm seriously going to like having you in the family." Jesse slapped him on the back. "Last I heard he's in your bedchamber. You'll point me in the right direction?"

"I'll do better than that. I'll lead you there." Connor smiled in anticipation.

He was just thinking that he rather liked this Jesse when Robert threw open the door and all hell broke loose.

Connor had only a moment to admire the damage his new brother-in-law could cause with his feet before he was set upon by one of the guards. He quickly dispatched the man and picked up his discarded sword, using it to carve his way through the next attacker.

"Connor," Jesse yelled from across the room. "Which doorway?"

He pointed to the tower where his bedchamber was located and headed that direction at a dead run.

Robert was just finishing off another of the guards. He quickly moved to the main doorway, grinning as he dropped the bar down to keep out any others who might try to join in the fight.

Duncan stood for an instant over the body of the guard nearest Rosalyn and then, holding his side, leaned down to cut her bindings.

Connor turned to run up the tower stairs. Jesse was three steps ahead of him, but the words from across the hall stopped them both in their tracks.

"Connor. Surely yer no leaving the party now. Not when yer lovely lady's just joined us again."

Lyall. A shiver of fear crawled up his back and into his stomach. He met Jesse's eyes and saw the same emotion mirrored there.

Jesse joined him and they moved together into the Great Hall. Bodies lay on the floor and across the tables. Robert slowly inched away from the door, moving closer into position.

They continued to move into the room, spreading apart, circling, until they were only yards from his cousin.

Lyall, flanked by three of his guards, held Cate in front of him like a human shield, once again with a knife to her throat. Her eyes were calm, focused on her brother.

The fear receded, leaving only the determination so necessary for battle.

"Let her go, Lyall. I'm going to kill you."

"No, I dinna think so." Lyall grinned like the madman he was. "I've changed my plans yet again. I'm going to kill you. By killing her." His arm began the slicing motion across Cate's throat.

The room erupted in chaos.

Jesse, running by his side, yelled, "Now. Do it now."

Cate threw herself forward, into the knife, and then slammed back into Lyall's face, just as he finished the slicing motion across her throat. Blood splattered everywhere as she fell to the ground.

The red haze of rage blanketing Connor prevented his full awareness of anything but reaching his Caty and the man who murdered her. Only dimly did his consciousness recognize bits and scenes of the action around him, all of which seemed to him to be in slow motion. His eyes riveted on the motionless body of his beloved.

Robert threw himself in front of the guard whose sword was aimed for Connor's heart. There was no need for that. What did it matter? His heart lay on the ground at Lyall's feet, her hair covered in blood.

Jesse flew through the air, his feet knocking a second guard to the ground as his sword sliced at Connor's neck.

Duncan, took the head of the third guard before he could move from behind Lyall.

Until there was only Lyall. Lyall, his face covered in blood, her blood. Lyall looking down at Cate's body, his face contorted in rage. And then, incomprehensibly, Lyall falling to the floor next to her, Blane's knife through his back.

Cate screamed, chasing away the red haze, bringing Connor back to his senses.

He fell to his knees, gathering her into his arms, crushing her to him.

"Yer alive." He said it weakly, barely able to form the words.

"I am." Her arms were around his neck.

"But how? I saw him cut yer throat. I saw the blood everywhere."

He wanted to pull her away from him, to check for himself she wasn't bleeding to death even now, but he couldn't bear the loss of her body next to his, not even for a moment. She felt warm and alive with her arms about him and that was all that mattered right now. The woman he loved was alive.

"You can thank the miracle of a Kevlar turtleneck." Jesse slapped him on the back as he passed, going to check on Robert. "We'll explain about that later. All that blood came from Lyall's busted nose. Great job on the head butt, Caty. Just like I taught you. I knew that bastard would go for your throat again." He squatted next to Robert, feeling for the pulse in his neck. "Shit. We need to get this guy out of here fast if we're going to."

Robert was bleeding heavily. Jesse applied pressure with his hand as Rosalyn came forward and tore off part of her shift to give him.

"That won't be enough," Rosalyn said quietly.

Cate pushed away from Connor, putting her hands on either side of his face.

"Remember the first time you came to me and you needed me to make a big decision, whether or not to come with you, and you needed me to make it fast?"

He nodded, still trying to come to terms with what had just happened.

"Well, Connor, it's your turn now. I'm taking you out of here. To Dun Ard in my time. You don't get a choice. History says that after the death of Artair, the MacKiernan brothers battled at Sithean Fardach to see who would be the next laird. I guess that's Blane." She smiled up at him. "But the knight living at Sithean Fardach and his lady were evidently killed in that battle. They don't show up again in any of the records. That's you and me. I'm thinking that guy Jesse knocked out, the one who made this slice on your neck, was probably supposed to be the one that got you." She shuddered at the thought of how close he came.

"Then what decision is there? I canna remain here without upsetting history."

He was himself again. He didn't care where he spent the rest of his life, as long as he spent it with Cate.

"Your decision is about Robert. It didn't appear that he made it through the battle either. He'll bleed to death here. But we could take him with us. Medical help will be waiting. He has a good chance there. What do you want to do?"

Connor moved to his friend's side. He was weakening rapidly, his eyes glazed with pain, but he was conscious.

"Robert? I realize you dinna ken the whole of what's being decided, but you heard Cate, did you no? You up for joining me on another adventure, old friend?"

Robert smiled weakly. "I never thought yer lady had the looks of one from Outremer. Aye. I'll take the adventure. I dinna think I fancy the other choice."

"He comes with us." Connor stood and helped Cate to her feet. "And Rosalyn?"

"I stay." She came forward and pulling Connor's head down, kissed his forehead. "This is my place, Nephew. I'm no supposed to go."

He looked at Cate and she nodded. "But who will protect you?"

"I'm of a mind to be the one who does that." Duncan stepped forward.

"And if he can't, I will." Blane joined them. "I'll no be steered from the course I ken to be proper again. I'll do the right thing, Connor. I give you my word."

"And Mairi? Will you look after Mairi as well?"

"He won't have to. We already have Mairi out." Cate pushed him over to her brother and Robert. At his raised eyebrow she laughed and threw her arms around him.

"I'll explain it all in a few minutes. We have to go now. Did you hear me, Fae? Go now." She turned to Connor. "You are in for a light show you won't believe."

He got a light show of amazing proportions. But he missed it all, occupied as he was with kissing his wife.

EPILOGUE

Seun Fardach Ranch
North of Grand Lake, Colorado
Five years later

Cate slowly rocked back and forth on the long front porch, watching little Dougal tear across the yard on his Hot Wheels. He was extremely well coordinated for a four-year-old, but considering who his father was, she didn't find that at all surprising.

"Dougal, be careful of Beast, honey. He's just a baby." Beast was their latest addition, a clumsy wolfhound puppy named in honor of the dog who had given his all trying to save her.

Her son got off his Hot Wheels to tumble around with the frisky puppy. They were already fast friends.

Large warm hands clasped her shoulders and she smiled up at Connor. He leaned down to kiss her cheek, nuzzling her ear in the process. Her stomach filled instantly with butterflies. She would never tire of his touch.

"I smell chocolate. Have you been in those brownies already?"

"It's no my fault. You left them by the phone. What's a man to do?" His eyes twinkled. He was addicted to chocolate.

"I take it you got your call then?"

"Aye. It was Gordon MacAlister at Dun Ard. He says they have our reservations all arranged for the lodge next month. It'll be grand to get back again and see how work is progressing at the old castle." He sat in the chair next to her, propping his cowboy boots on the porch rail.

It made her smile that he still referred to it as the old castle. They'd bought the land there and were rebuilding Sithean Fardach. Considering his personal knowledge of the original, they should have no trouble duplicating it accurately. Well, accurately except for the modern plumbing and electricity that would be installed. Cate wasn't up for spending summers in a completely authentic thirteenth-century castle. Once was enough.

Gordon MacAlister, it had turned out, was a descendant of Duncan MacAlister. On that amazing first day back from Connor's time, Gordon had been the first to approach them once he'd heard Connor's name. He'd then excitedly run off to get his wife and a very old box that had been handed down through his family, held in safekeeping for the day Connor and Cate MacKiernan showed up at Dun Ard. Inside the box had been the emerald necklace and the matching emerald pin, along with a very, very old note. The woman writing the note had indicated that in honor of her son's fifth birthday, she had decided to seal these items away, now assured that she would have family to pass them along for her. She went on to wish for them a long life and a true love as happy as her own. It had been signed by Rosalyn MacKiernan MacAlister. Cate was pleased that Duncan had finally recognized his calling as Rosalyn's true love

She and Connor had worn those matching emeralds when they were married for a second time in front of Cate's family at a beautiful chapel overlooking a picturesque valley in Colorado Springs. Her father hadn't been satisfied that the original wedding really counted.

Both Connor and Robert had adjusted well, and worked with her brothers at Coryell Enterprises. There were several more employees now, so Connor could be very selective about which assignments he took. He didn't like to be away from home much. On their ranch Connor raised, of all things, horses. Huge, beautiful, rare horses. He loved them. Cate, however, still didn't ride.

Robert bought the land adjoining their own and raised cattle. He was endlessly fascinated with the gadgets and machines of this time and owned many. They never knew if he'd show up for daily sword practice in a car or on a tractor. His latest passion was a new Hummer. The military model, not the commercial public version. Fortunately they made good money in their line of work and Robert never turned down an assignment. He was still a true warrior.

"What's that coming down the road?" Connor pointed at a small dust cloud approaching the ranch.

Cate lifted one hand to shade her eyes. "Probably Jesse." On the fastest, biggest, baddest motorcycle he could find. "He said he'd bring Mairi up from Boulder today."

"Good Christ," Connor swore, rising and leaning over the porch railing. "He's no got her on that monster machine of his again, does he?"

Cate laughed. "You know Mairi loves that motorcycle

of his. She begs him to bring that every time he comes to get her. She adores having the other girls see him ride up on that thing, all dressed in leather. They're all jealous of her hanging out with a real live bad boy."

"Aye, weel. So long as 'hanging out' is all they're up to."

Connor would always be the consummate big brother. It drove Mairi as crazy now as it had in the past. Mairi had excelled in her studies. Cate often wondered if it was the Faerie blood. Mairi was majoring in Medieval studies at the University of Colorado. Her professor said she had a gift for the field, as if she'd been there in another life. If he only knew. She had less than a year left until graduation and then she planned to work on her master's. Though Mairi had become a subdued version of her old self, she liked life in Boulder and thought she might like to teach there eventually. Cate had correctly pegged her as a Boulder girl right from the beginning. And she still only wore shoes when she had to.

Connor ambled off the porch, swooping their son into his arms and swinging him high into the air, causing him to giggle uncontrollably.

"Come with yer da, wee Dougal Pol. Let's go down to the gate to see what mischief is headed up our drive."

"Yay, Unka Jess." The little boy recognized the sound of his uncle's motorcycle, happily anticipating hours of roughhouse play and spoiling.

Cate sighed contentedly. She continued to rock slowly back and forth, unwilling to wake the little girl sleeping across her lap before she had to. Soon the house would be alive with activity and she would be up and running around. Rose had turned two just last week.

They had named her for Rosalyn, and since Rose's birth, Cate often thought of the woman who had been so good to her and without whom she wouldn't have this perfect family. This perfect life.

Jesse and Mairi pulled into the drive. Dougal was already begging his uncle for a ride, and Mairi was laughing at her brother's attempts to dissuade his son from the machine.

Connor turned to her, raising his hands helplessly, and catching Cate watching him, he threw her a kiss, accompanied by that wonderful warrior smile of his that still turned her knees to Jell-O. He was without a doubt the most gorgeous man she had ever seen.

Rose wiggled in her lap, waking as usual with a smile on her beautiful little face. She grinned up at Cate with large emerald eyes. Life was going to be so very interesting for this inquisitive, happy little girl. Perhaps one day Cate would even take her to that beautiful glen and introduce her to her more unusual relatives.

Cate rubbed her hand over her baby's bare shoulder blade, enjoying the feel of her soft skin, and she smiled at the deep, dark birthmark there. She wondered, not for the first time, what Rosalyn would have said about this particular Faerie kiss.

If she squinted her eyes and turned her head just right, it looked like a whole bouquet of flowers.

**POCKET BOOKS
PROUDLY PRESENTS**

Highland Guardian

Melissa Mayhue

*Coming soon
from Pocket Books*

Turn the page for a preview of
the next book in *The Daughters of the Glen* series. . . .

"The threat is over." Dallyn bowed to the assembled Fae dignitaries, long blond hair sweeping across his shoulders at the movement.

"Not over," Darnee corrected, her green eyes flashing in his direction. "Only suspended for the moment. The threat will never be over as long as a single Nuadian lives."

Dallyn acknowledged her point with a slight nod. "Granted, but we have disabled most of the portals. A guard has been set around the Fountain of Souls."

"We must do more. The souls on the Mortal Plain are still at risk. The Nuadians can gain limited amounts of the energy they seek by releasing souls from the mortals' bodies. Without access to the Fountain, that will be their next logical target."

"The Fae can no longer fight on the Mortal Plain. You know that." Dallyn scowled.

"True. But they can gain control of weak mortals, ones who will gladly carry out the destruction they desire. We must guard against that eventuality."

"What would you suggest, my child?" The woman seated at the center of the great table spoke up.

"Guardians, Earth Mother, placed at each of the remaining portals." Darnee turned to the woman who had asked the question. "Guardians drawn from the Mortal Plain itself."

"How can mortals possibly defend against Fae? Our kind

can only be seen by mortals when we choose." Dallyn faced her directly now.

"Not just mortals. Mortals who share Fae blood." She arched an eyebrow, scanning the assemblage. "Many of our kind have half mortal offspring."

A low murmur spread through the room.

"This is true, daughter." The Earth Mother frowned. "Our kind have not always demonstrated proper restraint in their dealings with the mortal race. Many of these offspring exist and the numbers will continue to grow through the generations. Even a small amount of Fae blood would allow them to see us. But most are unacknowledged. How would you find them?"

"I will seek them out."

"I agree that they would suit well, Darnee." Dallyn shrugged. "But mortals have such short life spans. They would barely learn their task before their time would be at an end."

"That's another advantage of their Fae blood. They'll already be longer lived. And we can easily enhance that by exposing them to the Fountain of Souls. The energy will add many centuries to their time."

Dallyn rubbed his chin thoughtfully. "I see the merit of this plan. It could work. And many of them will carry gifts bestowed by their bloodline."

"Exactly." Darnee nodded in agreement. "Second sight, extra strength, other perceptions unusual in the Mortal Plain. All of these things will make them easier to identify and more capable of the task."

"I can see you've given this proposition a great deal of thought." The Earth Mother looked around the assembled group. "We cannot allow the Nuadians to disrupt the timelines of the souls on the Mortal Plain. We know first hand the chaos that brings. Forcing too many of them from their chosen bodies before they are destined to leave could ultimately damage the very flow of time itself." She rose from her seat, lifting her hands to signal an end to the discontented murmur that swept the hall. "My decision is made. You two, Darnee and Dallyn, will share responsibility for choosing and training these Guardians. You will share oversight for their performance. Any questions? No? Then you will begin at once. There is no time to spare."

"Thank you, Earth Mother." The two bowed and hastily left the grand room, quietly discussing how to carry out their assignment.

CHAPTER 1

"Bloody hell."

Ian McCullough glared at the telephone receiver he had slammed into place. Nothing was going as planned this week. He needed to be in London, following up on the latest threat. Instead, here he was at Thistle Down Manor, waiting to play innkeeper to some stressed out American while Henry lay in a hospital bed recovering from knee replacement surgery.

How many times had he tried to discourage Henry from renting out the cottage? He'd lost count years ago.

"This one needs to be here, Ian." Henry had told him on the way to the hospital. "I know it displeases you when I let the cottage, but rarely does it have any impact on you or yer responsibilities."

"Well it does this time. Honestly, it isna like you need the income. I've seen to that many times over. These guests of yers always need watching. You know the primary responsibility is to protect the portal."

Henry had given him a sheepish grin. "I know, I know. But I have my own gifts, and I canna ignore them. I could feel it when I spoke to this woman. I believe her soul has been wounded. The peace of Heather Cottage, and the nearness of the portal, will do much to help her." He'd grimaced in pain as he shifted in his seat. "If no for this damn knee, I would no have troubled you with this." He'd smiled then, his wrinkled face reflecting his inner calm. "Dinna worry. I'll be up and around in a few days. Peter and Martha will be there to help keep an eye on her as well and you can get back to the things you need to be about."

Ian continued to glare at the telephone, his dark eyes narrowing, as if that inanimate object held full responsibility for his latest problem. Peter and Martha. They were the only hired help at Thistle Down Manor, although they were more like family than employees. Peter had taken over the position of caretaker after his father retired. When he married Martha, she came to work there as well, as housekeeper and cook. They really did shoulder most of the day to day care of the grounds and house. And now they wouldn't be returning until some time tomorrow, at the very earliest.

Their daughter had gone into labor early this morning. Her husband's call had come out of the blue, so there had been no time to prepare the cottage for their guest's arrival before they left. Now thanks to the weather, they were staying at the hospital overnight.

Just one more thing to complicate his life.

The intensity of the storm raging outside only added to Ian's irritation. The downpour that had begun hours ago would probably flood the valley below. That would most likely mean power failures again. From what little news he'd heard, the storm front was huge, extending north well beyond Glasgow.

Surely the American wouldn't try to navigate the narrow back roads in weather like this.

"Perhaps this storm is good news, after all," he mumbled to himself as he rummaged through the hall closet searching for the emergency supply of candles. He glanced at the clock. She was an hour past due. Chances were she had stayed in one of the larger cities once she'd run into the storm.

"Thank the Fates for that, at least." The very last thing he wanted was to deal with the vacationing American on his own. Now it appeared he wouldn't have to.

Ian smiled to himself, and, feeling somewhat relieved, he carried the candles back into the library. After building a large fire in the fireplace, he settled back into his favorite chair to read, relaxing for the first time all day.

* * *

"Good Lord."

Sarah Douglas slammed on her brakes to avoid the cows in front of her car. It wasn't the first time in the last three hours she'd almost collided with livestock. She had known driving would be a challenge here. After the first hour or so, even traveling on the wrong side hadn't been so bad. But since leaving the A76, she'd also had to contend with wandering animals and roads that were narrower than her driveway back home. By the time she added in the rain coming down in buckets for the last few hours, her nerves were almost completely frazzled.

Driving conditions alone would have been bad enough, but that was on top of twelve hours spent either on planes or in airports waiting for planes, not to mention the most horrible flight ever from Toronto to Glasgow. The woman seated next to her was traveling with two small children, one or the other of which was crying from the moment of takeoff until they'd landed. Sarah had literally been without sleep for more than twenty hours.

She should have stopped at one of the hotels she'd passed near the airport. Or even the one she'd noticed as she'd turned off the main highway, if you could call it that, at Dumfries. But she hadn't.

"Get a grip," she muttered and then chuckled in spite of her circumstances.

Oh, she had a grip. On the steering wheel. So tightly, in fact, that her fingers were starting to cramp.

Taking a deep breath, she consciously relaxed her hands and slowly accelerated as the last of the cows cleared a path in front of her.

It shouldn't be much farther now. Panic returned briefly as she again considered that she might be lost, but, taking another deep breath, she regained control.

The directions that nice Henry McCullough had emailed her were very thorough and she'd been careful. Well, except for starting off in the wrong direction when she'd left the airport. Once she'd gotten that figured out and headed back the proper way, she'd been very careful. That little scenic detour had only increased her driving time by an hour or two.

It was simply exhaustion wreaking havoc with her emotions now. Exhaustion and the storm. And the dark. It was intensely dark. Between the late hour and the storm, she could only see those areas lit up by her headlights or brief flashes of lightning.

As if on cue, lightning sliced through the sky, striking directly ahead of Sarah's car. Illuminated in its flash was the figure of a man, staring straight at her, his face a mask of surprise. Once again she slammed on her brakes, but this time she accompanied the action with a scream, as her car began to slide slowly toward the man. He stood as if frozen for only a moment more before leaping—actually leaping—over her vehicle.

The automobile came to a gentle stop, nestled against a high rock wall. Breathing hard, Sarah peeled her fingers from the steering wheel and looked around. There was no man anywhere to be seen.

Closing her eyes, she let her head drop back to the headrest, the sound of her pounding heart filling her ears. He must have been a figment of her imagination. Real flesh and blood men didn't leap over moving vehicles and then completely disappear.

Slowly, she opened her eyes. Through the rivulets of rain running down her window, she read the plaque on the wall next to her. Thistle Down Manor. At least she wasn't lost.

The car, firmly stuck in the mud, refused to move either forward or back. Sarah turned off the ignition. The absence of noise from the engine only magnified the sound of rain beating on the metal above her head. Now what?

Choices and decisions. She could sit here all night, waiting to be rescued, or she could get out and walk.

How ironic. Wasn't that really what this whole trip was about, choices and decisions? After all those years of having no choices, of following decisions required of her by others, she'd finally chosen to change her life, to take charge. She'd decided for the first time in her life to embrace, rather than ignore, the intuitive feelings that had plagued her from childhood. It was one of those feelings, a driving need to do something before it was too late, that had landed her in this very spot.

Now it was time for her to act. Certainly not the most convenient time to realize that action doesn't come easily to a natural born coward.

Peering through the gates, Sarah could faintly make out the looming form of an enormous old mansion, across a bridge and down a long drive. The little cottage she'd rented would be somewhere nearby on the estate, though she couldn't see any sign of it from where she sat.

The distance would make for a pleasant walk on any normal day. It didn't, however, look very pleasant right now. Of course, it wasn't a normal day. It was late at night in the middle of a storm. Not to mention the man she thought she'd seen earlier.

Taking one last look at the rain pouring outside the car, Sarah sighed and reached back for her shoulder bag and purse. Her choice made, she opened the door.

The rain's icy chill hit her as she emerged from the car. She'd left the headlights on to illuminate the path. The battery would be dead by morning, but that was the least of her worries right now. If that figment of her imagination showed up again, she wanted to see him coming since she doubted she would hear him over the noise of the storm. She scanned the trees and shivered. The back of her neck prickled, as if eyes watched from those woods. The feeling grew in intensity and she started to run.

The bridge was much longer than it had looked, and not until she'd crossed over it did the panicky feeling of being followed leave her. She stopped, leaning over to catch her breath. Glancing back, she saw nothing through the rain except the wavering glow of her headlights.

If this whole thing weren't so frightening, it would be funny.

Shifting the heavy bag on her shoulder, she turned toward the house and started walking up the long drive. Hopefully, Henry McCullough was still awake.

Ian awoke with a start. He'd been dreaming. Dreams were rare for him and, to his way of thinking, that was a good thing. He learned long ago—very, very long ago—that when he dreamed, it always meant something. The "something" was always a very accurate warning of the future and, more often than not, it warned of something bad.

He tried to recall the dream now. He'd been in the forest and there had been a woman, although he hadn't been able to see her clearly, and some type of danger. And that blasted pounding.

Pounding, he suddenly realized that continued even now that he was awake. He stood up, feeling disoriented. The book he'd been reading fell unheeded to the floor.

Where was that noise coming from?

Moving into the hallway, he followed the sound, his senses coming fully alert.

"Hello? Mr. McCullough? Is anyone there?" Muffled words reached him, followed by more pounding.

A woman's voice.

Damn. The American had come after all.

What was wrong with the woman? Didn't she realize how dangerous driving in one of these storms could be? Didn't she have any sense at all?

He strode to the door and threw it open, fully intending to give his visitor the tongue-lashing she deserved for her reckless behavior.

"Do you bloody well realize what time it is?" He'd begun to yell when the sight of her on his doorstep struck him speechless.

Standing there in the pouring rain, with her hair plastered to her face, she was completely drenched and shivering hard enough the movement was visible to him even in the dark.

At the sound of his voice, she drew back sharply, losing her footing in the puddle that had formed on the stoop. Only his grabbing her elbows prevented her taking a nasty spill down the steps.

"Sorry. I'm sorry." Her teeth chattered so violently he could barely understand her mumbled apology. "I . . . I didn't think about the time. The drive took so much longer than I'd planned."

She feebly tried to pull her arms from his grasp.

Rather than letting go, he tightened his grip, drawing her inside the entrance hall, where she stood, dripping, her eyes cast down as if studying the intricate patterns on the marble floor. She made no move to stop him when he slipped the strap of the heavy bag from her shoulder, and dropped it at her feet.

She glanced up then, almost furtively, and their eyes met.

Green, like the deep forest. Her eyes were an intense green that sucked him in, captured him, prevented him from looking away. They widened an instant before darting back down to resume their examination of the floor.

The contact broken, Ian gave himself a mental shake. *How unusual.*

"Stay right here. I'll get something to dry you off and we'll get you all warmed up."

He raced upstairs and grabbed an armful of towels, stopping only to pull a blanket off the foot of his bed before returning to his guest.

She stood as he'd left her, huddled into herself, shivering as a small puddle formed at her feet.

Wrapping the blanket around her shoulders, he guided her toward the library. She'd be much better there. Thanks to the fire he'd built earlier in the evening, it was the warmest room in the place.

"Here are some towels. I'll pop into the kitchen and find something warm for you to drink. Is tea all right, or do you prefer coffee?" She was an American, after all.

"Tea would be wonderful, thank you." Only a whisper.

She took the towels and began to dry her face and hair as he left the room.

While he waited for the water to boil, he let his thoughts drift to the woman drying off in his library. She intrigued him. A great deal. Which was most unusual in and of itself.

The old saying about eyes being windows to the soul hadn't become an old saying without very good reason. It was absolutely true. Catching a glimpse of what lived behind those windows, however, was extraordinary. Souls valued their privacy.

Looking into this woman's eyes, he'd felt an unusually strong energy pulling at him. Her windows had been wide open, her soul leaning out, demanding his attention like the French harlots he'd seen so many years ago, hanging out of the Barbary Coast bordellos.

He couldn't recall having run across anything like it in all his years. She was something entirely new.

A thrill of anticipation ran through his body. 'Something entirely new' was a rare experience for Ian. After six centuries spent shuffling between the Mortal Plain and the Realm of Faerie, he often thought he'd seen it all.

During that time, he'd also learned countless valuable lessons. One of those lessons was that the rare experiences were usually the best. Certainly the most important.

Yes, he was quite intrigued by Miss . . .

"Damn."

What was her name? He couldn't remember. He couldn't

even remember if Henry had ever told him her name. He'd spent so much time thinking of her as 'The American,' her name had been of no importance.

That was certainly changed now. Playing innkeeper to his little American tourist had unexpectedly become a much more stimulating prospect.

Bending over in front of the fire, Sarah vigorously scrubbed at her hair with the towel. She'd read all about Scotland's unpredictable climate in the bag full of travel guides she'd bought, but nothing had prepared her for the reality of it. In spite of the fire, the blanket, and the towels, she was still cold and soggy.

And enormously embarrassed.

One look at her host and she might as well have been a teenager again, completely tongue-tied and unsure of herself. That first glance had fairly taken her breath away, leaving her stammering and unable to make eye contact with anything but her own feet. It wasn't the sort of behavior she expected from a mature woman. Particularly not when she was the mature woman in question.

Handsome men had always had that effect on her, and this one was certainly a prime example. The classic line, "tall, dark and handsome," could have been written especially for him. He towered over her by a good six inches. His eyes, a brown so dark they might actually be black, matched his hair. Hair a bit too long, curling around his neck, just onto the cream colored turtleneck sweater he wore. The sweater clearly outlined a chest that belonged on a pinup calendar. He could be Mr. January, perfect start to a new year. A man like that might even get more than one month.

He was one outstanding specimen all right. And he was also a good ten years younger than she, at the very least, which made her reaction to him all the more ridiculous. What was wrong with her, anyway?

"Serious jet lag," she muttered, scrubbing harder at her hair.

"Pardon?"

Sarah jerked upright, dropping the towel to her neck. Her host stood in the doorway holding two steaming cups.

Oh great. He'd caught her talking to herself, a bad habit that had caused her problems more than once. Heat crawled up her neck and over her face.

"I didn't realize you were back already."

His only response as he moved into the room was a smile. And what a smile. It played slowly around his lips, growing, spreading to his eyes, where it shimmered like polished jet.

The heat on her face ratcheted up a notch.

"I've taken the liberty of adding a touch of honey to yer tea." He set the cups on a low table. "Please, sit yerself down."

Sarah started forward, but stopped, looking down at herself.

"Oh, no. I'd hate to sit on your sofa in these wet clothes. Maybe it would be best if you just direct me to the cottage where I'll be staying."

His smile altered, a look of chagrin passing over his features.

"Well, that needs some explaining, you see." He picked the folded towels up from the floor and spread them on the sofa. "Here. Sit." He held up his hand to stop her when she started to protest. "Sit. Have yer tea and then we'll get you into some dry things."

After carefully arranging herself on the towels, Sarah extended her hand to accept the cup he offered her, acutely aware of his penetrating gaze. Trying desperately to think of something to say to fill the silence, she was horrified to hear herself blurt out the first thing that came to mind.

"You're not at all what I'd pictured." If she got any redder, surely flames would erupt from the top of her head.

"No what you'd pictured? What were you expecting?" He was smiling again.

"Well, Mr. McCullough, you sounded much older when we spoke on the telephone."

"Ah, well, that explains it then. I'm no Mr. McCullough."

"What?" Had that squeak actually come from her?

He placed a restraining hand on her arm as she started to rise.

"Let me rephrase that. I am Mr. McCullough, just no the one you spoke to. That would be Henry, he's . . ." he paused for a moment, glancing away from her as he moved his hand from her arm to pick up his cup. "I'm Ian McCullough."

"Oh." That explained why he didn't look at all like the sweet old man she'd imagined Henry McCullough to be. "But you're also a McCullough. You're related?"

"Aye. We're as related as an uncle and nephew can be." He briefly flashed that brilliant smile again.

"Where is your uncle?"

"Henry? Oh, in hospital, actually. Minor knee surgery. He'll be home in a few days. In the meantime, I'm supposed to be looking after things, but I'm afraid I've mucked them up a bit." The smile reappeared. "Starting with knowing nothing about my lovely guest, no even her name."

"Oh." Her conversational skills were rapidly disappearing in his presence. The blush returned. "I'm Sarah. Sarah Douglas."

"Sarah." He repeated the name slowly. "It suits you. Now that we know one another, we've only the problem of the cottage, it seems."

Uh-oh. "My cottage?"

He nodded. "Regrettably, our caretakers were called away on emergency this morning, so the cottage isna prepared for you. With the storm, I dinna think it a huge problem. I was sure you'd stay in the city when you saw the weather. Which reminds me,"

His eyebrows lifted in a manner reminiscent of a school principal about to chastise an errant student.

"This is no night to be out on the roads, lass. Did you no think about the risk you were taking by driving here in this tempest?"

His tone implied lecture, not a conversational question. It might even have been offensive if not for his lovely accent. The lightly lilting brogue made everything he said sound good. The brogue and the deep baritone.

"I guess I didn't at the time. But I certainly recognize it now." She put down her tea. "Mr. McCullough—"

"Ian," he corrected.

"Ian." She briefly made eye contact and smiled. "If the cottage isn't prepared, then . . ."

"It's no worry. We'll put you up here in the main house for tonight."

He sat back, looking very satisfied, and took a drink of his tea.

"I was under the impression that you didn't rent out rooms here." Henry had been rather emphatic about that point, assuring her there would be no other lodgers.

"We dinna. You'll join us tonight as my guest. We'll get you set up in the cottage tomorrow. Now . . . ," Ian stood and held out his hand in invitation. "Let's get you settled. When did you eat last?"

"On the plane."

She rose to her feet, clutching the now damp blanket tightly around her. If he'd noticed she'd avoided his hand, he gave no sign of it.

"We'll remedy that right after we get you in some dry clothing." He paused, tipping his head to the side. "Come to think of it, I dinna recall seeing your auto in the drive."

"It's not exactly in the drive. It's down at the entrance

gate." She shrugged. "I sort of slid off the road and got stuck in the mud. I can go back down and get my suitcase."

As they neared the door, thunder rumbled ominously close, rattling windows.

"I'm thinking that's probably no the best idea. In fact, I'm sure we can find you something dry to slip into here. We'll collect your things, and your vehicle, in the morning when the rain's done."

He'd stopped talking so she risked a quick glance up. It appeared he was waiting for that, catching her eyes and once again extending his hand. Perhaps he had noticed her earlier evasion after all.

"Here. Come with me."

There was no chance this time to avert his touch without seeming unusually rude, and she couldn't bring herself to do that. He'd been much too nice.

Simply one hand against another. No way to prevent her unprotected skin from contact with his. No blanket or clothing to filter it through this time. She'd simply have to steel herself against the assault she knew would come with the touch, as it always did.

She'd learned to accept it. From childhood she'd suffered the trauma of absorbing other people's thoughts and emotions when she touched them, and the strange random "feelings" that assailed her, trying to direct her actions. Almost worse had been the pain of knowing she was "different" from everyone else. She'd accepted that long ago, too.

While her preference was, as always, to escape the unavoidable result, sometimes, like now, it couldn't be helped.

She took his hand.

* * *

DESIRE LURKS AFTER DARK...

BESTSELLING PARANORMAL ROMANCES FROM POCKET BOOKS!

NO REST FOR THE WICKED KRESLEY COLE

He's a vampire weary of eternal life. She's a Valkyrie sworn to destroy him. Now they must compete in a legendary contest— and their passion is the ultimate prize.

DARK DEFENDER ALEXIS MORGAN

He is an immortal warrior born to protect mankind from ultimate evil. But who defends the defenders?

DARK ANGEL LUCY BLUE

Brought together by an ancient power, a vampire princess and a mortal knight discover desire is stronger than destiny...

A BABE IN GHOSTLAND LISA CACH

SINGLE MALE SEEKS FEMALE FOR GHOSTBUSTING.... and maybe more.

Available wherever books are sold or at **www.simonsayslove.com**.

POCKET BOOKS
A Division of Simon & Schuster
A CBS COMPANY

POCKET STAR BOOKS
A Division of Simon & Schuster
A CBS COMPANY

15606

Not sure what to read next?

Visit Pocket Books online at
www.simonsays.com

Reading suggestions for
you and your reading group
New release news
Author appearances
Online chats with your favorite writers
Special offers
Order books online
And much, much more!

POCKET BOOKS
A Division of Simon & Schuster
A CBS COMPANY

POCKET STAR BOOKS
A Division of Simon & Schuster
A CBS COMPANY

13456